MW01129193

Reckless Magic

The Star-Crossed Series

Volume One

Rachel Higginson

1

Reckless Magic
The Star-Crossed Series
By Rachel Higginson

Editing services provided by Jennifer Nunez.

Printed in paperback May 2012 and available in Kindle and E-book format as of May 2012 through Amazon, Create Space and Barnes & Noble.

To my Daddy, who instilled the confidence in me
To write long before this daydream took form

To Kylee, my first reader and critic, who made
This possible from start to finish

To Zach, who was the first ever to believe
My dream could also be my work

Headlights lit up the dark living room as a black, unmarked sedan pulled into the driveway. A man sitting silently in the corner arm chair lifted his head from his fingertips and focused sharply on the late night visitor.

The man was used to hosting many guests, mostly dignitaries and officials sent on palace business. The guests would come and go with lots of pomp and circumstance, reminding the man that he was a servant. He was a servant, to the Monarchy, the palace, the King.

The guests would also come with lots of warning. The car parked out front came with no notice and it caused the man to focus. He wasn't afraid. He wasn't worried. He was just curious.

Standing up slowly, he felt the tingling of magic ignite in his blood. They couldn't disguise themselves, those that were like him. He could feel their presence before they were too close. Their similar magic, like a warning flare, always reminding him of whom he was, of whom he belonged to.

He expected the worst, the end to a too long life. The house he had made his home in recent years would be perfect for this tragic finale. An empty tomb holding centuries of memories, most of which he would have loved to forget. The expensive but empty house would be perfect to bid good-bye to this life. It felt like his over-lived existence: too large, too old and too empty.

He half wondered who they would send. He wondered who would be strong enough to finish the job no one previously had been able to finish. This time he wouldn't fight. He was tired of fighting. He was tired of victory. There was nothing left for him to win. The people he had believed in had let him down. The King he had expected the worst from hadn't. It was time to give up. Time to throw in the towel and let them destroy him; along with the cause he alone was defending. He was ready.

Finally, he was ready.

But as the magic moved towards the door, he was surprised to find it not threatening, but familiar, like an old magic, from an old friend. A friend from a different time and one that he had hoped to never meet again because he knew she must be desperate to brave this visit.

"Hello, Angelica," the man answered the door before the old woman could knock. Her long white hair glistened in the moonlight, and she returned his scowl with a gentle smile and sad violet eyes.

"Hello, Amory," Angelica's arms were full of something covered with blankets. She pushed past him; his tall, muscular frame took up most of the door way. The cold night of a winter turning into spring blew quietly into the house, but encouraged the man to shut the door quickly behind them.

Once the door was shut, Amory turned the lights on in the darkened house, planning to invite the woman in for the night. The house now lit, took on a different personality from before. What once felt like a stark and empty room was now warm and inviting with the soft glow of light. A simple burst of magic brought a roaring fire to life and warmed the room, as quickly as it was lit.

Angelica sat down on a large leather couch near the fire. Her arms were still full of blankets and her expression still sad.

"Let me take those from you," Amory offered, realizing Angelica looked frail and tired under her packages.

"I would love that," her face lit up just a little bit as Amory bent over to take the first bundle out of her right arm.

As his strong hands slipped underneath a blue blanket to lift the package from her, they stopped suddenly, paralyzed by the soft and warm body underneath. Pulling his hands away, he stared at her with fear in his eyes.

"What is this?" he asked, nearly choking on his words.

"Take a look for yourself," she nodded her head and encouraged him with tender eyes.

"Who? What? It can't be," Amory fumbled through words afraid of what was in either arm.

Eventually he found enough courage to pull the blue blanket away from a sleeping infant, not more than a week old. The little boy was perfect, tiny and soft with chubby cheeks and a thick head of dark curly hair that seemed too much for his little head. He stared at the child for several seconds recognizing his parents without ever needing confirmation.

He looked back to the woman who smiled even sweeter, a

tear escaping from one of her violet eyes, making their strange color stand out starkly against her pale and wrinkly skin. She nodded to the other bundle, one wrapped in a pink blanket. Amory shook his head and stepped back.

The baby boy had not scared the man; it was the second bundle that had concerned him so. Several seconds passed before Amory found the courage to pull the blanket away from the second sleeping child. Almost identical to her twin brother, with chubby cheeks, and dark, unruly hair, she was unmistakably a girl, but with almost an angelic quality and a sweet, small nose.

"It's not possible," Amory shook his head again, noticing the tiny buzzing of infant magic swirling around him for the first time.

"That's what I said," Angelica held out the baby girl and, shaking slightly, Amory took her into his arms, feeling like the smallest mistake would shatter the fragile child.

"How did they….? How did you….? How did they get here?" Amory stumbled through several half questions before settling on the most recent. Twins did not exist in their culture, or at least they hadn't in thousands of years.

"Two days ago, Justice came to me in the middle of the night with these two. He stayed for only a couple minutes, just long enough to explain that these were their children, their first and only, that they were twins, and that Delia and he were fine." She cuddled the little boy in her arms, pressing her cheek against his head gently. "And, Amory, he asked me to bring them to you. It was Delia's idea." She stared down at the sleeping child, afraid to look up into her dear friend's eyes.

Although Amory was infinitely older than her, no one would have been able to tell. His black hair showed no signs of gray, and his matching black eyes were as sharp as ever. She was nearing the beginning of old age and looked it. Her face was wrinkled and hair perfectly white; her hands were gnarled and she showed a lifetime of hardship that she was unwilling to admit to.

"To me?" His voice betrayed the fear he felt and took on the sweet cooing of a gentle soul speaking to a baby. The little girl sighed heavily in his arms as if perfectly content to be there.

"Yes, to you. They are choosing to stay hidden. The children would not survive if they stayed with them." Although

9

she was the younger of the two, Angelica's voice took on a stern maternal quality that showed her desire to protect the two infants fiercely.

"And you suppose they will survive if they stay with me?" Amory's voice did not lose the sweet, soft tone, but his question was valid.

"They have to. This is a miracle, Amory, an unbelievable miracle. They have to survive for the sake of our people," Angelica stood, walking to Amory and putting her free hand against his face.

Amory looked deeply into Angelica's lavender eyes and knew that she was right. The hope he had lost so many years ago was suddenly ignited again by these two seemingly impossible infants. The children continued to sleep in their arms, but made little noises only newborn babies did, oblivious to their surroundings, innocent of the world they were entering.

"Then we cannot keep them together, Annie. They cannot have anything to do with each other if we hope to keep them alive." Amory looked back at the little girl, already the spitting image of her mother. She opened her eyes at the sound of his louder voice and gazed up at him. She did not cry; she only stared back at the man now responsible for her future.

"Agreed," Angelica nodded with resolve. "Then we will leave now."

She covered the little boy again with his blue, fleece blanket and leaned over to kiss the girl on the forehead. The baby lifted her mouth to the human contact, looking for a bottle.

"I don't think I remember how to do this," Amory was suddenly swept with a different kind of fear as he realized the child, although necessary to the cause recalled in the old man's mind, had needs of her own; needs that a lonely bachelor was extremely ill-equipped to provide for.

"I have no doubt that you'll figure it out," Angelica reached for Amory's face again, offering an encouraging smile before kissing him on the lips.

"Where will you go?" he asked her as she walked towards the front door, that she had only just entered.

"Not home," she said sadly. "You?"

"I have no choice but to stay here," Amory said with all

the malice he was capable of.

"Then what will you do with the child?" The fear in Angelica's voice was unmistakable. She had made a choice in bringing the children to Amory, and it was too late to change her mind, but regret flooded her veins when she realized the danger she had put all of them in.

"I have a dear friend here that will help me, a human friend. She is young but immeasurably smart and capable." A sly grin crossed Amory's face; he felt confident in his plan.

"Ah. You mean she is in love with you," Angelica watched the embarrassment color her friend's face, but he didn't respond; no matter how long the man lived, he stayed humble and private. "I will contact you when we have settled somewhere."

She turned to leave, opening the door and looking out across the deserted neighborhood street.

"Angelica, these children are our only hope," Amory said quickly with more passion than he had felt in almost a century.

"I know," she replied with determination.

"Annie, wait. Please know," his voice broke with emotion, "please know what they mean to me."

"I know that too," Angelica did know, but it was with a sadder determination that she responded.

The man watched his friend carefully load the child back into the black sedan. Their departure was bittersweet, tearing at his determination to keep these children alive under any circumstance and his unwillingness to ever be separated from them again.

If this plan, this plan of survival born in the midnight hours were to work, his resolve would have to be strong. Magic swirled around him, as he watched her twin brother be driven away to safety, not knowing when the next time the siblings would meet.

He looked down at the little girl, wrapped in pink and sleeping again and smiled. There was hope again for his people. There was something worth living for, worth fighting for. And she was the key to it all. She just didn't know it yet.

Chapter One

"Well, here we go," I said softly to myself. I took a big breath and stepped out of the car. I gave a cautious wave to Aunt Syl as I watched her drive away. She waved back enthusiastically. I felt anything but encouraged.

I had to go to school, right? I did not have a choice. I was pretty sure it was against the law not to go.... I tried to think of other reasons to postpone the inevitable but came up empty handed. Social suicide.... I was well on my way.

I cringed inwardly, knowing I looked like a hot mess. I could feel my tan skin, turning translucent with nerves, and my unruly, dark hair, tangled and wild as I stood too long in the wind. It whipped around my face in the hot, humid breeze, partially blocking the impending view from sight. I brushed my hair out of my face, but it refused to obey and with another gust of unbearably hot August air, I was forced to walk forward to maintain my sight.

I felt sick and nauseous; I was practically on the verge of puking. I closed my eyes for several seconds and then opened them again, hoping I'd be someplace else, any place else. But I was right where I was supposed to be: staring up at my new school. The tall, ominous buildings clustering together, stared back. Their dark, red brick laughed at me silently, daring me to run away. The central tower, with its golden bell, and deep sweet chimes taunted me, mocked me.

Ok, maybe I was being a little over dramatic, but school had never been my, um, thing. It could have been because I was a complete social spaz; or it could have been because this was my fourth school in two years. Either way, I always seemed to have trouble adjusting to teenage normalcy.

Kingsley Preparatory Academy was a last resort of sorts. Well, really, it was the last prep school that would take me; God forbid I would attend public school. As the niece and only surviving relative of my aunt, the doctor, I was destined for a higher education.

If only I could have gone six months without being expelled. Kingsley was the last prep school in Omaha that had given me a chance, and that was only after a very generous contribution from my aunt and a promise from me that I wouldn't burn it to the ground. Although I harbored no ill will for the school itself, I was not sure if I could keep my promise.

Not that I would burn it down on purpose, but that kind of stuff just happened to me. The burning down of schools, the flooding of schools, and the infestation of huge, tropical insects of schools.... All fell into the category of been there, done that. It's not like I ever did it on purpose; it all just sort of happened.

So after another deep breath, I began my death march to the top of the hill and the large, brass, double doors that led into the Administration Building. The doors slammed shut behind me, making me almost jump out of my skin. The lobby was dimly lit; it took a while for my eyes to adjust from the bright sunlight outside.

Kingsley was immaculate; beautiful marble floors and elaborate lighted sconces filled the lobby. An intricate, crystal chandelier hung from the ceiling and gave the room a warm glow that reminded me of dusk rather than 8:00 AM. Plush, crimson divans lined the lobby, and oil paintings of elderly people adorned the walls. I reminded myself that this was a school building and not the sitting room to a luxurious Victorian home.

I forced my feet forward and adjusted my backpack straps. I stopped to fiddle with my uniform, afraid to make the wrong first impression. The front counter, located directly on the other side of the lobby was crafted from a beautiful wood, probably mahogany, that expanded the width of the room and stood elbow-high. I walked the rest of the way tentatively, as this was like no other school building I had ever been in, and I'd had my fair share of experience.

An elderly woman, with snow-white hair and small-framed glasses, sat behind a small desk made from the same wood as the counter that partitioned us. Her posture was perfect and her legs crossed properly, as she focused typing at her computer. A name-plate that read "Mrs. Truance" decorated her desk, facing me. She glanced my way from the top of her spectacles and gave a little sigh.

"You must be Eden Matthews," she declared more as a statement than a question.

"Yes, I am," I choked out.

"Welcome to Kingsley," she said tersely. Mrs. Truance stood up gracefully and walked over to me with some sheets of paper in her hand. "Here is your class list and map of the campus. It can be quite confusing, so please ask for help if you get lost."

"Thank you, I will," I tried to smile, but she had already turned away and headed back to her desk. So instead, I looked down at my class list and found my first hour of torture to be English.

I shuffled through the papers until I found a map of the campus. Junior AP English was located in the English and Arts Building, which appeared to be two buildings east of this one.

"Please hurry, Kiran. I don't want you to be late for our first day," a peculiar accent and heavy footsteps made me turn to see two figures walk through the brass double doors I had just come in. The bright sunshine illuminated the lobby; I was blinded for a moment as the doors slammed for a second time. My eyes took a moment to adjust again.

"Stop worrying; I'm royalty for God's sake!" barked the second voice with a strong, aristocratic English accent that sounded irritated. As they walked closer, I could see that they were dressed in the Kingsley uniform, and close to my age.

The first boy who spoke resembled a giant; he was at least 6'5 and extremely muscular. Good-looking with olive skin and dark hair, he seemed to speak with an Italian or Spanish accent. He looked a bit rough, like he had been in a fight or two. He leaned toward the other in a strange way, almost as if he was bowing slightly. Although his eyes were a bit far apart, they were deep brown, with glints of gold, and said something about him, but I couldn't determine what they might reveal.

As I watched the two boys walk closer, I eventually noticed the second one, who was almost overshadowed by his friend until he was nearly five feet away. My mouth dropped open as I looked at him. He was the most beautiful thing I had ever seen.

Not usually the type to objectify men, or even notice them at all, my reaction was almost as shocking as his beauty. He had thick, dirty blonde hair that was unkempt in a way that said movie star. He ran his fingers through it slowly, moving it away from his forehead; I could swear it happened in slow motion. He had clear

14

dark eyes, a color almost indefinable. They reminded me of the ocean, aqua at first; but the closer he got the darker they appeared. Suddenly they were turquoise and shining. A straight nose and perfectly full, but masculine lips completed his face. I hardly noticed anything else as I stared stunned and bemused into his eyes, eyes that happened to be staring back into mine.

"Excuse me, Ms. Matthews; you are going to be late for class if you don't get going. Can you read the map, or are you already lost?" the stern voice of the secretary pulled me out of my stupor.

"Um, no, I can read," I said, sheepishly, still unable to take my eyes off the mysterious boy staring back.

"Of course you can read," she said sharply, snapping my entranced head back to reality. "Now, get to class."

This time I obeyed, although hesitantly. I was thankful for my long hair, and let it fall in front of my face, hoping to hide my embarrassment. I could feel my tan cheeks burning with shame. As I started to walk past the eyes that had captured my attention, I began to experience the strangest, but not-so-unfamiliar feeling.

My skin started to tingle as if I were being shocked a million times; my insides began to grow increasingly warmer until I felt like all of my vital organs were energized from the sun. Instantly my blood began to warm and then rapidly heated to what felt like a strong boil. I picked up my pace and nearly ran out of the double brass doors into the fresh air, trying to catch my breath.

It was only the end of August, so the sun was still hot and the humidity already overwhelming, despite the early morning hour. I pressed my face against the cool brick of the building, gasping for air and mentally calming my insides.

I realized that I looked ridiculous, but the physical changes that had just begun to occur in my body were usually a sign of pending destruction. Although I had never been sure of why my body suddenly felt like a giant microwave, I could always be positive that it would end in a great travesty. I pressed my face closer to the brick, allowing the shade of the building to cool me, calming the electrical impulses tingling beneath my skin.

I was officially humiliated by my erratic behavior. I was sure I left those inside thoroughly entertained and confused. I was just thankful I was able to stop the electrical build-up in time.

The first time I felt the electric pulses underneath my skin I thought they were bugs. In the middle of second semester of my freshman year, I thought I had been attacked by a swarm of insects. During gym class, I began to freak out, feeling the creepy-crawly sensation of the electricity building slowly inside of me. I remembered my gym teacher rushing over to my side and then I remember nothing. Supposedly I passed out, but not before screaming something about bugs being everywhere. When I finally woke up, I was outside in an ambulance, surrounded by hazmat guys. Apparently my school had become thoroughly infested with tropical insects, the really big kind. Unfortunately, I had implicated myself in what the school board assumed to be a serious prank, and I was respectfully asked to leave.

After pleading a pitiful case to the next school, I was allowed to begin my sophomore year on the provision of absolutely no shenanigans. I lasted all the way through the year until finals week when I felt the electrical sensation again. This time I tried to restrain myself and get it under control; I wished only to wash the feeling off. Again I must have blacked out because I woke up to find myself in another ambulance; the school had flooded spontaneously. The school board did not ask so nicely for me to leave; but Aunt Syl forced them to give me passing grades by threatening a lawsuit, since there was no substantial evidence that I caused the flood.

Last week, the beginning of my junior year, I started my third prep school, only to experience what felt like my blood beginning to boil. I was warned it was my last chance to finish high school. Unfortunately for them, no one would be finishing anything at that school, since I magically burned it to the ground.

I couldn't explain what happened to me; I just knew better than to mess around. The powers in charge at Kingsley must have been brave souls to allow me entrance into their prestigious prep school, or had taken out an unusually large insurance policy.

I was just glad I was able to stop it that time. I had never felt the impulses react so strongly. More than a sweeping sense of unconsciousness, the electrical impulses had felt alive, as if they were reacting to something. Who knows what would have happened had I let them continue…. possibly the Apocalypse? I had no idea why those things happened to me, or what exactly they were. I just knew that I was always the one responsible for something catastrophic. And I was seriously hoping to avoid closing this school down for good.

I turned around, so that my back was to the wall, slid down slowly to the ground, and closed my eyes. I was utterly unconcerned with being late for class after all that; I had bigger things to worry about, like ensuring there was still a class to go to.

I compelled my nerves to calm down, and started slowly to relax. I forced my muscles to loosen up, mentally flexing them. My relaxation only lasted a second, though, as the Administration Building doors burst open. The two boys, from before, exited the building in mid-conversation.

I prayed they would not notice me and crouched even closer to the wall. I could not have felt more humiliated. Although the gorgeous one did look in my direction, he acted as though he couldn't see me and continued down the steps.

"What are we doing here, Talbott?" the one named Kiran demanded, almost growling.

"Please sir, you know what we are doing here," Talbott replied, almost too softly to be heard.

"No, I do not," Kiran snapped again. "Aren't there any qualified girls in London? This is ridiculous. I don't even know where we are. This is the ugliest place I have ever seen. I cannot possibly be expected to spend the next two years of my life here. I want to talk to my father," his voice had almost turned into a whine, but his accent was so sexy that I hardly noticed.

"There are none in London with her pedigree and power. Your father looked. Your father looked everywhere. And this place is called Omaha…. Nebraska. I'm afraid he will not be moved; this was his idea," Talbott said humbly but persistently. Although inferior in looks, he certainly seemed to be the more mature of the two.

"This is ridiculous. Where is she?" Kiran looked around himself with such pride and arrogance that I found his beauty quickly fading. Crouching closer to the wall, I could not believe they still hadn't noticed me.

"Please calm down. I believe you will meet her soon; but we must get to class now or you will be late on your first day," Talbott half smiled and started walking in the direction of the academic buildings; Kiran followed slowly behind, arms crossed, looking less god-like and much more child-like.

I breathed a sigh of relief and slowly stood up. Reluctantly, I collected my papers and adjusted my uniform, which consisted of a navy-blue, pleated skirt and white button-down collared shirt, knee-high navy blue stockings and of course the classic prep school tie: navy-blue with red plaid. I gathered my nerve and headed in the same direction as Talbott and Kiran, already afraid of the rest of my day.

Chapter Two

My thoughts were preoccupied as I walked into class, not realizing that English had already started until I stumbled clumsily through the door. Not only was I starting school a week later than the other students, but I walked loudly into a class that had already started.... awesome. The teacher, a skinny bald man, dressed in a tasteful navy-blue suit and tie, looked up from a textbook and glared at me.

"Why do I even bother to start class when we're going to have all of these interruptions?" he said, still staring at me.

"Um, I'm sorry, I'm new," I replied guiltily, my face turning bright red once again.

"Obviously. Are you Eden?" he asked, speaking through his nose.

"Um, yes, Eden Matthews," I clarified, just to be sure, but obviously he knew that. I could barely contain my nerves. Usually a shy person, I hated having the attention on me, and at that moment, the entire class was staring, probably laughing, at me.

"Nobody's laughing at you," the teacher declared unexpectedly. "I'm Mr. Lambert. Welcome to Honors English. Please take a seat over there." He tried to smile and pointed to the back of the classroom where an empty desk sat between none other than the two boys I encountered earlier.... fantastic.

Although I was oddly reminded by Mr. Lambert that nobody was laughing at me, I still felt all eyes were on me as I walked quickly, head down, to my desk and slid in as quietly as I could. I glanced around the room and realized, thankfully, that no one was looking in my direction; well, no one except Kiran who was sitting directly to my left and staring openly at me. I ran my fingers through my hair, pulling it over my shoulder and in front of my face. I hoped to build a wall of tangled curls to separate me from this curious stranger.

I fumbled through my backpack looking for the same book that everyone else was holding but I suddenly found it hard to concentrate. My bag was full of books for every class and the covers all began to look the same. My vision blurred, I squinted to give myself a clearer view. I could hear the lecture, but it sounded far off, and I was beginning to feel dizzy. My breath became quick and shallow; I grabbed on to my desk with both hands, trying to find my bearings.

As if from everywhere around me, I started to feel a wave of heat overcome me. My skin began to prickle again as if I were going through a low dose of electroshock therapy and there was a high-pitched sound resonating in my ears. I could feel my head hit the ground as I slid back out of my desk and onto the floor.

"Good grief, I'm never going to get through this lecture," sighed a very exasperated voice, I wondered what a nasal-sounding man was doing in my bedroom while I was trying to sleep.

"What did you do? This kind of thing is strictly prohibited, Mr. Kendrick. I don't care who you are. You will obey your father's ordinances when you are in my class," the aggravated voice kept going on and on. I thought, "Just let me sleep!"

"I didn't do anything!" a familiar English accent defended himself. Where had I heard that voice before? "I don't know what happened to her, she just fell over!"

"Ms. Matthews, Ms. Matthews, can you hear me?" It was the annoying voice again. I could hear him, but I didn't want to; I wanted to go back to sleep.

Then it hit me. Oh no! I did it again. Well, I didn't know what I did again, but I was too afraid to open my eyes and find out. Strong, small hands gripped my shoulders and began to shake me roughly.

"Maybe you should slap her," a high-pitched girl's voice offered. That got my attention.

"What have I done now?" I groaned, closing my eyes even tighter. I refused to open them and assess the damage I just caused. I also refused to be slapped, I wasn't unconscious anymore.

"You fainted," the English accent that I could now identify as Kiran's said plainly. I thought I could also detect a smile in his voice and maybe something else.... amusement?

"What else?" I groaned again.

"What do you mean what else? Well, you've also interrupted my class," Mr. Lambert's unmistakably irritated voice replied impatiently. "What's wrong with you, do you need to go to the nurse?"

21

I finally summoned enough courage to open my eyes. The world around me was perfectly intact, perfectly as it should have been and I was completely confused. This wasn't the first time I had awoken in a daze after experiencing similar feelings. This was just the first time I had awoken to things still normal around me. Usually, it was all mass panic and chaos, due to lethal insects or flooding waters, or even scorching flames. Truthfully, I much preferred a crowd of confusion. I was inwardly overjoyed there wouldn't be mass lawsuits and a new school in my near future.

"No, I am fine, thank you," I think I was actually smiling on the outside now too, because the entire class of faces staring down at me were more confused than ever. If only they had known what could have happened to them; if only they had known that miraculously their lives were saved. I could feel my smile get bigger and I knew without a doubt that I looked crazy.

I tried to push myself up onto my elbows, but was still a little shaky and fell back down. A nervous, almost hysteric laugh escaped me and it was the only sound in the room. I had officially begun my first day at my new school as a freak. A swarm of students stared down at me, a sea of white and navy-blue, with islands of hanging red plaid ties.

I decided to try to sit up again; I needed to move since everyone was still gawking at me. As I struggled, I could see that Kiran and Talbott, closest to me due to the proximity of their desks, attempted to help me. I watched as their arms reached out to grab mine and assist me in sitting up. As soon as their skin touched mine, I started all over again with the heat and electricity and I let out a mild scream.

Both sets of arms immediately dropped from mine and I found myself back on the floor, wishing I were dead. I had no idea what was going on, but I soon realized that everyone staring at me wanted an explanation. I wished I had one to give them; one that wouldn't completely brand me as nuts.

"Maybe I should go to the nurse," I conceded as I struggled to get up once again. I could see both sets of arms reaching out to help me in another attempt of chivalry and I overreacted a little by shouting, "That's Ok, I can do it on my own!"

I knew that I sounded like a lunatic, like certifiably crazy;

but for whatever reason these two boys were bringing out the scariest part of me and I didn't want them or anyone else to get hurt. I looked up at Kiran apologetically, but instead of looking concerned for this crazy person, like I expected, he just gazed back entertained, almost like he was about to laugh.

"Can someone help Ms. Matthews to the Nurse's Office, please?" Mr. Lambert sounded exasperated.

"I can," Kiran volunteered.

"No, that's all right," I blurted out; for fear that I'd faint again. "I'm sure I can find it on my own," I gave a weak smile, but finally stood up. I actually had no intention to find the nurse, I just needed to calm down and get some space. I grabbed the back of my chair to steady myself, and inhaled deep breaths of air.

"Lilly, can you take her?" Mr. Lambert turned to look at a fragile-looking girl with short, vibrant, red, curly hair.

"Sure," she answered sweetly. She took a few steps from the back of the crowd of students to wait for me by the door.

I grabbed my backpack, terrified to look at anyone until I was almost to the safety of the hallway. Once I reached the door, I took a brave look back only to see Kiran smile and wink at me from his desk. This had been the most bizarre day, and, unfortunately, it wasn't even the end of first hour.

Chapter Three

Once the door closed behind me, I headed straight to the nearest bathroom. Kingsley was a school for the privileged; the girl's bathroom reflected this. The stalls, sinks and hand dryers were all made of the latest bathroom technology and porcelain, I guessed. The mixture of class and technology seemed a little strange, especially in a bathroom. Conveniently, there was a plush sitting room adjoined where I could hide my shame in private.

I plopped down on the nearest divan, pulling my knees to my chest. I rested my head in my hands and let out an audible groan. What was wrong with me?

"Ugh. What is wrong with me?" I echoed loudly.

"Is there something wrong with you?" a soft, sweet voice asked. I had forgotten all about the girl who was supposed to take me to the Nurse's Office. I would have rather not had an audience during my impending breakdown, but it was a little late to think up an excuse now.

"It seems like it," I looked up and gave her a small smile. She was pretty, with bright green eyes and clear, pale skin. She was shorter than me, maybe 5'6 or 5'5, and had impeccable posture; which I was sure, was a sign of her upbringing. I expected her to look back at me as if I was crazy, but to my surprise, she only looked concerned. Her forehead had creased in worried lines and her plump red lips were pressed together in a frown.

"What happened back there?" She sat down beside me and waited for an answer. At least she hadn't tried to console me by assuring me everything was Ok. We both knew everything was not Ok. She sounded genuinely concerned though, and I was suddenly grateful not to be alone.

"I wish I knew. Sometimes I just, uh, faint," I knew it was a weak explanation, but I didn't think she would believe me if I told her that sometimes I felt my body turn into a giant microwave. "I am a freak show; I was kind of hoping to avoid drawing that much attention to myself today…. or like ever," I started to laugh; this was absurd.

"I'm Lilly Mason, by the way. And I know exactly what you mean," she thankfully didn't ask for more of an explanation, but I was one hundred percent positive that she had no idea what I meant.

"Nice to meet you," I said with a genuine smile. "Thank you for volunteering to help me. I know that you didn't have to, but I would have just died if Kiran witnessed anymore of my meltdown." I rolled my eyes, expecting her to understand.

"Oh, do you know him?" Her question caught me off guard because clearly I was new to this school.

"No, not at all. I don't know anyone here. I ran into him in the Administration Building."

"That's so strange. He's new today, too." The worry lines reappeared on her forehead.

"Why is that strange?" I remembered that Talbott was worried about Kiran being late on his first day. But if he was new too, then why would he offer to take me to the Nurse's Office?

"Well, Kingsley doesn't usually allow anyone to start classes late, let alone three students in one day. I can understand Kiran Kendrick, but why did they let you in?" Her question could be taken offensively, but the way she asked it seemed only curious. Her voice was so pure; and her eyes so innocent, that I could hardly believe this girl could ever have a hurtful thought about anyone.

"I'm not sure, actually. I'm not what you would call the ideal student," I confessed with a cynical smile, but offered no explanation to my statement. I wanted at least one friend in this place; admitting that I was practically a ticking time bomb seemed like the wrong way to make one. "You said three students, who is the other one?" "Talbott Angelo. He was sitting on the other side of you." Lilly started blushing as soon as she said the word "Talbott." Her cheeks turned a crimson red against the pallid tone of the rest of her skin, yet somehow it enhanced her beauty instead of diminishing it.

I gave her a slightly knowing smile. I had barely noticed Talbott, other than his size and stature, yet, Kiran's blazing blue eyes flooded my memory. I couldn't help but blush too, as I thought about his perfect features and the way he seemed amused at my discomfort. I should have been offended, or at least irritated, but I couldn't blame him.

Instead of being offended, I was more embarrassed at my

25

body's reaction to any close approximation to him. First, I stared unabashedly; then I acted clumsy and erratic. Next I had physical reactions that no one could explain and eventually I fainted. Clearly I needed a class on how to behave in the presence of the opposite sex, which I was sure they offered here at the prim and proper prep school I now attended.

The bell rang in the hallway, and we started to gather our things. I noticed that Lilly was wearing the best of every designer imaginable, which was hard to do considering we all wore the same, plain uniform. But her book bag was designer, her shoes were designer, and what little jewelry she was wearing screamed expensive. I looked down at the backpack I had carried since junior high and laughed at its…. um…. wear and tear.

I stopped to glance at myself in the mirror. My black eyeliner was smudged in the corner of my eyes, but I didn't bother to fix it. I probably had laid it on a little too thick to begin with; I had been in a hurry this morning. The black from the eyeliner matched the color of my dark eyes, making the white of the pupil appear almost neon. I grabbed my pink lip-gloss out of my pocket and applied it quickly, unsure of the reason behind it.

"What is your next class?" Only Lilly's clothes screamed snob. Her demeanor and voice were so sweet that I doubted she belonged at a place like this.

"Um, Drama with Mrs. Woodsen," I replied, looking at the class list Mrs. Truance handed me earlier.

"Oh, good, I have that too. Hopefully we'll have most classes together," Lilly smiled again and I could tell that she was truly happy we had the same class. I already felt relaxed now that I had a friend or at the very least someone who didn't utterly hate me; the rest of the day didn't seem so impossible.

We left the restroom and entered the throng of students hurrying to their next classes. We joined them, and Lilly took me through a winding hallway to a set of beautiful marble stairs, leading both up and down. The English and Arts Building of Kingsley was another red brick building, but much larger than the Administration Building.

Located on the first floor were the theater and dressing rooms; there was also a lavish foyer and an elegant, marble staircase that led up to the second and third floors. All other grade levels of English, honors or non-honors, were located on the second floor. The third floor was dedicated entirely to the Drama department.

Although this floor had many small rooms assigned to storage and props, the majority of the floor was taken up by a large, unusual drama studio. There were no desks or white-boards in the room. The room glowed with paint in effervescent colors: oranges, and reds, greens and blues; beautiful silk floor pillows were scattered around the room. Oriental room dividers stood in one corner, suggesting a dressing room, while various props and costumes cluttered together in another corner.

An exotic but frazzled looking woman stood in the front of the room, holding her hands wide, welcoming us into her classroom. The woman, whom I assumed to be Mrs. Woodsen, the Drama teacher, had frizzy, unkempt dark black hair and leather-like skin that suggested years and years in the sun, as she seemed to be in her late fifties.

She was wearing a deep purple kimono, with vibrant red dragons embroidering its floor length silk. Around her wrists were dozens of golden bangle bracelets that jingled with every small movement she made.

This teacher, who seemed more than human, transfixed me as I took a seat on the floor like everyone else. I had noticed that although the room would suggest chaos and confusion, all of the students entered the room silently and took their respective places on the floor. I sat close to Lilly, not sure whether to be terrified of what was to come next, or excited.

"Hello, my darlings," Mrs. Woodsen's voice purred her hello. As I looked at her thick eyeliner and dark red lipstick, she reminded me of a cat, or an Egyptian, or maybe an Egyptian cat.

"I understand we have new actors to join this vivacious cast today," she slowly moved her eyes to mine and held my attention for a few seconds before searching out Kiran and Talbott. I was horrified when I realized they were in this class as well, but as I looked around, I noticed that I recognized most of the students from English were here. "So before we begin our work with the one-acts, I would like for each of these newcomers to introduce themselves and enlighten us on their unique personas."

I was mortified; surely she didn't expect me to speak in front of this entire class of people. Not to mention the fact that almost all of this entire class of people witnessed the only unique thing about me already this morning. Thankfully, Talbott stood up first. I tried my best to shrink into a ball of nothing.

"Well, I am Talbott Angelo," he said in a strong, authoritative voice, his accent thick, making his words run together. "I am new to this place and this school. I come from London with Kiran. I hope to enjoy America very much," he gave a goofy smile and laughed a little, along with the rest of the class. He waited for Kiran to stand before he took his seat back on the floor. His huge frame seemed too big among the other, smaller-framed girls that had surrounded him.

"Welcome Talbott, we are so thankful you have been sent to us," Mrs. Woodsen purred to him. She turned her full attention on Kiran, gazing at him until I was almost embarrassed for her. He was not able to look fully at her face and I noticed a light shade of red creep up the back of his neck.

"My dear Kiran, you don't have to say anything unless of course you want to," Mrs. Woodsen's eyes became glassy with obvious adoration. Yuck.

"No, it's all right," he forced his eyes up and gave her a benevolent smile.

Kiran cleared his throat. His perfect posture and amazing good looks already set him apart from everybody else; but now with him standing and everyone else on the floor it almost seemed as if we were bowing down to him. Thinking that Mrs. Woodsen practically was, I smiled, and then realized Kiran was looking directly at me.

"Hmmm..." he continued to stare at me, while seemingly thinking about what he was going to say. "I am Kiran Kendrick. I am also from London," Unlike Talbott, Kiran's accent was light and crisp, making him sound like the perfect English gentleman. "We arrived yesterday. And let's see…. something unique only to me …." he was obviously dragging this out on purpose because a mischievous grin began to appear in the corners of his mouth. I found myself impatient with him, despite all of his looks and glory. Then he looked directly at me again, "Well, recently I caught a fainting, young girl, and saved her from imminent danger," he finished dramatically.

As his eyes locked with mine so intensely, and since apparently everyone in this class had already been a witness to my episode, all thirty voices burst out in laughter at once. The sound was shrill and mocking and I was once again humiliated.

"Quiet down my darlings. I apparently am not privy to the joke, so let us calm ourselves and our inner auras so that we may hear from our last new soul," her calming voice met with immediate success and all voices became silent. Kiran took his seat, but not without giving another roguish wink in my direction. I now found myself extremely irritated with him.

I struggled to my feet, not nearly as effortlessly as the two boys before me did. I looked around at my seated peers; my mind was blank and my face bright red. The faces staring back were exceptionally beautiful; their eyes unnaturally bright, and their hair unnaturally shiny. They were also exceptionally hostile and judgmental. It was nice to know I had once again been able to isolate and alienate myself just as quickly at this school as at any other.

"Um," I coughed to clear my voice and found Lilly's face, the only genial expression in the room. Even Mrs. Woodsen seemed to be eyeing me skeptically. "Um, I am Eden Matthews. I am from here, I mean from Omaha. And I recently fainted in front of my entire first hour class, but I don't remember anyone saving me from banging my head against the floor," I finished quickly and quite sarcastically, before plopping down cross-legged next to Lilly, unable to look up or at anyone. I thought for a second that I might come off funny or at least witty, but the deafening silence indicated otherwise. Lilly patted my knee reassuringly, but I was too mortified even to look at her.

"Well, I do hope you are all right, dear," Mrs. Woodsen eyed me even more suspiciously before turning her gaze on a few students who had begun to whisper. I looked over to see that it was the girls who had surrounded Kiran and Talbott. They stopped talking after receiving the evil eye from Mrs. Woodsen, but all turned to give me a dirty look. "Unfortunately for those of you who are new, we have already started working on our one-act plays, and the groups have already been chosen. I am afraid you three will have to work together quietly on busywork, until after the One-Act Meet, in a few weeks. I will have you grade papers from the younger classes. Please sit in a group behind the dividers, so that the other students can have room to work on their small masterpieces."

At this point, the entire class stood up and moved into their one-act groups. Lilly gave me an encouraging smile and went to stand with her own group. I picked up my backpack and shuffled slowly behind the dividers. This had to be some cruel joke. Mrs. Woodsen was now officially my least favorite teacher, even worse than Mr. Lambert was. Again, I was reminded that this was only second hour and the day was far from over. I had never regretted burning down a school more than I did at that moment.

Chapter Four

I took my sweet time walking over to the dividers and cringed when I looked behind them and found a tiny sitting area. I stared, mouth agape, wondering how I was going to get through this hour.

Kiran bumped, purposely, into my shoulder as he walked by and took a seat on the floor directly in the middle of the small space. Talbott followed close behind, although he was careful not to touch me as he entered. I was amazed at how quickly my infatuation with Kiran turned into disgust. Had I known he was going to sell me out in front of everyone, I doubted I ever would have found his faultless features so alluring before.

Regretfully I took my seat next to Kiran on the floor. I pulled my knees in as close as I could and disdainfully, rested my forehead on them. I gave myself hope that there was a way to avoid these irritating boys in the hole we had been banished to.

"So what are you?" Kiran asked pointedly. I lifted my eyes and found him staring at me intently. Avoidance was clearly out of the question.

"What do you mean?" I asked dryly. I had lost all patience with him. For the first time I noticed Talbott staring at me, as well.

"What are you?" he asked again, pronouncing each word crisply and clearly. If this was some weird game, I was not in the mood. I laid my head back down on my knees.

"What he means to say is.... which are you?" Talbott interjected, apparently hoping to elicit some type of answer from me; I, however, had no idea what kind of answer they were even looking for. After responding with silence, he continued, "We were not aware of you before we came; are you Witch, or Psychic?"

My head snapped up in reaction to his ridiculous question. I saw then that they were just playing another joke on me. How irritating. I was speechless, and my temper was slowly rising. I may have made a fool of myself before, but that did not mean these teenage boys needed to continue humiliating me.

"She's not one of you?" Kiran tilted his head towards Talbott and asked softly.

"No, not in the least. And I cannot get a read on her. Can

32

you?" Talbott responded just as softly. They spoke to each other as if I was not there and my patience drew thin.

"No," Kiran responded, almost as frustrated as I felt. The strangest thing was that they actually maintained a straight face as though they really were serious.

"I'm neither," I almost laughed as I said it. "I am actually an elf, a Christmas elf. Santa gave me some time off so that I could go to school. He's such a nice old man," I rolled my eyes, not just at them, but at myself, I couldn't believe I was playing their games.

They both laughed a little nervously and looked at each other. Kiran adjusted his sitting position and our legs bumped each other. I couldn't tell if he did it on purpose or not, but as soon as there was contact between us, I began to feel the prickles and heat like before. It wasn't intense and my pride promised me I could handle it. There was no reason to panic and flee from the room, at least not yet.

"Where are the papers we are supposed to grade?" I asked Talbott, seeing a large stack of loose-leaf notebook paper in his hand. "Can I have some, please?" I choked out manners, trying to be the better person, although they were making it extremely difficult.

"Talbott will do it," Kiran answered quickly, without even looking at his friend.

"I would rather grade my share, thank you," I suddenly felt sorry for Talbott, to have a friend like Kiran, but I shook my head trying to rid myself of the feeling. I needed to remember that he had been just as bad as Kiran. Ok, well maybe not just as bad, but the mere fact that he indulged Kiran put him in the same category.

"Really, Talbott will do them. He's actually probably already finished," Kiran insisted. I looked to Talbott but he just smiled. I realized that Talbott was going along with Kiran's orders happily and was not going to hand over any papers.

"Ugh. Fine," I resigned.

"Your last name is Matthews?" Talbott asked unexpectedly.

"Yes," I was getting tired of this.

"Nothing?" Kiran asked cryptically to Talbott.

"Nothing," Talbott responded just as cryptically.

33

"Do you have any questions for me?" I assumed Kiran was talking to Talbott, because I could not think of any nice question that I would have wanted to ask him. Any question I would have asked would surely get me into trouble. "Eden," he nudged my foot with his; there was instant electricity shooting from my toes up through my leg. "Eden, do you want to ask me anything?" He gave me another one of his impish grins and looked at me with such intensity that I found myself squirming.

"What? No," I said with surprise. "I don't have any questions for you," I let a little venom slip into my tone, and rolled my eyes again. "Except, why you felt it necessary to act like such an ass before?" I said it before I could stop myself.... I knew whatever I asked would not be kind.

Kiran let out a small laugh, but Talbott started to stand up next to him. His body had become tense and he was in a fighting position. I just stared at him completely confused. I cringed a little and pulled my knees in tighter. The last thing I wanted to do was fight Talbott.... No, sorry, the last thing I wanted to do was apologize to Kiran; maybe it would come to fighting after all, although I thought it was very strange that Kiran's friend would be so defensive over such a small thing. Maybe they were gay.

"It's all right Talbott, sit down," Kiran was still amused, and I guessed it was at my expense.

"She can't talk to you like that," Talbott growled. I was amazed at his devotion to Kiran. I found their relationship strange, and felt more uncomfortable than ever. Was he really going to fight me for calling his friend an ass? Truthfully, I could have said a lot worse.

I sat there silently, sizing them up. If they were gay, then the girls in this class were going to have an unhappy surprise, not to mention poor Mrs. Woodsen. Other than Talbott's overprotective aggressiveness and his obvious devotion to Kiran, they did not seem like lovers. Maybe Kiran was straight and Talbott was in love with him.

Kiran suddenly let out a roaring laugh, nearly rolling over in hysteria. I continued to stare at them, more confused than ever. Talbott sat back down, but his face was suddenly bright red. I realized he was having a hard time looking me in the eye.

"If she is who she says she is, of course she can. Now calm

down, you're not going to fight a human girl just for speaking her mind. I was rude, and for that I apologize," his voice turned to liquid and he reached out to touch my hand, resting it on top of my knees.

I pulled it away quickly. Both boys turned to look at each other; when Kiran returned his face to mine, I could see that his smile was now carefully controlled. He was frustrated with me. A wave of regret washed over me, and a small tingling of fear ran down my spine. I quickly shook it off. It made no sense to be scared of these bullies; surely, they were just playing another game.

"Don't be silly Eden, let's put this all behind us and become great friends," His voice retained a smooth fluidity, frustrated with me or not.

"You're right. It is silly," I thought of a hundred snotty things to say, but in the end, I lost my nerve. "I accept your apology. Thank you."

I could see that he wanted to say more, but the bell rang, so I stood up quickly and started to gather my things to leave. Before I could, he reached out his hand to grab my arm gently. A sudden, pulsating electricity overwhelmed me; I willed myself to continue to stand, doing my best not to show any signs of distress.

"As long as you are who you say you are Eden, I know we can be the best of friends," he tightened his grip on my arm as if to make a point. As he did, the electricity became stronger. My ears started to ring and my vision blurred, but somehow I managed to respond.

"Let's just try regular friends first," my voice was breathy and choked. He took his hand off me and I impulsively gasped for breath, steadying myself with a hand on the partition.

"Probably a good idea," he smiled widely and walked passed me, away from the oriental dividers. Talbott followed behind him, carrying the large stack of papers Mrs. Woodsen had asked us to grade.

I panicked slightly, not wanting her first impression of me to be a disappointment. I prepared a small apology in my head and followed the boys, hoping she'd believe my explanation: "They wouldn't let me grade the papers, but I tried. I promise!" It already sounded weak and I hadn't even said it aloud yet. However, as I got closer I could see Talbott handing over the papers already.

"Thank you Mr. Kendrick, I hope that I didn't ask too much of you," Mrs. Woodsen sounded slightly nervous as she addressed Kiran, although Talbott was the one who handed her the papers.

"Oh, no. Talbott was able to handle them just fine. I have to expect this sort of thing now that I am Stateside, I suppose. I will grow used to it. This way of life is just very unfamiliar to me," Kiran smiled generously at Mrs. Woodsen and then turned on his heel to leave.

I was shocked at his arrogance. His behavior made my stomach turn and I forgot all about his good looks. He was a completely despicable person. Who did he think he was talking to a teacher like that? Or talking about us….Americans? The Midwest might be different from jolly old England, but it was just fine for the rest of us, thank you very much. Clearly, he suffered from some sort of deranged class prejudice. My only hope in surviving the day was to manage to avoid him completely.

I searched out Lilly and saw her waiting for me by the door. I rushed over to her, thankful again to be in her calming presence. Her cheeks flushed as she scrunched her hair nervously with one hand.

"How was your One-Act practice?" I asked, trying to be as nonchalant as possible. I just wanted to forget all about my own hour of hell.

"Oh fine. I mean…. I am not very good at this kind of thing, so I always get nervous, even in practice. I know I'll just die when we get to the real competition," she tried to laugh it off, but I could tell that she was seriously unnerved.

"I'm sure you're great." I said, trying to encourage her. I actually had no idea what she was like, but any compliment felt good. I hoped that she was great; she deserved to be great.

"Thank you," she smiled, slightly more confident. "What was your hour like?"

"Ugh…. terrible. I cannot stand those boys!" I vented, a little more frustrated and a little louder than I would have liked. Her eyes dropped to the floor, and her expression became instantly strained.

"Now, now Eden, you promised we would be friends,"

36

Kiran chided me softly. He walked closer toward us, with Talbott following loyally behind. Maybe Talbott was a dog in his former life.

I immediately turned and walked out of the classroom. I had no idea where I was supposed to go next, but that didn't stop me from a fast escape. Thankfully, Lilly followed speedily behind me, although I could tell she was embarrassed of my behavior.

"Do you know what your next class is?" Lilly asked, a little out of breath from the quickness of my step. I could hear the boys following closely, so I picked up the pace even faster.

"I think French. Is that in this building too?" I needed a direction; I needed to get away from the golden boy and his golden retriever.

"No, it's not; it's in the History and Language building across campus. But I can take you, since I have Latin this hour," I was so grateful for Lilly Mason at that moment I could have just hugged her. I slowed down to a normal walking pace when we reached the marble staircase.

As we descended the steps, Kiran and Talbott took positions on either side of us. I could hear Talbott introduce himself to Lilly; she responded back in a terribly shy and shaky voice. I inwardly winced, imagining all of the horribly rude things Talbott would say to her. But to my surprise, he remained perfectly polite and sounded nearly as nervous as she did. Their voices dropped in volume and I tilted my head to listen in on their conversation.

"Did you say you had French next?" Kiran's languid accent pulled me out of my eavesdropping; I found myself relaxing a little.

"Um, yes. Why? Don't tell me you have that next as well?" Was this school playing some kind of sick joke on me?

"Yes, I do, actually. It looks as if we are destined to be together," his grin was back and I hoped that he was only kidding. I replied with a forced smile of my own.

"Does everyone in our class have French?" I realized that he was new too, but for some reason everyone seemed to know him already.

"No, I don't think so. I think that French is a last resort for us latecomers. The other language classes must have been filled," his accent was alluring, and I had to remind myself forcibly what kind of person he really was.

We exited the building and found ourselves in the warm sunshine. I hadn't realized how damp and chilly the building was, until I could feel the sun on my skin. I breathed in the fresh air. I pulled my thick hair off my neck and let the gentle, but humid wind blow through it.

I closed my eyes, hiding them from brilliant light of the morning sun. Lilly had led us out of the building through what appeared to be a back entrance. We were standing in a courtyard surrounded by identical brick buildings on every side. The beautiful campus felt more worthy of a university atmosphere than a horrible preparatory school.

"There you two are! I have been looking all over for you," a girl's smooth, but unfamiliar voice forced me to open my eyes and meet yet another student of Kingsley.

"Hello, Seraphina." Kiran's voice was all honey again as he addressed the girl approaching us. She was tall, even taller than I was; probably 5'10. Her long, thick, blonde hair bounced gently as she walked and her clear, unblemished skin almost glistened in the sun light. Her cherry-red lips were pursed and her cobalt blue eyes squinted, making a face that was less than happy. If it weren't for the expression on her face, she could have been a model walking down the runway.

"Hello," she said, careful to pronounce each syllable. "What is taking you so long?" she gave a disinterested look in my direction, and without waiting for an answer from Kiran, looked at me and declared, "You're the girl who fainted."

"Good memory," I responded sarcastically. I started to walk away, dragging Lilly with me when Kiran interrupted our getaway.

"These lovely girls were just showing us to our next class," we stopped moving and turned to look at him. I noticed Lilly's bee-stung lips formed in the exact "Oh" formation mine were.

"How nice of them," Seraphina slid her stick thin arm through Kiran's, suggesting some kind of claim she had on him. For the first time I noticed how similar they looked; they could have almost been twins. Despite my disgust for Kiran, and now,

Seraphina, I couldn't ignore the tightening in my stomach that felt something like jealousy.

Chapter Five

Welcoming all students and guests, the Administration Building sat in the front of hexagonally-shaped Kingsley. But leading out from either side of the building was a stone pathway connecting all six buildings. A large grassed courtyard surrounded a tall, brick, bell tower. The same dark, red brick architectural style dominated the buildings at Kingsley.

The English and Theatrical building was placed on the far northeast side of campus, and the History, Language and Arts building was placed on the southeast side. The walk along the brick path was short; we just had to pass the Gymnasium to get to it.

Green grass, green trees, and flowers still in bloom, embellished the beautiful campus. I would have loved to walk this alone, and take it all in slowly.

Unfortunately, I was not alone. I was forced to walk to French not only with Lilly and Talbott, who couldn't keep their eyes off each other, but with my new best friends Seraphina and Kiran as well. And to my ultimate disdain, Seraphina could not keep her hands off of Kiran, I realized this shouldn't bother me, and I hated that it did.

The walk was short however, and soon we had all climbed yet another marble staircase to find ourselves on the second floor of the H and L building. I glanced at Lilly who pointed me in the direction of French.

I entered into another class that had already begun; I was apparently unable to get to class on time today. A young, sophisticated, teacher glanced back from the chalkboard to glare at me. Her short, cropped, black hair was the same color as her short, cropped, black skirt suit. She wore bright, red lipstick and dark-rimmed glasses. She reminded me of something out of a bad adult film.

"Vous etes en retard," although she was speaking French, her irritated tone did not escape me.

"I'm sorry. I'm new," I tried in English. I had never had a French class in my life. At my previous schools I took Spanish; but that was not even offered at this school and, so I was stuck with French because it was the only open class. Aunt Syl promised me it was very similar to Spanish, but after what Kiran said, I was sure it was the last available space.

"Excusez-nous s'il vous plaît. C'est toute ma faute," Kiran and Talbott finally made their way through the door behind me and of course, Kiran took the initiative to introduce himself to the teacher; and it appeared he was speaking in perfect French, although I had no clue what he was saying. "Eden est nouvelle aussi et nous avons perdu notre chemin. Pardonnez-nous s'il vous plaît."

"Il n'y a pas de problème. Je suis heureuse que vous nous ayez trouvé," the adult film school dropout responded to Kiran in the most pleasant voice. She had completely transformed from the woman who spoke to me only seconds earlier, to another adoring fan of our one and only Kiran. "Accueillez, accueillir."

"Eden, you look confused," she turned her attention to me, and although she was not completely rude, she was not friendly either. Her English was marked by an unmistakably French accent. I wondered cynically if Kingsley had all of their language teachers directly flown in.

"I'm sorry, I just, um, I don't speak French. I've only taken Spanish," I tried to look as apologetic as possible, while wondering silently if you could be kicked out of this school just for irritating the bejeezus out of every teacher.

"Cela ne peut pas être?" she said again in French, shaking her head. "Why would they put you in this class if you cannot speak the language?" Without waiting for an answer, she continued. "Well, you are just going to have to learn. I refuse to dumb down my curriculum because one student is ignorant."

She looked at me as if she expected me to fight her on this. I didn't expect her to "dumb" down the class either. Although, I thought she could have said it in a nicer way; but that was what I had come to expect of this school, of its teachers, and of its students. I just kept looking at her in the same apologetic way as before.

"Well, I suppose the best way for you to catch up is by full immersion. I am Ms. Devereux. We speak only French in this class, and although I will give you some grace, I expect you to catch up quickly. You will need a tutor as soon as possible. You will sit at my desk, until I feel you are ready for a partner. Go quickly," she waved her arm in the direction of the teacher's desk and didn't give me another look. "Kiran and Talbott, I am so glad you have chosen this class. Please sit down anywhere," she spoke her instructions so quickly and with such a thick accent, I had trouble understanding, but I did as she told me.

I took my seat at her desk and pulled out my French books. I knew that I was the center of attention and again felt completely humiliated sitting in the front of the class, all eyes staring at me. Worst of all, Kiran was barely able to contain his laughter.

I opened my books and forced my eyes on to the page. Even the introduction was written in French. I rolled my eyes and groaned inwardly, while Ms. Devereux spoke rapidly in a language I was afraid would be the reason I would never graduate from high school. All of the students answered her questions without missing a beat; including Kiran whose flawless French rivaled even Ms. Devereux's.

I tried to avoid staring at him the entire class, but found myself glancing in his direction more than I would have liked to admit. Every time I looked up from my book, I found him staring back, making me blush for reasons I couldn't understand. I thought I found him completely horrible?

The class flew by; I spent most of the hour just trying to find words in the book that I heard spoken in class, although I was sure not one French word was spelled phonetically. It appeared that all of the students could already speak French fluently, and Ms. Devereux was out of her mind if she thought that I would ever be able to catch up.

When the bell finally rang, Ms. Devereux lectured me again on the importance of finding a tutor quickly. But as the entire class was gone by now, I didn't see that happening today. Kiran and Talbott were the only two people I recognized in that class and I'd be damned before I asked either of them.

I found history on the third floor of the same building and realized that except for French, the same people were in all of my classes so far. This had to be the entire junior class. I had been hoping to meet new people, to be given a second chance at proving I was not the idiot everyone in my class thought I was. But it didn't look like I would get that opportunity.

Thankfully, Lilly saved me a seat and I took it, grateful

once again that she was willing to be my friend. Mr. Emerson, my "A History of Europe" teacher, was an elderly man, with an all-white beard and all white-hair. He did not even bother to acknowledge Kiran, Talbott, or me, which actually surprised me. He was so far my favorite teacher, although I couldn't admit that he did much teaching.

We spent the entire hour listening to him drone on and on, not once looking up from his lecture notes. His voice was a gruff monotone that I found very hard to listen to. I struggled to take notes, but noticed that most of the students were either sleeping on their desk or passing notes back and forth.

Several of them ended up on Kiran's desk, and I observed his smug smirk after he read each of them. I could only imagine the important messages the girls in this class found necessary to send him. Talbott had his fair share of notes as well, although he had abstained from reading a single one. All the while, Mr. Emerson was oblivious to it all.

The bell rang, and we were off to lunch. The cafeteria was located exactly one building over from the Administration Building. Only seniors were allowed to take lunch in the courtyard, and as Lilly and I walked back across campus, we couldn't help but feel jealous. They sat basking in the sunlight, and again I noticed that all of them, without exception, were extremely beautiful. The same characteristics that defined my class, defined them as well, uniquely bright eyes and flowing hair. They all seemed to be ready for a photo shoot despite the drab Kingsley uniforms.

Lilly and I walked slowly behind the mob of juniors in front of us, watching the other students gather around Kiran aggressively. Talbott stood close to him as if to protect him from the overzealous girls. The seniors, who had thus far ignored the passing underclassmen, seemed just as enthralled with him as all of the others. Several of the girls and boys stood up and approached him, shaking his hand and taking pictures with their cell phones. These people were seriously delusional.

The cafeteria was more like a great hall, with long, thick, oak tables set up all over, than a typical lunchroom. I turned to Lilly for direction, but her blushing red face looked down at the ground. We hadn't talked since we left the other building, and I couldn't imagine what had upset her. I wondered if she was just as astounded over the scene in the courtyard as I was.

"Are you ok?" I asked, trying to be as nonchalant as possible.

"Um, it's just that, well, I don't usually sit with anyone else at lunch," her voice quivered slightly. She was embarrassed because she assumed I would think less of her. However, I couldn't have been more thrilled at the news.

"Oh thank God!" I blurted out. We both immediately started laughing and got in line for lunch.

After picking our way through the large buffet-like selection of food, which resembled more of a Thanksgiving feast than cafeteria food, we found an isolated table and took our seats. I looked around at the lunchroom full of people, sitting together in their own respective cliques. I noticed that Kiran and Talbott found a table near the middle of the room surrounded by girls, including Seraphina and several seniors, all giving Kiran their undivided attention.

"So what's the deal with that girl from earlier?" I tried to sound casual.

"Which girl?" Lilly looked up from her apple.

"The one that could be Kiran's twin," I mumbled, allowing the sarcasm to drip into my tone. I was embarrassed by the pang of jealousy punching me in the stomach.

"Oh, that girl," Lilly rolled her eyes and took another bite of apple. "Well, her name is Seraphina Van Curen. Her family has been part of this school forever, like since it opened a thousand years ago," Lilly was obviously not impressed with her either, and I breathed a sigh of relief.

"Huh," I said a little distracted, wishing I were brave enough to ask Lilly to spill all of the dirt.

"Apparently Talbott is impressed with her," Lilly looked over at the table and the blood immediately rushed to her cheeks.

"I don't think it's Talbott that she's after," I said sardonically, hoping to reassure Lilly that Talbott was still available, although I had no idea what she saw in him.

"Those girls are the rest of the girls in our class. The one with short black hair is Adelaide Meyer, and the one wearing all of the diamonds is Evangeline Harris. They and Seraphina, make up the holy trinity," she rolled her eyes again and I laughed. I'd been in enough high schools to understand the social order of things. "The rest of the girls are just followers, with no minds of their own."

"Wonderful," I mumbled under my breath.

"Just steer clear and they won't bother you…. most of the time," she looked down at the table, in a way that hinted they probably bothered her more times than she would like to admit.

"Well, this is the side of the cafeteria I prefer to sit on," I smiled at her reassuringly; it could not have been more truthful.

The bell rang before I finished but we got up to clear our things anyway. I wasn't sure if I was ready to get back to all of the humiliation. We double-checked to make sure we had the next class together, Calculus, something I was destined to fail at, and made our way to the exit. Mrs. Truance was standing in the doorway eyeing me. Great, the school board had already decided I didn't fit in and should be expelled promptly.

"Ms. Matthews, Principal Saint would like to see you in his office please; wait here and you can follow me there," she directed, appearing less than happy to be running this type of errand. I stopped to wait beside her; I waved to Lilly, as she walked by, giving me an apologetic smile. "Mr. Kendrick, please come with me as well."

Kiran and Talbott approached us with their group of lackeys; Kiran rolled his eyes when he left them. Kiran walked over to us slowly; I noticed his eyes were looking me over approvingly. Unexpectedly, a wave of nausea and a tingle of excitement ran up and down my spine; slowly, but surely, I began to feel the tiny prickles I knew would soon overwhelm me.

"Mr. Angelo, your services will not be needed, unless, of course, you are not able to continue on to class alone?" Mrs. Truance's snide and demeaning voice addressed Talbott, and I couldn't help but let out a small snicker that got me a very dirty look from everybody.

Mrs. Truance turned on her heel and stalked off toward the Administration Building. I allowed Kiran to pass, and followed in step behind them. What had I done now?

Chapter Six

The Principal's Office, located on the second floor of the Administration Building, was accessed by a stairway right inside the front door. I had not noticed it when I entered the building earlier in the morning. The small and slightly winding stairway triggered a claustrophobic sensation as I followed Kiran, who was following Mrs. Truance, to the second floor.

The small pricks I felt while near the cafeteria grew stronger in the small space, and I was getting very uncomfortable. The electrical pulses buzzed inside of me; my blood was slowly rising to a boil. This was a different kind of an energy that I felt I could manage. Struggling to contain myself, I tried to place the energy into a specific area of my body. My hands trembled. I clenched and unclenched my fists, struggling to gain control. The stronger the electricity grew, the more I could control it, so the logical place for me to concentrate was on my hands. As I did this, the collective energy rushed down through my body into my fingers. I experienced the electricity through my palms and fingertips, almost as if I was holding it.

By that point, we exited the stairway and entered onto the second floor. Teachers' offices surrounded us on either side of the hallway. At the end of the long corridor stood the Principal's Office with a gold nameplate that read "Dr. Amory Saint."

Now that the energy saturated my hands, it felt too much for me. My entire body shook from the force, and I struggled to contain the power of it. I had no idea what that meant; all I knew was that I wanted these people to continue thinking I was a normal teenage girl, especially if I was on my way to plead my case.

Two potted ferns sat on either side of Principal Saint's doorway. As we approached, I thought of the logical thing to do, although, in reality, this entire experience lacked any kind of logic. As casually as possible, I pointed my hands in the direction of one of the pots and let the energy go. This seemed the only natural course, although I was unsure of what prompted me to do it.

A bright light shot from my hands, and to my shock and horror, the potted plant exploded. Dirt, leaves, and shards of ceramic flew everywhere. I let out a loud scream and stopped dead in my tracks. That was not at all what I had expected to happen.

My body stopped shaking; the electricity was gone. I felt wonderful, the best I had felt in years. It was as if whatever had built up inside of me and caused all those terrible things to happen was finally gone. I let out a small smile of triumph.

My elation however, only lasted a second. Thoroughly proud of myself, and realizing how good I felt, I looked up to see that not only Kiran, but also Mrs. Truance, were covered in dirt and leaves.

Mouths tightly closed, mimicking each other, they turned around to look at me, and waited for an explanation. Mrs. Truance's burgundy suit and her glasses, covered in grime, were completely worthless. She let out an angry sigh, spewing dirt from her lips. Kiran's dirty blonde tussles, turned black from dirt; white dust and shrapnel from the ceramic covered him from head to toe. I held back a laugh when I noticed a fern leaf resting precariously on the top of his head.

"Oh, my gosh. That was the weirdest thing I have ever seen! Are you guys Ok? What happened?" Words and lies rushed out of my mouth. Feeling ridiculous, I just prayed they bought it.

"You did this," Kiran glared at me, angrily and accusingly.

"How could I have possibly done that?" I laughed aloud, hoping to pass myself off as incredulous. I sounded more hysterical than anything. "I was way back here. How could I have done that?"

"Mag-" Kiran started.

"Oh my, must have been a prank," Mrs. Truance interrupted Kiran. "Those nasty little underclassmen are always pulling stunts like this." She physically pushed him out of the way of the office door. "Mr. Kendrick, go clean up. Ms. Matthews, since you are unscathed you will see Dr. Saint first." Her voice, void of emotion, confirmed that she didn't believe a word she had just said. I doubted Kiran did either.

I followed the direction of her pointed finger and entered Principal Saint's office. Small bits of dirt and ceramic littered the floor; I was careful to walk over them.

"Close the door behind you," a deep, sophisticated voice ordered me.

I obeyed, moving the debris out of the way with the sliding

door. The door closed with a final click as I turned to look at the man who had spoken.

Dr. Amory Saint, a man in his late fifties; his dark, almost black hair complemented his even darker eyes. He was handsome, or maybe more distinguished than handsome; but either way he seemed to be a man that got things done. He actually resembled one of the bad guys in a James Bond movie.

"Please sit down, Ms. Matthews," He pointed to one of two, elegant leather, sitting chairs opposite his large, mahogany desk. Again, I did as I was told.

"Welcome, Eden. May I call you Eden?" I nodded my head, afraid to make a sound. I never felt more intimidated and I wasn't sure if it was because of the thousands of books lining every available wall space and cluttering the gigantic, opposing desk, or if it was because I knew this man held my fate in his hands.

"I hope you are making yourself at home in our humble school," he looked to me again, and I nodded, although I would have called Kingsley anything but humble. "That's good.... I wanted to check in with you, just to see how you are adjusting," Here he looked to me and paused; I could tell he was waiting for a verbal response.

"Um, yes, I'm adjusting, um, just fine. Thank you," I stammered.

"That's good." he repeated. "And everything is to your liking?" again he waited for me to respond.

"Yes, everything is just fine," I managed a small smile, hoping that maybe if this wasn't a meeting to expel me, then I could go.

"So nothing strange has happened to you today? Nothing out of the ordinary?" his face remained perfectly calm, but I began to panic.

"What do you mean?" I asked in a barely audible voice.

"I apologize if I've confused you. I just want to make sure everything is going smoothly on your first day here. It is my job to make sure every student feels well-adjusted," he smiled calmly, waiting again for my response. Was this some kind of test?

"Everything's fine," I blurted out. "If you mean the plant, I mean what happened in the hallway; Mrs. Truance said that it was just a prank. I didn't do it. It wasn't my fault. I don't know what came over me this morning, I didn't mean to faint. I'm sorry, it won't happen again. I guess I was nervous and…." he cut me off with a shake of his hand.

"Calm down, please. I didn't mean to upset you, I was simply inquiring about your first impressions of Kingsley. You may go now," he motioned towards the door and I got up quickly to leave. With my hand on the doorknob, he stopped me again. "Oh, Eden, one more thing, please don't hesitate to speak with me if something is on your mind."

Dr. Saint's last comment caught me off guard and I hurried through the door, feeling very uncomfortable. I felt the anxiety growing inside of me, along with the electrical pulses. I was so concentrated on his last words that I was not paying attention to where I was going and ran face-first into the chest of none other than Kiran.

I looked up to apologize, but something happened when our entire bodies met. Quicker than I realized, the electrical pulses seized my whole body causing stronger and more painful sensations than anything I had experienced before. As a gut reaction I forced them out of myself just like I did before, only this time, their target was not a potted plant, but Kiran.

Kiran suddenly flew through the air and across the hallway. The strong impulses that exited my hands hit poor Kiran directly in the chest. He landed fifteen feet away on his back looking up at me. I stood there shocked, completely unharmed. At least he didn't explode.

"What the hell was that for?" he demanded, scrambling to his feet and rushing over to confront me.

"I, um, I have no idea. Um, I am really sorry," I was mortified; there was no way, I could ever explain that to him.

"How dare you!" he yelled at me. I hung my head, not having a clue how I could make any logical excuse for my behavior.

"Mr. Kendrick, please come into my office," Dr. Saint, standing in his doorway, remained calm.

"Did you see what just happened?" Kiran shouted incredulously.

"What I saw, was an accidental collision. Ms. Matthews

49

meant no harm, nor did she do it maliciously. In fact, I already heard her apologize to you. Now, please, come in to my office." We both stood there, staring at Principal Saint. "If you please, Mr. Kendrick," he asked again with less patience. Dr. Saint opened his arm wide, directing Kiran beyond his office door.

Shaking his head, Kiran walked by me, and as I made my way back down the hallway towards the staircase, I heard Kiran shout, "Who is she, Amory?" before Dr. Saint closed the door behind him.

Chapter Seven

Knowing at any moment he could demand the explanation I could not give him, I survived the rest of the day hiding from Kiran. To my surprise, he appeared to avoid me as well.

All of my extra "energy" was gone for right now, and I was able to relax. Because of Kingsley's full, eight-period day, the afternoon dragged on. Lilly and I sat together in most of our remaining classes. Thankfully, our other classmates preferred to ignore us.

I understood why they wanted to avoid me; I was fully aware that I was a total freak. But I didn't understand why Lilly had no other friends. She was drop-dead gorgeous and completely sweet, yet all of the other girls in the class acted as if she didn't even exist. Only the teachers talked to her and even they seemed to do it out of necessity. The exception was Talbott, who found any excuse necessary to say something to her. Maybe the other girls were just jealous.

All of my teachers, demanding and irritable without exception, appeared to hate their profession in some unexplainable way. They showed favoritism to a select group of students; but no surprise, it happened to be the Seraphina-Kiran crowd. Oh well, I'd never been much of an honor student.

The students were the real enigma. They gravitated around Seraphina as if she were the sun. Even her supposed friends, Evangeline and Adelaide reverently worshiped her. So, it shouldn't have been surprising to me that Kiran and Talbott were victims to her gravitational pull. It was disgusting really.

The constant flipping of her long, blinding-blonde hair and the incessant giggling were enough to make me want to burn down this school as well. If it weren't for Lilly, I would have never made it through the day.

It was as though we were made to be friends, and similarly made to be outcasts. I wondered what she did before I came; and then I realized probably the same thing I did at all of my other schools: sit alone, stand alone, and eat alone.

Lilly could have been my exact opposite. She didn't have to fill in the silence with needless conversation, like I did, but didn't seem annoyed if I babbled on and on either. I lashed out at anyone who gave me a dirty look, but even though other kids bothered her, Lilly's sweet demeanor remained unaffected.

Lilly and I said goodbye to each other after our last class, chemistry. She promised to save me a seat in homeroom tomorrow morning. With something now to look forward to, I watched her climb into an elegant, black SUV and drive away. She seemed much too small for the oversized monster truck she was driving and I imagined her barely able to see over the steering wheel.

Looking around the student parking lot, I realized that everyone drove an elegant, black something or other. All of the cars exhibited class and style; all of the students driving them were obviously born to privilege. The extraordinary colors the students exuded bore a stark contrast to the dark, glossy veneers of their automobiles.

I wondered if a black car was part of the dress code as Aunt Syl drove up in her cherry red convertible. I smiled widely, happy not to fit in, and jumped in the passenger's seat. As we drove away, I felt slightly embarrassed for being picked up from school, but relieved that we were leaving the looming towers of Kingsley behind us for now.

"How was your day?" Aunt Syl asked, glancing at me from behind her oversized sunglasses. Her shoulder-length hair whipped around her face in the wind, but she barely noticed.

"Oh, you know," I sighed, thankful to be on my way home.

" Actually, I don't know." Aunt Syl gave me a longer look, and I realized she was looking for assurance that I would be allowed back tomorrow.

"Well, I didn't set anything on fire," I smirked, keeping the exploding fern episode to myself. Aunt Syl smiled sweetly; she always put up with my sarcasm.

"Well did you make any friends?" she questioned further, very maternally.

"Um, yeah, one. Her name is Lilly Mason; we sit by each other in most of our classes," I prayed she wouldn't ask about the rest of my class; I had no idea what I would tell her.

"Well, that's nice," she paused, glancing at me quickly. "What about the boys?" a mischievous grin flashed across her face, and I couldn't help but smile too.

"Oh, I don't know…. There are some good looking boys, but they all seem too immature." Kiran's perfect face passed through my mind, but remembering his antics, I shook it out quickly.

"Sounds like high school to me," she laughed, "So what do you want to do for dinner?" I realized then, that she was dressed nicely, in a light-blue short-sleeve blouse and black, pencil skirt with killer heels, precariously pressing on the gas. It was a nice change from the doctor's scrubs she was usually in.

I sometimes found it hard to believe we were related at all. Aunt Syl, or Dr. Sylvia Matthews, was very tall, very tan, and very blonde. I was naturally tan as well, but only moderately tall. As blonde as her hair was, mine was black. She made me keep it long; she claimed it was something about my natural color and volume being a crime to cut short. I didn't mind; at least I could hide behind it. Likewise, my eyes were black, very black; hers were crystal blue. She looked like the stereotypical California beach babe, and I looked like the Adams family. How we both could be related to my mother was beyond me, but since I'd never even seen a picture of my mother I guess I didn't really know how it was possible.

"I'm in the mood for steak," I sighed whimsically.

"Steak it is. But first, pedis, unless of course you have homework?" Only Aunt Syl would put a pedicure and steak dinner before homework.

"No, nothing I can't finish later," I lied; but honestly who really expected me to learn the entire French language in one night? I looked down at my beloved backpack filled with so many odious books. I had enough homework to last me several weeks; a few hours of procrastinating would not get me any farther behind than I already was.

"Great," she headed in the direction of her favorite nail salon and I laid my head back against the seat and completely relaxed, for the first time all day.

After a pampering spa pedicure, and a giant steak dinner at

our favorite Omaha steak house, I sat down to what looked like hours, maybe days, of homework. Aunt Syl had been called to the hospital, as usual; I had the house to myself. Her on-call schedule gave me a lifetime of freedom; I enjoyed the solitude and independence.

My house, a cozy Tudor style, four bedroom, three bath, sat in the middle of one of the most beautiful neighborhoods in Omaha. All of the houses, built in the same style, looked uniquely different. The tall trees embellished this part of town, and overshadowed most of the houses and streets of our mid-town, Happy Hollow neighborhood.

Although Aunt Syl made enough as an ER doctor so that we could live almost anywhere in town, she preferred it here, as did I. The neighborhood was safe and since there was only the two of us, we didn't need anything bigger.

Sitting at the desk in my room, overlooking the street, I could see my yellow Land Rover looking back at me. I stared back longingly; one day I'd be able to drive it again, hopefully one day soon.

I was never the child that needed much discipline and Aunt Syl wasn't the type of adult to administer much anyway. I did, however, lose my car after being kicked out of the third prep school; I couldn't really blame her.

I rapidly tapped my pencil on the desk, knowing I should get to work, but lacking the will power. I did everything I could to avoid French; but I was running out of options. I did the dishes, even though we ate out. I worked through my yoga DVD twice and I even finished all the other homework I had, which was a considerable amount.

French was too overwhelming, and after just finishing Calculus, my brain was fried. Besides, I really needed a tutor. A pit began to form in my stomach as I remembered the students in my French class, mentally picking them off one by one. I learned from Lilly during 8th hour Chemistry that French 101 was an underclassmen class, and the majority of the students were freshman. So not only was I unable to function normally at school, I now needed tutoring from a freshman.... awesome.

I could ask Kiran.... or Talbott. My stomach tightened at the thought of asking either one of them for help. Talbott seemed harmless enough, but his devotion to Kiran was disturbing. The way he followed Kiran around and could be so protective of him was not normal. I thought of Lilly and hoped that eventually his loyal energy transferred to her.

That left Kiran. Barring the fact that he wouldn't talk to me again after I threw him down the hallway with my inexplicable electrical powers, we didn't exactly get along. Something about him both excited me and terrified me.

With swirling thoughts of all of his exciting and terrifying qualities, I drifted off to sleep at my desk. I couldn't escape him; he was even in my dreams. Subconsciously I knew that I was dreaming, but there he was staring at me, as real as anything else.

He moved closer to me; instantly I felt the electricity coursing through my veins, but because it was a dream, it was even more intense. I turned and ran away, but he chased me. I could hear him only steps behind.

We were running in a forest of thick trees and uneven ground. In my dream, the night stars shone bright enough to light the landscape despite the thick canopy of the trees.

Although I was running, I wasn't scared. I knew that I was running because Kiran wanted to ask me a question, and I didn't want to answer it. But, he was too quick for me.

He grabbed my arm, and the force of the electricity from his touch pulled both of us to the ground. I found that we were now laying on our backs in a meadow, looking up at the million stars lighting up the sky.

I wanted to get up and run again, but I couldn't. My limbs felt weak and although the electricity hadn't left my body yet, a dull humming kept me very conscious of Kiran's hand intertwined with mine.

My hair fanned out around me; I noticed that I wore the shorts and tank top I was in while I did my homework. A warm breeze swirled around us, lifting my hair off the ground and then laying it gently to rest again. I could feel Kiran's eyes on me.

I looked over at him, unable to speak a word. I was transfixed to the ground, but it was not an unpleasant feeling. Kiran reached over with one hand, still holding my hand with his other to brush the hair away from my face.

"Eden," he whispered in a hypnotic voice. "Will you

56

please tell me what you are?" he smiled sweetly. I couldn't help myself; I wanted to tell him what I was, because I knew that I was something, something different, even though I didn't know what it was.

I opened my mouth to speak, but no sound came out. He leaned closer to me and I inhaled his intoxicating aroma, something earthy, something herb-like, but something sweet as well. He placed the palm of his hand against my cheek and electricity surged from his touch. The feeling was heady and overwhelming.

I wanted to struggle, to get away from him, but I couldn't move. Someone was invading my mind, my soul, or both. The intensity of the pulsing confused me. I trembled under the force of it.

Suddenly a deep and commanding voice spoke, "Eden, wake up." I lifted my head to see Principal Saint standing at the edge of the meadow, dressed all in black and with a terrible, foreboding expression on his face.

And then I awoke, reaching out in the darkness for a hand that remained holding mine only in my dreams.

Chapter Eight

With thoughts of my bizarre dream from the previous night swirling in my head, I stepped out of Aunt Syl's car unsteadily. Not only was my body psychologically shocked from the sense of realness of my dream, but I was also physically exhausted. My head felt very cloudy from the dull sense of electricity pumping slowly through my veins. Weak and tired, I forced myself forward.

Slowly, I walked up the hill towards the Administration Building. Students passed me as they hurried to class, but my feet felt clumsy, the electricity made me wobbly. At the top of the hill, I took a left on the brick path towards the English Building, and to my surprise, Principal Saint stood on the path, blocking the way.

"Eden, may I speak with you for a moment?" His entire presence exuded a dignitary-like respect, and I was sure people did not tell him "no" very often. Despite the request, he stepped in front of me, giving me no other option. At that moment, all I wanted to do was get to class and sit down. I entertained the thought of walking right past him, pretending I didn't hear. "Please, it will only take a second," he asked again, noticing my hesitation.

"Have I done something wrong?" I asked out of habit.

"Not that I am aware.... have you?" he flashed me a smile. He made a joke, but I was too exhausted to respond. He continued, "I am only concerned that Kingsley might be a bit overwhelming for you at first. Are you feeling all right? Has anything strange happened that would give you cause for concern?" His voice was slightly strained, and I saw real apprehension in his eyes. Suddenly *he* became something to be concerned about. This was getting kind of creepy.

"I'm fine, thank you," I kept it short and to the point. The last thing I wanted to do was confide in the Principal of the school from hell.

"Of course you are," he took a quick look around us before finishing with, "If you ever need anything, or if you ever have questions about anything, please feel free to find me immediately." Before I had a chance to respond, he walked away back toward his office.

That was strange. I wondered for a second if he knew about the weird things going on with me; but then I shook it off. How could he? I never told anyone, not even Aunt Syl. The only thing that could really have alerted him was the mysterious exploding plant, but I was not even sure if he saw what happened, although it was extremely out of the ordinary. I had to admit that.

I continued toward class, realizing now that I was the only student left standing outside. I tried to pick up my pace, but after my brief encounter with Principal Saint, I was more unstable than ever. The pulsing electricity was steadily growing stronger, and my blood felt like there was a current of energy rushing through it.

By the time I entered the English and Arts Building I could barely stand up. I needed to empty myself completely before I continued to class. I looked around quickly. Although no students occupied the lobby, I was afraid to cause a scene. My fingers crackled with the sound of electricity and my skin sizzled from the climbing temperature inside.

As quickly as I could, I ducked into the theater doors, across the hall from the marble staircase. I took a moment to let my eyes adjust to the darkness and started frantically looking around for a place to dispose of my building energy. A sudden burst of electricity surging through my heart made me double over in surprise. I tried to stand up, but only half succeeded. As fast as I could I hurried down the aisle, looking for anything that could be quietly destroyed.

On the stage I recognized the form of an almost hidden tin trash-can. I heard the last bell ring, informing me that I was late for class, so I took the stairs on the side of the stage two at a time and headed straight for the can. Looking around once more to make sure there were no onlookers, I pointed my hands toward the bottom of the can, hoping for a quick second, there was nothing disgusting in it, and released the energy.

The trashcan exploded. Its contents scattered across the stage, along with shredded pieces of tin. I felt much better and although I was sure the explosion was loud, I was confident it couldn't have been heard upstairs. I brushed what pieces of debris remained on me and ran for the exit, out the double doors of the theater, and toward the marble staircase.

I didn't make it far however, before I noticed Kiran and

Talbott entering the building. They talked quietly, but heatedly, until they looked up and noticed me leaving the dark theater. They instantly stopped talking and gave each other a quick glance.

"What were you doing in there?" Kiran asked suspiciously.

"Nothing.... I got lost," I gave a sheepish grin and slowed down to a fast walk, hoping to make it to the stairs before them. I felt much better after discarding the electricity and felt an entirely new kind of energy, a natural kind.

"I don't believe you," Kiran said bluntly, eyes squinting accusatorily.

"Kiran, let's just get to class," Talbott interrupted.

"Good idea," I agreed over my shoulder, passing them while they still stood in the lobby. I made it to the stairs, sprinting the remaining distance to class. By the time I reached the door to English I was completely out of breath.

"Oh, Ms. Matthews, late again, I see," Mr. Lambert acknowledged my entrance with disdain and irritation. "At Kingsley we try to make promptness part of our daily routine. I hope this will not be a regular occurrence." He gave me a snide smirk, but allowed me to take my seat in the back without further commentary. Lilly looked back and rolled her eyes.

A few minutes later, Kiran and Talbott arrived to class. They were both a little red in the face and clearly had continued their argument after I left them. Mr. Lambert offered a genuine smile and said nothing about their tardiness as they took their seats. Now I was the one that was irritated.

English seemed to drag on under Mr. Lambert's lecture; I struggled to pay attention. He droned on and on about Shakespeare, but my only thoughts lingered on the evidence I left in the theater. At the time I dreaded the consequences of being late for class over the consequences of what would happen to me if the school figured out who trashed the theater.... literally. I groaned inwardly, as I realized I should have cleaned up my mess and destroyed all evidence first and worried about class second.

"Pssst," Kiran whispered in my direction. When I refused to look at him, he tried again, "Pssssst." I pulled my hair over my shoulders and blocked my view of him.

"Eden," he tried a little louder, causing several students

around us to turn and glare. "Eden."

"What?" I whispered back as sharply as I could, peeking out from behind my wall of hair.

"Why were you late this morning?" he smirked, proud that he was able to get my attention.

"Why were you?" I avoided his question. The theater incident was just one of the many reasons I was running late that morning.

"I'm allowed to be late. Didn't you sleep well last night?" his grin widened into a proud smile and his perfect, straight and white teeth glistened at me.

I let my hair fall quickly back in front of my face, and slouched a little lower. My cheeks burned with the memory of my dream from the night before, being near Kiran with my hand in his, his eyes piercing me, as if he was looking into my soul. Thoughts of how inviting and seductive Kiran appeared in my dream conflicted with my fears of him finding out how crazy I was, more specifically about the trashcan. I heard him laugh softly, and a surge of electricity made my blood feel hot beneath my skin. He completely confused my emotions. I didn't know what I was feeling anymore.

The bell finally rang and I took my time standing up out of my seat. I gathered my books slowly; all of the time my dark hair masked my face. Eventually, the next class started to file in. I looked up, relieved to be the last junior left. I headed slowly for the stairs, afraid of Drama.

Unfortunately, I didn't need to wait until class for the drama to begin because Kiran was casually sitting on the black and white marble staircase, blocking my path. He sat in the middle of the fifth step, looking like a model waiting for the photo shoot to begin. His face wore the familiar smirk I had grown accustomed to seeing as he watched me awkwardly approach. I was not totally sure I understood his infatuation with bothering me.

"I was worried you would get lost," he said smugly as I walked closer.

"Where's Talbott?" I asked, realizing his absence was strange.

"He didn't want to be late for class," Kiran rose to his feet, waiting for me to ascend the steps.

"Me either," I breathed, picking up my pace, but brushing shoulders with Kiran as I passed. As soon as our bodies connected, the strong shocking sensation seized my shoulder, forcing me to grab it with my other hand for support. I gasped for air and pulled my body away, but I still felt the impression of his skin hot underneath my shirt.

"Are you alright?" he asked, his English accent sounding more like mockery than concern.

"I'm fine," I steadied myself and continued up the stairs as quickly as I could, although I was still out of breath from what felt like tiny lightning bolts in my blood. The shocking sensation encompassed my entire circulatory system and I cursed underneath my breath, determining that I would not faint today.

"Eden, you are ridiculous!" Kiran sounded exasperated as he caught up with me on the stairs and grabbed my wrist with his hand.

The force of his touch was too much to handle. The electricity surged through my body at an alarming rate, causing my heart to beat wildly. I forced myself to focus, but my vision blurred and a high-pitched ringing sound pierced my ears. I tried to say something but the world darkened around me. I felt myself falling and wondered for a moment if fainting down a flight of stairs would hurt.

"Eden…. Eden…. wake up, Love…." a soft, foreign voice pulled me out of darkness.

I opened my eyes slowly, but shut them swiftly when blinded from the light of the crystal chandelier hanging from a lofty ceiling. My blood flowed at a rapid pace and burned with a strong current of electricity. My heart, beating quickly, but somewhat controlled, made me realize that I was lying in someone's arms.

"Come on…. let me know you are all right," the voice turned stern. Obeying, I opened my eyes slowly and let them adjust to the light around me.

I groaned audibly when I looked up to find Kiran looking

back at me. His expression read concerned, and when I finally focused on him, I watched his facial muscles relax. His piercing aqua colored eyes gazed into mine; I started to remember what happened and how I ended up in his arms.

"Did I faint again?" I mumbled as memories slowly started to come back.

"Mmmm…. hmmm…." Kiran smiled and I realized that we were still positioned on the marble staircase. He must have caught me before I fell down the entire flight.

"Thank you," my voice was a little hoarse. I found that I was very comfortable lying in his arms. Despite the temperature and activity of my blood, I was hesitant to get up. I groaned again, milking it just a little longer.

"How can you really not know what you are?" Kiran's voice was soft and soothing, and although I didn't understand his question, he seemed to find it amusing and laughed a little.

"Mr. Kendrick, Ms. Matthews I believe you are supposed to be in class right now," Principal Saint hollered at us from the middle of the lobby. Unaware that anyone was around, my cheeks blushed with embarrassment.

I tried to sit up quickly as I heard Principal Saint's footsteps come closer, but Kiran held me down. I looked at him with pleading eyes, mortified by the predicament Principal Saint had found us in. Kiran laughed again, but slowly helped me into a sitting position.

"I apologize, sir," Kiran addressed Principal Saint, disdainfully. "You see, we were on our way to class, when Ms. Matthews fainted and nearly took a tumble down the stairs." I could hear the amusement in his tone and felt like punching him in the shoulder.

"Is this true, Ms. Matthews?" Principal Saint stopped walking when he reached the bottom of the stairs, and eyed me skeptically.

"Yes, it is true." I defended, terrified of the consequences I was about to face. "Luckily, Kiran, um, Mr. Kendrick was here to catch me," I stood up, shakily and looked as grateful as I thought I felt; although I realized it was all Kiran's fault to begin with.

"Hmmm…. I suppose it was lucky," Principal Saint did not look completely convinced and eyed Kiran with more suspicion. "Ms. Matthews, are you all right to continue on to class?" I nodded silently. "Fine, then go on. I will inform Ms. Woodsen of the incident. Mr. Kendrick, please come with me, I have an errand for you to run."

Principal Saint turned on his heel without waiting for a reply from either of us and headed for the doors that exit the building. Kiran gave me a roguish look and a familiar smirk before following behind Principal Saint. More confused than ever, I stared after them, before turning in the opposite direction to Drama class. Electricity still rushed through my veins, leaving me overwhelmingly weak and shaky.

By the time I arrived at lunch, I was exhausted. My nerves were completely fried and my hands could not stop shaking from the violent current in my bloodstream. Every small physical contact with another student sent more electricity running through my body, and my head buzzed from trying to function through it all.

When I finally took a seat next to Lilly at a table in the corner of the lunchroom, I was physically ill from the trauma that racked the inside of my body. I knew that I looked like a terrible mess. Beads of sweat dripped down my temples and the back of my neck. My hands, shaking so violently, caused me to clasp them together tightly to keep from making a scene.

"Are you Ok?" Lilly looked at me, concerned.

"Um, I think I might be coming down with something," I lied, but knew there was no better explanation. This feeling defied explanation and I preferred not to let Lilly know just how crazy I was. I tried to think of a way to sneak back into the theater after lunch. I needed to blow something up, before I blew up instead.

"You're lying," Kiran's stern voice accused unexpectedly. I nearly jumped out of my seat. He sat down next to me, so close that our bodies almost touched. Electricity pulsed through me in waves now and I realized I could be sick at any moment. The close proximity to Kiran had sweat pouring down my face and I could feel my blood boiling.

"About what?" I deflected. My shoulders begin to shake

more violently. It was hard to believe; I was still trying to play this off. My hand reached up instinctively to wipe my forehead, but I quickly brought it down again when I saw how badly it was shaking.

"I saw what you did in the theater," he whispered. He leaned in so that only I could hear him. "And we both know what happened on the stairs. Now look at you; you are clearly about to go into some type of shock." I should have been grateful for his discretion, but his nearness caused my vision to blur from the intensity of energy. His warm breath tickled my ear, but a cold shiver ran down the back of my neck.

"I don't know what you mean," I tried to deflect again, but now I realized Kiran and Talbott weren't late to English because they had continued their argument; they had gone to investigate the theater after I passed them. It was stupid of me to rush up the stairs so quickly, and it was stupid of me to linger on the stairs with Kiran. Why was he so damn nosey?

"Yes, you do," Kiran leaned in closer to my neck, his lips nearly touching my ear. His silky and soft voice lost its edge; his lips brushed my hair. "What's wrong with you?" He sat back quickly.

I began to convulse, and wondered to myself if this was a seizure. Surely, I was too coherent for a seizure, but my body shook so violently, I could barely stay seated. A small part of me wondered if I should bite down on a spoon, but before I could react, I felt myself falling backwards, slightly aware I was causing a scene.

I fully expected to hit the floor, but instead, I felt strong arms reach out and catch me. I looked up assuming to see Kiran, but instead I was shocked to see Principal Saint looking down at me. His eyes were full of concern and I could see his mouth was moving, but the ringing in my ears drowned out the sound. That was the last thing I saw before I lost consciousness for the second time that day.

Chapter Nine

I regained consciousness in an unfamiliar place. My head was pounding and my mouth felt like sandpaper. The electricity inside me slowed to a soft hum and my blood temperature cooled down a bit. I must have been in the Nurse's Office because I was lying on a soft cot and a metal medicine cabinet sat directly to the left of me.

As I slowly pulled myself into a sitting position, I realized I was not alone. I rubbed my eyes and moved my tongue around in my mouth, but it was no use. I needed a glass of water.

Arms folded, Principal Saint sat at a desk, staring. A wave of trepidation swept over me.

"Are you feeling alright, Ms. Matthews? You took quite a fall," his distinct, elegant voice was crisp and serious. He stood up and reached over to hand me a glass of water. I took it, my hands trembling a bit, and drank it quickly.

"I think so," I still felt weak, and my head was especially fuzzy. "Thank you," I said hesitantly. He took the cup out of my hand and walked over to fill it again at a sink positioned behind him.

"For what?" he sounded surprised.

"For the water.... and for not letting me fall," I replied matter-of-factly.

"I did no such thing. You did fall; you fell hard. The student, who brought you here, said you possibly had a seizure. I am here to make sure that you don't have another," his voice was full of conviction, but I could have sworn I saw him catch me.

"A seizure?" I said pretending to be confused. Although confident that I was conscious of what was happening to me, I was not so sure now. I didn't remember hitting the floor at all. I rubbed the back of my head, but nothing felt sore or tender.

"Yes, Mr. Angelo said you began shaking uncontrollably before passing out; you were fortunate he was near and able to act so quickly. Do you not remember any of this?" he looked at me skeptically.

"No," I said simply. I leaned my head forward to look at the ground, letting my long hair fall in front of my face. I could not look at this man in the eye when I lied to him; he seemed as if he would be impervious to a dishonest student. Obviously still confused, I didn't remember Talbott being there at all.

"Hmmm…" he clearly didn't buy it; but I wasn't sure I bought it either. "Well, the important thing is that you are alright. Do you have any idea of what could have caused this? Has this happened before? What is the last thing you remember?"

"I don't know," I paused, trying to remember what happened. What made me convulse so terribly? "I remember talking with Kiran and then nothing."

"Mr. Kendrick?" Principal Saint's voice raised in alarm, although I had no idea why. "This is worse than I thought," he mumbled cryptically under his breath. "Eden, I am afraid there is something we need to discuss. This has gotten out of control," he looked at me gravely, but did not attempt to stand or come closer. A feeling of dread washed over me, but before he could continue, Mrs. Truance stepped through the door.

"Eden's aunt is here, sir. Would you like me to send her in?" I was amazed at the tone of respect Mrs. Truance used with Principal Saint. Her quiet, subservient demeanor was nothing I had ever seen her exhibit before.

"Yes, that would be fine. I am sure she is anxious to see her niece," Mrs. Truance left the room and Principal Saint turned his attention back to me. "Our discussion will have to wait. I am sending you home for the day, and strongly suggest you take the rest of the week off to recuperate. Kingsley does not tolerate sick and fainting students." He said it with finality and stood to take his leave.

"Oh my word, Eden are you all right?" Aunt Syl was through the door and in front of my face before I could react. She was still in her green doctor's scrubs, and her hair was frazzled. She reached out to put my face in her hands and I inhaled the strong smell of hospital soap.

"I'm fine, really, I'm fine," I tried to reassure her, but she reached into her pocket and pulled out a small flashlight to begin examining my eyes. I attempted to push her away but she was persistent.

"They said it was a seizure, I was so worried," she exclaimed, finally giving up the impromptu checkup and hugging me tightly.

"Aunt Syl, I can't breathe," I said, struggling for oxygen.

"Oh, I'm so sorry dear," she pulled back, but didn't take her hands off my shoulders.

"I have excused her for the day, as well as the rest of the week," Principal Saint interrupted from the doorway. "Please, take this time to recover, and we will see you back here on Monday, healthy. I will have Ms. Mason bring over your homework and make sure you are caught up on classes." With his final instructions, he left us alone, closing the door behind him.

"What happened?" Aunt Syl asked exasperatedly. "The school called me at the hospital and I rushed over here right away."

"I guess I had some sort of seizure or something.... I don't really remember to be honest. But I feel much better now; I think I'm fine. Let's just go home," I looked up at her with pleading eyes, giving her my most charming smile, hoping to convince her.

"Nice try, but seizures are serious Eden. I am going to take you to the hospital for a full checkup, and then we will go home.... Ok? Who is Ms. Mason?" Aunt Syl was serious. I knew there was no getting out of all of the tests I was about to have run on me. I inwardly groaned, not sure if I was up to being poked and prodded. Still, I wondered if there was a diagnosis for blood made out of lightning.

"Lilly, the girl I was telling you about yesterday," I hopped off the cot and adjusted my uniform. Aunt Syl checked out with Mrs. Truance before we left; but we eventually made our way down to her car, parked slightly askew in front of the school.

Before we could begin our escape and to my utter despair and frustration, I noticed Kiran jogging down to us from the Administration Building. I cringed, unsure why he just couldn't leave me alone. Since I was still not feeling like myself, I was in no mood to deal with him.

"Eden," he called from a few feet away as I tried to slide into the passenger's seat as quickly as my trembling appendages would let me. "Eden!"

"Who is that?" Aunt Syl was both impressed and confused by the unbelievably good-looking boy jogging in our direction.

"What?" I shouted exasperatedly, stepping back out of the car and closing the door, hoping to shield, whatever this was about, from my aunt.

"Are you Ok?" he came to a stop too close for comfort, but thankfully I only felt the soft hum of electricity that had come to be normal.

"I'm fine," I said quickly, hoping he would just get to the point.

"Are you sure?" he reached out to hold my hand, reminding me of the dream I had about him last night. I let him hold it for a moment, feeling butterflies instead of overwhelming energy, before taking it back. He smiled slightly.

"Yes, I'm sure, but my aunt is taking me to get a checkup anyway," I said with slight irritation. "What do you want?" I hoped he was not here to ask me about the trashcan in the theater again.

"I just wanted to make sure you were Ok," he smiled wider and I found myself smiling back. I couldn't help it. He was just beautiful with his perfect white teeth, surrounded by perfect lips and perfect dimples. Even his eyes smiled at me.

"Thank you," I said softening a little. "But really, I'm fine. Like I said, I'm going to the hospital, and I am sure they will tell me that there is nothing wrong with me. So.... I'll see you later," I tried to turn away from him and get in the car, but he was not finished.

"I brought you your backpack," he blurted, never taking his eyes off mine. I reached out to take it from him, willing myself to look away from his shining turquoise eyes. I felt the heat rush to my cheeks, and let my hair fall in front of my face to hide the embarrassing blush.

"Thank you," I mumbled again. I took the backpack and our fingertips brushed softly together. Butterflies and electricity surged through my body this time, and I realized it was time to get out of there before Aunt Syl would witness one of my "episodes."

"Can I bring you your homework tonight?" his eyes wavered for a second and I realized that he was nervous.

"Um, actually I think Lilly is going to bring it," I replied in a rush.

"Mr. Kendrick, get back to class," Principal Saint's voice called from the top of the hill. Clearly annoyed, Kiran looked up, and then looked back at me. His entire body tensed; I could see

69

that he was torn. Surprised by his reaction, I could still relate to it. Every time that Kiran tried to talk to me, Principal Saint showed up out of nowhere to keep us apart. Maybe it was just a coincidence, maybe not.

"We'll see about that," he whispered before turning around and jogging back up the hill. I stood staring after him for a moment, wondering if he was talking about class or my homework tonight.

Kiran left me once again confused, but excited at the same time. With so many mixed emotions, no wonder I couldn't keep control of myself. Thankful I would have something to distract me the rest of the afternoon; I climbed back in the car. I was almost looking forward to the promised MRI and CT scan; maybe Aunt Syl would even throw in a PET scan just for good measure.... one could only hope.

Chapter Ten

I never thought I would miss school, especially Kingsley, but sitting in front of my window Sunday night, I could not wait to get back there. Or rather, I could not wait to get out from under Aunt Syl's watchful eye.

The tests at the hospital all came back normal. I knew they would, I knew that whatever was wrong with me was not going to show up on a hospital chart or graph, unless maybe it was a mental hospital.

Aunt Syl was less than convinced when they told me everything was fine and I could go home. Since she decided to use some of her accumulated vacation days just to be sure I didn't die, I was under constant supervision.

My week was full of manicures, pedicures, hair appointments and hours and hours of yoga. I had done enough up-dog, down-dog, Warrior-two for a lifetime. I enjoyed spending so much time with Aunt Syl, but so much relaxing proved hard for both of us to accomplish.

My aunt, an important ER doctor, was most comfortable with constant movement and nights of sleeplessness. I was accustomed to her absence for days at a time, and taking care of myself. I wasn't sure if we had ever spent that much quality time together. It was nice at first, but we were both in the habit of being alone.

Finally, that afternoon, she could stay home no longer and found an excuse to go to the hospital. Since I had never experienced an episode at home, I was sure she believed I'd be Ok by now.

The only other person I had seen was Lilly. She faithfully brought me my homework every night and stayed for supper. She also sat with me for hours explaining it, especially French. She was just as fluent as everyone else; having already finished her required French classes and moved onto Latin. Why I didn't think to ask her for help to begin with was beyond me.

Lilly was what Kingsley called a "boardy"; which meant that her parents lived elsewhere and rented her an apartment during the school year. Apparently, most of the students at Kingsley lived like that. Their parents, all super important and super rich, sent their children far away and provided them with all of the teenage necessities: food, lodging, chauffeurs, cooks, maids, tutors and no-limit, black, American Express cards.

I had heard of that sort of thing before, but my idea of a prep school, worth all that trouble, was located usually near an ocean, not in the middle of nowhere. When I asked Lilly why these students didn't go somewhere like New York, or North Carolina, she informed me that Kingsley was the trifecta for people of our stature. Since that only confused me more, she explained that Kingsley was not only the best of the best in the world of academia, but it was located where students couldn't find too much trouble and most of the parents were either close friends with the school board or Principal Saint.

I doubted that I fit in to any of those categories for attending, but remembered Aunt Syl's sizable donation to the science department before my admission forms were accepted. Despite all of her freedom, however, I could tell that Lilly was lonely. Thankfully, Aunt Syl loved her just as much as I did, so she spent most of her time at our house, refusing only to spend the night. Eventually I figured I would just convince her to move in with us.

The flash of headlights in my driveway pulled me out of my musing. Aunt Syl must be home from the hospital. I threw an oversized navy-blue Kingsley sweatshirt on over my tank top; it hung down over my shorts, making me look like it was the only thing I had on. I gave up on my Calculus homework and headed down to the kitchen, hoping she brought home something to eat with her.

The cooler weather brought a nice breeze through the windows, giving the house a freshly mowed grass smell. I inhaled the pleasing aroma, thankful the humidity was finally letting up a bit. Soon the leaves would be turning colors and the rain would come; fall was my favorite time of year.

Just as I entered the kitchen, the doorbell rang. I turned around and walked back through the living room to the front door. Wondering why she chose the front door instead of the garage, I flung the door open, expecting to see my aunt. To my utter shock, Kiran was standing in the doorway looking like a page out of magazine. What was he doing here?

"What are you doing here?" I blurted out, completely aware of what I was wearing and the mess of hair piled on top of my head.

"Don't you look cute?" he said mischievously, in his crisp English accent. He gave me his signature smirk and let his eyes drift over my legs. His wavy blonde hair, slicked back away from his face and wearing a black motorcycle jacket, he could have been cast in a scene from "Rebel without a Cause."

"What are you doing here?" I repeated, stunned and practically drooling.

"I came to see if you were Ok. You haven't been at school all week; I thought maybe something terrible happened to you," he stepped past me into my house and I inhaled his scent, feeling suddenly dizzy.

"Um, come in then," I still managed some sarcasm though my mind was swirling and I could feel the pin pricks of electricity start to return.

"So are you... Ok?" he turned back around to face me, his smirk still playing at the corners of his lips. His voice relayed no real emotion of concern and I could tell that he knew I would be fine before he came.

"I'm fine," I answered, or, at least, I was fine until he showed up.

"Good," he took a step closer. I pushed the door closed and leaned back against it, not really sure what to do now. I glanced around the room, debating if I should ask him if he wanted something to eat, or if I should just kick him out.

"Yep," I replied shortly, filling the awkward silence. I looked around the room again; hoping some piece of interesting information would come to me, and noticed he was still looking at me. "What?" I said half-laughing, half-humiliated.

"What are you wearing?" he took another step closer and lifted the hem of my sweatshirt with one finger, letting his other fingers brush lightly against my thigh.

I couldn't move. I couldn't think. I couldn't do anything with him that close. Although his fingers were barely touching me, they were completely weighing me down. The excitement his touch brought, scared me and I found myself trying to remember how to breathe.

74

"Eden," he breathed softly, almost whispering. I willed myself to look up into his eyes. His gaze was so intense I couldn't look away; he smiled softly. "Why haven't you called to let me know you are all right? After saving your life on numerous occasions, I think I deserve at least a phone call.... A friend would have called," he pouted sarcastically but leaned his face in closer. It was too bad for him that I saw through him.

"I apparently need to remind you that we are not friends," I retorted quickly, snapping out of my daze. "Plus, I don't your phone number...." I mumbled hastily. His eyes flashed with something that looked like frustration, but instead of offering his number, he softened his gaze and refused to look away. A wave of embarrassment washed over me; he shouldn't be able to manipulate me so easily just because he was the most gorgeous thing I had ever seen.

I tore my eyes away from his and walked across the room, leaving him to face the door alone. Maybe he would take the hint. I definitely did not need to be reminded of how often I fainted in the last few days.

I didn't care if I had to stand ten feet away from him at all times, I was not going to let him get to me so easily. His face flashed with frustration, before he put his seductive mask back on. Apparently, he thought I would be easy.

"Oh come on," he crooned, "We're friends. I thought we were going to try to get along."

"You thought wrong," I said flatly. Now that my emotions had calmed down, I could feel the slow tingling of electricity making its way through my veins. It was days since I had to deal with the energy, I almost forgot how uncomfortable it was.

"Eden, what do you have against me? Why all the hostility?" he gave me a playful smile and walked over to one of Syl's oversized, leather couches and plopped down. Great.... How did you get rid of somebody who refused to be gotten rid of?

"What hostility?" I questioned, feigning innocence.

"I just don't understand why you won't confide in me," although his posture was relaxed, his gaze remained intense and I watched his jaw flex and un-flex. I wondered at his use of the word "confide." Weren't we just talking about my gratitude?

"Kiran, there is nothing to confide. I have no idea what

you are talking about. If you want a thank you, well then, thank you. I appreciate all of the concussions you saved me from," I laughed a little, trying to pretend he was as ridiculous as he sounded.

"You're lying. You are more than what you seem," he sat up straight and folded his arms across his chest. He looked like a little kid pouting. "I could help you, you know."

"Oh, you want to help me?" I mocked, mimicking his accent, although it came out very badly. I wasn't sure exactly what ethnicity I just impersonated... Indian, perhaps? "Now, I'll tell you. Oh wait, there's nothing to tell." I finished sarcastically.

"Are you expecting someone?" he stood up abruptly and glanced around the room.

"My aunt," I said, looking around as well. We were standing at opposite sides of the room, but the electricity coursing through my blood grew steadily stronger.

"No, someone else," he squinted his eyes and walked around the room. "I'm getting tired of this, old man," he mumbled it so quietly, and his accent was so thick that I was not sure what or who he was talking to.

He turned away from the window and walked straight over to me, dropping all pretenses. His eyes were hungry and his face said something I didn't recognize.... maybe desire? I backed slowly away from him, not sure what he was about to do. My foot bumped into the fireplace and I knew that I was pinned. Electricity and anxiety washed over me.

Kiran let me struggle; I saw the familiar smirk returning to his lips. He looked over me until his eyes finally settled on mine. I lost myself in the depth of his ocean-blue eyes and worried that I would say or do anything he wanted now.

"You're not crazy, you know," he placed his hands on my arms and pulled me slightly closer. My stomach erupted with butterflies, making me forget about the energy that nearly knocked me off my feet.

"I wish I knew what you were talking about," I lied, but I knew the conviction didn't reach my voice.

"Sure," he leaned in closer, hesitating for a moment, our lips just barely apart. Kiran looked at me for a second longer before changing his mind and kissing me tenderly on the cheek.

He let his lips linger on my face, while the warmth of his body heat warmed me all over. I felt my body tremble as his sweet breath tickled my face.

I was not sure how to react, or even if I could react. Since this was the first kiss I had ever received from a boy, ever…. I was completely frozen. His lips left my cheek burning, and my body began to overheat. I couldn't tell if it was from his kiss or the electricity surging through me at an alarming rate.

He looked into my eyes again, watching my reaction. Unfortunately, for him, all I could do was stand perfectly still while willing my body under control. He laughed gently, then turned around, and walked out the front door.

I placed my hands behind my back and pointed them towards the fireplace. Not entirely sure why I felt the need to be discreet in my own home, especially now that I was alone, I let the energy escape through my palms and into the open hearth. Thankfully the only damage was to my ears, from the loud popping noise of the small explosion that I created; otherwise, a large fire was the only evidence of the electricity I let escape.

I heard the garage door open and knew that it was my aunt coming home for sure this time. I was too shell-shocked from Kiran's surprise visit to want to see or talk to her, so I headed for the stairs. My weak body and a stomach still full of butterflies, affirmed that I didn't understand my feelings for Kiran. It was no wonder that I could barely control my actions either. A shiver ran over me, and I couldn't decide if it was from excitement or fear.

Just as I passed by the living room window, however, I saw somebody or something move from behind a tree in the front yard. I stood there staring for a few seconds, one foot on the staircase, one on the wood floor, expecting Kiran to jump out from behind the large oak or something. But instead of Kiran, a tall, masculine figure walked out from behind the tree, clearly not Kiran.

In a long trench coat and bowler hat, he walked slowly and purposefully across my yard and down the street. A shiver once again traveled up my back, but this time I clearly recognized it as fear. Somebody was watching me.

Chapter Eleven

I parked my car in the long line of black something or others, taking up two parking spaces. My sunflower yellow Land Rover stuck out terribly, but I could have cared less. I took a big breath, thankful that I didn't fit in there. But even more thankful that I was allowed to drive myself that morning.

Of course, that was only due to the fact that Aunt Syl was called into the ER in the middle of the night. Feeling slightly sorry for her, but still happy to have my independence back, I grabbed my backpack and stepped out of the car.

Although I was running significantly late, I stopped to take another deep breath and mentally prepared myself. I had no idea how my body would handle returning to school after my short hiatus. I was definitely concerned about the whole fainting thing, and would have rather avoided it for the rest of my life.

I was pleased that my close encounter with Kiran brought no immediate spells of unconsciousness, and hoped that my previous behavior was all just a phase I was now, hopefully, over. I still could not mentally wrap my head around Kiran's unexpected visit or his even more unexpected exit. I unconsciously brought my hand to my cheek and smiled. I felt the heat rise beneath my fingers and quickly shook my head, physically trying to forget last night's intimate moment.

The student parking lot sat on the back of campus, near the football and soccer fields, so I bypassed the Administration Building and headed straight for English. A nice change from being dropped off at the front of campus like all of the other students who were too young or too rich to drive themselves.

A handful of students were in front of me, scrambling to get to class on time. All of them dressed in their navy blue and white uniforms; the only change today was the addition of navy blue or cardinal red cardigans, signaling the change in temperature. I was always amazed at the ability some girls had of changing a dowdy school uniform into a stripper piece from some teenage boy's wildest fantasy; I was not one of those girls.

I clearly picked out Kiran and Talbott in the throng of students ahead of me since they were walking much slower than everybody else. I slowed my pace slightly, not sure if I wanted to pass them, or be brave enough to join them. I mean Kiran and I were friends right? Or something more? Or something entirely different all together? I actually had no idea what we were.

I noticed how much taller Talbott was than Kiran, how much taller than everybody he was, and how strong he was built. I had a hard time picturing him in a bowler hat, but realized it must have been him behind the tree last night. An instant wave of relief washed over me. I had no idea why he would wear a disguise to accompany Kiran to my house, but it was the only thing that made any sense.

I was still pondering whether to pass or wait them out when they simultaneously turned around to look at me. Kiran gave me a small wave and an almost sheepish grin. I noticed near embarrassment in his eyes; it was the most endearing he had ever looked. I gave a small wave back and felt my cheeks burning from the memory of last night.

Talbott noticed our exchange and slapped the back of Kiran's head. My mouth dropped open from shock and amusement. Kiran stopped dead in his tracks and Talbott followed suit. They stood there staring at each other, both refusing to say or do anything more. For a second I thought they were going to fight.

"Enough of this Kiran, go to class," Talbott demanded.

"Who do you think you are?" Kiran shouted hostilely. They were both angry enough that their accents were making it difficult to understand them. The remainder of students, running as late as we were, turned to watch the exchange. I wiped the smile off of my face and realized this could get serious.

"Go to class," instead of shouting, Talbott's voice was a low growl.

"You cannot talk to me like that. I won't forget this," Kiran snarled back, but obediently and without looking at me again, walked on. Talbott did not continue walking however, but stayed where he was. His demeanor remained calm, and he turned his body to face me. After I refused to walk any closer to him, he signaled me with his hand.

"You can't keep playing this game with him," he started speaking to me as soon as I was close; a look of sincere determination on his face.

"I don't know what you're talking about," I replied,

79

slightly offended, and feeling like I used that phrase an awful lot lately. If there really was anything between Kiran and me, who was Talbott to get in the way? More importantly, why was Talbott getting in the way? And even more importantly, was there anything between Kiran and me?

"I'm afraid you do," he alleged softer, making his accent thick. I continued walking and he matched his strides with mine. "Listen, we are all curious about you, I'm sure you understand, but Kiran is taking this too far. It's not fair to him and it's definitely not fair to you. You are only going to get hurt."

"Thank you for your concern, but really there is nothing for you to worry about," I tried to stay polite, but get the message across at the same time. The soft undulating energy that was only a hum a moment ago was steadily growing stronger the longer I talked with Talbott, making my temper even harder to control.

"I am warning you for your own good," he persisted. "Stay away from him."

"I am trying to stay away from him. Maybe it's him you should be having this conversation with."

"I've tried to talk to him….. He is focused. When he finds something to…. entertain him, it is hard to refocus him; and you Eden, are turning out to be much more than mere entertainment. I am afraid the game is getting dangerous," When I opened my mouth to say something he continued quickly, "You should know that he has a girlfriend," he looked at me out of the corner of his eye and I knew that he was waiting for me to react. So I played it as cool as I could, continuing en route to English class.

"Really. Who?" I tried to ask coyly, but I could feel my blood temperature rise and not from the electricity this time, for whomever the girl was. The energy rushing through my veins centered unexpectedly and surged out through my fingertips into the grass, creating a small fire. I stopped suddenly to stomp it out, hoping Talbott didn't notice. And he didn't, or at least he pretended he didn't.

"Seraphina. That is why we are at Kingsley. He moved here to be closer to her," he reached out to open the door for me and the gesture gave me a second to recover.

"Figures," I sighed under my breath. "Listen, I'm really not into him. As far as I'm concerned, there is nothing for you to worry about. Seraphina and Kiran make a nice couple, really, they deserve each other," I finished through gritted teeth. All anger had vanished; instead I could only feel disgust for myself. Clearly, I was making something out of nothing.

"So I have your word, you will not distract him anymore?" his language was confusing to me, I was not going to give "my word" about anything; the promise seemed too binding. Besides that wasn't really up to me, right?

"Whatever Talbott, I won't bother him anymore," we were almost to class and I could not wait to be finished with the conversation; for some unexplainable reason I was suddenly depressed. I hoped I wasn't jealous of Seraphina. I found that especially degrading.

Before I could get through the classroom door however, Talbott put a soft hand on my shoulder, stopping me. "Eden, he can be quite persistent. He is very intrigued by you. He has never met anyone quite like you, so you will have to give him a clear message," I turned to look at him in the face, hoping that he was joking, but I was met with frighteningly serious eyes. "Even if you are human, Seraphina will not be very forgiving if she senses any competition," he tightened his grip on my shoulder, sending lightning bolts running down my arm. I was officially irritated.

"Listen, this doesn't sound like my problem. If Kiran is unhappy with his relationship then let them work it out. As far as I'm concerned, none of this has anything to do with me," I was finished with this, so I pushed passed Talbott into the classroom. I was late again and I could hear Mr. Lambert lecturing me as I headed straight for my seat. Wasn't it just last night that I was looking forward to coming to school?

The rest of the day went surprisingly quick. I was very prepared to ignore Kiran completely, but as it turned out, he was the one to give me the cold shoulder. This irritated me more than anything.

All day I began plotting what I would say to him if we happened to bump into each other. But I soon realized all of our previous run-ins must have actually been on purpose, because

81

suddenly he was nowhere to be seen. By the time I was sitting in eighth hour Chemistry, I felt terribly mopey.

The most irritating thing of all was that I had never noticed Kiran and Seraphina were a couple. Seraphina was loud and obnoxious, always drawing attention to herself; never once had I looked up to see Kiran at her side, worshiping her like the rest of the sheep.

Occasionally they would sit next to each other in class, and always at lunch, but I just thought those were their social obligations, since they were the cool kids and all. Now, every time I looked up they seemed to be side by side.... Laughing.... Touching.... Was I so consumed with myself I couldn't see what was going on around me?

On top of everything I could not figure out why this bothered me so much. Or why I felt like Kiran lied to me. It's not like I had asked him if he had a girlfriend and he said no. And he never really pursued me, or said that he liked me. Most of the time, he made me angry.

I doodled on my paper, resting my head on my arm. The electricity was at a medium hum, but my energy level was much lower. I recognized my depression and it depressed me even more. I shouldn't let this get to me as much as it was.

Suddenly, I snapped out of my funk and saw everything clearly. I was a game to him, just a game. Nothing was real, not even last night. It was just like Talbott said, I was only entertainment.

I bought into the whole good-looking, charming accent, playfully-mischievous persona and allowed myself to get emotionally involved. I was sure that if he didn't have that damn accent I would have seen through him immediately. Oh, those Brits could be so charming and manipulative with their proper way of talking.

I tried to sort through my feelings further. I never really felt anything more than physical attraction.... did I? I mean sure, the whole kiss thing last night left an impression, but I was sure any girl would have had the same reaction. He was the one who was practically stalking me; he showed up at my house uninvited. I never wanted anything to do with him; he forced himself on me.

What may have been construed as jealousy or resentment

for Seraphina was really just pity. I felt bad for her; she had no idea what kind of person she was dating. He was probably just using her too. He seemed like that type of guy....

I was no longer depressed; there was no more reason to feel sorry for myself; because I was livid, absolutely livid. I saw Kiran for who he was now, a disgusting, narcissistic pig. Albeit a completely gorgeous, perfect pig; but definitely a pig. And I certainly didn't want anything more to do with him.

I was interrupted from my epiphany by someone knocking on the classroom door. Mr. Hayman looked up from the chalk board at the front of the class and walked across the room to open it. A tall, athletic man in a black track suit entered, carrying a clip board and wearing a whistle.

"This couldn't have waited until the end of class?" Mr. Hayman asked the man.

"Who is that?" I whispered to Lilly.

"That's Mr. Lawly, our P.E. teacher," she whispered back.

"We have P.E.?" I said shocked. I didn't realize I had signed up for P.E., and I was sure I would have found a different elective if given the choice.

"Upper classman have a special kind of P.E.," she replied, but didn't get a chance to explain. The two men had stopped talking to each other and Mr. Lawly called for the attention of the class.

"As you know our camping trip was scheduled for later in the quarter. But due to unforeseen problems in scheduling and the fact that I am worried about weather if we wait any longer, we are going to take it this weekend. The arrangements have been made and your parents notified. I am happy to say I spoke to all of them personally and not one of you has a legitimate excuse to miss," audible groans were heard throughout the classroom. "You can pick up permission slips and a list of what to bring on your way out of class. And may I remind you, all of you are required to attend," when he said this last bit, he looked directly at Kiran. I found that amusing.

"What camping trip? I don't remember signing up for a camping trip," I looked, panicked and wild eyed to Lilly, hoping she would have some answers.

"It's on your class schedule as Special Elective," she rolled her eyes. "The camping trip is our P.E. class. The school board wants us to get 'real life' experience."

"So the whole class is over in one weekend?" I asked hopefully.

"Hardly…. Kingsley believes itself too important to fill our day with a menial class like P.E. So to fulfill the requirement they send us on one of these god-awful trips every quarter. I think next time we go rock climbing or something as equally terrible as camping. Everybody hates them, but there is seriously no way to get out of it. They think of everything, trust me."

"I have never been camping in my life," I was terrified. The only thing I knew about camping, was that every camper in any scary movie I had ever seen was always hacked to pieces.

"That's the idea," she rolled her eyes again. "The trips are meant to get us out of our comfort zone, make us do something we would never choose to do."

"Oh. Fantastic," It was my turn to roll my eyes.

A weekend trapped in the woods with this group of people sounded exactly like a horror movie to me. Could I request specifically that they check everyone's bags for chainsaws and hockey masks? Because surely, I would be the first one to die.

Chapter Twelve

"We're here," Lilly sighed despondently and I opened my eyes. I hadn't really been asleep, but there was nothing else to do on the four hour journey to the middle of nowhere.

"This is it? Please tell me we don't have to hike for hours into that jungle," I whined. Our bus was parked in the middle of a gravel parking lot surrounded completely by trees. There was literally nothing else but trees. I searched frantically for a gas station, or convenience store nearby, but all I could see were trees. I was not even sure if this was a legal camping area.

I yawned widely and had a feeling that my breath smelled awful. I glanced down at my wrinkled sweats and t-shirt and realized I looked as bad as I felt. I was pretty sure this was what the rest of the weekend was going to be like: sloppy clothes and bad breath. Our 4:00 AM. departure time didn't help the fact that I had been perpetually grumpy since I set foot on the bus. Mr. Lawly seemed like such a nice man at first until I realized he was a drill sergeant with the intention of fully entrenching us in the wilderness. My idea of camping entailed an RV and heated swimming pool; it was obvious I was about to be sorely disappointed.

"I think it's a forest, and yes, there will be some hiking involved," Lilly gave me a dejected look. "Your shoes are cute though," she offered me a bleak smile.

"Not for long….. Is it too late to go home?" I rubbed my bleary eyes, trying to focus on my brand new hiking boots.

"Afraid so. Come on," we grabbed our things and followed the rest of the students out of the bus.

Someone started pulling backpacks from the luggage compartment and Lilly and I found ours and strapped them on. Aunt Syl and I had to go on an emergency shopping trip since I owned none of the essentials. Normal people don't keep things like sleeping bags, hiking backpacks, portable stoves, canteens and two-person tents lying around. Ok, well some normal people did, but not me.

I looked around at the other thirty students and doubted any of them did either. Everything looked brand new and high tech; I even saw a random price tag still attached. We might as well have been a commercial for Coleman.

Lilly looked so tiny underneath her gigantic backpack I was convinced she was going to tip over. Her bright red hair covered by an army green hat, she peered out from underneath it barely able to see. But she bore the burden surprisingly well as we made our trek into the wild unknown.

Mr. Lawly appeared to know where he was going, and he was constantly consulting a compass, but after an hour of ruining my brand new hiking boots, I was skeptical. That a group of thirty or so students were following this man blindly into the wilderness did not seem like the brightest idea to me, but I guessed he was trustworthy. And if something were to happen to our only chaperone, I was sure the thirty of us would know exactly how to rough it in the wild until someone came to find us..... yeah, right.

"You're not afraid are you?" a familiar English accent had come to walk beside me, creating an equally familiar electrical buzzing throughout my veins. And so the shock therapy began.

"Of what?" I asked dryly, not sure what to expect and completely positive I didn't want to be bothered.

"Of bears and mountain lions and such," Kiran said seriously.

"There aren't any bears in the middle of Nebraska," I laughed incredulously, although inwardly I was cringing.

"Are you sure? We're close the Niobrara River. I'm pretty sure there are bears, mountain lions and wolves. I hear they like to prey on unsuspecting girls who have clearly never been camping before. This is their home you know, you are the intruder," he grew more dramatic with every syllable and although I knew he was just trying to scare me, I hated to admit that it was working.

"Oh, and you have been camping?" I glanced at him skeptically, but noticed that his hiking boots looked well worn. "But yes, I am sure, now go away," I didn't have the patience for him and I couldn't afford to faint if we had much longer to go. My pack was getting heavy and my sweat pants were starting to get too hot.

"But who's going to protect you from the big bad wolf?" I could hear the smile in his voice but I refused to look his direction as I trudged on past him.

"I can take care of myself.," I called over my shoulder and caught back up with Lilly.

"What was that about?" she asked softly, always the discreet one.

"Ugh. Kiran, playing his games again," I knew that Lilly wouldn't understand what I was talking about, but she was polite enough not to ask. Although I considered her a close friend now, I had never been one to open up much to others. I expected she was the same way, since she had never said a word about Talbott, but I saw the way they looked at each other.

I scanned the wilderness in every direction, telling myself over and over that Kiran was just joking, but a small amount of fear crept its way through my body. And then the worst thing possible happened; Kiran snuck up behind me grabbing both of my shoulders and shouting "boo" loudly in my ears. I screamed bloody murder and jumped at least five feet. The entire class turned around to see what the commotion was and all I could do was hang my head in embarrassment. I could hear Kiran's snickers behind me and I had half a mind to turn around and punch him.

"Alright kids, we're here," Mr. Lawly called out from the head of the group. We walked into a clearing in the middle of a dense forest. I could hear running water not far away and assumed it was a creek or a river or something. The space was wide enough to accommodate all of us although I saw no outlet for electricity. The realization that this far out there was no possibility of real plumbing also occurred to me. Welcome to hell.

Although all of the upcoming "P.E. classes" were a bit more involved, this particular one was basically just about surviving. I would have been terrified of what the other ones entailed if I could have been sure I was going to make it through this one. However, the outcome of this weekend was looking more and more pessimistic.

The rest of the morning was spent setting up the campsite and going over the rules. Mr. Lawly talked on and on about what to do with food, and trash and how to go to the bathroom. Yuck. He also gave a long lecture about not wondering off, not pulling pranks and not swimming in the river alone…. or naked. Blah, blah, blah.

After Lilly and I had successfully set up our tent, and gotten sufficiently dirty we headed over to the river with our fishing poles. Mr. Lawly's idea of camping included "catching" our lunch. This was going to be interesting.

The entire class was set up along the bank, every student holding some type of fancy fishing rod. We found a quiet space at the nearby stream and set up our own respective poles.

Well, we tried to set up our fishing poles. Eventually Mr. Lawly made his way over and explained what we needed to do, and then eventually he just ended up doing it for us. If I wasn't so frustrated with my freaking fishing pole, I would have found the image of thirty very privileged, very snobby prep school kids trying to catch their own food hilarious. I had just learned why fishing was considered a sport.

I stared into the stream for what seemed like hours, but in actuality was probably more like thirty minutes. I was starving, I was dirty and I was never going to catch a fish, and even if I did the chances of me actually eating it were very slim. Well, at least I wouldn't have caught a fish if I had the chance.

As I watched the water, hoping for a glimpse of anything fish-like, and tried to ignore the humming of electricity running through my veins at a steady rate I noticed Seraphina approaching out of the corner of my eye. Her habit was to usually ignore Lilly and me, so I didn't think anything of it, until she stopped directly behind me.

"Stay away from Kiran," she growled threateningly.

I half turned my head to say something snotty, but she didn't give me the chance. I felt her palm on my back and with surprising force she shoved me straight into the stream of ice cold water. My head just barely missed a rock in the shallow end of the riverbank, as I went face first beneath the surface, drenching myself completely.

I rolled over quickly into a sitting position with my knees sticking out of the water, not entirely sure what to do. I was horrified and humiliated. I looked around to see everyone laughing at me and somewhere I could hear Mr. Lawly yelling "What did I say about swimming!"

"You're right Mr. Lawly, I felt like a swim and therefore dove into the freezing cold, three foot stream, with all of my clothes on, on purpose," I thought to myself.

From where I sat, water flowing over me; I could see Seraphina and her groupies all laughing and pointing. I couldn't say that Talbott didn't warn me, but really was any of this my fault? I thought I had left Kiran alone, though clearly not soon enough.

My eyes continued to roam until I found the boy in question, standing away from the crowd staring at me without any smile on his face. I couldn't make out his expression, but I knew mine was one of pure disgust.

The electricity already shaking my body began to rise with my temper. The angrier I got, the stronger the energy pulsed through me. I had never felt it that strong before. Anger turned to fear when I realized I didn't know what I was going to do with it. I was so unsure of how my body was going to react to that much force that I was terrified to even stand up. My hands began to shake and I was fully aware I was about to look more like a freak than ever, if that was even possible at this point.

I had to get out of there, I had no other choice. Even if I fainted, at least maybe I could get to shore first. It would have been better than drowning in the middle of the cold shallow stream with an audience whom I doubted would even come to my rescue.

I slammed my hands in the water, to push myself out of the slow current, but that, unfortunately, turned out to be a big mistake. As soon as my palms touched the cool water, energy erupted out of them and what I created was beyond bad.

A giant tidal wave, of what seemed to be the entire river engulfed the shore. I watched in terror as all of my classmates and Mr. Lawly were suddenly and unexplainably covered head to toe in a torrential downpour. Well, at least no one was laughing anymore.

In fact, no one said anything, they all just stared at me....dripping wet. Fish lined the shore, but most of the students continued to hold onto their poles, completely shocked. Seraphina gave me a death stare, even Lilly looked less than happy.

I stood up as the riverbed began to fill again and walked straight through the crowd of people. No one said anything or even attempted to stop me. I didn't know what I would have done if they did. There was no explanation I could think of that would make sense; there was no explanation I could even give them period. I couldn't explain what just happened myself.

And so with head down, I marched straight back through the woods and into my tent. I realized it was just a tent, that the only thing separating me from the outside world was a thin layer of canvas, but it would have to do for now.

I ripped off my wet clothes and flung them outside the tent opening. I grabbed my sleeping bag and used it for a towel, regretting the action as soon as I realized it now smelled like river water. I finally found some new clothes and threw myself down on my air-mattress.

Eventually I would have to face them again, but now was not the right time, I was positive of that. My hair was drenched, still dripping and smelled like fish. I closed my eyes and breathed in the solitude, even if it only lasted a minute. I might have destroyed what little illusion of sanity I had left, but at least I had expelled the electricity for now and maybe, just maybe could get a few minutes of rest.

Chapter Thirteen

Eventually everyone dried off. Mr. Lawly made several small fires for all of the students to sit around. He also gave everyone a dried food packet he had brought along for emergencies. I doubted he expected he would need them so soon.

Thankfully Mr. Lawly didn't banish me. He was actually surprisingly nice; he even built Lilly and me our own fire so I wouldn't have to face the other students yet. I supposed dealing with thirty vengeful high-schoolers was enough punishment for one girl to endure.

Our activity for the afternoon was supposed to be a long hike through the wilderness. Thanks to me, and the fact that everyone's shoes needed to dry out, it would only be a short hike through the wilderness. Just in time to get back and try to catch our dinner, hopefully tsunami free.

Mr. Lawly called us to our feet and we formed a wide line. Lilly and I hung back slightly, so we could take our places in the far back. I was not ready to look anyone in the eye yet; I couldn't even look Lilly in the eye. She hadn't asked me any questions about my accidental tidal wave, and I appreciated her more than ever.

Mr. Lawly started walking in the direction of the river, before stopping suddenly and turning around. The students in front of us followed his lead, making a semi-circle through camp to adjust our course. My guess was that Mr. Lawly was just not ready to face the water again. I couldn't blame him; I didn't think I was either.

So instead of walking along the river we took a route in the opposite direction, to the East of how we hiked to our camp this morning. The terrain was rough and uneven. I had to focus on the ground to keep my balance. Or at least that was what I told myself I was doing, but really I was not ready to face all of the snickers and glares from my still angry class-mates.

Our hike followed a winding path through a beautiful forest. The trees were thick and the leaves were just beginning to turn colors for fall. The sound of the creek had silenced completely and the only noises we could hear were birds and squirrels or the occasional insect flying too close. I was lost in my own thoughts when I heard Lilly gasp softly. I looked up immediately, not knowing what to expect; maybe Seraphina had organized for me to be taken to the mental institution, or better yet, burned at the stake.

Instead of physical death, however, it was only physical torture. Kiran and Talbott had stopped walking and were apparently waiting for us to catch up. I glanced at Lilly to see her porcelain cheeks stained red from blushing. I didn't understand what she saw in Talbott, but as his cheeks were an equal shade of crimson, I'm guessing he also saw that same something in her.

"That was some temper tantrum back there, Love," Kiran fell in to step next to me. I was surprised to see Talbott choose to walk next to Lilly instead of Kiran.

"Back where?" I played ignorant hoping to avoid the conversation and glanced back behind my shoulder. I realized it was impossible, but a girl could hope.

"I told you Seraphina would not appreciate competition," Talbott said softly, ignoring my sarcasm and joining the conversation.

"I'm not competition. Seraphina can have him," I growled, frustrated with Kiran, he was the reason all of this had happened. Seraphina could have him; I was certainly not going to fight over him.

"You're not competition huh?" Kiran asked softly, letting our arms bump gently together as we walked. "And here I thought you were madly in love with me," Kiran whispered over-dramatically, his perfect accent articulating each syllable. The electricity under my skin flared for a moment and I felt a surge of heat rush through my body.

"No, I'm not. Seraphina has nothing to worry about, trust me."

"Well that just hurts," Kiran shoved me gently and I realized that he was flirting with me, although I was doing everything in my power to disengage him.

"Stop it," I commanded firmly. "You're going to get me into more trouble. Just leave me alone so Seraphina will leave me alone."

"That's not very likely on either account," Kiran mumbled.

93

"Besides, you're done for now. I wouldn't be surprised if the whole class wasn't plotting their revenge."

"Well, you could at least stop," Talbott looked directly at Kiran, but his tone was hopeless.

"Yes, you could stop," I repeated and gave him an irritated glance.

"Yes, I could stop, but then I wouldn't have any fun," Kiran whined defensively. "If I left you alone, who is going to blow things up when they get nervous? Or nearly drown thirty people in a poor attempt at vengeance? I can't count on any of them to do it." He pointed his chin towards the group of students walking in front of us.

"Very funny," I responded dryly.

"Really though, you need to control your magic. You are out of control," Talbott said seriously, although I knew he was only mocking me.

"If only it was that simple," I muttered under my breath.

"Well you could at least try; I think the teachers are going to stop believing that it is all accidental behavior, especially when you involve them in your anecdotes," Talbott was always the advice-giver, if only he had a solution as well.

"You're right about that. But I think when that happens, when they finally stop believing it's all on accident, they will finally send me where I belong," I laughed bitterly.

"Oh yeah? And where is that?" Kiran asked.

"The loony bin," everyone probably assumed the worst now anyways; I couldn't hide the fact that I was crazy any longer.

"I told you, you're not crazy," Kiran put a protective hand on my shoulder, sending both butterflies and electricity soaring inside of me. After today's outburst and the strength of energy I felt in the river, at least the electricity had become easier to control.

"Oh right…." Sarcasm dripped from my voice, "This is completely normal behavior; all teenage girls can empty riverbeds with just the touch of their hand."

"It is normal behavior if you go to this…." But Kiran didn't get to finish his sentence. All of a sudden I was hit in the face with a giant ball of earth. Rocks, dirt, mud and leaves splattered all over my face, into my mouth and covered my hair.

I was blinded for what seemed like minutes as I tried to scrape the mud from my eyes, nostrils and tongue. Not only did it hurt, but it was also disgusting. My mouth was open when the attack came, meaning I had eaten and tasted more than anyone's fair share of dirt for the day.

I could feel the mud caked in my hair, in my eyelashes, up my nose, and I thought there was even some in my ears. I was sure Seraphina was the one to thank for this, although I couldn't be positive because I never saw who threw the mud ball in the first place, and I certainly couldn't see anything now. I coughed up rocks and leaves, gagging violently, doing everything in my power to keep from puking. A few wet clothes did not even compare to the grossness of this retaliation.

"You could have helped her," I heard Talbott accuse Kiran.

"If I would have seen it coming, I would have gladly taken the bullet for her," Kiran said bravely, while laughing hysterically.

"Thanks a lot jackass," I grumbled threw bouts of spitting out mud. I heard Mr. Lawly yell something about keeping up with the rest of the group; clearly he thought this prank was well deserved.

"I wish I had a towel or something to give you," Lilly offered helplessly. "Would you like some leaves or something?"

"Yea, I guess," wishing more than ever I had worn a sweatshirt; instead of just a tank top and jeans. I thought about using my socks, as unpleasant as that sounded.

"Here, you can use my shirt," Kiran finally decided to be a gentleman. He handed me the red cotton polo he was wearing and I cringed while using it to wipe off my face. After glancing down at the expensive designer tag, I felt guilty for punishing the poor thing by turning it into a filthy rag.

"Thanks," I mumbled into the shirt, peeking out from behind it to make sure I hadn't left him shirtless. Thankfully, he was wearing a white v-neck undershirt.

I wiped as much off with Kiran's shirt as I could, feeling the dirtiest I had ever felt. Since Lilly, Talbott and Kiran waited with me while I cleaned up, we had to walk a little faster than before in order to catch up with the rest of the group.

Not sure what to do with Kiran's polo now that it was

completely ruined; I held it awkwardly in my hands. I glanced up and gave him a sheepish grin. I could feel small pebbles and bits of mud still in my mouth, so my grin quickly turned to disgust and I tried to spit it out as quickly as humanly possible. Not very lady like, but what other option did I have?

"You just invite trouble, don't you?" Kiran goaded, but handed me a water bottle I hadn't noticed him carrying before. I took it, very grateful I was able to rinse my mouth out.

"Looks like it," I said through bouts of gurgling and spitting.

"What are we going to do with you?" he laughed again lightly.

"Ugh. Mud tastes awful," I changed the subject to what was really on my mind. The constant grinding of dirt and pebbles between my teeth had me beyond nauseous.

"How are you going to get them back?" Kiran apparently lived for my humiliation.

"Are you kidding? I'm not. I would like this all to just end," I nearly whined.

"What? With your kind of power, they're no match for you."

"Thanks for reminding me what a freak I am," I was all of a sudden irritated. "This thing is ruining my life; I'm certainly not going to use it against anyone else."

"Don't be such a baby. Seraphina could never have done that with the water and she certainly hasn't held back against you. You could get her back so good. Come on, rain down hell!" Kiran pushed.

"I'm not just here for your entertainment. And isn't she your girlfriend?" I spit harsher than I had intended, electricity building with every emotion. "I can't control what is happening to me and it's not some joke for you to use to pit me against Seraphina. You are crazy if you think we are going to battle it out all over you," I picked up my pace and refused to look back at him.

"You're wrong, you can control it," Kiran yelled after me. That was not really the point I had hoped to leave with him and that irritated me even more. What stung the worst however was that Lilly stayed next to Talbott, leaving me to walk alone through the never-ending wilderness.

Chapter Fourteen

The day ended and slowly the sky turned to dusk. Mr. Lawly had been to every tent, making sure all of our fires were strong and we would be able to make them last through the night. Lilly and I sat around ours on a couple of rocks. Most of the other students were doing the same.

There were thirty students on the camping trip and all of them were assigned to groups of four, except Lilly and me. Thankfully we were the only two to get a tent to ourselves, well besides Mr. Lawly, but his little one-man lean-to hardly counted.

All of the tents formed a circle around a large campfire set up in the middle of the clearing, but occasionally Mr. Lawly set up smaller fires closer to the tents. This seemed like a forest fire waiting to happen; but Mr. Lawly was confident he had things under control.

Some people actually caught fish after we returned from our hike and that was what we were nibbling on now. Our lesson was how to gut and cook a fish over an open flame; I had never done anything more disgusting. I am not exactly sure how this trip was teaching us to survive in the real world.

I couldn't think of one situation where I might be stranded in the wilderness and have to depend on fresh fish and berries to survive. Except maybe if I was some type of fugitive on the run or something; I guessed with my track record that didn't seem so impossible after all. I took a big bite out of my smoked catfish and tried to enjoy the taste of my future.

Mr. Lawly passed out cans of baked beans and ingredients for s'mores all to be cooked over the fire. I knew that this was the ideal camping cliché but I wasn't buying it. I was filthy dirty, my long hair was in endless tangles and I was tired of being picked on. I wished I could say I was the outdoorsy type, but I would have done almost anything for a shower right then.

Lilly and I sat silently, consumed with our own thoughts. I pushed the food around on my tarnished tin camping plate and wondered what Seraphina had planned next for me. I looked over at Lilly and saw a small smile on her face, clearly her thoughts were elsewhere and infinitely more enjoyable.

I wanted so badly to ask her if anything was going on between her and Talbott, but I couldn't bring myself to do it. She had been so great about giving me my privacy that I just couldn't invade hers. If she wanted to talk about it with me, she would.

I looked over at Talbott; he was sitting in the middle of all of the "cool kids," right where he belonged. His olive skin was darker from the sun today and his black curly hair was pushed out of his eyes. His posture was perfect and his white teeth glimmered in the coming darkness. All around him sat equally as beautiful girls staring at him, but he happened to be staring at Lilly. I didn't understand why he was so tied to that group of followers, clearly he liked Lilly. Was he that much of a robot?

I glanced over at Kiran sitting next to him. He too was staring in our direction and so I quickly looked back at the ground. I didn't get him, plain and simple. He was apparently dating Seraphina, yet barely had anything to do with her. She was gorgeous and popular; the very girl high school social standards required him to date.

But me, the social outcast and resident freak, Kiran wouldn't leave the hell alone!   Either this was just some really messed up game he was playing, or he wasn't as attached to Seraphina as she was to him. It didn't really matter which one it was, I was getting sick of being in the middle. And I was definitely tired of providing tonight's entertainment.

I pulled my knees closer to my chest and laid my head between them. My dark hair spilled over and made a pool on the ground. Normally I would have worried about dragging it through the dirt, but since it was probably dirtier than the ground, I decided not to get upset about it.

I contemplated revenge against Seraphina, but I couldn't think of anything legal. I was already in enough trouble with Mr. Lawly anyways and I was pretty sure his list of rules said something about an ongoing prank war being forbidden. A small jolt of electricity shocked my system and made me sit upright; I looked over to see Kiran about five feet away and coming closer…. great.

"Go away," I picked up a rock and threw it at his legs.

"Don't be so grumpy," he caught my rock effortlessly and tossed it back at me.

"You're going to get me into trouble again," I complained, catching the rock and throwing it back at his shoes. He didn't try to catch it that time, but I doubted he could even feel it through his thick hiking boots.

"You are trouble," he sat down next to me, a little too close for comfort. Electricity shot like sparks in my veins and gave me goose bumps all the way up my arms. "Listen, I've negotiated a cease fire on your behalf. Seraphina has agreed to stop this nonsense as long as you can agree to as well. I think you officially owe me now."

"I don't owe you anything, you're the reason I'm in this mess," I stood half way up and moved the rock I was sitting on over, away from Kiran. I didn't need this right now; I didn't need him right now. And it irritated me that he was right: I was grumpy.

"Eden…" he scolded tauntingly. I couldn't help but love the sound of my name when he said it with his seductive accent. I laid my head back down between my knees to hide the smile I was having trouble keeping off of my face. The roller coaster his presence sent my emotions on was overwhelming.

"What are the terms?" I asked, my voice muffled underneath my massive amount of hair.

"Oh, right. You leave them alone, they leave you alone."

That was way too easy. I peaked at them through my wall of black hair and realized that none of them were looking this way. Seraphina and all of her groupies were laughing, but not at me, they were thankfully completely absorbed with themselves. It seemed I had faded into oblivion once again. Thank God.

"What about you? I'm sure this is some breach of contract," I turned my head to the side and laid my cheek on the tops of my knees, allowing me to have a full view of Kiran. He was still in the white undershirt he was wearing earlier, after I destroyed his polo. The soft, cotton t-shirt clung to his body. His arms were strong, each muscle clearly defined from bicep to forearm. His tanned skin looked faultless in the fading sun; he could not have been more perfect.

"I do what I want Eden, Seraphina knows that and you should too," he looked directly and deeply into my eyes, causing me to blush.

"So she is really going to leave me alone, even if you won't?" I asked, not sure if I really wanted him to at that moment. I inhaled deeply through my nose, willing my nervous body to relax.

"Yes of course, I asked her to," still looking into my eyes, he smiled.

"Oh, I see, your girlfriend obeys your every command." I asked sarcastically. Obviously he was deluded.

"She is not my girlfriend, but I think you get the gist of it."

"Sure she's not," I rolled my eyes before positioning my face back into my knees. I couldn't look at him anymore; I was finding it hard to think straight. Energy was vibrating through my heart at an accelerating speed, feeling more and more like a defibrillator.

"She's not," he softened his voice and sounded dejected, like he didn't really believe what he was saying either.

Dusk turned to dark and the air became cool. I was still in my muddy tank top from earlier and shivered under the night breeze. I looked up to notice the fire was getting smaller because of the wind and silently wished I knew how to "kindle" it.

My blood suddenly began to boil and the energy became pin pricks underneath my skin. I felt a little faint and then the fire burst out into a larger version of itself. I stared after it stunned, thankful for the warmth and even more thankful I didn't injure anyone.

"Did you do that?" Kiran half laughed at me.

"What? No. That's weird," I mumbled, still unable to accept the fact that it was me. I mean, was it me? I was certainly thinking about the fire, my body had the strangest reaction right before it happened; but it couldn't have been me. A person cannot do things like that. I mean, I may have been a freak, but I was certainly no magician.

Kiran laughed longer. He scooted over closer to me and I realized for the first time, that he was not freaked out by me at all. In fact, in some weird way all of my strangeness was making him more attracted to me. I decided the poor thing loved crazy people.

"What are you laughing at?" I demanded, determined to prove it wasn't me. The heat felt good on my bare skin and the energy that was strong inside of me just moments before had dwindled down to a soft buzzing.

"I want to know who you are," Kiran replied cryptically.

"Me too," I muttered under my breath. He looked over at me and smiled. I was coming to terms with the fact that I was comfortable around him and it actually felt good. He seemed to understand me in a way that I didn't even understand myself.

"Hey, let's go for a walk," he jumped to his feet excitedly; realizing that I had let my guard down, I instantly put it back up.

"Why?" I asked, eyes narrowed, feet planted firmly on the ground.

"Because a walk will be fun, we can explore the great Nebraska Wilderness," it was hard to say no to his accent, or his eyes, or the child like excitement he was suddenly full of.

"I'm not so sure. Are we even allowed to leave?" I looked over at Mr. Lawly who was exiting his tent, guitar in hand. I panicked a little. There was no way in hell I would be singing "Kumbaya" with this group of people.

"We won't get into any trouble, I promise. I am pretty sure Mr. Lawly is scared of you," he smiled wider and I saw he had already made up his mind. Lilly, whom I had nearly forgotten about was looking at me like I was crazy if I didn't go.

"Fine. Let me get my sweatshirt." I ducked into my tent and grabbed a gray hooded sweatshirt from one of my old schools out of my backpack. I threw it on over my dirty tank top and knotted my hair high up on my head. I contemplated lip gloss, but quickly disregarded it.

I had no idea what I was thinking saying yes, but I supposed there was no turning back now.

102

I exited my tent, energy buzzing and a little nervous, but ready for my walk with Kiran through the woods. I noticed that Talbott and Lilly were standing close together at the edge of the forest, whispering to each other and giggling. Apparently it was a double date.

I exhaled and realized I had been holding my breath. Kiran waited for me by the fire and I joined him, following the 'love birds' into the dark woods. Hello "scene from very scary movie."

I stumbled my way around, unable to see anything through the crowded trees. The night was cloudy, but the high canopy of branches would block out any light from the stars or moon anyways. I stayed close to Lilly, grabbing on to her for support every once in a while. She didn't seem to have any problem making her way in the dark; in fact, none of them did. I was the only one staggering around blindly.

I had always scared easily and so this scenario without a doubt had me terrified. Every little noise, every little break of a twig and I was nearly jumping out of my skin. I couldn't remember why I had thought this was such a good idea. An owl hooted nearby and I let out a tiny scream.

"Calm down Eden, I was only kidding when I told you there were bears out here," Kiran sounded slightly exasperated and I couldn't blame him. I was pathetic.

"I know.... I'm fine," I tried to sound confident, but my voice wavered.

"There's nothing to worry about," Kiran walked from the other side of Talbott and Lilly to be next to me, and put his hand on my arm, steadying me. "I won't let anything happen to you," he leaned in to whisper, but I could hear the sarcasm in his voice.

"Thank you, but I am just fine," I ripped my arm out of his hand a little too dramatically.

"All right, suit yourself," he didn't attempt to touch me again, but he didn't leave my side either.

We wandered silently through the dense wilderness. The night was very still, even the animals and insects had seemed to quiet down. The sky was overcast, but every once in a while the moon would break through the clouds and shine down an eerie glow around us.

I began to relax after my eyes had adjusted and I could see where I was going a little better. Lilly and Talbott had managed to walk ahead of us; I could hear them talking quietly. I smiled at how relaxed Lilly was around Talbott; they seemed to be really good for each other. I thought Lilly might even have made Talbott relax a little as well.

"I think he would leave me for her," Kiran said softly.

"I didn't realize you two were a couple," I smirked, satisfied with my insult.

"Oh, you think that's funny do you?" Kiran laughed out loud and then reached over to tickle me. I stumbled in the dark, trying to get away from him but tripped. Electricity began to steadily hum underneath my skin as I took Kiran down with me, falling to the ground.

He sat up and shoved my shoulder gently with the palm of his hand. I could tell he was getting ready to say something but suddenly I felt a surge of electricity that I could barely control. I slammed my hand over his mouth, every one of my muscles on edge.

We had been walking for a while, maybe thirty minutes and we were pretty far from camp. We had come to a dead end of sorts as our path was blocked by a tall cliff and wall of boulders. We would have had to change directions to continue on our walk.

The energy abruptly surging through my blood warned me that we were not alone. I hesitated, wondering if maybe Seraphina or one of her minions followed us, but I usually could recognize the level of electricity brought on by another Kingsley student. The pulsing energy I felt now alarmed me of a greater danger.

"Lilly, Talbott get down!" I half whispered, half shouted. They obeyed instantaneously, and I was surprised they didn't ask any immediate questions.

"What is going on?" Kiran wiggled out from underneath my firm grasp, talking at full volume.

"Shh," I whispered with force. "I heard something, or felt something.... something is definitely not right," I was as confused as I sounded. The hairs stood straight up on my arms and the back of my neck. I didn't know how, but I knew something was terribly wrong.

"You're right," Kiran's voice had softened to a whisper now and he crawled into a crouching position. "Talbott do you feel that?"

"Yes I do. I think we should get you back to camp," Talbott was suddenly next to us, along with Lilly. His arm rested protectively on Kiran and he had positioned his body in front of him. I was surprised to see that Lilly had also taken a defensive crouch blocking Kiran's rear.

Electricity began rushing through my veins, sending my senses reeling. At first the sensation made me nauseous, but I adjusted quickly. The very first awareness I noticed was how vivid my eyesight became. Everything around me sharpened into the clearest image, as though I was in the middle of daylight, only more intense. I could see everything now, every animal hidden up high in the trees, every insect crawling, and every speck of dust on the ground.

The electricity pounding through my veins was intense, but it was also focused. Every one of my senses was heightened in an unnatural way: my sense of smell, my sense of sight, hearing, touch and even taste. I felt another sense as well; although it was unfamiliar and unidentifiable to me, I knew it existed and I was suddenly aware of how to use it.

My sixth sense, as it were, was hypersensitive to the physical nature of the world outside of myself. I could feel everything move around me. I could feel the leaves move in the trees from the light breeze, and the rocks crunch under oncoming feet. I felt the moon in the sky and the stars that were millions of light years away. I felt the center of the earth pulsating with the rhythm of the universe.

And then I realized that we were not alone. The change in my nature was a result of other people surrounding us. I could "feel" distinct entities making their way towards us, trying to be discreet. Each individual carried their own dissimilar electrical field, warning me of their approach.

"Someone's coming!" I whispered fiercely, but by the tense and crouched postures of my friends, I knew they already realized this. I could feel the negative aura of the oncoming force. Whoever they were, they meant us harm.

Before we could react, we were surrounded. Five hooded figures stood surrounding us, faces all masked. If it were not for my heightened sense I would have assumed this was another practical joke, but the focused energy surging through my veins told me that this was a very dangerous threat. The heat in my blood readied me for battle, and I barely recognized myself.

I looked at Kiran; he stood to his feet, arms wide, and ready to fight. Adrenaline pumped through my bloodstream, allowing me to feel no fear, but did nothing for my confusion. I glanced at Talbott and Lilly and to my surprise they had both taken the same stance as Kiran. I had no idea who these people were, but realized a fight was imminent.

Lilly stood with her back facing Kiran as if to protect him from a rear attack. She looked miniscule alongside Talbott and Kiran. Even our attackers were large and tall figures. Although I couldn't be for sure that they were all men by the way they were dressed, but if I had to have guessed I would have assumed they were.

I positioned myself in the protective circle with the rest of my friends, unsure of what I was capable of. I would do anything to protect these people, but if push came to shove, I realized I was going to be the one that needed protecting. I mimicked their stances, hoping someone would shout out instructions.

The fight would happen at any moment, of that I was sure. The only thing we were waiting on was for someone to make the first move. I considered rushing one of the men in black, but decided it was probably too risky and definitely too stupid.

We stared at each other for what seemed like an hour. I had never witnessed a fight except on TV, and although I expected for them to pull out guns or some other type of weapon, nothing appeared. They clearly pursued us, but I was unclear of how they would begin their attack. Instead of a weapons fight however, something so unexplainable happened that I could only stand there staring at all of those around me, mouth opened wide.

The cloaked figures had surrounded us on every side. We had our backs towards each other, in a protective circle around Kiran. The tension was thick and my muscles twitched in anticipation.

Finally the first move was made; it was like nothing I had

ever seen happen in my life. One of the masked men jumped forward into the air, seemingly trying to hurdle over Talbott to reach Kiran. Although the jump at first appeared impossible, as soon as his body was lifted off of the ground he inexplicably transformed into a mountain lion. My mouth dropped open and I shook my head frantically, unwilling to believe that what I thought I saw actually happened.

To my amazement though, instead of getting torn to shreds, Kiran met him in the air, forcing him to the ground underneath him. They were not alone for more than a millisecond before Talbott jumped into the wrestling match pounding the human turned animal until he bled.

I hoped that this was the end of it, but there were four other cloaked beings surrounding us and I had an ominous feeling this fight was far from over. Two more of the strange men immediately transformed into similarly dangerous animals to assist their friend; one a bobcat, the other a leopard. Snarling, growling and biting, they attacked Kiran and Talbott over and over. I watched, with disbelieving eyes at a fight that seemed doomed.

The animals ripped into their skin, biting, clawing, tearing away pieces of flesh, but I never saw blood. I used my heightened sense to search for the terrifying sight of torn and bloodied flesh but could not find it. My stomach lurched at the sight of Talbott and Kiran in a battle for their lives, but I remained a bystander unsure of how to help.

My mind refused to process what I could feel was reality around me. Lilly let out a battle cry of her own, jumping into the air and turning herself into a tigress. Her animal form maintained her petite size and the vibrant red color of her hair, but her claws and teeth had suddenly become the most ferocious weapons I had ever seen. She joined the fight, tearing and biting the other animals involved. I covered my mouth with my hand, unable to move, paralyzed by confusion.

Kiran threw the mountain lion off of him with such an unimaginable force; the animal was thrown at least thirty feet away. Quickly the animal, once a man, was back on his feet taking three quick bounds and jumping back into the fray. Talbott was desperate to keep the animals away from Kiran, throwing one, and then two off of him, but they were persistent, always returning with even more vigor.

The two remaining masked men remained men, but were none the less dangerous. They joined the fight as well, uprooting trees and hurling large boulders at my tiring friends. They had yet to touch anything however, accomplishing it all with what seemed to be just an outstretched hand.

The fight was creating a clearing of its own in the once crowded forest. Trees and boulders were constantly hurled at my friends, some finding their mark; some stopped midair and dropped to the ground by a mere glance from Kiran. The only problem was that the animals continued to attack him, making it impossible for him to see every obstruction coming his way. My friends were being beaten to death and I still stood there helpless.

I swallowed the bile rising in my throat and I couldn't help the feeling of panic washing over me. I had been forgotten, a simple bystander to the unreal destruction happening all around me. My tired and outnumbered friends were frantic to win their survival but the attacking men seemed even more bent on their demolition.

My blood was hot with electricity surging through my veins, my heart beating wildly out of control. My fingers and muscles twitched with the desire to join and my senses heightened to a crystal clear state. I inhaled deeply of the battle around me and I realized that I wasn't helpless.

And then it dawned on me. The energy coursing through my veins must be the same force with which these men were using. Its very nature sharpened into a treacherous weapon by their presence. I could feel anticipation mingled with bloodlust as though the electricity itself were a life form. I had never felt more empowered as the electricity I had tried to oppress for so long rushed through my blood giving me a sense of strength I had never experienced before.

I forced my mind to focus on the fight, appreciating that all of my senses were already finely in tuned. I watched as mammal ripped flesh from mammal, and masked men performed feats of strength that should have been utterly impossible. Kiran and Talbott seemed to possess the same power that the two remaining humans did; the landscape around us was ripped to pieces as they tried to destroy one another.

I tested my own strength with a nearby rock. I willed it to be lifted into the air with my mind and the small bolder obeyed easily. I decided the course of destruction and the rock flew through the air crashing into pieces against a small tree. Again I tested my strength with the same tree, ripping it out of the ground and lifting it easily into the air; its limbs and roots hung precariously over the two standing strangers. With a thought, I dropped the tree onto them and watched as they were crushed beneath it. I heard the revolting crunch of bones breaking as they were buried beneath the branches.

The men did not give up however, and threw the tree off of their mangled bodies scrambling to their feet, bones completely restored. My mind refused to believe what my senses had already accepted as reality. Again I tested my strength, electricity building with every mental movement.

Merely thinking of a basketball sized boulder, I lifted it with my mind, the energy growing even stronger and hurled it with all of the mental power I had at the nearest shrouded figure. Everyone had written me off, clearly I had been frozen by fear, but as terrifying as my new found powers were, I was the only hope we had for victory.

The man I hit was not expecting an attack from me, and I realized they did not comprehend where the first tree I dropped on them came from. I hit him directly in the temple, causing a sickening skull-crushing thud. He lost his balance and fell over, letting out a scream of frustration.

For just a second Kiran had the upper hand and brought another tree branch down on him. Momentarily he was trapped, until the other standing figure reached out his arms sending Kiran flying through the air in the opposite direction and isolating him from the rest of the mêlée.

I decided to try the same effect, and it was my turn to send the other attacker flying. I was more than angry, I was furious. All of the energy building up inside of me had come to an alarming climax, I let it loose on this one man, sending him thirty feet away and head first into a thick tree. I expected the energy to dissipate after releasing so much at one time, but it rushed back through my blood stronger and more powerful, sanctioning me to do more damage.

I saw the battle clearly, more clearly than I had seen anything else in my life. It was as if I was created specifically for that moment. The deathly encounter made me more alive than I had ever felt. I could no longer fight against my ingrained electricity, but worked with it to wield the destruction I saw all around me. The energy rushing through my body set me on a war path, my blood turning to an uncontrollable fire, and I found that I was willing to fight at any cost to win the battle.

I took a moment to assess the situation around me. Lilly, although in the form of a tiger had her back to the cliff wall, trapped by both the leopard and the mountain lion. She was a capable fighter, but the two animals were closing in on her and I knew it wouldn't be long.

Kiran had come face to face with the very man I threw and they were circling each other, both waiting for the other to make the first move. Talbott was in a wrestling match with the bobcat and had barely escaped his throat being ripped out twice. It was only a matter of time.

The man I trapped underneath the tree branch had thrown it off and was standing, ready to attack me. I took this all in, in a single breath, but understood with certainty that this fight could not last any longer. We were outnumbered and they would not stop until each one of us was dead.

I gathered the energy inside of me, letting it build and build. The man who had intended to attack me slowed to a stop and tried his attack at a distance. The electricity in my blood became a sort of energy field around me, blocking the attacks from the cloaked man standing only a few feet away.

I felt myself growing stronger with every small molecule of electricity in my veins. I took energy from everything around me; borrowing from the trees, the ground, the stars, the moon, the very breeze that remained soft despite our deathly battle. I sensed myself becoming an unstoppable force. Even my enemies couldn't hold on to their own energy as I took it from them and added it to my own.

My body was nearly bursting. I had created such a force of energy, I could barely contain it. I looked around again and saw all of my friends in imminent danger, unaware of the oncoming storm I was about to rain down.

With controlled thoughts and determined power, I let loose my building tempest. Every cloaked being was sent flying through the air, all coming to rest in one final heap on the ground. I felt their energies dissipate quickly and their lifeless bodies move no more.

Four bodies, piled carelessly on top of each other in the middle of our destruction were the evidence of what I was capable of. One of the attackers however was able to escape. He did not wait around to be certain of his friend's fate, but fled through the woods; his energy growing fainter and fainter the farther away he ran.

Only one of them escaped through the forest, only one of the five. I could sense each of his feet hit the hard ground and his body panic from the terrifying image I ingrained into his mind until eventually he faded away completely.

There was no way I could catch him now, my body had no more strength to move. I collapsed onto the ground, shaking in violent tremors. I lifted my head to see Kiran, Talbott and Lilly back in her human form, were all alive. I rejoiced silently, unable to even say anything. They stared at me with the strangest mix of emotions on their face, all hesitating to move.

Chapter Sixteen

I might as well have been drained of all life. The strength I
expelled to put an end to the fighting was more than I knew I was
capable of; not to mention all of the other crazy stuff that I didn't
know anyone was capable of. I lay on the hard ground, barely able
to lift my head, let alone my limp limbs.

I was aware of what just happened; a small part of me
accepted that the events that occurred were in fact real. But the
fight I partook in only moments ago felt more like a distant
memory than reality: like a dream I just woke up from and could
barely remember. The exact details of everything were fading
from my mind quickly and I wasn't sure I cared.

"One got away," my voice came out hoarse and shaky. I
pointed in the direction I felt him run in before he disappeared
from the tracking device I knew was my mind.

"Talbott, go," Kiran demanded, rushing over to my side
and kneeling down. He leaned in close to my face, seemingly
examining my pupils, although I had a hard time believing he
really knew what he was doing. He took my hand into his and held
it tightly in his grasp.

"I can't leave you. Damn it. We should have brought the
entire Guard, damn it Kiran," Talbott yelled. "I knew this was a
bad idea. Damn it," he repeated over and over and started to walk
in circles. "Kiran are you alright?"

"I'm fine," Kiran looked down at me concerned. He
inspected me again by lifting up my arms and head, looking for,
well I didn't really know what he was looking for, but he
eventually seemed satisfied. All the while, he never let go of my
hand.

"Damn it Kiran, are you all right?" Talbott shouted at him
louder. I watched Talbott continue to pace back and forth from my
peripheral. I could tell that he wanted to pursue the attacker, chase
him down. I could also tell by the way he glanced at Kiran every
other second he was not going to leave his friend alone.

"Yes, I'm fine, I'm really fine," Kiran spoke louder and
with confidence. I saw Talbott relax his shoulders a little, but
continue to pace. "Lilly go back to camp and tell Mr. Lawly that

we have to leave now!" Kiran demanded of the human-again Lilly. She did not speak a word, but obediently took off running through the forest, her bright red hair disappearing into the darkness.

The logical part of me objected to Lilly trying to make it back to camp by herself. The attacker could still be out there, he could have easily circled around to our other side to finish the job and I was too exhausted to pick him up with my new found powers. After what just happened, somebody should go with her, whether he was out there or not. I was too weak to contest. I tried to verbalize my concerns, but only a moan came out.

"She will be fine," Kiran looked into my eyes intensely and I saw his passion and concern. "Lilly can take care of herself it turns out. She will have no problem making it back to camp." Kiran's voice was soothing and calm; it felt like medicine to my fried nerves.

"I don't think you should be so close to her," Talbott stood over us, gruffly assessing our position.

"She just saved our lives," Kiran growled.

"And look at what she did to everyone else," Talbott was calm, but I heard the tension back in his voice. Kiran looked around and let go of my hand to stand up. I began fading in and out of consciousness, fighting to stay awake, but the fatigue was making it impossible.

"Have you ever seen this before?" Kiran asked Talbott, and I knew they were talking about me. My eyes had closed and I was breathing evenly, I was not even sure if I was conscious anymore.

"No, never. I had no idea she was capable of this. I had no idea anyone was capable of this. Four Immortals at once…… it doesn't make sense," Talbott replied.

"I thought you said that she wasn't one of your kind?" Kiran asked softly.

"She's not. She's not…." Talbott repeated. "We must tell your father immediately, she is clearly a security threat. Kiran, she did not even realize she had this kind of power. What else is she capable of?" Talbott sounded almost scared, and I began to lose awareness completely.

"No, that is the last thing we are going to do. You will tell

115

him nothing of her power. Do you understand?" Kiran's voice started to fade, "That is an order Talbott."

I knew they were talking about me, and talking about what I did, but I didn't understand what they were saying. Clearly I wasn't as much of a freak as I thought I was, because they were capable of the same things. I was just lucky enough to be overlooked at first. Surely any one of them would have been able to do what I did with more power and quicker.

I began to regain lucidness as reality set in. I tried to process what just happened, but I could not wrap my mind around it. I saw human beings, real human beings, turn into animals. I saw Lilly turn into an animal. And these were no ordinary mammals; they turned into dangerous creatures thirsty for blood. Human beings posed as animals trying to rip each other apart.

I saw men move things with their minds. I saw them try to kill each other without ever touching the other. Their strength being one thousand times more dangerous without ever physically coming into contact with one another than any other human being I had ever seen. The power these men wielded was beyond comprehension; but these were not just strangers, Kiran and Talbott were capable of the same feats of extraordinary. Kiran and Talbott, only teenagers, were capable of murder, even if it was self-defense.

And then I realized that it wasn't just them that did those things, it was me. I moved things with my mind. I hurt people. I killed people. I was capable of everything the others were, if not more. And I finished it all.

A rock seemed to drop in my stomach and I was suddenly sick. I sat up quickly and emptied everything I had eaten that day on the ground next to me. My body shook violently as it tried to rid my mind of the crimes I just committed. The electricity in me was not only powerful, it was evil.

What had I done? How could I have killed anyone? And not just one person, but four? I pulled my knees to my chest and began to cry, fully awake, but fully unaware of what was happening around me. I drowned out any sound nearby with my sobs. I wanted it so badly to be a dream that I could wake up from, but there was the terrifying fact that I just lived through a real life nightmare I would never be able to forget.

116

Somehow I made it back to camp, either Kiran or Talbott carried me, I wasn't sure who. Between sobbing and blacking out I didn't remember much. My body was so weak that I was barely able to lift my hands, let alone walk or sit up. My voice was hoarse and my throat on fire. When I was conscious I either cried or puked. Unconsciousness was a sweet black hole of nothingness my body and mind longed for.

Mr. Lawly already had the campsite cleaned up before we arrived back at camp. All of the tents and equipment had been packed up and the students organized to leave. I heard people talking around me, but I couldn't understand their words. I was unable to comprehend anything; the only sounds I truly understood were that of my own uncontrollable sobbing.

Someone carried me the entire way back to the bus which was running and waiting for our arrival. A hike that took over an hour just that morning seemed to take only minutes on the way back. We were loaded onto the bus and I was deposited in the very back, left alone to sob as silently as I could.

If only the extreme force of the energy I held were enough to cope with tonight it would have been enough. But it wasn't just that, my friends were attacked tonight, attacked by people who had intended to kill us. I had to watch my friends fight for their very survival.

I was physically weak and inundated. But the realization of what I had done to other people, enemy or not was the truly crushing reality. I took four lives tonight. No one asked me to, and no one else could be held responsible. With the suggestion of no other person I chose to destroy those people. Despite the fact that I saved my friends lives in return for theirs, the truth remains: I was a murderer.

They weren't even ordinary men, they were men like me. Whatever I was, they were. They possessed the same energy, the same electricity; we were the same, and I killed them. Their lives are over and for all I knew they were still lying there, piled on top of each other, in the middle of the wilderness.

I continued to sob until I was at last too exhausted to even

117

cry and fell into a deep, dreamless sleep. I could finally feel nothing and think no more. The sweet rest seemed to last forever and consumed my whole consciousness. I was aware of the bus arriving back at school, and I was aware of being taken to my aunt's car, but through it all I refused to open my eyes and acknowledge reality.

Somehow, someone eventually placed me in my bed. It was there, under my thick comforters and surrounded by soft, feather pillows, that I let the sweet nothingness consume me entirely. I would have been perfectly happy to never wake up again. But of course, that was asking for far too much.

After what seemed like days of sleeping I finally could not keep my eyes closed any longer. Although if it had been up to me; I would never have opened them again. But fighting against my selfishness was the conscious knowledge that I had a moral responsibility to pay the consequences of my actions. I sighed deeply and contemplated whether I wanted to get out of bed or just call down for Aunt Syl.

The warm sunlight from my bedroom windows enveloped me as I lay on my overly soft, overly large bed. I was wrapped in warm blankets and surrounded by my favorite pillows. I rubbed my eyes as they adjusted to the light they hadn't seen for what seemed like a very long time. I could feel how puffy and swollen they were, a consequence of the large amounts of sobbing I had accomplished lately.

I started to sit up, but still felt drained of all energy. I laid my head back down and wished I could stay there forever. I tried to swallow, but my throat was dry and scratchy. I didn't attempt to move, unquenchable thirst seemed the least of my problems.

"Aunt Syl," I called out, but my voice was nothing more than a harsh whisper.

"Sshhh…" she responded, entering my room with a glass of water in hand. Either she was a mind-reader or just a very good person. I sat up a tiny bit, taking the water from her. "I figured you would get up soon, and I thought you would need this," I took a small sip and my eyes filled with tears; for being both grateful for the water and for having to face her.

I realized that she had been sitting just outside my door, waiting for me to get up. I wondered how long I had been asleep and how long she had been sitting there. I couldn't hold back my tears as I thought about the pain I must be causing her. How could I explain any of this to her?

I gratefully gulped the glass of water down, spilling it all over my face and on my surrounding covers. I tried to speak again, but this time no sound came out. Tears continued to spill from my eyes and I hung my head in shame. Aunt Syl soon started crying as well.

She took the water from my hands and set it down on my night stand. Still crying she pulled me into her arms and hugged me, rubbing my back with her hand. She had never felt like much of a mother type before, but at that moment it was exactly what I needed. I felt like a small child, unable to comprehend anything that was going on outside of my own feelings.

"It's alright Eden, everything is going to be alright," she cooed soothingly, pulling my shoulders away from her and staring directly into my face. She brushed the tears away from my eyes and then her own eyes as well. She handed me a tissue from her pocket and I gratefully wiped my face with it. "There is someone here who needs to speak with you," She tried to smile reassuringly, but I saw the trepidation in her eyes.

Without being asked, a man entered my room and cleared his throat. I looked up to see Principal Saint standing in my doorway, looking very grim. All of the horrors of the previous night rushed back to me and I was filled with dread. A sense of foreboding gripped my nervous system, and the tingling electricity filled my veins once again.

Chapter Seventeen

"Hello, Eden," Principal Saint said in his usual distinguished voice, then cleared his throat. "I am glad that you are feeling better."

He assumed I was feeling better without even asking. I was not feeling better, I was feeling worse. The cloaked figures passed through my mind again and I bit my lip to hold back the tears. A wave of nausea crept over me and I glanced around in search of a trash can.

"First things first, those men are not dead," Principal Saint continued. He paused as if waiting for his words to sink in. "They may have appeared that way to you, but Talbott was able to revive them. They were simply unconscious. You children were very lucky to have survived such a brutal attack." He cleared his throat again. Principal Saint was a very tall man, and since he had not moved from my door way he appeared overly large and intimidating in his double breasted, brown, tweed suit.

"They were dead, I know they were dead," I protested. "I killed them," I looked down and covered my face with my hands. I couldn't hold back the choking sobs.

"Eden it's alright, what Dr. Saint says is true," My aunt put her hand against my cheek and spoke in a soothing manner. I looked up at her unbelieving. "There are a lot of things that have happened to you that need to be explained," she continued, "Amory would like to talk with you, and maybe shed some light on all that has been happening recently," she gave me an encouraging smile and stood to leave. I grabbed her hand unwilling to be left alone with him.

"I saw those men lying on the ground. They were dead. I know they were dead," I struggled to speak through my tears, my voice was deep and course, but I refused to believe them. I committed a horrible act, and I knew that I must pay for my actions. They were not going to sugar coat it for me. Surely the police would be here any minute anyways.

"Eden, the police are not coming," Principal Saint seemed to read my mind and answer my very thoughts. His voice was more constrained and I could see that he was frustrated with me.

"The police will never be involved. We have our own way of dealing with issues such as these. Now trust me, those men were not dead. They probably appeared that way to you, maybe even felt that way; but as I said before, Talbott was able to revive them and they are currently being held for questioning."

"Why didn't you call the police? Those men are dangerous. They tried to hurt us, they tried to kill us!" I was fully ready to face the consequences for homicide; but I was also more than ready to plead self-defense. As awful as I felt for taking another man's life, I did realize that it was necessary. The fact that these men were not even in police custody made my actions meaningless.

"Trust me, those men are in custody. However, it is a different type of legal system than you may be used to. I'm afraid they will face a judge and jury very soon. A trial has been set for them and they will face their accusers soon enough," a look of sadness passed across Principal Saint's face and I was not sure if it was meant for me or for the men who would stand trial.

"So I will get to testify against them?" I asked, unsure if I was even ready to face them again.

"No, absolutely not. That is out of the question," Principal Saint reacted quickly. I was instantly confused, but before I could ask any more questions, he continued, "What I mean to say is that Kiran Kendrick and Talbott Angelo will act as both witness and prosecution. Their testimonies will be more than enough to seal your attacker's fate. Trust me," Principal Saint wore the same look of sadness he had a few moments ago and I was positive this time it was meant for the attackers.

"But why can't I speak on my own behalf?" I felt obstinate; those men tried to kill my friends.

"Haven't you been through enough? Besides the trial will take place in Romania."

"Romania?" I blurted out, much louder than I had intended. "What does Romania have to do with what happened here… in Nebraska? Isn't there something about jurisdiction or international law or something?" I was now completely confused. Surely a Romanian court system could care less about what happened to a bunch of teenagers in the middle of America.

"They will not be tried by a Romanian court system,"

Principal Saint once again answered the questions in my head and I was sure now that he was reading my thoughts. "We have our own judicial system and they will answer to us. Like I said, their fate, I'm sure, will be much worse than any human justice system is prepared to give them, trust me," Principal Saint looked down at his shoes and shook his head slightly as if ashamed.

"Ok, I have no idea what you are talking about," I looked at Aunt Syl, hoping she would shed some light on this bewildering conversation. "You are really starting to freak me out."

"It's alright Eden. You need to start trusting me," he approached the bed and pulled my desk chair closer so that he could sit near me. My aunt stood up and crossed the room to look out my window. My throat began to close in nervous anticipation. "Sylvia would you make us some tea? This might be harder than I imagined." Aunt Syl left the room silently and obeyed.

"How do you know what's been happening to me? How do you know what I'm thinking? What do you mean by our justice system?" my questions tumbled out quickly and all at once. Principal Saint obviously knew much more about what was happening to me than I did.

"What is happening to you is completely normal," when I rolled my eyes he continued, "Well it's completely expected anyway. It's completely expected for someone in your position," he clarified. "You see Eden; you are special, very special."

"If by special you mean crazy and this is some sort of weird intervention then just let me know where you are sending me and get on with it!" I couldn't hold back my tears this time; they came in waves of choking sobs. All of my fears and anxiety finally manifested themselves in a very real manner. The strange things that had been happening to me and the inexplicable things I was responsible for were not normal, but more than that, they were scary.

"You are not crazy," Principal Saint replied a little disdainfully, but even more impatiently. "You did the only thing that anyone would expect you to do and that was to protect yourself and your friends. From what I've heard it was a very dangerous situation; you are lucky to be alive," he said this with finality, as though this should be enough. "And I will say it again, you are not crazy. You drained those men of their magic; it was

122

not a pretty task, but a necessary one," he paused to let his words sink in. "I'm sure the magnitude of force you used on those men felt like murder, it probably felt worse to them, but Talbott was able to revive them. They are in custody now and soon we will find out what their exact purpose was. Then we will know why they attacked you children…. although I am sure I already have a reason in mind."

"Drained them of their magic? What are you talking about?" I asked, highly irritated. I thought I was the crazy one? My emotions were at a level I had never experienced before and I felt as if I were on the verge of a breakdown; maybe I'd been on the verge for a while and this was finally the breaking point I'd been waiting for.

"Yes Eden, magic. I am sure you are aware that you are different from other humans, that you possess a set of skills that appear…. super-human. We have all been a witness to your erratic and unexplainable behavior; and after last night you can no longer deny it to yourself. I had hoped that somehow through your experiences you would become aware of what your powers are capable of and see that others around you possess the same set of skills. However, I see now how stubborn and self-absorbed you can be and can wait no longer. If something were to happen like this again, you need to be aware of what you are capable of," he was a stern man, and I didn't know whether to feel offended, shocked, or like a fool. This had to be some type of joke.

"This is not a joke," he said louder, and with more conviction. "Open your eyes, Eden," he shook his head and I knew he was frustrated with me.

"Amory, please, she's just a child," my aunt entered the room again carrying a tray of hot tea. She handed me a steaming cup and I took it from her gratefully. "This is new to her, she's never been around anything your people can do until now; of course she's going to deny it, to her it doesn't make sense," she walked over to hand Principal Saint his cup of tea, but turned back to address me soothingly, "It didn't make sense to me either the first time I saw what your people could do," Aunt Syl sat back down with me on the bed and put an arm across my shoulders. I knew that I should feel comforted by her gesture, but my mind was still reeling.

"What are you talking about?" I asked, my head spinning.

"Eden, I am not your real aunt," Aunt Syl began. And Principal Saint gave a small chuckle. "You were given to me at a very young age after your parents had disappeared, I never knew them; I have always told you that, and that has always been true. But you see, we're different, you are extremely special and I am only human," she smiled at me and something stirred deep inside my soul, something that told me I should listen closer.

"You keep saying that I'm special, that I'm different, that I'm not crazy, but what does that mean?" I demanded; it was my turn to become impatient.

"Like I said earlier, you possess a set of skills that make you more than human, that make you different," Principal Saint rejoined the conversation.

"If you're talking about how I am able to burn down school buildings, or create tidal waves, or make things explode, then yes, I suppose I do possess a certain set of skills; but the last thing I wanted was for any of that to happen," I folded my arms across my chest and shook my head. I was relieved in a sense that someone would finally be able to tell me what had been happening to me; but even more, I was angry that they felt the need to wait this long.

"Well, I suppose that's part of it. But a better example would be what happened last night," Principal Saint's tone had softened. "You see all of the things that happened before, when your school flooded, or burned down, or you made a trashcan explode in the theater, oh yes, we know about that, those were all manifestations of your magic. Eden, you have refused to use your powers, you continue to ignore their very existence. Because of that, the magic builds up inside of you and forces you to use it in less than ideal situations. Last night when you finally used your magic, instead of letting it explode meaninglessly, you saw what it could finally do; what you could finally do."

"You're saying all of the terrible things I have caused could have been avoided if I had been using my magic all along?" I cringed as I used the word "magic;" as if it were a real thing. "All of this could have been avoided if we would have just had this conversation a long time ago?" I was livid. I thought about the three schools I closed down before Kingsley and winced, knowing it could all have been prevented.

"You're right, dear," Aunt Syl rubbed my back gently, in an attempt to soothe my boiling anger. "We had no idea those things would happen though. And we certainly never expected them to keep happening. You see, you are the first of your kind to ever be raised apart. We knew the magic would manifest eventually, we planned to deal with it when the time came. When it did appear however, it was so much stronger then we could ever have anticipated. We weren't quite sure what to do, and we definitely weren't sure if it was safe to integrate you into your kind. Finally we made the decision to send you to Kingsley, but it was a last resort, and even then you were in such strong denial. Magic was happening all around you, people were constantly reading your thoughts and you still refused to see the truth about who you are. We were not sure how to approach the subject."

"Why would you talk to me at all, when you could just send a group of dangerous men to try to kill me? I understood that message loud and clear!" I said sarcastically. I knew that I should be asking other questions, more important questions, more realistic questions, but I couldn't get over the fact that all of this time I could have avoided destroying everything I touched.

"Please don't be angry Eden; we had no idea that would happen," Aunt Syl looked as if she was going to cry and I instantly regretted my outburst.

"She's right, child," Principal Saint glanced at the doorway and then back at me. "I don't believe those men ever meant you harm. And I would never have let you go on that trip had I known that you would be involved. We assume that they were after Kiran and Kiran alone; you, unfortunately for your attackers, were there to teach them a lesson." He half grunted a laugh and gave me a wink. "Eden, in my wildest dreams, I never imagined your magic would manifest so powerfully. At this point I am unsure what you are even capable of; but I do know that you are very, very powerful. It is time that you learned how to use your magic, not just for your sake, but for Kingsley's sake as well," his grin had turned a bit mischievous.

"So what am I then, some sort of Witch?" I asked, still not losing my sarcastic edge, but softening my tone a little.

"Yes, I think that you are a Witch," I almost laughed, but

realized that Principal Saint was completely serious. "Moreover though, you are an Immortal," he said the word with a deep reverence, and I knew instantly, that this word…. "Immortal" meant something greater than I could comprehend.

"Immortal?" I asked in a whispered breath.

"Yes, an Immortal. We are your people, you're kind. You are not human as you have been raised, you are an Immortal," every time he said the word an electric pulse surged through my veins and I was struck with the same reverence that Principal Saint spoke with.

"So I am a Witch that lives forever?" a small part of me began to believe him.

"Well, the real sense of the word Immortal was taken from us a long time ago, but yes, you possess the attributes in which describe a Witch. The way you are able to control or create events and circumstances with your thoughts, the powers that you possess, all point to Witch-like attributes. Or as our people call your kind: the Lamia. It is just another term for Witch though," he gave me a genial smile. I found myself slightly out of breath, my head spinning. I could hardly understand his words, but the harder part to understand was that I actually did believe him.

"The term Immortal today, really describes a set of four distinct super-human races," Principal Saint continued. "Immortal is a way of life set apart from ordinary human life. We have our own justice system, our own Monarchy, our own schools and our own belief system. You are a part of us, as much as we are a part of you. As a Witch you occupy a specific purpose for our people and it is important that you investigate who you are and what you are capable of. It is also important that you no longer identify yourself as a human, but learn our laws, and standards. I believe if you do, you will finally come to terms with who you are. You will finally find your destiny," something stirred inside of me and the electricity or magic or whatever began to rush through my veins. For the first time in my entire life I realized that I had just been told the truth.

Chapter Eighteen

"So last night was, um, normal for someone like me? I mean someone like us? I mean um…. an Immortal?" I got confused saying the word out loud. Principal Saint had basically just relayed the impossible to me. If what he said was true, then I was not human, or like he explained I was more than human, I was a Witch, or what he called an "Immortal." The enormity of what that meant began to sink in as my blood pumped charged and furiously throughout my body.

"Yes, well kind of. The extra energy or electricity as you call it you feel in your blood and unexplainable phenomena that you seem to be responsible for are parts of what it means to be an Immortal. When you move something just by thinking about it, or create something from nothing, these are all part of your….. powers. Each Immortal is different and unique. We usually classify ourselves into four different categories, but your powers manifested a little stronger than what should be normal for someone your age, someone who did not even know what she was capable of."

I was trying to take what Principal Saint said as truth, but it was difficult. Everything I held to be true about my life, about me, about the world in general was not true. I was something different; something I assumed only existed in comic books and action movies. My mind was having trouble wrapping itself around the enormity of Principal Saint's story; yet at the same time my inner being seemed to believe him without any hesitation. I had a thousand questions that needed to be answered.

"How many Immortals are there? What else can I do? Does this mean I'll never die? Does this mean I'll never age? Why are my powers so strong? Can I fly?" he cut me off with his hand and a small chuckle.

"No, you can't fly. Well, at least I don't think so," his eyes twinkled, he was relieved to have gotten passed my anger. His smile softened his face and I saw him in a different light now, almost paternal. "Let's see, there are thousands of us, living all over the world. There used to be more, maybe millions, we equaled the humans, but over time we have begun to die out," his expression was suddenly full of sadness. "And you can die, eventually, and you will age. 'Immortal' was a term given to us a long, long time ago," his smile had completely disappeared and he suddenly seemed older… ancient. "Thousands of years ago we did live forever, or at least it seemed as if we would live forever. We outnumbered the humans, although we lived in peace with them. No one knows exactly how we came to be, we were born into this world like everyone else, but we simply did not die. Our people would reach an age of maturity and we would age no longer; and we bore children that were like us, Immortals like ourselves. But eventually we began to die like humans, although our lifespan is considerably longer and we have been able to hang on to our special attributes," I took each word in, feeling as though my head would soon explode. "I'm sorry to go over this so quickly but we don't have much time."

"Oh," is all I said, my brain was on overload.

"We of course keep ourselves a secret from humans now that so few remain; they would have a hard time accepting us," he smiled at Aunt Syl, who didn't seem offended.

"But obviously Aunt Syl knew. So why didn't I?"

"Well, your parents were gone and I thought this would be the best way for you to…. live," Principal Saint folded his hands together and looked at me seriously. I realized that he didn't actually give me an answer, and I had a suspicion that he was hiding something from me, but there was so much information to take in that for the moment his answer was sufficient.

"So I am a Witch? Is everyone at Kingsley a Witch as well?"

"Yes and no, you are a Witch," he chuckled slightly, "But not everyone is a Witch. There are four distinct types of our kind. All four display very unique qualities and have been given different names; it is much like the different ethnic races in human kind. We are different, but of the same species. At first we did not have names for each other, but over time we have adapted names from the slang that has been associated with us; the names also help us distinguish between ourselves. Recently they have meant the difference between life and death," he smiled sadly again, "There are the Lamia, or Witches in today's terminology, the Mediums or Psychics, there are the Transmogrifiers or Shape-

129

Shifters and then there are the Proeliators, they have been called anything from gods, to angels to super-heroes; usually we refer to them in English as Titans."

"But everyone can refer to themselves as an Immortal?"

"Yes of course, just like any of the different races of humanity are still referred to as humans; what makes us stand apart, but also stand together is the magic that we have in our blood. The tingling sensation or what I think you refer to as 'electricity,' that is your magic. You would be unable to function without it; it is your life blood. It defines who you are, I squirmed thinking about the men I supposedly drained of their magic. I may not have killed them, but it sounded like I had given them a fate worse than death.

"How did you know I call it electricity?" I asked, realizing I had always been very careful to never share that with anyone before.

"One of the special skills of our Psychics is mind reading," he smiled, and my face flared up from embarrassment. Slowly I remembered every time I felt my question was answered without asking it, from teachers and other students to Kiran. I buried my head in my hands; this had to be a teenager's worst nightmare come true.

"Don't worry; we can fix that for you. I can teach you the skills you need to protect your mind against others."

"So everyone at school has been able to read my mind…. know what I'm thinking?" I whispered the question, completely mortified.

"Well only the Psychics and I suppose, only those who were interested," he acted so nonchalant I had a hard time believing he grasped the trauma associated with a sixteen year old girl's private thoughts.

"Kiran?" I asked in an even softer whisper. I could feel my aunt smiling beside me.

"Yes, I'm sure Kiran has been able to listen to your thoughts. Prince Kiran is very gifted; it was probably no challenge at all," he spoke so matter-of-factly, while my stomach took the roller coaster ride of its life. I felt overwhelmingly nauseous.

"What? Prince? What?" I barely got the words out. Did he say Prince Kiran?

130

"Yes of course. Kiran Kendrick is our Crown Prince. I told you earlier we have our own Monarchy. His father Lucan rules over us; he is our King and Kiran is the Crown Prince. Please remember, we are not bound by human law," he reminded me. Excuse me, but up until twenty minutes ago that was the only law I knew existed.

"So the King is like my King too? I mean I like should respect him and bow and all that?" I laughed; it all seemed too medieval for me.

"Well yes, you're supposed to, but I don't think you've respected royalty as of this far, so I wouldn't be too concerned just yet," Now it was Principal Saint's turn to laugh.

"They won't like execute me or put me in prison or anything for that will they? You'll explain to them that I didn't know, won't you?" my hands flew to my throat and I held onto it as if it were about to be chopped off. All of the times I was sarcastic and rude to Kiran flooded my memory…. oops.

"No, don't be so dramatic," he chided. "The royal family hasn't put anyone to death in a long time, or at least a couple years," his eyes looked out of my window and slightly glazed over. I knew he was thinking about something else, but I was too afraid to ask what it was and apparently lacked the skill to read minds, like the rest of Immortals. "No, you're not in trouble, but please try to be more respectful in the future. In fact, I think it would be best if you have no more contact with the Prince at all."

"Why not?" I wondered if that was possible for me. Hadn't I tried to stay away from him since the beginning?

"Well, he's really here for only one purpose, and I'm afraid you have been a bit of a distraction. There are other reasons why you should avoid him of course. For one, your friend Lilly is a Transmogrifier attending Kingsley against the law. You see, Shape-Shifters were banished a long time ago. They are the…. lepers of Immortal society, so to speak. Lilly was attending school illegally and hiding her true identity. After last night they have taken her away to await trial. If you were implicated as having known of her true identity, you too would be sent away," his voice was melancholy and he continued to stare out of the window.

"Lilly is what? What do you mean banished? How can they just take her away? Who took her away? She was trying to protect us! Where is the trial, I'll go and tell them the truth!" I half stood up, ready to leave at that moment; I couldn't believe that my one and only friend was gone, for reasons I couldn't even comprehend. How could someone really be banished? Where did they go? What happened to them if they were caught? My throat tightened with anticipation and I mentally willed my nerves to steady.

"Please, Eden, calm down. Lilly is a Shape-Shifter; the Monarchy banished her kind a long time ago. They are the outcasts of our society. They are to have no contact with the Immortal world," I watched the pain flicker in his eyes and instantly realized that he did not agree with the edict. "And no, you will do no such thing; the trial will be held in Romania as well, in front of the royal family. If you were to testify on her behalf and she was found guilty you would receive the same punishment as her. We cannot afford that mistake."

"So those men that attacked us, who were they really after?" I changed the subject, knowing it was a battle that I would not win, at least not then. I decided to think about it later, when I was alone. But the thought that Lilly would be tried the same as those disgusting men who tried to kill her made me physically sick.

"It appears they were after the Crown Prince. They were apparently making an attempt on his life and had assumed he would be alone, with only his body guard. I'm afraid you girls took them quite by surprise."

"His body guard?"

"Yes, of course. Talbott Angelo is Kiran's personal body guard. He is a Titan; they are the royal family's personal guard and personal advisors."

"Of course he is," A light bulb went on in my head, and I finally understood Kiran and Talbott's weird friendship.... or relationship.... or whatever.

"Talbott and a handful of others are the only Titans that have been allowed to leave the King in a very long time. They had hoped it would be enough to protect the Prince; I think they were quite surprised when it was you who saved them all," Principal Saint chuckled softly. "Talbott is the only one young enough to go to school with you. The rest of Kiran's guard try to remain

132

undetected, and unfortunately were completely absent during yesterday's attack. Luckily for them it was by the Prince's orders."

"Stop calling him that. He's not like real royalty is he? It's like I don't know...." I tried to search for the right word.... pretend, make-believe, fairytale? Kiran was the Crown Prince of what was now the world that I lived in. How was that even possible?

"I'm afraid my dear, that the Immortal Monarchy is as real as it gets. They have been a ruling Monarchy longer than any institution in history. And as immature as Prince Kiran is, he has the power over your life and death," Principal Saint's expression had turned grave, and I knew that he was serious. But I couldn't be. Prince Kiran.... what a joke.

"So what, I have to bow, and curtsy.... call him your Majesty?" I couldn't hold back my sarcasm.

"I'm afraid the best course of action is for you to avoid him completely. He is here, like I said before, for a very specific purpose and you are only getting in the way. If you don't leave him alone soon, his father is going to have something to say about it," I blushed defensively. Wasn't he the one always bothering me? Besides I didn't see how I was getting in the way of anything. Moreover, I wasn't sure if I wanted him to stop bothering me....

"Principal Saint, did you know my parents?" I nearly whispered, trying to change the subject, but almost afraid to hear the answer.

"Hmmm...." he smiled softly, "Please call me Amory outside of school grounds. Yes, yes I did know your parents. A long time ago, I knew them." He looked up at me and an expression I couldn't define settled on his face. "You look so much like your mother, Eden," he continued to stare at me for several moments longer and I began to feel a little uncomfortable. "Now, let's work a little on your powers alright? Let's make sure no one can read your mind again."

I nodded my reply. I had no idea what it meant to "work on my powers," and I was not completely sure I wanted to know. I felt completely overwhelmed by everything and I wasn't sure if I could take anymore. The electricity pulsating through my veins would suggest otherwise however and I felt almost itchy to exercise the supernatural force that was, as Principal Saint said before, my Life Blood.

Chapter Nineteen

"Try it again," Principal Saint…. Amory commanded me.

I closed my eyes, letting in every sound, every movement, and every breath. The magic flowed through me, putting every nerve on edge. My senses were sharpened like I didn't think was possible and my breathing even.

My blood felt hot under my skin, as if it was boiling my insides, but it wasn't an unpleasant feeling. I welcomed the sensation, understanding it was the magic finally unleashed. The hairs on the back of my neck stood up straight and I could feel the magic wanting to escape, wanting to be set free.

Now that my senses were heightened, I felt the extra sense that came with being an Immortal. My sixth sense was the perception of nearby magic. What felt like electricity rushing through me whenever I was around another Immortal, was my perception of someone else's magic. When I was near another Immortal's magic my blood began to tingle and pulsate. The magic that consumed me now alerted me to not only Amory's presence but that he was at this moment trying to read my thoughts.

I closed my eyes tighter and concentrated. I could not clear my mind, because then I would lose focus. I allowed it to be full of everything I could think of in order to practice for day to day activities. Closing my mind to outside forces must be natural to me or I would never survive another day at Kingsley. A small blush rushed to my cheeks as I thought about all of the days before and how open my mind had been to everyone else.

I allowed the magic to build inside of me, feeling as natural as breathing. Now that I knew the magic was a natural part of me I no longer felt the need to oppress it. I finally understood that when I would push it down before I would only make things more difficult for myself; I was not human, I could no longer act like it.

I felt Amory's magic prying the outside of my mind. It was as if someone was trying to cover my head with a heavy blanket. Slowly he worked his magic around my mind, trying to slip under or through any way that he could; but the longer I kept him away the easier it became. My magic grew stronger and I stood up straighter. The force field I had built around my thoughts became fortified and I relaxed, this was becoming natural.

I glanced at the clock, careful to maintain my defenses, 3:00 AM. We had been working on this for hours and finally I was getting the hang of it. I felt Amory pull his magic back and I looked over to see that he was finally wearing a smile. After hours of disappointment I was thankful I could finally come through.

"Good Eden. That was excellent!" he clasped his hands together. "Do you think you can keep that up at school?" his smile faded and his expression became worried.

"Yes, I think so. It's getting easier," I smiled reassuringly.

"I would not risk it if I didn't think your absence would cause suspicion. Everyone is going to be asking questions and we can't afford one mistake. It's bad enough your only friend at school was a Shape-Shifter, but then to display your powers in such a way as to make the Crown Prince look weak is an entirely different matter," he wrung his clasped hands together and began to pace. I didn't exactly understand what he was talking about, but I did trust him.

I watched him silently, realizing how similar we looked. He had the same oversized onyx eyes that I did and a tall frame topped with almost black, wavy hair. I went over the story he told me once again in my mind: my parents died when I was a baby and Aunt Syl found me while she was on a hike in the woods; I had been raised as a human until now when by accident I discovered I had powers. As vague as the story was and maybe a little farfetched, it was the only one I had.

"There is one more thing I would like to try with you. It will require your full concentration, and it will not be easy," Amory stopped pacing and looked at me full in the face.

"It can't wait? I'm exhausted," I yawned in reply and sat down lazily on the edge of my full-sized bed.

"No it cannot," Amory snapped. "Do you realize what is at stake here? There is no time for sleep; you must master your magic as quickly as possible. Now stand up and focus."

I obeyed, feeling a little like a zombie. I stood to my feet, the magic moving with me. It was almost as if I could feel my very blood circulating throughout my body. The magic moved with it, pumping from my toes to my heart to my head and back down.

"Now build your shield again," Amory continued. I threw my force-field around my mind and realized how easy it was becoming. "I want you to hold on to your own mind-defense while trying to read mine. Let your magic leave you slowly searching for my thoughts. Concentrate on me, on being me, on what you want to know," he stood still, focusing on a framed picture of Aunt Syl. I realized that he had built his defense and was waiting.

"I thought only Psychics could read minds? Aren't I a Witch?" It was late. I was tired. I felt like I couldn't keep my thoughts together.

"Yes, you are a Witch, but after what happened last night, I just want to see exactly what you are capable of. There have been Witches in the past that have been able to read minds and I would like to see if you are one of them," Principal Saint explained. I was too tired to argue.

I did as he said, thinking first of my magic, bringing it into my mind and creating a heady feeling. I swayed slightly, feeling a tad bit drunk, and tried to refocus. I concentrated on Amory moving my invisible and silent magic to the place where I imagined his mind to be.

I closed my eyes and focused harder. Suddenly it was as if my magic ran into a brick wall. With my mind, I moved it from side to side and up and down. I at least had found his mind; not that that was hard, a mind was where most people imagined it to be: in the head. I worked to penetrate it, to slide underneath his defenses but nothing seemed to work.

I formed the information I wanted to know as a single strain of thought, sending it through my invisible stream of magic using it as extra force against the wall Amory had created. I probed and probed, finding myself tiring from the exertion.

"Don't give up now Eden, work harder," he commanded, and I realized why he was the principal of a high school. Yikes.

Again, I did as he said. I stood up straighter, focusing my body as well as my mind. There had to be a loophole here. If there was a way to pierce his force-field it wasn't going to be from straight on. I continued to search what felt like a square energy field. I moved my magic, like fingers brushing themselves over a smooth surface, until I finally found it; a small, but real opening where his energy field met at a corner.

The hole was tiny, almost miniscule and I was not surprised I had brushed over it so many times before. As I was investigating the catch, Amory realized what I had found. Quicker than I could react, it was gone.

I searched again, with renewed vitality. Now that I knew what I was looking for, I began to find more and more of them. They felt like little rips in my magic, almost like getting a small splinter caught in smooth silk. The more I searched for them, the clearer they became, but whenever I went back to one Amory had already covered it.

I realized I must give up thinking and let my magic take control. I blanketed his mind with my magic, allowing it to completely envelope. This took more energy than I thought it would and I found myself out of breath.

From what I could sense, there were three separate, small openings, but if I hesitated they would be gone. All at once I let my magic infiltrate them, forcing my way into his mind and revealing all of his thoughts. As quickly as I could, I searched for the one thought I wanted to know most: what my mother and father looked like. I flicked through his mind like a flip-file, searching through all of his past memories.

Being in someone else's mind was almost overwhelming; it was like I had become him. His thoughts and my thoughts were one and the same. I kept my mind protected, but his was completely revealed. I found myself embarrassed as I not only thought his thoughts but felt his emotions. I refused to stop however, until I found what I was looking for.

I searched and searched, realizing that although I had surpassed his force-field, he was still capable of hiding things from me. Suddenly I saw a small glimmer of what I wanted, a long dark haired woman. The image was ripped away from me before I could make it out clearly and my searching became a game of tag.

The minute I found the image I was looking for, another menial image was thrown up in its place. I got tired of fishing trips and old books; I was almost hungry for the image of my mother. I flipped through his memories quicker and quicker, as if I was watching his entire life on fast forward. I felt him growing weaker.

And as he grew weaker, so did I, until I nearly collapsed. A deep longing sensation welled up within me and I couldn't tell if it was from Amory or if it was from me. I remembered who I was searching for and began again with new vigor.

Suddenly they were before me: my mother and my father. Although nothing had been said out loud, the very fibers of my being told me who they were. My mother was the most beautiful woman I had ever seen. She was strongly built, but had a tiny frame. Her eyes were the same eyes that I had, deep coals that were almost too big for her perfect, porcelain face. Plump, bright red lips were turned into a smile as she looked at my father with overwhelming affection. Her dark hair fell in long waves down to her waist and covered her pale figure, making the memory appear to be in black and white.

I tore my thoughts away from my mother to look at my father who was looking back at her with such a loving expression that I began to cry. He was tall and strong; his very being defined the word "Immortal." He too had dark hair, but it was much curlier and cropped close to his head. His skin was darker than my mother's; it had the same olive tone that Talbott had. His lips were pronounced on his face, but stretched in the form of a smile. A long, angular nose sat underneath the greenest eyes I had ever seen. As he gazed at my mother they glimmered like emeralds.

I examined the scene they were in; they stood gazing at each other in the middle of a crowded room. My mother was placed next to a man at first I assumed to be Kiran; the same dirty blonde hair and piercing blue eyes. But on longer examination I realized that he was older, taller and meaner looking. The man wore an embellished gold crown upon his head and draped his arm around my mother protectively. My father stood on the other side of him, tense as if ready to attack at any moment. Although the blonde man was speaking, my mother and father stared intently at each other as if he did not exist at all.

Suddenly I was ripped away from them. I reached out with my hands as if I could grab on to that memory and hold it close to me. After it was gone I felt lost; I fell to my bed sobbing. The strength I used to enter Amory's mind was gone and I felt weak

140

and somehow exposed.

"Very good, Eden," Amory whispered in a hoarse voice. I heard the emotion in his voice, and I wanted to apologize, but all I could do was sob.

The parents I never knew I had, the parents I never thought about were suddenly in front of me. Every molecule I was made of hurt from the exertion of so much power; every emotion in my soul completely exhausted. I unexpectedly felt such a longing for something I had never known, I did not know if I would ever recover.

"It's normal to feel this way. You accomplished something just now that only the most skilled of us all could hope to do." I looked up at him, tears streaming down my face, in confusion. "What you did just now is called Complete-Mind-Manipulation. I did not ask you to do that. I asked you to read my thoughts. That is much simpler and requires not near the effort. Reading peoples thoughts is more like reading a newspaper headline, you literally read their thoughts with your magic; there are no images involved. I will not ask you to try it right now, but tomorrow at school I think you should practice on some of your classmates. Reading thoughts does not make the other person aware of what you are doing, most people are sending out their thoughts in one way or another, you are simply catching them. What you did was entering my mind and becoming united with it. You were able to not only know what I was thinking, but what I have ever thought. You saw everything I have ever seen and felt every emotion I have ever felt. This is a very invasive process and rarely accomplished without the permission of the other person. Everything that you feel now, is multiplied by a hundred in me. Most Immortals find it difficult to recover from the process; but thankfully for us tonight I have undergone this process before," his voice cracked and I realized how weak he suddenly was. Amory was slumped over in his chair, resting his head in his hands, staring down at the floor.

"I am so sorry," I blurted out, bursting into more tears.

"It's not your fault; I should have explained more of what you were looking for. I just never assumed you had that kind of power," he shook his head, and stood up unsteadily. "I will leave you for tonight, please remember everything you have learned today and use it tomorrow. Well everything except…. this," he walked slowly, shakily to the door and closed it behind him. I had nothing left and could no longer control my emotions; I laid my head down into my pillow and let out everything I never knew I felt.

Chapter Twenty

I arrived at school the next morning to another full parking lot. Magic under control, Aunt Syl had given me my freedom back. Thank God. I couldn't say that I blamed her; waiting for me to figure out I was superhuman had its disadvantages. But no more blowing things up on accident, now I could do it on purpose.

I parked my car in the last remaining spot and paused a moment to take a deep breath and check myself. My mind was protected and my magic flowing through me naturally; well at least what I had been told was natural. It seemed as if I'd known this secret my whole life, but in actuality it had only been about twenty four hours; I guess I wasn't really an expert.

I made it to class on time, excited to see Lilly and have someone my age to talk to about this crazy new life. Instant disappointment met me however when I opened the door and realized she wasn't there. Although Principal Saint or Amory or whoever told me she wouldn't be, I still had held out hope. The hardest part about learning your true identity is coming to terms with the very real legal system you never knew existed.

I found it ironic how easy it was for me to believe the whole super-human, magic skills thing; but how hard it was to take the Monarchy, governing council, rules and regulations part seriously. Maybe because I'd never personally experienced a ruling class in action it seemed more fiction than reality. I wondered if I had some interaction with the Monarchy if it would feel real or not.

And then I remembered that I had. I walked into class and quickly made it to my seat before the bell rang. Kiran sat to my left in all of his pomp and circumstance. I understood now why the girls fawned over him; it was the idea of a crown.... and maybe his amazing good looks. But I wasn't falling for it. At least that's what I kept telling myself.

"Well, well, well.... look who it is," he whispered snidely as I sifted through my book bag looking for my copy of Romeo and Juliet. A fleeting memory of Principal Saint telling me to leave Kiran alone crossed my mind before I just as quickly dismissed it.

"Hello, your Highness," I responded sarcastically. He may have been the Crown Prince, but he was still a jackass.

"Finally, you've caught up with the rest of us. Congratulations," he clapped his hands quietly in mock applause. I gave him a sharp look and found the constant smirk he wore already in place.

"Well, we can't all have parents who are um, alive," I sighed, still trying sarcasm, but regretting the words as quickly as I had spoken them.

"I guess not," his tone softened and I thought for a second I made him feel bad. "It's a pity though; I had so much fun watching you struggle," Cue the smirk. "Thanks for the other night," he whispered even softer and I heard real emotion in his voice, I turned to say something to him but found that I was speechless looking into his eyes.

The door to the classroom opened and then slammed. In walked Mr. Lambert and another teenager whom I had never seen before. The sight of Mr. Lambert usually made me feel uneasy and nervous, always like I was about to be yelled at; but today when he walked in, an overwhelming feeling of serenity passed over me. Not only that, but I felt more focused than usual; my senses became heightened and the magic became more alive in my blood. The feeling reminded me of the other night in the woods, sending a shiver down my back.

"Excuse me," Mr. Lambert cleared his throat in an attempt to draw the attention of the class forward. He tried again a little louder. "Class, please give me your attention; this is Avalon St. Andrews. He is a transfer student from Brazil, please welcome him to Kingsley."

Mr. Lambert directed him to Lilly's seat and my heart dropped into my stomach. As the new student sat down, I realized the very real possibility that she might never be coming back. I watched Talbott for a moment and though his expression was frozen in place I imagined I could see the sadness in his eyes.

I turned my attention back over to Avalon St. Andrews, thankful that I was no longer the newest kid in school. By the looks of things however, he was going to have a lot easier time fitting in than I did. He was almost too big to be a high school student; although he was wearing the same white collared shirt and navy blue tie every other boy was wearing, the muscles in his arms were clearly defined through the light cotton. His dark curly hair was long, maybe to his shoulders, but he had it tied in a messy pony tail, giving him the appearance of a biker or something. His nose was pronounced and vaguely familiar, although I couldn't place it. And his eyes were clear green and penetrating.

His most interesting feature was almost invisible, but my eyes drifted there immediately. Under his hairline, covering the entirety of the back of his neck and clearly marked was a very intricate and elaborate tattoo. What looked like angel wings were spread wide covering all of the skin between the base of his shirt collar and hairline. Complex, but beautiful feathers fanned out into wings I imagined belonging to the angel of death. A symbol sat in the middle of the two adjoining wings, but the way his hair was positioned made it impossible to identify. I glanced down at the rest of his body, expecting leather pants or spurs or something and noticed that underneath his white cotton button down were more lines of the green tattoo ink. Although I couldn't make out what they were in the shape of, they clearly covered his torso and forearms. He reminded me of someone and I continued to stare at him, wondering who it could be.

"Ms. Matthews…. Ms. Matthews," Mr. Lambert called loudly from the front of the room. I looked up to see that while I was staring at the new kid, the entire class had turned to stare at me. My face blushed red and I cleared my throat instinctively.

"Ms. Matthews, now that I have your attention, please read the part of Juliet," I silently came to the conclusion I would never cease to disappoint Mr. Lambert.

The lunch room seemed a much more daunting place without Lilly. I grabbed a tray of food and headed to the back of the cafeteria. I was a little bit earlier than everyone else today since I did not stay after class to crowd around Kiran with the other girls and make sure he was Ok after his near death experience on the camping trip. I also refused to throw myself at…. I mean introduce myself to the new kid.

146

I sat down to an empty table and relished the few moments of silence I had. Now that I was not threatened with the possibility of losing all control, I had been able to observe my surroundings today. All throughout the day I noticed students and teachers using magic.

In small ways and in big ways they used it for everything they did. Students used magic to pick up a pencil off of the floor, and teachers used it to close a door that was left open. Mrs. Woodsen used magic to close the windows in her classroom and then again to open them when I was pretty sure she had a hot flash. Kiran used magic constantly; to write, to open books, to get a drink. At first I thought everyone was just lazy, but after a while I began to realize that the magic was so much a part of them that there was no other way they were able to function. It truly was the essence of their very existence, and I supposed mine too.

A small portion of me was jealous. I had to remind myself that the magic was at my disposal too and then I had to remind myself that I needed to use it. When I didn't use the magic that was when I began to have problems. And although I knew I was just like everybody else, they apparently hadn't gotten the memo because I was still a social pariah. Not that I really minded; I couldn't really imagine that a girl like Seraphina Van Curen and me would ever be friends.

Speak of the devil, Seraphina entered the cafeteria on Kiran's arm and suddenly the granola bar I'd just taken a bite of was threatening to resurface. I saw that now too, not just the magic but the respect and reverence Kiran demanded. His very presence elicited sycophantic behavior from everyone, both student and teacher. I also noticed how protective Talbott was, but in a more natural, body guard way; he never left Kiran's side. I saw him always on the defensive, and after last Saturday night I could hardly blame him. Kiran looked my way and I quickly bit into my granola bar again, staring down at the table. I rechecked my mental force-field and found all intact. I breathed an audible sigh of relief, but it appeared premature. A uniformed boy plopped down across from me. I refused to look up from my lunch.

"Go away. Your minions are waiting for you," I said through bites of an apple.

"Oh, I'm sorry. Was this seat taken?" a polite and

surprised deep voice sans cocky English accent asked. I looked up quickly, horrified.

"Oh, no! I am so sorry!" my face turned a shade of crimson red. "I thought you were somebody else," my hand flew to cover my mouth after I spit apple all over the table and all over Avalon St. Andrews.

"It's alright. No worries," he laughed, while wiping a bit of apple off his cheek. How terrible.

He gave me a genuine smile that I returned immediately. The same peaceful feeling from earlier filled my entire body and my senses were once again sharpened. I could hear every conversation, every fork touch the plate, and every small chewing sound in the cafeteria. I did my best to drown it out; it was actually kind of gross.

"You don't have an accent," I said bluntly.

"Were you expecting one?" his skin was tan, tanner than most of the students here. His sleeves were rolled up and I could see a deep shade of olive glistened beneath the green lines from his tattoos; it had to be from living in Brazil.

"Oh, I just thought, since you transferred. I'm sorry, I just expected an accent," I blushed again, not really sure why I felt embarrassed.

"I'm American, just like you," he smiled as if he had made a joke, but if he had I didn't get it. "My parents were working in Brazil until last week. We only lived down there for the last two years."

"That's nice. Accents can be so irritating anyways," he looked up at me confused, but I didn't dare explain.

"Do you mind if I sit here?" he asked.

"Oh, no, not at all. As long as you don't mind the outcast table," I gave him a sardonic grin.

"I don't mind; I'm pretty sure I prefer it," he glanced over his should at Kiran and all of his fans; he shook his head and took a big bite of his turkey sandwich. I was pretty sure Avalon St. Andrews and I were going to get along just fine.

"Me too," I rolled my eyes in the general direction of the Monarchy.

"I'm Avalon by the way. And you're Eden?" when I nodded my head, he continued, "So I heard a rumor that you like

148

saved his life this weekend?" he jerked his head in Kiran's direction.

"Where did you hear that?" I asked mortified.

"All of the girls were talking about it this morning. You'd think they'd be grateful, I mean they still have their precious Prince to worship," he grunted in disgust.

"You'd think," I agreed with another mouthful of apple. I realized how disgusting my eating habits were around Avalon and I quickly swallowed. The bite was a little too big and I began to choke a little. The apple stayed lodged in my throat as I continued to cough and gulp my bottle of water.

"Use your magic," Avalon suggested, sounding confused.

Oh right. I held up my finger to him and focused on my magic. The electricity was flowing through my blood at a steady pace. It only took a minimal effort to determine that the apple would no longer be stuck. And just like that I was able to swallow the detrimental piece of food and cough no more.

"Thank you," I cleared my throat, feeling like an idiot.

"Do you enjoy choking?" I heard the laughter in his voice.

"Ha. Ha. No. It's just that, well this whole magic thing is new to me," I gave a sheepish grin and took another swig of my water, just in case.

"What? New to you? How can that be?" Avalon stared at me intently, his green eyes sparkling.

"I was raised by humans," I explained dramatically. I wiggled my fingers a little, to add a theatrical flair.

"I've never heard of that before," Avalon sounded skeptical.

"Well, I had never heard of this before." I gestured to the room filled with my peers, my Immortal peers.

"So you didn't know about magic? You didn't know what you were capable of?" He still sounded skeptical.

"Well, I knew I was capable of something. But I just thought I was crazy. I guess I figured it out Saturday night, when people started turning into animals and I could move trees with my mind," I said it all very casually, but the truth was I still could barely get past what I was able to do.

"Huh," he grunted. "You mean to tell me, that you were able to save the Prince's life and do what you did to those Shape-

Shifters and you had never even used your magic before?" he squinted his eyes at me, unbelieving.

"I guess," I looked across the room to where Kiran sat, surrounded. He met my eyes, and I realized that he was watching me. I quickly turned my attention back to Avalon.

"That seems impossible," Avalon was still skeptical.

"Yeah, to me too," I looked down at the table, ashamed of what I did and worried for Lilly.

"What are you doing later?" Avalon asked suddenly.

"French homework." Ugh.

"That seals it. We are going to practice your magic later tonight and that's final," he leaned back in his chair and folded his arms across his chest as if his decision was the final authority.

"I told you, I have French homework. It's going to take me all night," I protested; although the thought of sitting down to learn a language that completely escaped me made my head spin.

"Eden, there is no more homework. Don't you get it? You are Immortal! Your magic can do the homework for you," his voice was stern as if I should have known this forever.

"I can't cheat!" I protested louder.

"You're unbelievable. And you have so much to learn. You're lucky I'm here, you really are. I have so much to teach you!" he gave me a playful smile and I guessed he won, because I couldn't think of any other reason not to let him help me with my magic.

Chapter Twenty-One

"Do you want to follow me?" Avalon was suddenly behind me as I dug through my backpack looking for my keys.

"Follow you?" I replied confused, pushing my things around inside of my book bag and reaching deeper beyond the books and loose leaf paper.

"We're going to work on your magic, remember?" Avalon stood next to me, fidgeting a little, as if his muscular frame was having a hard time containing all of the energy within. He rocked back and forth on his heels and bit his thumb nail nervously. I noticed that his right hand was constantly drumming a beat into the side of his Dockers and imagined that he was playing a rhythm to god-knows-what kind of angry rock music I was too innocent to listen to.

I squinted at him, trying to figure him out. The same feeling of peacefulness and tranquility passed over me again and once more I felt completely focused. I had no reason to fidget or wiggle at all. My energy seemed to be completely balanced.

"Magic, Eden," Avalon nodded his head in the direction of my backpack and heat quickly rose to my cheeks. How could I keep forgetting the magic when it was so helpful in situations like this?

"Oh yea, I forgot," I finally focused my magic on the missing keys and used it to direct my hand where to go. I pulled them out of my worn book bag, feeling quite triumphant. "Do you want to go to my place?"

"Just follow me. We have to go somewhere where no one will bother us," he smiled wide and pointed to his car: a bright red, four door truck, with an extended cab and monster wheels. It not only stood apart from the rest of the black something or others, but stood above them as well. I couldn't help but laugh out loud.

I followed Avalon for twenty minutes. I could tell he wanted to speed, but drove painfully slow so that I could follow him. We drove over the bridge and into Iowa up into the bluffs that looked down over the Missouri River.

Eventually the road ended and we continued on a dirt path through some trees. I had never been more thankful for my Rover as I bounced along behind Avalon's ginormous truck.

We continued for miles on a dirt path barely wide enough to accommodate Avalon's massive vehicle. Every once in a while a tree branch smacked down on the roof of his truck and I fully expected him to eventually get impaled.

After a while Avalon stopped his truck. His was parked precariously near the edge of a one of Iowa's famous cliffs. I kept my Land Rover a little ways back and in a more secure area. I loved my yellow SUV and was totally not ready to watch it plummet into the Missouri River just yet.

Avalon hopped down from his cab and I noticed that he had changed out of his school uniform. I looked past him to see a winding path that snaked carefully around his truck and into a clearing surrounded by trees on one side and the cliff's edge on the other. The sight was beautiful, but I couldn't help the small tremors of terror making their way across my arms and legs. The familiar acceleration of electricity surged through my veins, reminding me that I was a scaredy-cat.

Avalon wore a short sleeved black t-shirt and loose fitting jeans. His hair was out of the pony tail and hung wildly just below chin level. His jet black hair was semi curly, creating the image of chaos carefully framing his prominent two-dimpled grin. My suspicions from earlier were confirmed and I could make out green tattoo ink tracing his forearms up to his biceps and beyond the shirtsleeve.

I shut my engine off and exited my car as well. Still in my school uniform, I felt oddly out of place next to Avalon, who looked like he belonged in a juvenile detention center. A chill ran up my spine reminding me of Saturday night and the last time I was in a wooded area. Images of murderous men flooded my memory and I shook my head to bring myself back to the present.

"What's with all of the ink?" I jutted my chin at Avalon's sleeved tattoos, hoping I sounded a little bit cool.

"What, this?" he held up his arms and shrugged. "I guess I like to define exactly who I am."

153

"Ok…." I wished I knew what he was talking about.

"Like this," he pointed to his right forearm and then suddenly took off his shirt. Although I was surprised by his gesture, I finally understood the strange markings on his arm. The entire right side of Avalon's torso and arm were covered in an intricate and large tree. The tree was amazingly defined and detailed.

The branches of the tree started at his shoulder and wrapped themselves around his arm and to the front and back of his body. The branches and trunk of the tree were thick and gnarled looking. The trunk of the tree wrapped itself from his lower back, around to the right side of his stomach, covering his rock hard abs.

The tree's branches had no leaves, and were barren, but strong. One branch in particular wrapped its way down Avalon's arm and to his forearm, breaking off into smaller branches along the way. It was as if someone took a beautiful painting and wrapped it around half of Avalon's body. The image was powerful and beautiful at the same time.

I walked closer to him, letting my fingers trace the lines running down his forearm. "So what does it mean?" I asked, a little breathless. I had never seen such a vivid tattoo before, although I was not completely sure why it was so powerful to me. Maybe to see such a detailed image on a human body was unusual.

"A tree is the symbol of Eternity, or Immorality. It has been since the beginning of time," his own fingers traced the lines of the branches.

"Ok, so what is on the back of your neck?" I remembered the first tattoo I saw from that morning.

"Oh that?" he lifted up his hair in the back and revealed the two strong wings I had seen earlier. In the middle of the two wings was a snake wrapped in a circle eating its own tail. The same image of the snake eating his own tail wrapped around his left wrist as well, creating a tattooed bracelet.

"What does that mean?" I asked, not sure if I was grossed out or in awe again of the detailing that went in to each of his tattoos.

"That literally defines who I am. Someday you will

understand," he spoke cryptically and I wasn't completely sure I wanted to understand.

"Ok, so this one is pretty self-explanatory," I pointed to his left forearm; a picture of a beautiful bird rising out of an intricately drawn fire. The bird looked commanding and angry; its wings were spread, but remained close to his body as the tattoo sat long on his skinny, but muscular arm. The one wing reached out across his chest until the image of the tangled tree met it and the other one across his shoulder blade.

"Is it?" he asked and cocked his head a little to the side.

"No, I guess not. I mean at least I know it's a bird," I responded defensively, realizing that I had no idea what the meaning was.

"I'm just giving you a hard time," he gave my shoulder a rough but playful push. "This is a phoenix," he pointed to the bird; "It's just another symbol for Immortality."

"But we're not really Immortal, right? I mean we're not really going to live forever?" I remembered Principal Saint telling me that Immortal was not a literal meaning for our people.

"No, we'll never live forever as long as Lucan is in charge," Avalon spat on the ground in disgust. I searched my memory for Lucan and remembered that he was supposedly our King…. my King.

"What do you mean?" I asked innocently.

"As long as Lucan tries to control the magic and keep our people separated, we will never live forever. Our magic isn't strong enough. But he doesn't care about us. He only cares about himself, his bloodline and his damn prejudices," he spat again and I was more confused than ever.

"I have no idea what you're talking about," I tried honesty. Maybe Avalon would give me some explanation.

"The King," he said, frustrated. When I gave him an even more confused look he continued, "Lucan is the one who has taken away our freedom!" he exclaimed heatedly.

"We're not free?" I asked in a very small voice.

"No we're not free, and we're dying as well. As long as we live under his bondage, we will continue to die. But he could care less. All he cares about is that his blood remains pure, and the blood of his line. The Monarchy must never become tarnished," I

155

could almost feel Avalon's disgust as an oppressive force weighing down on me.

"Ok, you need to explain.... now," I tried to be forceful, hoping that he remembered I was new to this whole thing.

"Sorry," he grunted, not sounding sorry at all. "Derrick is the King that outlawed intermarriage, well for everyone but his precious line. This happened a long time ago. Derrick was the first King, the first Immortal to rule our people. The people cried out for a King and they were given one. Too bad the first thing he did was execute the Oracles."

"The who?" I interrupted; trying to stay focused and keep my head from spinning out of control.

"The Oracles, they were something like prophets or advisors to our people before the King. There were four of them and they represented one of each of us, and together they were all powerful. They were also the first to die. So anyway," he shot me a serious look that let me know not to interrupt again, "After Derrick executed the Oracles, he banished the Shape-Shifters. He claimed they were deceitful and manipulative because they were able to take any form. He turned the other Immortals against them and those who didn't escape were hunted and thrown into prison until their magic was weak enough that they could be killed. And since the Titans had pledged their allegiance to protect the King before one had ever been elected they were forced into service and remain there today as nothing more than glorified prisoners." He took a moment to spit on the ground once again. "The only free people are the Witches and Mediums, but I would hardly call what we have freedom. We live under tyrannical rule and a King who is just as heartless and sick as his forefather. And who knows what the next King will be like; he seems even more clueless than those who came before him. Our people are going to die and they do nothing about it."

"But what could they do about it?" I thought about Kiran and found it hard to believe he would actually want us all to die. He may have been immature, but he was not a ruthless killer.

"They could break the ban on intermarriage for one. They could allow the full magic to flow between us and they could release us from their dictatorship," the whole Monarchy thing might have been new to me, but I knew enough about world

156

history that if what Avalon just told me was true, then I also knew that what he was saying could probably get him killed.

"What marriage ban?" I asked, feeling more confused than ever.

"The one that got us into this whole mess to begin with. We are not allowed to marry outside of our own kind."

"You mean, like humans?"

"No, well, yes, but mainly a Witch has to marry a Witch and a Titan has to marry a Titan. They keep us compartmentalized that way, and they restrict the flow of magic. See before King Derrick, an Immortal could marry whomever they chose and no matter who they married their child was always unique. Like a Witch could marry a Titan and then have a Medium for a child. It was all allowed and the magic flowed freely. But since Derrick, our magic is deteriorating and the royal family could care less," Avalon laughed bitterly.

"But isn't their magic deteriorating as well? Won't they eventually have to intermarry?" I asked, feeling like I was beginning to understand the whole thing and realizing the people I was a part of had just as many problems as humans.... if not more.

"They are the royal family. They can marry whomever they choose," Avalon said slowly as if I were having trouble understanding his words. I didn't really blame him. "Not that they would marry just whomever, they only choose the best of the best. And for them that means either a Witch or a Psychic. They rotate between generations. Up next is a most promising Psychic, I'm sure."

"What? So Kiran has to marry a Psychic?" I had a hard time getting the actual word out.

"Yes, that's the law. Just to ensure the royal blood stays strong. His father of course married a Witch, and now it's his turn to carry out the imperial edict."

"Huh...." was all I could say. I knew Avalon had just enlightened me on an overwhelming amount of new information; but the hardest part I found myself unwilling to accept was that by law it was illegal for me to marry Kiran. Not that I would even think that far ahead, or have those kind of feelings for him; but the fact that it was against the law, that I was not even an option, was making me a little resentful.

157

I thought about Lilly then and realized what she was up against. A wave of fear flooded my entire body and I realized that I had to do something to help her. I shuddered at the thought of the court inevitably finding her guilty. My mind began to reel with the crushing feeling of hopelessness that settled on me. I had to talk to Kiran about it, he had to do something.

"So anyway," Avalon changed the subject, still sounding riled up from his tangent. "Move that tree."

"Excuse me?" his command brought me out of my inner freak out.

"Move that tree," he said it slower, but firmer.

"You're not very nice you know," I gave him a playful pout.

"I'm sorry, you're right. I just don't like those damn Kendricks," he smiled playfully back. "Please, move that tree."

I focused my energy on a medium sized tree that sat about twenty feet away from us. I let the electricity surge through my blood and build, using my mind to direct the tree. I lifted it out of the ground slowly; the roots and branches hung limply down on the ground below where it was now suspended in midair, completely unearthed.

"What now?" I faked a yawn, as if holding the tree in midair was the easiest thing in the world.

"Now put it back," he smiled smugly as the tree wavered a little bit while my mind grasped the task.

Blowing things up and ripping things apart was easy. I had never had to put something back together before. I focused my energy back into the ground. I lowered the tree slowly with my mind until it was positioned just above the earth. I let my mind snake through the roots of the tree, my energy focused completely. I let them dig back into the soil, searching for their homes once again. Slowly and methodically I returned each root and branch to its original position and let the tree rest peacefully, balanced once again deep within the earth.

"Good," Avalon admired quietly. "You're better than I thought you'd be."

"Well, thank you," I gave a sarcastic bow, but was actually very thankful for the words of encouragement.

We spent the rest of the afternoon like that. Avalon giving

158

me task after task, each one getting more difficult. I completed all that he assigned me and continued to impress him. I would think that after hours of using my magic I would have felt fatigued or depleted; but instead I felt more empowered. The more I used the magic, the more magic I had to use. I was filled with a never ending supply of omnipotence.

Chapter Twenty-Two

"Pssst….." Avalon tried to get my attention during French, but I did my best to ignore him. "Hey, Eden." He whispered harshly.

"What?" I whispered as softly as possible, realizing I could never be quiet enough to escape Ms. Devereux's stern glare.

"What are you doing tonight?" Although Avalon sat directly behind me during the hour of horror known as French, Ms. Devereux had positioned me at the front of the class; always under the watchful eye of the firm French teacher. I had done my best to catch up, but the woman could not understand a world in which French was not spoken fluently in every home. Since I didn't grow up with parents who spoke multiple languages and summered in the South of France, I thought I had ample excuse to be a bit behind; she saw it differently.

"Nothing. Leave me alone," I whispered even quieter back.

"Good," Avalon replied a little louder than I felt comfortable with.

I turned my attention back to my book work and concentrated as hard as I could on my conjugations. I was sure Avalon had some great plan for the evening. Over the past week and a half I learned to just go along with the adventure; which usually meant an isolated area, usually forestry, working on my magic. Avalon was always very concerned that I was practicing what powers I had.

I never complained and always had fun. I enjoyed learning all of the super-human feats I was capable of. But even more I enjoyed spending time with Avalon. He was always amusing and always adventurous. He was like the exact opposite to how careful and easily-scared I was. We complemented each other well.

"Do you own anything sexy?" Avalon whispered hoarsely to me, striking up another in-class conversation.

"What?" I blurted out, too loudly. My cheeks flamed red and I dropped my pencil on the ground.

"Mr. St. Andrews, Ms. Matthews please continue this inappropriate conversation after class. Merci beaucoup," Ms.

Devereux seethed through her strong French accent. I blushed even redder and averted my eyes back to my homework.

As I stared down at the foreign language I could barely understand a small ball of paper landed right in front of me. I expected it to be an apology from Avalon, although I could hear him snickering behind me. I unrolled the wrinkled piece of paper, curious more than anything.

Maybe you should save the dirty talk for private....

I glanced over at Kiran to confirm the sender. He was staring at me with a smaller version of his signature smirk, but something was different about his eyes. I rolled my own eyes at him and gave him my own playful version of a smirk, but he just looked back down at his homework. Instead of feeling irritated like I would have expected, I felt a little bit sad, missing the days when he would have made more sport out of embarrassing me. I realized this sounded twisted, but I was suddenly nervous I had lost his attention.

"I'm sorry, Avalon, did you want to ask me something?" I asked Avalon sarcastically, as he sat down at our regular table. "Because I would appreciate it if you asked me your inappropriate questions here, alone; not in the middle of French class where the teacher already hates me and the entire class is listening in," I pretended to be really upset, but Avalon realized a while ago I was incapable of getting angry with him. He did enjoy trying to make me mad though.

"Oh, calm down," he shook his head and gave me a wide smile, accentuating his dimpled cheeks. His mischievous baby face contradicted strongly with the rest of his toned physique. "If you would use your magic and let me communicate telepathically with you, I wouldn't have to say things loud enough for the entire world to hear."

"Oh, I see. It's my fault. You know that I'm not supposed to um, let my guard down," I said softly, still not sure why Principal Saint had been so insistent upon my mental defenses.

"I know that, I'm just giving you a hard time. Chill out. But what I really need to know is if you have something nice to

161

wear tonight…. something um, more grown up?" Now that he was forced to ask me his bizarre question face to face, I realized that he was a little shy. I inwardly felt satisfied to witness Avalon's small embarrassment; although it could never equal my seemingly constant humiliation.

"That depends on what you have planned," I doubted any good could come from whatever scheme he was devising.

"I, of course, can't tell you," he replied dramatically. "It's a surprise," he looked around us as if to make sure no one was paying attention. "And really, it's no big deal."

"Oh but you expect me to get all dressed up?" I asked hoping to get more details.

"Well, it's just that….." he hesitated, and looked around again. "Do you have something sexy or not?" he was barely able to say the word now that we were face to face.

"You are awesome at asking a girl out," I was a little irritated with his funny behavior.

"This is not a date!" Avalon blurted out a little too loudly. My face flooded with heat immediately and I couldn't look him in the eyes.

"I was just joking." I mumbled pathetically. I knew that it wasn't a date from the beginning. It wasn't like that with Avalon…. but he didn't have to react so strongly.

"I'm sorry," Avalon calmed down and said softer, "Eden, I'm really sorry. I didn't mean to hurt your feelings. It's just that, you know, we're only friends right? I mean good friends… best friends…. but just friends," I nodded my reply, instantly forgiving him, but I fully planned on milking this just a little longer. "Besides, this is a mission."

"A mission?" curiosity made me completely forget feeling sorry for myself. "For what?"

"You'll just have to wait and see," Avalon responded mysteriously, flashing his big dimples at me again. "Remember, look like a grown up. I'll pick you up at eight," he stood up and headed for the door. I was once again left to wonder at the strange behavior of high school boys.

162

I checked myself in the full length mirror once again, not fully buying what I saw. Aunt Syl was working tonight and so I had full access to her "grown-up" wardrobe per request from Avalon. I obeyed his appeal to find something more mature, but left him waiting impatiently in his truck while I found the courage to leave the house.

The dress I chose to wear could have had many descriptions; some might have called it "sexy"… I called it "midnight hooker." Somehow I thought Avalon would approve. The all black dress was simple, maybe too simple, but definitely mature. The short skirt covered just enough, leaving my legs bare, but looking extra-long. The dress covered nothing behind me above my low hip-line and I prayed it would remain tactful although completely backless; I was thankful that the neckline of the dress was just below my throat. My arms were sleeveless and the only thing keeping the dress on my shoulders was a thin ribbon that tied at the base of my hairline.

I resisted the urge to let my hair hang down covering the open back, and instead pulled it over one shoulder in a loose and low pony tail. I stepped close to the mirror and applied some bubble gum pink lip gloss. Looking over myself for a final time I realized I had forgotten shoes.

I ran back into Aunt Syl's closet. My eyes quickly assessed the racks of designer heels and fell on a pair of six inch hot pink stilettos. I pulled them on immediately; fully aware I would regret the decision later. I grabbed a silver clutch on my way out of the massive room and went as quickly, but as carefully as possible down the stairs and out the door.

Using magic to lock the house, I made it to Avalon's truck before I realized there was no way in hell I could make it up into his cab with class. I opened the door of the truck and eyed the step. I looked back down at the long heel on my beautiful shoes and then at my short tight skirt and laughed out loud.

"You have got to be kidding me." I turned my eyes to Avalon and shook my head. "This is impossible."

"You're right," Avalon turned off the engine and jumped down. "I said look grown up, not like a prostitute," he hurried across the street to a silver Lexus parked on the curb. "Whose car is this?"

"I think my neighbors. You don't have to be rude. I can go change," I called after him; my insecurities confirmed.

"Nah. You're fine; I was just kidding," he opened the door of the car easily; I had expected it to be locked. Avalon took another look around and sat down in the driver's side seat. "Come on."

I walked over to the car with my mouth open. There was absolutely no way I was stealing this car. I half expected Avalon to rip the wires out of the steering column and do some fancy trick to hotwire it. Of course he just used his magic and turned the car on without any sign of vandalism.

"There is no way I am going to be an accessory to grand theft auto!" I shook my head and crossed my arms stubbornly.

"Come on, we're going to be late," Avalon ignored my objections.

"I'm serious, Avalon," I tried again, but he threw the passenger's side door open and revved the engine.

"Seriously Eden, we will bring it back completely unharmed. If you like, I'll even fill up the gas tank. Now get in," he said it firmly and I realized that he was going with or without me so I decided to get it in. Hopefully my magic would be enough to repair any major damage Avalon was able to incur.

Avalon played with the dial of the radio, until he found something he deemed suitable. The loud music reinforced the point that this was definitely not a date and I realized once again that I was totally fine with that. My interest was raised however, and I couldn't even imagine where he was taking me.

Avalon drove out of my neighborhood and towards downtown. I lived nearly exactly midtown, in an area called Dundee, so it only took fifteen minutes or so before we were driving on the old brick streets through the Old Market. Shops and restaurants surrounded us on both sides of the old fashioned part of town.

We drove slowly to avoid the meandering pedestrians and occasional horse and buggy. Cops sat on street corners talking casually with street artists and a group of musicians played the blues with an open guitar case set out in front of them.

Although the weather was still fairly warm, the days were growing shorter and it was already dark outside. My magic was

164

pulsating and my senses were heightened. I could feel the pull of strong magic in the direction we were driving causing my heart to beat even faster.

Eventually Avalon pulled over in a more deserted area of downtown. My pulse quickened as we stepped out of the car. I could tell where we were going now from the draw of magic beneath the ground, but I let Avalon lead the way.

I followed Avalon to a darkened doorway that appeared to be locked; the door was made out of a strong wood but had been painted black. A brass door knocker sat in the middle shaped into the same image that Avalon had tattooed on his left wrist: a large snake wrapped around an apple, eating its own tail. A chill ran up my spine; I was not entirely sure what I had just gotten myself into.

Avalon gripped the doorknocker in his palm and held it for a few seconds. The brass turned to gold and then illuminated the doorway for only a second before dulling back into the brass we first encountered. I heard the lock click and the door opened partway. I followed Avalon into the building realizing he had given me no explanation as to what was behind this door.

A long and lighted hallway surprised me, as I had expected something dark and dingy. Candelabras on mahogany tables were placed evenly down the length of the hallway; the carpet was plush and burgundy and the wallpaper, a beautiful and intricate gold-leafed. Although the entrance was not what I had expected, it still offered no explanation as to where I was.

"Follow my lead." Avalon turned his head and whispered to me. "And stay close," the look in his eyes helped me understand his seriousness. I nodded my head, swallowing the huge lump in my throat and continued down the hallway.

At the end of the passage was a large mahogany door with a similar brass knocker as the first door; only this snake was much skinnier and wrapped around a scroll. Avalon wrapped his hand around it and the same effect as before occurred. This time however, beyond the door was a set of stairs winding downward, but significantly dimmer than the hallway.

I could hear many voices below us and the strong drag of magic left me certain this was our destination. I followed Avalon down a twisting path of stone stairs that seemed like it would never end. My stilettos made a clicking noise with each step.

At the bottom of the stairs was a surprisingly large room full of people. The room must have covered the entire block underneath the streets up above. The people all dressed extremely well, milled around the room on plush couches and chairs covered in ruby and gold thread. Small tables sat in between them and I noticed in one corner of the room larger tables, set up for poker. A counter ran half the length of the back of the room serving drinks and I realized that this place was a bar, or a club, or Ok, I didn't really know what this place was yet, but something along those lines.

Avalon walked straight over to the long counter and ordered two drinks; I stayed close to his side and took the brown liquid he offered to me. I sipped the strong smelling liquor, pretending I knew what I was doing, but nearly spit it out in the same breath. The strong, woodsy whisky burned as I struggled to swallow it and then gave me an instant heady feeling, making the room spin around me.

"Use your magic," Avalon whispered to me through gritted teeth. I forced a smile and then worked harder to force my magic into control. I calmed my nerves and cleared my head. I would just pretend to drink whatever it was.

Avalon looked around the room nervously and I wished I knew what he was looking for. I did my best to pretend to be bored; mimicking the stance of the other scantily dressed women I saw standing around the room. Avalon stood on his tippy toes to get a better look and I contemplated telepathic communication to get some answers, but decided against it.

The force of magic radiating around the room and my blood, hot and boiling, combined with the energy buzzing inside of me confirmed my belief that everyone in here was an Immortal. I was at once thrilled that there were so many others like me, but then cautious again when I realized they were still all strangers. They however, all seemed to know one another. Maybe this was some type of Immortal club that I hadn't been inducted into yet.

"Stay here," Avalon commanded and turned to walk away.

"Wait," I demanded. "Where are you going?" I was suddenly nervous and shy.

"I'll be right back…. I promise," Avalon softened his tone

166

and gave me a reassuring smile. I tried to trust him, but this whole night had just been too weird.

I attempted to follow Avalon with my eyes, but I quickly lost him in the crowd. For a while I could follow his trail of magic, but the overwhelming quantity of mixed energies in the room made me lose that as well. I looked down into my glass and swirled around the golden liquor, contemplating another sip.

"Well, well, well…. look who it is," A familiar English accent whispered into my ear with equal parts menace and mischief. "What are you doing here?"

"What do you mean? What are *you* doing here?" I avoided his question and leaned back against the bar. I took a miniscule drink from my cup, noticing Kiran had an identical one in his hand.

"Hmmmm…." Kiran's eyes drifted over my "mature" outfit and heat crept onto my face. "So this is what Avalon had planned for you…. not very exciting."

"Then why are you here?" I asked again, realizing that although I hadn't given him an answer, I hoped he would give me one.

"I have to be here; royal duties and all," he shot me a roguish look and took a long drink from his tumbler. His usually clear blue eyes looked a little duller than usual and I noticed black and blue bags under them.

"Must be tough to be King," I pretended to take an equally long drink.

"Not King yet," he said simply. Kiran looked me over once again and I crossed my arms self-consciously. He stepped closer, resting his hands on either side of my body. I could smell the woodsy scent of liquor mixed with his sweet, almost herbal scent and the electricity picked up strength through my veins.

"So really, what are you doing here?" I tried one more time, my voice trembling from Kiran's close proximity. His hands slid up my arms and he pulled me in closer until our bodies were touching. Electricity almost overpowered my senses and I forgot the rest of the world around us.

"This is where I conduct my business, Eden. You are in my American office," he smiled a little. I wished I could look around the room once again, but I couldn't tear my eyes away

167

from Kiran's. "Oh, Eden you've so much to learn," he smiled a little wider and leaned his face even closer to mine. I was transfixed in his arms, completely unable to move. I was certain he was about to kiss me and I closed my eyes in anticipation. His grip tightened on my arms and I felt the heat from his face; his sweet breath tickling my nose.

And then…. A throat cleared in my ear and my eyes instantly popped open. Kiran's body stiffened next to me and all intentions changed. Principal Saint and Talbott stood there side by side, both sets of arms crossed, both men visibly seething. I gathered myself and regained my senses quicker than I thought possible.

Chapter Twenty-Three

"Damn it," Kiran growled and slammed his hand against the bar behind me. I jumped, startled by his outburst of anger. He turned to face the interrupters, but did not leave my side. "Can I help you gentlemen?" he asked through gritted teeth.

"Forgive us for the interruption sir, but Ms. Matthews is not allowed in your private club," Principal Saint ended his sentence with a small bow. His manner was respectful, almost subservient.

Outside of school, the roles were reversed. Kiran was in command here, and Principal Saint must obey Kiran's orders. I may have had a hard time wrapping my mind around the Monarchy before tonight, but the facts of Kiran's power were clearly displayed in front of me. I was forced to understand the role of the Monarchy in my life now. My face flushed with embarrassment, as I noticed all eyes in the enormous room focused on us.

"I granted her entrance," Kiran said softer, noticing the onlookers as well. His voice however, was none the less menacing.

"I'm sorry sir; by your father's order she is not allowed here," Talbott interjected himself and I couldn't help but despise him a little more.

"Mr. St. Andrews is waiting upstairs to take you home," Principal Saint addressed me for the first time and then angled his body as if to tell me I should leave immediately. I began to move, but Kiran stopped me by putting his hand on my waist.

"There's no need for that. I was leaving anyways. I will take her home. Please tell Avalon, he is free to go," Kiran took me by the arm a bit roughly and began walking towards the door.

"Excuse me, Prince Kiran; there is still business to attend to," Talbott again interrupted, but this time I could hear the small amount of trepidation in his voice.

"What business?" Kiran growled quietly without even turning to look at him.

"I am not at liberty to say in front of.... her," Talbott referenced me with a disdain that let me know exactly how he felt.

"Fine," Kiran stood still for a few seconds longer, but did not let go of my arm. He left his back turned on Talbott and Principal Saint, apparently trying to decide what to do next. I was too afraid of him to speak. I could feel the heat of his anger swirling around us. The electricity pulsed between my skin and his fingers wildly. "I will walk her to the door," before anyone else could object, he began walking again, pulling me along beside him.

"I'm sorry," I stammered out; not exactly sure why I was apologizing.

"Don't be. You did nothing wrong," he mumbled through gritted teeth.

He did not let go of my arm the entire walk upstairs. I hurried along beside him as quickly as I could in the shoes that I was wearing. Kiran rushed up the long flight of stone stairs and through the long, brightly lit hallway. He did not stop moving until we reached the door to the outside.

If I was surprised by his behavior downstairs, I was even more surprised by his behavior on the way back to the front door. But nothing could have prepared me for what he did next.

Once we reached the door, I grabbed for the handle, hoping to escape to the safety of the car Avalon had stolen. I was perplexed by Kiran's behavior, but more than anything I was humiliated by my exile from his private club. I wanted to put this night behind me and crawl into a ball, forgetting about this entire experience. Kiran however had a different idea of how to end the night.

Although I reached for the door, Kiran stopped me by grabbing me firmly around my waist. His hands were hot against my skin, even through the material of my dress. He pushed me roughly against the wall and pressed his body against mine. One hand stayed on my hip, but the other he raised above my head to plant firmly against the wall. The magic flared in my blood, making it boil beneath my skin.

Kiran stared into my eyes for several seconds looking for something I was not sure I possessed. The intensity of his expression left me breathless and the closeness of his magic made me dizzy. The electricity ran between us wildly, igniting a lightning storm in my veins.

Suddenly, his lips were against mine, and his hand was tangled in my hair. He kissed me hungrily, pressing me against his body and wrapping me up in his magic. I kissed him back as if I couldn't breathe without him. Every place our bodies touched felt like a thousand degrees; he kissed me passionately, leaving my mouth for only a second to kiss my neck and jawline, but then he was back to my lips with even more passion. I heard him sigh sweetly as though he had waited for this kiss for a very long time. Our magic connected with an almost violent force and I fought to keep consciousness. Our souls were united in that one moment, and I never wanted to leave it.

Kiran's sigh turned to misery as the door at the end of the hallway slammed shut. Another magical entity was present and our perfect kiss was forced to a close. Kiran was across the hallway in milliseconds. He gave me one more intense look of longing and then turned around to walk in the other direction. I was left staring after him with swollen lips and messy hair.

Principal Saint waited at the end of the hallway for Kiran to approach and respectfully opened the door for him to pass through. The door closed behind him with a loud finality, leaving me to feel cold and alone. Kiran's magic was no more a part of mine; I felt drained and empty. Although my own magic was still pulsing through my blood at a rapid rate, without Kiran's to set it on fire, it left me something to want.

Principal Saint stayed on my side of the door as if protecting the entry way from the likes of me. The thought of forcing my way passed him crossed my mind, but the other side of the door offered no hope to reinstate the kiss anyways. I tore through the door to the street instead, running as quickly as I could to the safety and loneliness of Avalon's stolen Lexus.

I found sanctuary in the passenger's seat of the sedan. I plopped down on the seat, very unlady-like and completely out of breath. I barely paid attention to Avalon, but out of the corner of my eye I could tell he was equally as emotional as I was.

I touched my fingers to my still swollen lips, expecting Avalon to drive away. Instead of making a getaway however, he rolled down his window and I saw the figure of Principal Saint resting his hands on the open window frame.

"How dare you bring her here," although Principal Saint

172

didn't use my name directly, it was crystal clear who he was referring to. His fingers gripped tightly to the window sill. Clearly he was angry, but I was confused why my presence here would conjure such rage.

"Nothing happened," Avalon defended himself loudly, and accentuated his point by slamming his hands on the steering wheel. His fingers wrapped themselves around the leather and gripped the steering wheel equally as tight as Principal Saint's. "We're all fine."

"Something did happen." Principal Saint spat back. I realized I preferred a much more docile school teacher, than this angry and scary version of Principal Saint. Everyone was clearly livid with me, but I could not figure out why. Maybe I wasn't allowed in the club, but were these reactions really necessary? "The entire room noticed who she is because of the Prince's damn affections for her. Now not only do you risk discovery but the entire Kingdom will soon be aware of her effect on the Prince. Damn it Avalon, what were you thinking?"

"I am stronger with her near me. I can't just run reconnaissance without some type of protection. You send me into the lion's den and you expect me to kill the beast, unarmed," Avalon nearly shouted at Principal Saint; he grasped the steering wheel tighter and glared out the windshield.

"Never mind that now. Get her out of here," Principal Saint touched the steering wheel underneath Avalon's firm grip and the car instantly turned on. "Take her straight home; we will talk about this later," the two of them had yet to address me personally. If only I could stay mad, but the burn of Kiran's sweet kiss still lingered on my mouth.

Avalon stomped his foot down on the accelerator and my head slammed back against the headrest. He peeled out of the parking space without slowing down. It was my turn to dig my fingers into something and I found the edge of my leather seat and held on tight.

"Damn it. Damn it. Damn it," Avalon repeated over and over; and then another long stream of expletives poured out of his mouth. I was not sure how to react, but felt strangely responsible for the demise of whatever he had planned tonight. "Why can't you just stay away from him?" he practically shouted at me.

173

My temper flared up immediately. "If I remember correctly, you were the one who dragged me along to that place, and you were the one who left me completely alone! Kiran approached me. I did exactly as you said and did not move from the bar. He came over to *me*. I didn't even know he was there!" I yelled back, suddenly over emotional and definitely sick and tired of being blamed for Kiran's actions.

"You cannot talk to him anymore Eden; you have to end whatever there is between you." Avalon softened his voice, almost pleading with me.

"There is nothing between us," I replied just as softly; but my lips burned from the memory of our kiss. I looked out the window and watched the scenery fly by as Avalon drove a hundred miles an hour.

"Do not lie to me," he said sternly. "Eden, don't lie to yourself. He is dangerous and.... evil. You have no idea what you are getting yourself into. You cannot be so reckless," Avalon's eyes turned hard as he stared at the road ahead of him. I didn't know how to respond to his allegations; I didn't know why he hated Kiran so much. But I did know that Kiran was not evil and that he was not dangerous; at the same time an uneasy feeling washed over me and a small pit of fear began to grow in my stomach.

"There is nothing between us, really," I tried to sound confident, but my voice was tiny and far off.

"Promise me you will not let it get farther than what it is right now. Promise me you will stay away from him," Avalon turned to face me and the look on his face was enough to make me promise anything. I quickly shook my head "yes" and reached out to grab his hand. His skin was cold and when I touched it the magic easily flowed between us. My senses became even clearer and my magic became instantly stronger, rushing quickly throughout my body.

"He will take that away from you," Avalon said sadly, and I understood that he was referencing our magic. "You have to trust me Eden."

"I do," I said simply, knowing that it was the complete truth. Whatever it was about Avalon, and whatever happened to our magic when we were together, I knew it was no mistake. I

174

trusted him completely, and I knew he would only do what was best for me. I did not know however, if I could keep my promise to him and stay away from Kiran.

The rest of the drive home was made in silence. Avalon's eyes never softened. I could feel his magic on edge and irritated. I could feel him always searching our perimeter, looking for other signs of magic. I was not sure what he was looking for, but it made me nervous.

Avalon pulled into the same spot on the street that he took the Lexus from what seemed like hours ago. He parked it perfectly and I relaxed a little, realizing he brought it back in excellent condition. We got out of the car, silent still and he walked me to the door.

I expect to say goodbye to him at the doorstep, but when I unlocked the front door and turned around to say goodnight, I realized he was following me inside.

"Where's Sylvia?" Avalon asked. He began to search the downstairs of my house as if expecting to find an intruder. My throat closed in nervousness, wondering what exactly he was looking for.

"Um, I think she'll be at the hospital all night," I noticed that Avalon called my aunt "Sylvia" and I couldn't remember ever giving him her full name.

"I better stay here tonight. Do you mind?" he didn't wait for an answer, but walked over to the wicker basket of blankets behind the oversized couch and pulled out a large, warm quilt.

"I guess not," I debated whether to be annoyed or scared, but in the end I decided I trusted him; and so I walked over to the linen closet and grabbed him a few feather pillows.

"Goodnight, Eden," Avalon plopped down on the couch and pulled the blanket over him without even taking off his shoes.

"Goodnight, Avalon," I replied and made my way up the stairs and into the quiet safety of my bedroom. What a night.

Chapter Twenty-Four

"It looks like you've made a new best friend," Kiran's crisp accent whispered in my ear from behind. He scared me so I turned too quickly to face him and our noses bumped. A shot of electricity rushed through my blood as we were less than millimeters apart from each other. And then I blushed as I remembered our kiss from the other night.

"What do you mean?" I asked, praying my breath had recovered from lunch.

"The new kid, it looks like you two are getting along well," he sat down next to me at the lab table. Lilly was usually my chemistry partner, but because of her prolonged absence I was alone today.

"Avalon is um, nice," I was not quite sure what Kiran was getting at; but almost positive he was just trying to extract some reaction from me.

I turned my attention back to my work, not really sure what to do. Both Avalon and Principal Saint had told me countless times to keep my distance from Kiran and I'd done my best, but Kiran hadn't been given the same directions.

Well, actually he had been told to stay away from me; he just had the luxury of being able to do whatever he wanted. I found that a tiny bit irritating.

"I bet he is," Kiran grunted and I realized for the first time that Kiran was jealous of Avalon. I couldn't hold back a smile. I looked over at Avalon who was partnered with Adelaide Meyer, extricating her from her usual table with the "holy trinity". Despite her separation from Seraphina and Evangeline she seemed completely at ease. Well at least she was completely drooling over Avalon, finding any excuse possible to touch him; my stomach churned violently, but not from jealousy.

More like I had an internal need to protect him. I found this weird, since we just met not that long ago, but the feeling remained despite that fact. I stared at them for a few seconds longer wondering if Avalon enjoyed the attention or was as annoyed with her as I was just watching them. Yuck.

"Have you met him yet?" I asked, half joking. I pretended

to focus more intently on the busy work Mr. Hayman assigned, carefully looking up answers from the Table of Elements.

"No, not yet. I mean he did manage to break into my private club and all, but I wouldn't say that we have met properly. Would you care to introduce us?" his English accent was the epitome of gentlemen-like behavior, but I noticed his eyes roll and shoulders slump a little.

"My pleasure," I mumbled. I glanced again at Avalon understanding why all of the girls fawned over him, but that didn't mean I necessarily felt the same way. He had turned into my only friend since Lilly's absence and we had a lot of fun together, well at least a lot of excitement together. But he was definitely only a friend.

I had tried to like him. I had tried to play his games; but I couldn't keep up. Besides I was pretty confident he was not the least bit interested in me. We were it seemed, just friends. Actually I didn't even know if I could say that. He at least preferred to talk with me more than the other girls, but I just couldn't figure him out.

If I understood Kiran's feelings for me, or non-feelings for me, maybe I could have understood his jealousy, but at the moment it didn't make any sense. Avalon and I usually sat together and talked together, but it was completely platonic. Kiran hadn't tried to do very much of either since he kissed me. I guessed since he figured out who I was, I was no longer a curiosity; he probably got bored.

I touched my fingers to my lips remembering his passion. The back of my neck got hot suddenly and the electricity surged through my veins. Confusing or not, the memory of his lips against mine made me dizzy. I noticed that Kiran's eyes were also on my lips and he was wearing his signature smirk.

"Is he taking you to the Fall Equinox dance?" Kiran pried, forcing his eyes from my mouth deep into my own.

"Hmmm…. I don't know," I tried to be coy, but knew that I would say no even if Avalon did ask; dancing was not really my thing. "Who are you taking?" I asked, taking the attention off myself. I already knew the answer though; in fact, the whole school knew the answer. It wasn't like Seraphina was very quiet about their relationship anymore.

I was not totally sure if it was because she thought I was a threat to her precious relationship, or if she was scared that Kiran really wasn't that into her; but whatever the reason, she was no longer reserved about her feelings. Every chance Seraphina got, she was all over him, or bragging about him. She loved to talk loudly about what Kiran bought her, or where he took her. Kiran remained silent, but was always by her side lately.

"Are you going to the dance?" he avoided my question.

"No, probably not." I decided to be honest. I couldn't play these games; I wasn't any good at them.

"Why not?" Kiran asked sounding a little panicked.

"Well dances are not really my thing, besides I don't want to go alone. Avalon and I really are just friends," I put my pencil down and looked out the window. I'd been talking to Kiran for too long and felt like I was going to get into trouble.

Principal Saint warned me every time I saw him to stay away from Kiran, especially since he caught me at Kiran's club the other night. As helpful as he had been in finally shedding some light on who I was; I found staying away from Kiran the hardest thing he had asked me to do. I understood that he hadn't asked much of me, but there was something about Kiran that I was unable to keep myself from.

"Well you don't have to go alone. You could um, come with us," he sounded sincere, and I flashed him a grave look. He had got to be kidding me. A third wheel to a date between Kiran and Seraphina, no thank you.

"Sounds fun, but I think I'll pass. Besides what would your girlfriend have to say about that?" I rolled my eyes.

"Well, maybe you could double with Talbott?" he suggested softly. "He doesn't have a date yet." This was getting ridiculous.

"Yeah…. maybe," I laughed sarcastically, "Thanks, but no thanks your Majesty." The bell rang and I was thankful to be done with Kingsley, at least for the day.

"That's not funny," he said defensively. I gathered my things, hoping that this conversation was over. If he followed me out the door and Principal Saint saw me talking to him, I was going to be in big trouble. "Eden, please wait," he grabbed my wrist gently and I turned to look at him. Something in his eyes looked sad, like he was sorry for something.

"I just think that you would have fun if you came to the dance," he gave me a saddened version of his custom smirk, and his eyes twinkled a little bit. The rest of the class was quickly leaving and I was afraid we would be alone in a second.

"Really, I can't dance. If I went, it wouldn't be fun for anyone…. trust me," I tried to sound sincere, but my voice was breathy as Kiran pulled me a little closer, his fingers left my wrist and intertwine themselves with my fingers.

"Eden, are you ready?" Avalon was beside me and in an almost defensive stance. Oh no. I remembered my promise to Avalon and felt guilty for indulging myself with Kiran too long.

"Yes, almost," I turned and smiled at him, refusing to drop my hand from Kiran's. What was wrong with me? My magic flared at the memories of the last time we were this close and I regretted the fact that we were at school.

"Come on, let's go," Avalon's voice was anxious and I was surprised that he was so impatient. The usually focused and clearer sensory perception that came from being around him felt tense and put me on edge. Avalon glared at Kiran, but every once in a while he turned to give me an impatient frown.

"She said she'll be right there Avalon," Kiran pulled me closer to him, blocking me with half of his body, and took an equally defensive pose. I could see Talbott out of the corner of my eye begin to make his way over from where he had been waiting for Kiran in the doorway.

"Let go of her," Avalon nearly growled.

"No," Kiran growled back and Talbott took his side, clearly protective.

"Alright, everybody just settle down." I made my voice light, trying to soften the mood. What was going on?

"Back off Avalon. I wouldn't do anything that would get you into trouble if I were you," Talbott tried to step in front of Kiran but Kiran didn't let him. He stepped forward as if he to challenge Avalon. Avalon mimicked his movement and stepped forward too.

"He's right Avalon, you wouldn't want to get into trouble…. again," Kiran mocked him.

"Are you sure about that?" Avalon threatened in a deep,

growling voice.

"Alright, I'll see everybody tomorrow," I dropped Kiran's hand and headed for the door quickly. I was not going to get in the middle of some ridiculous boy fight.

I could feel Avalon's presence behind me, but I refused to turn and acknowledge him. I headed straight for my car as fast as I could, hoping he'd get the hint.

He didn't and continued to follow me, but he also didn't try to say anything until we reached my car. He never even tried to walk beside me, although his long legs could have easily outpaced mine. He stayed behind me almost as if he was protecting me from whatever else was back there. I became even more irritated.

"I'm sorry about that Eden," Avalon finally broke the silence as I searched for my car keys deep inside my book bag. "He just, ugh, he's just so infuriating," Avalon punched one of his fists into his other hand and I watched him clench his jaw.

"Well, he's not the only one," I gave him a fierce look and dug deeper in my bag for the keys to my Land Rover.

"Why do you even bother talking to him? I thought you weren't allowed," he looked at me with an intensity that I didn't understand.

"It's not like I try to talk to him. He is just always there! What do you mean I'm not allowed?" I defended myself, but wondered at Avalon's use of the word "allowed." I searched through my memories, trying to remember a time when I had been outright forbidden to talk to him.

"Oh nothing, I mean, it's just that, like the whole betrothal thing," he blurted out and I didn't know what he was talking about.

"What do you mean?" I repeated.

"The betrothal between Kiran and Seraphina. I thought everyone knew. They are engaged to be married," I stared at him confused until he continued, "I thought that was the whole reason he was at this school; he's like supposed to get to know his future wife." And then the meaning of the word "betrothal" sunk in. Kiran was going to marry Seraphina; no wonder she thought she was his girlfriend: she was. In fact she was more than his girlfriend, she was his freaking fiancée. Freaking Monarchy with their freaking tradition. What century did we live in? Betrothal?

Out of control.

Talbott's warning suddenly made sense, in fact, a lot of things suddenly made sense and I felt like such an idiot. He really was just using me for entertainment this entire time. I felt sick; how could I have not known.

"Oh," was all I could manage, and my lips stayed formed by the word. But my heart dropped into my stomach.

"Hey were you planning on going to the Fall Equinox dance?" Avalon asked out of the blue, changing the subject quickly.

"Not anymore," I reminded myself to breathe and willed myself to forget the nauseous feeling rising in my throat. "It's not really my thing anyways." I said softly, hoping I wasn't letting him down. My mind was still reeling from the wedding news.

"Oh good…. Yeah, those things are dumb anyways," his face looked visibly relieved and I didn't understand why.

"We could hang out though; you could come over tomorrow night and we could like rent a movie or something," I said, not wanting to sit at home, alone on a Saturday night, when the guy I had kind of liked or kind of hated or whatever I kind of felt was out having a great time with his future wife. Ugh.

"Oh no, I can't, sorry, I already have plans. But you should definitely stay home and not go to the dance," his expression was completely serious, and I was completely confused. "I hear it's going to be really terrible. See you Monday, Eden," Avalon turned and walked away to his car, leaving me standing alone, completely baffled. Boys could be so confusing.

Chapter Twenty-Five

"Eden…. Eden," A gentle voice encouraged me to wake up and I tried, but I found myself in a very heavy sleep.

"Eden, come with me," I grudgingly opened my eyes slowly and took in my surroundings. I was in the middle of a forest, unlike any forest I had ever seen before, although vaguely familiar at the same time. Tall flowering trees surrounded me; all unique, all yielding a distinct, but beautiful blossom of every color imaginable. The forest floor was covered in wild flowers as unique as the blossoms on the trees. Butterflies and dragonflies buzzed energetically around me, never intrusive, but fun to watch.

I found myself sleeping on a long boulder, but I was not uncomfortable, in fact I was very relaxed and felt slightly sedated. A carpet of vibrant, green grass surrounded me, layered with the petals of flowering trees. The petals in all different colors floated tenderly down to the earth like a beautiful and colorful snow. The sun shone brightly above me, warming my skin and casting rainbows on the rock. I felt completely at peace.

"Eden, come with me," the voice beckoned to me again and I forced myself to stand, legs unsteady and my head somewhat dizzy. I did not want to leave this enchanted place. However, I followed the voice into the trees, searching for the body it belonged to. I noticed I was wearing my pajamas and felt faintly out of place in a black tank top and plaid, baggy bottoms.

In the trees it was slightly darker, the blossoms blocked out the light of the warm sun. The petals continued to fall around me, tickling my arms as they made their way to the plush ground. Bursts of light shone their way to the forest floor through gaps in the trees, illuminating the way for me. I heard a stream nearby and the sound of the water rushing over rocks gave a soothing lullaby to this perfect place.

I wandered aimlessly, forgetting about the voice. This place seemed familiar, but new at the same time. Vaguely I realized that I was dreaming, but the magic still rushed through my veins awakening my mind more and more.

I walked through a patch of flowering trees and found the stream. The water was breathtaking. The aqua river glistened and sparkled as it flowed over rocks and a shallow bottom of golden sand. The stream itself wasn't very wide, but created a treeless path that allowed the sun to freely shine down. On the other side of the brook were more glorious flowering trees and behind them I could see the beginnings of foothills.

I dipped my foot into the cool water and let my toes sink into the sand. The sand glistened like diamonds over my toes. I thought about crossing the river to wander among the trees on the other side, but got distracted by a butterfly that landed on my hand. It floated effortlessly from my fingers to my shoulder and then back into the trees; I contemplated following it, but was interrupted.

"There you are," Kiran stepped out of the trees and approached me. He had never looked more beautiful. His dirty blonde hair glistened from the sunlight and his perfect blue eyes were clearer than the water. He stood tall against the background of the forest. He was wearing a t-shirt and athletic shorts and his muscular build was clearly defined. I smiled, taking him in and realized that I was not at all surprised to see him.

"Where were you?" I asked as if he should have been here all along.

"I was looking for you," he smiled, taking my hands. "Should we go for a walk?" he asked, pulling me along, intertwining our fingers.

I leaned close to him, stepping out of the water and laid my head on his shoulder. I inhaled his scent, sweet yet masculine, and felt as though this were the most normal thing I had ever done. He wrapped his arms around me tightly, pulling me even closer. I heard him sigh sweetly; the same sigh I heard during our kiss.

"What are you hiding from me Eden?" his voice was sweet, almost laughing.

"I'm not hiding anything," I replied without emotion. A feeling of paranoia crept up my spine sending the magic shivering through my veins. But I refused to leave his embrace. Whatever his question meant was not important enough for me to let go of him.

"Hmmm…" he sighed, contentedly, pulling me away from him so that we could continue to walk.

We moved silently through the trees; I allowed him to lead as he seemed to be walking in a specific direction. His fingers tightened around mine and I felt his body stiffen. My magic became more and more alert, awakening my senses and sending suspicion through every blood vessel.

"Where are we going?" I tried to keep my voice even, but it cracked with anxiety.

"We haven't got much time," Kiran replied breathlessly. "Eden what are you hiding from me? Quickly, I need to know," he stopped moving and faced me, taking my other hand in his. His sapphire eyes searched mine, looking for the answer to his question.

For a few seconds I pondered his question, deciding what to tell him. With my hands in his I began to feel a sense of calm wash over me. My magic slowed down to a normal rhythm and my suspicion began to fade. My senses seemed dull and slow and I couldn't think of a good reason not to tell him.

I opened my mouth, not sure of what I would say, but nothing came out. I didn't know what I was hiding; I could feel there was something that I shouldn't tell him, but I had no idea what it was. His cobalt eyes gazed into mine intently, willing me to speak, but I remained silent.

"Eden, what is it? You have to tell me so that I can keep you safe. I need to protect you, Love." He begged quickly.

"There's nothing to tell you," I stepped back from him, trying to free my hands from his grasp, but he held on tightly.

Suddenly my senses were clear again and the magic pulsed through me at an alarming rate. Instantly I became ready for battle; my muscles flexed and I tore my hands away from Kiran's. A hooded and cloaked figure stepped through the trees and I immediately was aware that he meant us harm.

"I am stronger than you in this place," Kiran spoke calmly and measured, but I could hear the underlying current of rage in his tone. At first I thought he was speaking to me, but when I looked up at him, he was facing the masked man, arms stretched out as if shielding me.

"It doesn't matter; I'm not here to kill you; only to protect her," he nodded with his chin in my direction and a surge of magic rushed through my veins.

"I should kill you," Kiran growled while stepping in front of me and blocking my body almost completely from the other man's view.

"Don't touch her," the dark figure lunged forward, but caught himself before he was within Kiran's reach.

They stood there staring at each other menacingly. The petals continued to fall from the trees sweetly and calmly. Complete silence surrounded us; I wasn't sure what to do. Seconds ago I felt the urgency to flee from Kiran, but now I felt as though I must protect him; he clearly had the same instinct for me.

Confusion washed over me. Although I didn't know who the cloaked man was, I could feel with every fiber of my being that he meant me no harm. A vague sense of familiarity flowed between the hooded man and me; his magic was very memorable. Despite the man's peacefulness towards me however, I did recognize that he meant Kiran harm, and I refused to allow that to happen.

"Eden it's time to wake up," the hooded man said firmly, and I knew somehow that he was right. There would be no happy ending to this dream if I stayed.

"Please don't be angry with me," Kiran turned around to speak to me, his eyes pleading. With his back to his enemy, completely exposed, he gave me his signature smirk and leaned down to kiss my cheek.

I closed my eyes, feeling the magic turn to electricity, making every hair stand on end. Kiran's warm lips on my cheek made me forget about the other man, the man that meant him harm. Such a small gesture, but his gentle kiss had me reeling with dizziness. The last thing I heard in the dream was the other man shouting a scream of rage; I felt Kiran disappear and knew that I could now wake up.

My eyes shot open and I felt the bed all around me. I was in my room, in my bed, striped comforter surrounding me, pillows piled everywhere. I took in a big breath to slow my rapidly beating heart. The dream felt so real, the forest so vivid, Kiran's touch so authentic.

I touched my fingers to my cheek, and a slow blush rose to the surface. Usually my feelings for Kiran were so confused, but in that dream they were crystal clear. I smiled, remembering that in my dream his feelings were the same for me.

I forced my mind to remember reality, his crown, his girlfriend, and their betrothal. My smile disappeared and I slammed my head back down against the pillows. I covered my face with my arm and audibly groaned.

My dream was not only about a sweet moment between Kiran and I, it was about his betrayal. My dream was also about his desire to know something I knew I could never tell him, although I didn't even know what it was myself. Finally, my dream was about the hooded figure that we'd met in the forest; the man that haunted me even in sleep.

Chapter Twenty-Six

"Good morning, Eden," Aunt Syl sat at the kitchen island sipping a cup of coffee in her white pajamas. Her hair was a mess and she was wearing her glasses; it was such a comfortable feeling. I loved having breakfast with her in the morning; it was something we rarely got to do. "I'm surprised to see you up so early. Isn't today Saturday?" she turned to look at the clock, and I knew her question was sincere.

"Yes, today's Saturday. I don't know, I had the strangest dream and then I couldn't fall back asleep," I rubbed my eyes feeling like I had had no sleep at all last night. "Have you been at the hospital?"

"Yes, since sometime yesterday.... or the day before. I can't really remember anymore," she yawned big, causing a chain reaction, and I yawned in response. "The days are starting to run together. Do you want a cup of coffee?"

I nodded my reply and she stood up to get a big black coffee cup from the cabinet. I sat down next to her seat and inhaled the aroma of the strong Columbian coffee she was pouring into my cup.

"Did you want me to make you something for breakfast?" she asked while handing me the hot cup and taking her seat next to me.

"No thank you, this is fine," I smiled and looked over her shoulder at the newspaper she had been reading. While she may have been an expert surgeon, pancakes were a little out of her league.

"Hey, how are you doing with the whole Immortal thing?" she looked up from the business section of the Saturday morning World Herald and gave me a concerned look.

"I'm fine; I mean.... I'm coping," I gave her a reassuring smile and contemplated my feelings. I hadn't really thought things through; I'd just accepted everything at face value. I knew there were lots of things I needed to learn and sort through, but at the moment, all I could do was accept who I was and what I was capable of.

"Well, if you ever need to talk about it, I'm here," she

patted my back and kissed the top of my head. She was the reason I never felt the need to think about my parents until now.

"It doesn't freak you out?" I asked, taking a nice long sip of the steaming hot coffee.

"Oh no, not at all. Amory and I have been friends for years, long before you came along," she gave me a wink and I didn't think I wanted to ask her any more questions about that.

"But you didn't know my parents?" I wondered out loud.

"No, I never met them. Amory and I were—" she was interrupted by the doorbell. We both looked at each other and rolled our eyes; mentally calculating which one of us was dressed enough to answer the door. The familiar tingling of electricity pricked the back of my neck and a feeling of anxiety washed over me.

"I'll get it," I groaned, standing up and regretfully setting my coffee down. I made my way through the large chef's kitchen to the front room; my slippers made a padding sound as I walked over the hardwood floors.

Not bothering to look at who it was first, I threw the door open, and sent a rush of cool air into the house. I didn't know who I expected to see on the front porch, but Talbott Angelo was probably the last person I wanted to see. He stood in front of me, dark hair combed, green eyes blazing, holding a bouquet of pink chrysanthemums. My mouth dropped open.

"Hello Eden," he said calmly, accenting each syllable to clean up his accent. I tried to mouth something in reply, but couldn't make a sound. What was he doing here? "May I come in?"

I moved out of the way silently and allowed him to pass; this was so strange. I instantly regretted not asking Aunt Syl to answer the door instead.

He walked casually by me and then turned around to face me again in the foyer. I glanced through the door one more time, looking for Kiran or the mailman or anyone else to rescue me from what I expected was going to be a very awkward conversation.

"I am sure you are wondering what I am doing here at such an early hour. I apologize for not giving you advanced warning. I didn't have much warning myself," he smiled apologetically and I

189

subconsciously covered my stomach with my arms, wishing I had a sweatshirt nearby to throw on.

"Prince Kiran sent me over this morning insisting that I made sure you were unharmed. I see that you are," he cleared his throat and glanced back at the front door as if wanting to escape through it. I wished he would and wondered why he didn't.

"What? Why? What is Prince Kiran so worried about? And why didn't he just call?" Surely there was a student directory he could use to get my phone number. I flashed back to my dream and found it strange that after such a vivid dream of him, he would send someone to check on me.

"Prince Kiran was worried about your safety. When he woke up this morning he demanded that I personally check to make sure you were alright; he seemed to think you were in some sort of danger," he shook his head a little, as if annoyed. "And I don't know why, but he said it was urgent. However, I can see you are just fine," Talbott continued to stand there awkwardly holding the flowers. Despite Talbott's efforts to be nice, I saw glimpses of the side of him that hated me. I was reminded of how rude he was to me at Kiran's club.

"Yes, I am fine," I said sounding more defensive than I had intended. "I still don't understand why he didn't just call."

"Prince Kiran has been forbidden from talking with you. He sends his apologies," I couldn't help myself and let out a small laugh. I could deal with the whole Immortal thing, but all of these royal rules and standards of conduct were an entirely different matter. Talbott shot me a confused look, but I didn't have an explanation for him and so I stayed silent. "Do you have a message you would like me to relay to him?"

"Is this because of Seraphina?" I blurted out.

"Well yes in part, I tried to warn you," he shook his head again.

"What's the other part?" I asked, ignoring his 'I told you so.'

"His father. You are a Witch, isn't that right?" I nodded my head yes, feeling odd to have this conversation with someone other than Principal Saint or Avalon. "Kiran is not allowed to marry a Witch; he must marry a Medium by royal edict," he said this with finality; I decided not to indulge Talbott by asking any

190

more questions.

"Who said anything about marriage?" I grumbled under my breath.

"Eden, you must understand that Kiran has responsibilities; responsibilities that he has so far failed to take care of. He will one day become King and that requires discipline; you are only a distraction to him."

I flinched from his words, and then instantly regretted looking weak in front of him. I was surprised by his boldness however; not many people were very open and honest with me. Despite my malicious feelings for Talbott, I could at least appreciate his honesty.

I noticed that Talbott felt bad for his harsh words and could no longer look me in the eye. He didn't offer an apology and I half wondered if he was waiting for me to give him one.

"That is beside the point," he cleared his throat and offered me the flowers. I didn't take them right away, but glared at their pretty petals instead. "Eden will you please go to the Fall Equinox Dance with me tonight?"

"You've got to be kidding me," I held back my laughter and eventually took the flowers from him, not knowing what else to do.

"I wish I was; please understand that this is Kiran's idea.... no, Kiran's order. I have been ordered to make sure you are protected this evening," he clasped his hands behind his back and I saw a hint of his military training.

"Protected from what? No thank you, I will be just fine.... here.... alone," this was ridiculous.

"Please go to the dance with me," he softened his voice, but hardened his tone. "Kiran has ordered me to stay with you; but I am afraid that he is the one in danger. I need to be near him tonight," Talbott looked down at the ground.

"You're right, you do need to be near him, and you're definitely not staying here with me. And I am definitely not going to that stupid dance," the man in black passed through my mind again and a feeling of uneasy started to grow in the bottom of my stomach.

"Eden, you don't have a choice," Talbott said exasperated. "He's the Crown Prince; you have to do what he says."

191

"You are kidding me," this was ridiculous. I was almost too angry for words.

"No, I'm not. Please be ready by seven," he walked passed me and opened the door.

"What is going to happen to Lilly?" I called after him, fuming.

"I don't know," he replied softly.

"Well, aren't you going to do something?" I accused, tired of being told what to do.

"Lilly Mason lied to me, and she lied to the Crown Prince, she is on her own. I cannot help her.... no one can help her," he nearly growled the words before closing the door behind him.

I stood in the foyer, flowers in hand, staring at the door. I was so angry I could spit.

"He's right dear; you do have to do what Kiran asks," I turned to see my aunt standing in the door-frame leading to the kitchen, arms folded, with a concerned look on her face.

"Ahhh!" I let out a small scream of frustration, threw the flowers on the floor and stormed up to my bedroom. If I was going to be treated like a child, then I was going to act like one.

Chapter Twenty-Seven

I rummaged through my closet, throwing piece after piece of clothing into a pile on my bedroom floor. I couldn't decide what to wear, against my will, to the dance. My nice clothes seemed too dressy and my casual clothes seemed too dumpy. I contemplated wearing the Kingsley uniform just to spite Talbott, but decided that he wouldn't care and I would look like an idiot.

I'd never been to a dance before and I didn't know what to expect. My high school experience had thus far been a disaster and the last thing I wanted to add to my long list of high school embarrassing moments was an opportunity to willfully show off what lack of dance moves I had. The only thing, in fact, that could get me to go to the dance was a royal decree, which was apparently what I was up against.

I was not sure if I even took the whole Monarchy thing seriously yet. It didn't seem real and the truth was I had a hard time believing there was a King out there that actually had authority over me. It was even harder to believe that one day that King would be Kiran.

I rolled my eyes and began to rummage through another section of clothes. I paused on a black strapless dress I had worn to a funeral for one of Aunt Syl's coworkers. The dress was tight-fitting, but had a ruffle that started mid-thigh and ended at the knee. To the funeral I wore a black, cardigan to cover up my shoulders, but I could go without one for the dance. I stomped my foot, frustrated, realizing that this date was the last thing I wanted to do tonight.

I found it hard to believe that Kiran was doing this with my best interest in mind. It seemed more like a way to torment me more than anything else. A date with Talbott, who completely lacked personality and didn't like me anyway, all while watching Seraphina Van Curen throw herself at Kiran sounded more like torture than a high school rite of passage.

"How are you doing sweetie?" Aunt Syl peeked her head in the door and talked softly, soothingly. She had probably heard me stomping my foot and grumbling for the last couple of hours to know that I was just a little upset.

"I have nothing to wear," I pulled my head out of the closet and glanced at the clock: 6:30. At least I had already showered.

"This came for you," she said tentatively and stepped all the way into my room, pushing the door aside with a large white box, wrapped in a soft pink ribbon.

When I didn't respond, she walked over to the bed and laid the box on top of my rumpled covers. I could see her watching me out of the corner of her eye, while she opened the box and revealed soft pink silk wrapped in silver tissue paper.

Since I didn't move to examine the contents of the box, Aunt Syl did the honors by slowly unwrapping the tissue paper and pulling out the garment. She held it up, with a soft gasp. The dress was absolutely stunning; the material completely pink silk, with gold embroidery at the hem. The top cut into a deep v in the front and in the back with wide cap sleeves, while the bottom flowed out into an a-line skirt with detailed pleating. Left in the box I could see a pair of gold strappy stilettos.

"Who's it from?" I asked, although I could probably assume.

"Oh here, this came with it," she handed me a piece of ivory cardstock, embellished with an elaborate snake circling around to eat its own tail; surrounding the snake were dainty lilies and intertwining with the snake was an ornate golden crown. I realized I had seen a lot of snakes recently and pondered their meaning as I grudgingly read the hand written note.

I wanted to be the one to take you tonight.
Know that I'll be thinking of only you.

"What a bunch of bull-sh--"

"Eden," my aunt cut me off sharply. "It is a nice gesture, and a beautiful gown," she held it closer and sighed softly. The dress was beautiful. I stepped closer to examine it and rubbed the soft silk between my fingers. I couldn't find a label and wondered what designer was responsible for this magnificent creation.

"No. I am not going to play these games," I said firmly, letting the material drop from my hands. I walked back over to my closet and ripped the black funeral dress from the hanger.

"Absolutely not," my aunt shook her head. "Come with me if you're going to be stubborn."

Aunt Syl laid the pink dress very carefully onto my bed, laying it out perfectly. She touched it one more time and gave another soft sigh, before turning on her heel and beckoning me to follow. We walked down the hall into her bedroom.

The master bedroom was gigantic and looked like a page directly out of pottery barn. Her bed always perfectly made, was adorned with a lavish comforter and probably fifteen pillows. I imagined that it was also gathering dust since she was never here to sleep in it. We walked past her settee and 52" flat screen TV and entered her bathroom.

The bathroom itself looked like a spa, but the real treasure was in the back…. her walk-in closet. Aunt Syl's only vice was clothing. She loved shopping and had a closet full of clothes to testify. Aunt Syl was really quite the bombshell. Her thin frame and trendy sense of style made it easy for us to share and swap, so I was excited to see what she had in mind.

She took in a big breath as if paying homage to the closet gods and let her fingers slide across the racks of clothes until she reached the back. I saw her slowly, and carefully, picking her way through the many formal dresses she had accumulated. Her fingers brushed softly, almost reverently over their various materials, moving them out of the way gently. Finally, she came to rest on one. She pulled the hanger down and turned around to face me.

I smiled. This was one of her favorite purchases. She picked it up in the middle of the summer and hadn't had a chance to wear it yet. The emerald green dress was strapless and short, with a curving bodice. Small black and gold beading covered the front, giving it the look of a corset, while the waist was cinched even smaller with an oversized black belt. At least it would give me curves.

I took the dress from her and gave her a small kiss on the cheek. I turned to head back to my room, but not before I grabbed a pair of killer black heels. Once in my room I dressed in seconds, maneuvering my body in ways I didn't think possible to get the zipper all the way up in the back. I slipped on the heels and pulled my black waves into an unruly bun at the base of my neck. It was messy, but it would have to do.

I headed to the bathroom, where my makeup awaited. I was in the middle of painting on a quick retouch of bright pink fingernail polish when I heard the doorbell ring. They were just going to have to wait. I smudged my black eyeliner on, while Aunt Syl answered the door. A little bit of mascara and some bright pink lip gloss and I was ready to go.

I grabbed a beaded black clutch and stuffed it with the essentials, and made my descent down the staircase. I always imagined the walk down the tall, wooden staircase, to be somewhat magical on my first date when I was a little girl. Unfortunately, I never imagined my first date to be with someone who despised me, to a dance where I was sure to make a fool of myself, by orders from a Royal Prince who likes me but has been forbidden to talk to me; but I never had much of an imagination.

Talbott waited at the foot of the stairs, more pink chrysanthemums in hand; well, they used to be my favorite flowers. As my heels clicked on the staircase, Talbott looked up to take a look at me. The moment his eyes took me in, they nearly bugged out of his big head. His mouth dropped open and I could see that he was struggling for words. I would have taken it as a compliment except the look on his face made me more self-conscious than anything.

"Y-y-y-you can't wear that," Talbott stammered out.

"Why not?" I asked defensively and finished my descent down the stairs.

"Because, you can't," he said simply, not really giving me a reason.

"Yes, I can," I argued back with attitude.

"Where is the dress Prince Kiran sent you? You have to wear that one," Talbott took a step forward and I thought for a moment he was going to push me back up the staircase.

"No, I don't have to wear that one. I don't have to do anything. You're lucky I'm even going to this stupid dance," I brushed passed him and out the door, leaving him to stare after me completely unsure what to do.

"Eden, behave tonight," Aunt Syl called after me, fidgeting with a camera she never got to turn on, as I made my way hurriedly towards Talbott's retro limousine.

The chauffer tried to get out of the driver's side quickly, but I beat him to it, leaving him just as confused as Talbott. I yanked open the door and threw myself in to the back seat, landing on something soft, but not quite a car seat. I looked up and saw Kiran looking down at me, confused and surprised.

"Excuse me," I said irritably, and maneuvered quickly, and as lady-like as possible in my short skirt off of Kiran's lap.

"You're excused," Kiran replied slowly and somewhat befuddled.

"I didn't expect anyone to be in here. I mean, I thought it would just be Talbott and me," I tried to explain, and crossed my legs self-consciously. Suddenly, I was rethinking my choice of evening attire.

"It's a double," Kiran cleared his throat, never taking his eyes off of me. Talbott finally began to make his way down the walk and towards the limo. "Didn't you like the dress I sent you?" his smirk was suddenly there and I watched his eyes appraise me.

"No," I replied simply.

"I think I like this one better too," Kiran cleared his throat again and I couldn't tell if he was nervous or annoyed. "Thank you, for coming tonight," he said sincerely.

"I didn't think I had a choice," I looked out of the window, hoping for a distraction. Kiran was dressed in a nicely tailored black tuxedo, shiny shoes to match. His dirty blonde hair was slicked back away from his face, accentuating his strong facial features. I had never seen him look so handsome; it was distracting me, and making me forget how mad I was.

"Don't be so grumpy Eden," Kiran scolded playfully, before half standing to sit next to me on the seat that was facing him. Talbott burst through the door of the limousine and I noticed for the first time that he was wearing a tuxedo as well. Apparently this was not just an ordinary high school dance.

"Wouldn't you prefer to sit over here Sir?" Talbott had not yet recovered from my dress and was still awkward as he took a seat across from us.

"I will Talbott, stop worrying so much," Kiran scooted closer to me as if to spite Talbott before turning towards my face and wrapping his arm around me.

My heart began to beat wildly and my magic was barely under control. Kiran's touch brought an electrical storm through my blood and I felt it begin to boil just below the surface of my skin. I saw Kiran smirk once again before leaning his lips close to my neck, breathing softly on my neck.

"You look beautiful tonight, Eden," Kiran whispered delicately in my ear, his breath tickling my throat gently. I felt dizzy from with him so close. "Will you save a dance for me?" I was flooded with overwhelming magic, making me forget how angry I was. I would have said yes to anything he asked, until....

"Driver, to Ms. Van Curen's, please," Talbott instructed the driver with authority. I suddenly remembered why this night was so preposterous and snapped out of my hypnosis.

"I don't think so," I said, half standing up as quickly as I could, moving across the limo and onto the seat next to Talbott. I folded my arms stubbornly and stared out the window, vowing to ignore Kiran Kendrick completely. He was not taking both Seraphina and me on a date; clearly he needed to be reminded.

To my irritation however, he only laughed, as if my rejection of him were somehow entertaining. I fumed silently; the blood that was boiling from desire now boiled from fury. I could feel the magic radiating off me as if putting up a guard that no man could cross.

Any and all hints I tried to throw Kiran's direction apparently flew right over his head because he purposefully scooted over in his seat and sat directly across from me. He casually slid his feet next to mine, our ankles touching in the smallest of ways. I tried to maneuver my feet away from his, but the space in the limo was too confined and anywhere I moved my feet, he simply stretched his longer legs to accommodate. I saw the smile on his lips and realized this was just another one of his games. Talbott sat next to me, head in hands, afraid to watch.

The driver came to a stop in front of an elaborate mansion on the northwest side of Omaha. The house was gigantic, with immaculate detailing. The walk up to the house itself was a good 50 yards. The entry way, surrounded by tall white columns, was large enough to accommodate an elephant.

Kiran stepped out of the car and walked the long way alone. I breathed a sigh of relief and stretched my legs from out of their cramped position. Only a few minutes went by before Kiran returned with Seraphina, whom he opened the door for and helped into the seat across from Talbott. I expect her to scoot down and across from me so that Kiran could also climb in the car, but to

199

my disappointment he walked around to the other side of the car and took his place, legs stretched out before him and all, across from me.

"You look nice," Seraphina said sarcastically, after only seconds of entering the vehicle. Her eyes appraised me in a much less flattering way than Kiran did, and I once again felt self-conscious.

"So do you Seraphina," I tried to return it sarcastically, but I knew the sincerity shined through, because she genuinely looked stunning. She only rolled her eyes and slipped her arm through Kiran's as if marking her merchandise.

Kiran glanced at her approvingly before giving her a small peck on the cheek. I couldn't blame him, although I wished I could, but she looked like a goddess tonight. Her long blonde hair was wrapped into an intricately woven side ponytail, her golden locks hanging curled and shining. She was dripping in diamonds from her earrings to her necklace to her bracelets. They complimented her floor length, bodice hugging, silver gown, and gave her the illusion that she was sparkling. Her silver gown accentuated every one of her curves and was low cut in the front, but maintained the class and sophistication my dress did not. The entire bodice was beaded and embellished and had almost a 1920's look to it.

I understood now, why the pink gown was more appropriate. I once again was walking into an unknown situation looking like a tramp. I rolled my eyes and continued looking out the window, internally cringing. This dance felt less and less like a high school extra-curricular activity and more and more like a witch trial; unfortunately for me, it turned out I actually was the Witch.

Chapter Twenty-Eight

The limousine pulled up to the driveway of Kingsley behind numerous other stretch, luxury vehicles. I was full of anxiety and beyond irritated. Thankfully, I didn't think Talbott was going to expect too much dancing out of me.

I watched the other students exit their cars, all of the boys in tuxedos and all of the girl's in elegant gowns, most of them dripping in jewels. My perception of this dance was apparently dead wrong. I expected this type of style and flare at prom, but wasn't this just the fall dance? I tugged at my short skirt, trying to cover my bare legs unsuccessfully. If I didn't want to stand out, a miniskirt was the wrong way to go.

I glanced up and noticed Kiran watching my failed attempts at last minute modesty and laugh. I gave him a wry look before rolling my eyes and turning my attention back to the students entering the gymnasium. At least the dance was still on school grounds and not some exclusive country club, or likewise ridiculous venue.

Eventually it was our turn to exit the vehicle. The driver came around to my door and opened it so we could exit properly. I felt like I was playing make-believe, this all seemed like some massive pretend production instead of reality.

Kiran and Seraphina exited first and she was immediately on his arm. They walked regally into the gym as if they were king and queen of Kingsley. I supposed one day they would be. Yuck.

Talbott nodded that it was my turn to exit the car, but I hesitated for a moment longer, afraid to leave the confined, but private space. He cleared his throat and looked after Kiran like a worried puppy. Fine, I thought, let's get on with it.

I exited the car with as much grace and class as I could muster, hoping to avoid a peepshow on my way out of the car. Talbott was quickly behind me. I heard the door to the car slam shut; there was no turning back. Talbott offered his arm and I looked at it with a mild sense of humor.

"Really, we don't have to pretend," I said curtly.

"Please, Eden; just humor me with some manners," he offered back haughtily. I took his arm a little too forcefully and we walked the rest of the way in silence.

The gymnasium could not be farther from what I pictured had I thought of the wildest scenario. This being my first time in Kingsley's gym I expected basketball hoops, bleachers and maybe some streamers to decorate the place for the dance.

As soon as we walked through the wide double doors my mouth dropped open and I stood their dumbly not sure how to react. Beautiful, and elaborate black chandeliers hung from the ceiling every ten feet or so. They were adorned with white candles and dripping with colorful floral arrangements. Along the walls in every direction, candelabras in the same fashion sat evenly spaced, lighting up the room and giving the large space a dim glow.

A DJ in the far corner, spun music that reverberated the floor. Tables and chairs took up half of the space, while the remaining space was used as a dance floor. On each table were eight place settings and in the middle were replica center pieces of the chandeliers hanging from the ceilings. Colorful flower arrangements intertwined with the candle lit centerpieces over black silk table clothes.

Talbott pulled me along to our table where Kiran and Seraphina already had found their seats. Most of the tables were full already and waiters began to bring out silver platters covered in food. The food looked as elegant as the decorations. Unfortunately, my dress didn't leave much room for expansion.

Besides Kiran, Seraphina, Talbott and me, our table was also home to Evangeline and Adelaide and their respective dates. Both of whom looked equally bored and unimpressed as the girls gushed over the dance and each other's outfits. Not surprisingly, I was completely ignored.

I stood next to the table unsure where to sit or what to say. Talbott released my arm and pulled a chair out for me next to Evangeline. She gave me a side glance and a little snicker before returning to her conversation.

I began to sit down but was interrupted by a subtle cough from Kiran. I looked over and noticed him give a suggestive head nod to Talbott who then stood up straight, pushed in the chair he had just offered and pull out the chair directly next to it, but located side by side with Kiran. If possible I noticed Talbott become even more exasperated and Seraphina scoot her chair ever closer to Kiran. I took my seat feeling much like a criminal or leper or something equally unwanted.

"Is it what you expected?" Kiran turned his body to face me and spoke quietly; his blue eyes simmering and slicked back hair gave him a seductive quality I was having a hard time ignoring. I cleared my throat to focus.

"Not quite," I said simply, forcing my eyes away from his. I noticed Seraphina take his hand in hers, and although he didn't turn his body away from mine, he allowed the possessive gesture.

"Seraphina," I found courage deep within me to pull her into the conversation. I refused to be a bizarre secret date to the spoiled Prince. "How often does Kingsley have these kinds of dances?"

"What do you mean?" she asked snidely, turning her head but not her body to face me. The look on her face made me tremble beneath the surface and I reminded myself to be brave.

"I mean, that this dance seems so extreme, is this like Kingsley's version of prom?" I cleared my throat again, feeling more insecure than ever before, but praying my plan to involve Seraphina into our conversation worked. I couldn't stay irritated and angry at Kiran if he continued to stay so damn sexy.

"I don't know what you mean by extreme; this is the way a Kingsley dance always looks," she rolled her eyes, but her tone was less derisive than before. "I guess it is nice though," she turned her body to face us then and pulled Kiran's arm even closer to her body.

"It's beautiful," I said softly, more to myself than anyone else.

"And we have one for every equinox and solstice, plus there's Christmas and prom too," she smiled ever so small and I felt encouraged to be braver.

"I didn't know people celebrated those holidays," I tried a joke.

"You didn't know people celebrated Christmas?" she asked dryly, and her attitude was back.

"No, I mean, I know people celebrate Christmas. I didn't know people celebrated like the fall equinox," I did my best to clarify, but she just looked at me like I was speaking a different language.

"You're so weird," she rolled her eyes again and then turned back to Adelaide to pick up where they left off.

"Trying to make new friends?" Kiran asked smugly under his breath.

"Well, you're certainly no help," I turned my body completely away from him and looked out into the tables of students.

"Did it ever occur to you that maybe I want you all to myself?" Kiran's hot breath tickled the back of my neck when he whispered in my ear. His accent was very alluring, and I shook my head to regain focus.

I stood up frustrated and practically stomped away from the table as quickly as I could. I couldn't sit next to him anymore; and I couldn't be party to his sick games. I was going to be the one that got hurt in the end.

I searched for the bathroom or a dark corner or something, but settled with the punch table. I just needed something to occupy my hands. I noticed a familiar figure pouring himself some punch as I approached the table and was suddenly very grateful to see Avalon.

"Hey!" I blurted out a little too loudly, overcome with joy to see him. "I thought you told me you weren't coming to this thing?" I nudged him with my elbow playfully. He turned and faced me with a horrified expression on his face that quickly turned to anger.

"What are you doing here?" Avalon demanded, practically dropping his punch.

"Um, I don't know," I responded tentatively, unsure what to make of his reaction.

"You're not supposed to be here, Eden," his tone was accusing and I could not figure out what he was so mad about.

"You told me you weren't coming either," I accused back, not half as mad as he was, but at least it was something.

"I changed my mind," he growled.

"Well, me too," I folded my arms stubbornly, not sure if I wanted to stand here any longer, and not sure if I was ready to head back to the table. Thankfully, it looked like couples were beginning to dance.

"Don't tell me you came here with him," Avalon squinted his eyes in disapproval and looked in the direction of Kiran.

"He came with his girlfriend," I mimicked Avalon's facial expression and realized I sounded jealous.

"Then who are you here with?" Avalon turned to face me, his expression still hard and angry.

"Talbott," I said softly and fearfully.

"Oh, like that's any better," Avalon raised his voice and gestured with his arms wildly, spilling his punch. He looked down at the puddle on the floor frustrated and instantly it was gone. I felt his surge of magic as he cleaned up the mess with only a thought.

"I don't know what you want me to say. I was forced here against my will! I'm not happy about it either," I raised my voice and hardened my eyes. How dare he blame me! I didn't want to be here anymore than anyone wanted me here.

I pushed past Avalon and fought back tears. I had never felt so alone. I was tired of apologizing for things I did or people I talked to. Why couldn't I just have a normal life with no magic, no exiled friends and no freaking Prince?

I ran through the closest door and found a staircase leading upwards. I took it not knowing where it would lead to. My six inch heels click-clacked on the wooden staircase, eventually drowning out the house music below. Soon the dance was only a faint hum as I made my way to the top.

At the top of the staircase there was only a heavy metal door with a push bar for a handle. I contemplated rejoining the party, but decided quickly against that. I also contemplated just sitting down at the top of the stairs to have a good cry, but decided quickly against that as well. In the end, curiosity got the better of me and I pushed through the heavy door.

I half expected some type of alarm to go off, but only the quiet of the evening greeted me. The cool fall air wrapped itself around me and I found myself on the roof of the gym. I took off my shoes, stepping gingerly over the cool concrete and to the ledge of the building.

All of Omaha surrounded me and the sight was breathtaking. The tall, lighted buildings of downtown sat to my east and the quiet suburban neighborhoods were located to my west. I could see St. Cecilia's Cathedral towers to my North and the Mutual of Omaha building to my South. Despite being in the middle of a big city, the stars still shone brightly overhead. I inhaled a big breath, finding serenity for the first time all night.

"Stop being so over-dramatic. There's no need to jump," Kiran's clean accent sounded amused as he entered through the roof top door.

"Go away!" I whined, exasperated, covering my face with my hands.

"Oh come now, you don't mean that," he walked slowly over to me, hands in his pockets, letting his eyes float over my figure.

"Where's Talbott?" I asked, looking past him. I wasn't sure if I wanted him to leave or not. I had never been more emotionally confused; I felt frustrated, irritated, nervous and excited all at once.

"Dancing, I expect," Kiran glanced over his shoulder and then continued to walk towards me.

"I better join him," I decided on my escape route. "He's probably wondering where I am," I walked quickly towards the door, but Kiran stepped in front of me before I got too far.

"I doubt that," Kiran gazed into my eyes intently, his signature smirk flaring up. He took a step towards me, and instinctively I took a step back until my heels touched the ledge of the building once again. "What's with all the hard-to-get nonsense; I thought we were passed that," his fingers brushed my arm gently, sending butterflies and magic racing inside of me.

"That was before I learned you were engaged," I held my ground, despite the dizziness his closeness was causing.

"I'm not engaged," He said firmly. When I gave him a doubtful look he continued, "I'm betrothed. And the two are very different things."

"Oh, really? How so?" I challenged.

"An engagement would suggest that I asked her to marry me; that it was my idea to get married or that we had been in a relationship prior to the proposal. But a betrothal is an arrangement made by parents; I had never even met her before I came to this school." He jutted his bottom lip out and looked up at me from beneath his eye lashes. He reminded me of a little boy,

207

and I couldn't help but melt at the sight of him.

"Oh," I gave in a little, leaning back against the building's ledge and relaxing. "But you are going to marry her?" I asked glumly.

"Well that is what my father expects," I heard the sadness in his tone and felt sorry for him.

"When?" I sunk down against the ledge and managed to sit down, legs stretched long without ripping my dress.

"If father had it his way we would already be married, with little ones on the way," he joined me on the ground, and although our current position was not as seductive, he still sat close enough so our bodies touched. "We compromised; that's why I'm here. I'm supposed to get to know her."

"How is that a compromise?"

"The Kingdom wants stability; they want to see that their future King is steady and responsible. It doesn't matter that I will live forever, or that my father will for that matter. They can be quite demanding," he gave me his smirk again. At least he could joke about it.

"The Kingdom... oh brother," I mimicked his expression.

"Yes, the Kingdom," he gave me a playful nudge with his elbow. "And how is it that you didn't know about our betrothal? This whole time I thought you were defying royal law on purpose!"

"Of course it wasn't on purpose! I'm new to this whole Immortal thing, remember?" It was my turn to give him a nudge, I found his rib bones and he squirmed.

"How could I forget?" he rolled his eyes teasingly and then laid his head on my shoulder. The gesture was so unexpected, but so charming that I simply allowed it. "So, I suppose I have no chance with you now?" he picked up a rock and skipped it across the rooftop.

"Nope, absolutely no chance," I blurted out defensively, although I was not sure if I believed myself. "What kind of home wrecker do you think I am?"

"I was just hoping that we could...." he lifted his head off my shoulder and leaned in until our faces were only millimeters apart. I knew he was about to kiss me again and no matter what I just said I was powerless to stop him.

Unfortunately, instead of butterflies and lightning storms, the magic suddenly became overwhelmingly alert and my senses focused sharply. I sat up straight before any contact was made and noticed that Kiran had done the same. We struggled to our feet just in time to meet five cloaked bodies burst through the roof top door.

Chapter Twenty-Nine

The men surrounded us quickly with the roof's edge to our backs and readied themselves for battle. Four of the men were different from our first battle, I could tell that because their magic felt different. But one man stood apart, but familiar, the same man that escaped the forest before, and the same man that was in my dream last night. He stood directly in front of us clearly leading the attack.

Our bodies mimicked our attackers and we awaited an assault at any moment. Kiran positioned his body in front of mine as if protecting me; but the carnal instinct to fight flooded my veins. I cursed my short, tight, expensive dress underneath my breath.

"It's time for you to go Eden. This fight doesn't concern you," the leader of the men addressed me and I flinched when I heard him say my name. Murderous intent mingled with magic and I was completely focused on the looming battle; but something familiar about the leader forced me to second guess myself.

"I'll stay, if you don't mind," I growled through gritted teeth. I had no doubt that I would win this battle, although I was unsure yet of how I would succeed. Unlike the forest that was full of natural tools and props to use, the rooftop was bare and the fall to the ground below long.

"Get out of here," the leader growled back, surprisingly emotional. I wanted to believe that he was asking me to leave because of the powerfulness of my skills, but something deep inside told me it was for different reasons.

"Let her stay if she wants to fight," a different masked man, to my right taunted. "If she wants to try and protect the spoiled brat, let her," disgust filled his voice, and there was no doubt in my mind that he meant to kill Kiran.

"Eden, go. If they are willing to let you go unharmed, then go," Kiran commanded me. His magic was strong and I could feel the heat from his boiling blood radiate off of his skin. He was not going to give up this fight easily, but neither was I willing to let him. "What do you want with him?" I deflected Kiran's command

210

and addressed the leader once again. Nothing in my body was willing to settle this dispute calmly; talking it out was only a decoy until I figured out what to use to my advantage.

"We want a new King," another cloaked figure to my left shouted. "A King who will give us our magic freely."

"A King who will let all of our people free," Another man roared louder. Their response was turning into their war cry.

"We want to destroy this bloodline and end the bloodshed and prejudice. We want what we were promised," the leader spoke softer, but equally as menacing.

And then the battle began. One of the men to my right let out a battle cry before shifting into a grizzly bear, towering over the still human rest of us. He crossed the distance between Kiran and himself in less than a second. I closed my eyes expecting the fight to be over before it began, but I heard the roar of the bear and opened my eyes to see that Kiran had eluded him.

Kiran was fast, much faster than the overly large bear; but he would not last long. Another man joined his companion, shifting into a chocolate brown wolf. Kiran used his skill and power, making it impossible for either attacker to touch him, but there were three other men closing in.

I focused my magic, making it palpable in my hand. The three men, who were apparently going to remain men, were circling Kiran waiting for the opportunity to strike. The men who chose to ignore me had made their first mistake. I threw the magic at them with force, sending out a type of pulse, knocking them off their feet and surprising them all.

Unfortunately for Kiran, I distracted him just long enough for the wolf to get a hold of his arm and bite down hard. He let out a shout of rage and threw the animal-man off of him and into the wall with such force that he crushed the red brick, sending shrapnel flying around him. He sunk to the ground before shaking his head and rejoining the fight.

Blood dripped down Kiran's arm as he tried to keep the grizzly bear at bay. The three remaining men stood to their feet undeterred by my weak attempt at disabling them. I tried the pulse again, but this time they were ready for it. The man, who had challenged me to stay, sent me his own version of a pulse; it was not as strong as mine though and I was able to block it with a defensive surge of magic. He continued on the path to fight me, while the other two men did their best to out maneuver Kiran.

I once again focused my magic, feeling the electricity surge through my veins. This time when I centered it in my hands I could see the white heat from the force of it. Just as I was about to send my powerful blow, the man on his way over, threw another one my way, knocking me off of my feet.

My hands flew apart and the magic was sent up uselessly into the sky, illuminating the dark clouds above. I struggled quickly to my feet, ripping the seam of my dress at the thigh. I sent quick pulses of magic his direction as rapidly as I could. They were small since I was unable to take the time to focus my magic firmly, but they did the trick in keeping him from advancing farther.

Kiran, with four men surrounding him, was struggling to stay ahead of them. Although he was super-humanly fast, there were just too many of them to stay untouched. The bear caught him by the back of the neck, shaking him roughly, before Kiran was able to break free. Blood dripped down his back, covering his torn tuxedo in thick crimson stains.

He fought on, defying all odds. He continued to block pulse after pulse from the remaining humans, while keeping the animals at a safe distance. My fight with my one attacker intensified as he got a blow past me, punching me in the stomach and knocking the wind out of me. I fell to one knee, ripping my dress further and tearing the skin away from that leg. I stood up quickly sending a stronger pulse in his direction throwing him against the metal door, and denting it.

I turned to Kiran's defense and centered my magic quickly but effectively. I threw my arms their way sending all men flying in different directions. The men recovered quickly; but the quickest of all was their leader. He stood to his feet, walking directly over to Kiran and surprisingly punched him in the mouth and then again in the eye.

No one was expecting such a human gesture, especially me. When the leader thrusted his fist into Kiran's face, the sleeve of his cloak slid up the length of his arm and I painfully realized why he was so familiar. Around his wrist was a thick tattoo of a snake eating his tail and around his bicep, the lower half of a phoenix rising from flames. They were the unmistakable tattoos belonging to Avalon.

My mouth dropped open and I stood dumbfounded amid the bloody battle. If I would have known how to react or continue I would not have been given the chance. The mouthy and vengeful attacker from before recovered from the last blow I sent him and sent me one of his own. The electric pulse hit me with such force that I was blindsided and unfortunately unprepared.

The wave of magic threw me flailing over the side of the building and towards the ground below. Time slowed down and I felt as if I was watching the entire experience in slow motion. All five of the attackers' heads poked over the ledge of the building as if to watch me fall to my death. But most surprisingly was Kiran, who himself came flying over the edge, diving in my direction.

Before I could realize how long the deathly fall was taking, Kiran was diving towards me and gathering me into his arms. Once in his arms, we seemingly were going to float to the ground. I relaxed, grateful to be wrapped in his protective hold.

My reaction was premature; I heard a guttural scream from the top of the building and witnessed the electric wave of magic fall from the sky and on top of us. Our descent was quickened to a sickening speed and we hit the ground with such momentum that we indented the cement sidewalk that served as a landing pad.

I closed my eyes expecting to open them to severed or paralyzed limbs. The landing was painful, the ground crumbling around us. Somehow Kiran managed to land on bottom, giving me a softer landing via his body. I heard several bones snap and wasn't sure if they were mine or his.

I heard him groan underneath me and forced myself to assess the damage to my body. Upon opening my eyes and wiggling my toes and fingers, I realized that I was generally unharmed, except for some bruising and the gash on my leg from earlier. I awkwardly peeled myself off Kiran and struggled out of the hole we created with the impact of our body.

By this time the students and teachers from the dance began to exit the building, investigating what must have sounded like a car crash to them inside. I looked down at Kiran's limp and unconscious body and let out a scream I didn't realize I was capable of. I turned my head to be sick and heard other students around me gasp and let out cries of their own.

Someone came to my aid and began asking questions, but the only sound I could make was a throaty sobbing noise. I watched the men teachers bend over and pick Kiran up out of the hole formed around his body. They carefully carried him inside and I was left on the sidewalk watching after him, feeling more than helpless.

I knew he wasn't dead, I could still feel the small pulse of his magic; but I didn't know what kind of damage was done. He looked peaceful but mangled in his unconscious state. For the first time I realized that I had no idea what the word Immortal actually meant. What kind of destruction could we actually withstand?

The students filed past me, following Kiran's limp body into the gymnasium. Principal Saint knelt down beside me, offering his tuxedo jacket. I took it, grateful for something to wrap around myself. The jacket was enormous and thankfully hung down past my miniskirt which had been ripped to an indecent state.

"Were you attacked again?" Principal Saint asked grimly.

I nodded my reply and heard him curse under his breath. He said something about calling my aunt. I didn't object, but realized that I was missing the sound of sirens in the distance.

"Has someone called 911?" I asked in a hoarse whisper, barely able to hear my own voice.

"No Eden, we have our own ways of healing," no sooner had he spoken this then a long black limo pulled in front of the school and the teachers once again carried Kiran's limp body over the hole imprinted in the shape of our fall and into the back seat of the car.

"I must go with him. Your aunt will be here soon," Principal Saint put a hand on my shoulder and squeezed it gently. "I'm glad you're alright Eden." I watched him quickly get into the passenger's seat of the limo and then the vehicle drove away.

The rest of the students waited until Kiran's "ambulance" was out of sight before walking to their own respective limousines. An eerie silence settled over us, except for a few of the other girls who cried like me. One of them in particular, who could not control her tears, was Seraphina. Adelaide and Evangeline helped her to a limo alone and I realized that Talbott must have gone in the other car with Kiran.

A pang of guilt hit me and my heart dropped to my stomach as I realized that I was the reason Kiran was on the rooftop to begin with. If he had been with Seraphina like he was supposed to, the attackers probably wouldn't have found occasion to assault him. It was because we were alone on the roof without his body guard that they found their opportunity. And then it was because of me again that Kiran sacrificed himself over the ledge of the building.

"Are you alright?" Avalon, dressed in his tuxedo again, was at my side.

"Don't," I said simply, but my one word was filled with all of the rage I felt.

"Eden, there are things you don't understand," he knew I had figured out it was him on the roof.

"I don't want to understand. I don't want to be anywhere near you," I spat out the words like venom. I saw Aunt Syl approaching in her red convertible and looked around, realizing Avalon and I were the only ones left standing in front of the gymnasium.

"It's time that you do understand. I can't lie to you anymore," his voice was soft and sad, but it wasn't enough for me to listen to. I waited impatiently for Aunt Syl to drive up. "Kiran has to die, Eden. We have to destroy his bloodline in order to survive."

"I don't know what you're talking about," I refused to turn and look at him; all of the energy from the battle had turned to hate and focused completely at Avalon.

"His bloodline is the reason we are so weak. The reason we die. They've closed off the magic. By not letting us marry whomever we choose the magic is confined to one type of Immortal or the other. The magic can't be free, and because it can't be free we are all going to die. Maybe not today, maybe not tomorrow, but eventually every Immortal will fade out of existence. And if that is going to happen, I'm going to start with the source of the problem," I shook my head as if refusing to believe what Avalon claimed was truth. "They take and kill whomever they choose and then imprison the rest of us to ensure their bloodline and their Immortality. But it affects them too and

215

so I call for their blood to be shed. Every King before Kiran has made it worse for our people. I want to cut it off at the source before we all die, can't you see that Eden?" his voice was pained and full of emotion.

"Why him? Why not his father? Kiran's not even King yet," I finally addressed his accusations.

"But he will be one day. And he will be no better than his father. Probably worse. Have you asked him about Lilly? Have you asked him what his father is going to do to her? Have you asked him why he won't testify on her behalf even though she fought to save his life? No you haven't. You've bought into his lie just like the rest of them," he raised his voice with passion.

"Oh, but I should buy into your lie. I should just believe exactly what you say, although you're the one trying to kill me!" I shouted, enraged myself.

"I have never tried to kill you; I've only tried to protect you! And yes you should listen to me, because after all I'm your brother damn it! Your twin brother!" That was it. I couldn't listen to him anymore. I was overwhelmed with information I couldn't discern from fact or fiction. The events of tonight had been too traumatic to even process his words, let alone believe them.

Thankfully Aunt Syl pulled up the drive. I put my hands over my ears like a little girl and ran away from everything I didn't want to face anymore. I threw myself into Aunt Syl's car and yelled at her to drive. After she obeyed, I let out all of the emotion once again in fitful sobs, trying to wrap my head around the words Avalon just shouted at me. Could he really be my twin brother?

Chapter Thirty

"Eden, there is someone here to see you," Aunt Syl's voice whispered softly but firmly in my ear.

My room was completely dark, and I was comfortably wrapped in my comforter, surrounded by feather pillows. I groaned a response and rolled over. She patted my back maternally, before standing up to open my bedroom door and allow whoever was here to see me, inside.

I heard Avalon's familiar voice and a wave of nausea swept over me. He was speaking to my aunt about accommodations or a spare room or something I couldn't quite make out. I heard my aunt turn the lamp on, creating a soft glow of light not strong enough to hurt my still sleepy eyes. I peeked one eye out from the pillow I had my face buried in and saw Avalon fidget tentatively in the doorway.

"Well you might as well come in; you have a lot of explaining to do," I struggled to lecture through a hoarse whisper. In the last twenty four hours I had begun to accept the fact that he was my brother. This was the first time he had tried to speak to me himself since he told me, but I decided it was something I always knew deep within. At least I understood there was something internal that tied us together, although I was unable to put a word to it. Much like when Principal Saint came to explain my Immortality to me, Avalon was now here to explain our connection.

"You're not mad at me?" he asked quietly and walked to the end of my bed, standing awkwardly and playing idly with the bed frame.

"I wouldn't say that. But at least I'm not planning on turning you over to the authorities," my voice grew stronger than a whisper, but maintained its' hoarseness.

"Would you like some tea, my dear?" Aunt Syl offered from the doorframe.

"Yes, please," she gave me an encouraging smile and disappeared down the hallway. "We'll be down in a second." I called after her, feeling suddenly awkward with my brand new brother alone in my room. Who knew what I had lying around on the floor?

I crawled out of bed stiff and sore. My knee and shin throbbed dully from the bloody gash covering them. My hair was tangled and wild, I had yet to shower; and my skin was filthy. Aunt Syl was kind enough to let me sleep through the day; I supposed sleep was how I emotionally healed.

I staggered out of the bedroom, but not before grabbing a hair tie that I worked my human-kind-of-magic with; pulling my tangled locks into some type of vice grip on the top of my head. I noticed the green dress from last night in a crumpled heap by my door; I glanced down quickly to make sure I was actually clothed. Thankfully I had an oversized sweatshirt and shorts on. I didn't remember putting them on, but it didn't really matter at that point, at least I was dressed. I grabbed the dress off of the floor with full intentions of burning it when I got to the bottom of the stairs.

Avalon followed me silently. On the way to the stairs we passed the guest bedroom and I noticed suitcases in the middle of the floor. I was not sure what to think of them, but was completely focused on the warm cup of tea waiting for me in the kitchen.

I tossed the dress into the fireplace casually as we walked by it on our way to the kitchen island. I lit the wood with a flick of a switch positioned on the wall next to the fireplace and glanced back to make sure the dress worked as kindle for the flame.

Once in the kitchen, I pulled out a stool and impatiently waited for the water to boil on the gas stove. Avalon followed my example and sat down on the stool next to me. Aunt Syl brought out a plate of fruit and cheese and crackers; some of my favorite munchies. I gratefully grabbed some grapes and shoved them into my mouth. I was starving.

"Amory is bringing over some Chinese food…. King Fong's," Aunt Syl explained tentatively and then smiled sympathetically. Great. Although I was excited for the lo mein en route, I wasn't especially ready to rehash the rooftop battle for Principal Saint, especially when it indicted Avalon.

"So…. spill it," I commanded of Avalon, giving him a sideways glance before reaching for some more grapes.

"I don't even know where to begin," he replied almost nervously, running his hands through his long locks. I realized now that our hair and skin were the same color; our noses nearly identical and our smiles the exact likeness of each other. Only our eye color was different; mine almost black like our hair, and his green like the color of emeralds.

"Start with why you have tried to kill me…. twice," I inquired casually, holding up two fingers before grabbing some Wheatables and gruyere cheese.

"I have never tried to kill you!" Avalon nearly stood up defending himself. "I've only ever tried to kill him; you just give us good opportunities to attack, I guess," he calmed down a bit and flashed an amused grin. "You always get him alone, where he is unprotected. Unfortunately you're still fighting on his side. But I'm hoping that will change."

"I don't think it will," I disagreed. "There will never be a time when I can just sit by and watch you kill Kiran," I nearly choked on my words; realizing my brother's true intentions for a person I had strong, but indefinable feelings for. Albeit I was not sure what those feelings were, but without a doubt they were definitely not murderous.

"We'll see," he argued back and when I opened my mouth to say something, he continued quickly, "Like I was saying, I have only done everything in my power to protect you; that includes doing my best to keep you away from him," Avalon refused to use Kiran's name.

"Everything in your power… does that include throwing me off a building?" I rubbed my sore bones to prove my point.

"Eden, you don't have to be in pain. It's called magic. Why don't you try using it?" he nodded in the direction of my cut up leg and I felt like an idiot. Oh, yeah. I focused my blood, allowing the magic free reign to flow. The electricity pulsed through my veins, heating my blood and healing my body. Instantly I felt restored and rejuvenated. The gash on my shin and knee completely disappeared in seconds; and the bruises that moments ago painted my skin, vanished.

"Thanks," I mumbled.

"I didn't throw you off any building. Jer- my companion got a little overzealous. He was just pissed that he was getting beat by a girl. He fully expected you to recover, but you, I think, forgot to use your magic again," I blushed, realizing that my fall from the top of the gymnasium didn't have to be fatal. I had had the power to be just fine. "We all were shocked when you just kept falling. I don't know what would have happened to you if that half and half hadn't Time-Slowed to catch you; but then again Jericho got a little too excited. And if it weren't for you, he could have finished the job, but you absorbed the majority of the blow, protecting him," Avalon just used so many words that I didn't understand and I had so many questions now I didn't even know where to begin.

"Half and half? Time-Slow? What do you mean absorbed the blow? Speak English; and for goodness sakes, who is Jericho?" I squinted at Avalon confused, but he only laughed at me.

"I forget that you were raised human," Avalon laughed again. Aunt Syl gave him a side glance, disapprovingly. It's not like I was raised by wolves, give me a break.

"Explain," I demanded simply.

"Ok, let's see. Half and half is like a slang word we use to describe someone like Kiran. Someone who is half Witch and half Medium; his family specifically breeds this way in order to ensure their bloodline and their power. They think if they use the two dominant Immortalities they will stay more powerful than the rest of us minions," his voice dripped with sarcasm and irritability. "Time-Slow; that's like something only Mediums can do. It's one of the things that separate Witches and Psychics. Kiran has the ability to slow time down without slowing himself down. He caught up with you in air because he slowed you down. They can only do it for a limited amount of time, but you can see why it would be useful."

"And Jericho?" I asked, mentally ticking off my list of questions.

"I shouldn't have used his name. But anyways, he is part of the Resistance," Avalon grabbed a handful of crackers and shoved them into his mouth like he was suddenly hungry.

"The Resistance?" I asked; a looming feeling of foreboding washed over me. If a Resistance was involved, there was no such thing as an easy solution.

"Yes, the Resistance. The only people left brave enough to stand up to this tyranny," Avalon exclaimed patriotically, cracker crumbs flying out of his mouth. He smiled apologetically, and swallowed quickly. After washing it down with a long drink of tea, he continued, "A lot of Immortals are unhappy with the King and have been since they instituted the Monarchy. Lucan has done nothing but divide us up and kill us off. And your boyfriend is the next executioner in line for the throne. We plan to change that."

"Ok, slow down again. So who is in this Resistance? Are you only trying to kill Kiran? Or the whole royal family? What exactly is the purpose of this… Resistance?" my list of questions just grew longer and longer the more Avalon tried to explain.

"I can't tell you who is in the Resistance until you join it," he paused to wink at me and give a suggestive raise of the eyebrows. "It has to be kept completely secret otherwise they would hunt us down and execute every last one of us. I'm serious Eden, me telling you this is a gigantic risk; even saying the word 'Resistance' is enough to get us thrown into a Romanian prison. You can't just run off and let your boyfriend in on all of our secrets. I mean it: mental lock-down," he looked at me with such distrust that I felt ashamed.

"I'm not an idiot Avalon; I understand that," I rebuffed, defensively.

"I know you're not an idiot; I am just not sure whose side you're on," when I gave him a dirty look he answered more of my questions. "And yes we are going after Kiran. But it is mainly to send a message to his father, who would, of course, be our next target. The kid can't do much damage yet, especially when he is so distracted with you; but one day he'll hold the keys to this Kingdom and I refuse to leave the fate of all Immortals in the hands of a Kendrick," I blushed at his reference to me; completely in denial that I could be that much of a distraction to anybody.

"Avalon you haven't answered her last question. What exactly is the purpose of our Resistance?" Principal Saint entered the kitchen arms full of brown paper bags. The smell of Chinese food filled the room and as soon as he set the bags down on the counter I snatched one and pulled out a paper parchment filled with Crab Rangoon. I tore the legs off of the crab shaped pastry and devoured the fried goodness.

"Why don't you do the honors Amory?" Avalon addressed Principal Saint with a strong familiarity, and slid a box of fried rice over to himself, digging in with a set of wooden chopsticks.

Chapter Thirty-One

"So you know about the Resistance?" I asked Principal Saint tentatively, not sure where he stood on the issue. He entered the kitchen uninvited, and made himself at home to no one's objections, his arms laden with paper bags of hot Chinese food.

"I believe I was the founder," Principal Saint smiled at me widely when my mouth dropped open from disbelief. As the principal of my high school, I found it hard to imagine him plotting the death of one of its most prominent students. "That was a long, long time ago however. I've been able to take somewhat of a backseat position for quite some time," Avalon rolled his eyes and I could tell that Principal Saint was not being entirely truthful with me.

"Sure, sure," Avalon mumbled, shoving more rice mixed with Mongolian Beef into his mouth.

"Well, at least for the last sixteen years. You kids have been quite time consuming," he grinned again. I was a little taken aback by his casual appearance. His black hair seemed a little looser; and instead of the double breasted suits I was used to seeing him in, he donned a pair of jeans and navy blue polo.

"What?" I asked, my disbelief growing.

"That has been my task since you were born: to make sure you both survived. So far, so good, but I think Eden here is bent on destruction," I gave him an acerbic squint of the eyes, but half wondered if he was right. "In truth however, it has been the greatest task I've ever been given," his expression turned serious, and something in his eyes gave me a foreboding anxiety that I couldn't explain.

"Why is that?" I choked out.

"Well, let's just say that you two are very important to the survival of our species," I opened my mouth to ask him to explain further, but he continued quickly. "Back to your question concerning the King, or Lucan. He's the same as his father and his father's father, and the King before that. They are all tyrants. They care only for the survival of their bloodline and have been chasing Immortality since the day they lost it."

"So we really can't live forever anymore? Kiran could

have died last night?" I asked quietly, afraid of the answer.

"Anything is possible. Some of us have definitely lived longer than others," he smiled almost humbly as if he were embarrassed of something.

"And we all live longer than them," Avalon said "them" with such disgust that I had no doubt he was referring to the Kendricks.

"You haven't lived longer than anyone yet, Avalon," Principal Saint addressed him with authority and I saw Avalon look down at his food with a half-smile on his face; as if he didn't quite take Principal Saint seriously. "But it would have taken a lot more than a long fall to kill Kiran Kendrick. He's just fine Eden, you'll see him at school tomorrow, I'm sure."

"So what can kill us?" I asked, once again afraid of the answer.

"Only another Immortal can kill us and in very dire circumstances," Principal Saint shook his head as if refusing to say more. "And then there is something we call the King's Curse; but so far it seems to only affect a person after a long life. It is much like dying of old age, only a little more gruesome than that I suppose."

"Why is it called the King's Curse?" I asked reaching for an egg roll.

"Because that is exactly what it is," Principal Saint's voice hardened. "It is a curse brought on our people by the first King, Derrick Kendrick, and grows stronger after every consecutive Kendrick that rules," when I gave him a curious expression, he continued. "You see before we had a King our people had never experienced death. For a couple thousands of years we had walked the earth without death. Nothing could be done to us that we could not heal from, and no sickness or plague affected us. We simply lived, our powers growing stronger every year longer we survived. Finally, however, there were too many of us, we outnumbered the humans, and we were spread across the globe. Instead of thanking God for our blessings, the people grew complacent and cried out for a King. The Immortals wanted to live like the humans; even though we lived with abilities the humans couldn't even comprehend; even though the humans lived in war and hunger and under oppression, still our people called for a King. So they elected one. One of the strongest Immortals to ever walk the earth; and how did he thank them? By destroying them. First order of business, he hunted the Oracles down and executed them."

"Not all of them," Avalon interrupted.

"All of them died that day," Principal Saint growled back.

"Avalon has mentioned the Oracles before, but I guess I still don't get it. And how did he execute them if no one had died?" I asked naively and confused.

"The Oracles were elders who guided the people before the King. They acted as a referee for disputes, and other issues that arose. They were one of the first and strongest of our species. But at that time, every kind married each other; there was no distinction between races. Because of that, the magic was much stronger than it is today. You see a Witch could marry a Titan and together they could have a Medium for a child. The magic was mixed; but each individual would display certain attributes defining what they were capable of. Derrick killed them by first draining their magic and then they were easily murdered just like any normal human being would have been," I thought for a moment Amory was going to be sick. A look of pure nausea passed across his face, but then it was gone and he continued, "The second thing Derrick did was to cut off the magic from mingling. Each race, by King's edict, was henceforth forbidden to intermarry. This singled the magic out, not only weakening its power, but cursing us for generations to come. The King's Curse spread wildly, destroying most of the older generations first, and then working its way down, cutting our numbers by millions. It hit the King's household the hardest however. And to this day every King we have dies young comparatively, and worst of all they are only gifted with one male heir. It has been like this for King after King after King. Yet, they continue to oppress us, enforcing the rules even more harshly these days."

"So that is why Kiran has to marry a Psychic? Because he's a Psychic?" I asked, thinking very selfishly of my own problems.

"Well, in order to prolong their lives and strengthen their powers the royal family is both Witch and Psychic. They alternate what type of wife they take. Lucan took a Witch, and now Kiran must take a Psychic in order to ensure the equality of magic,"

Principal Saint explained this as if it made perfect sense, but I found this entire history lesson a bit confusing.

"So if the royal family is responsible for all of this, how come the Resistance has to be a secret? Why don't we all just rise up against them and take over peacefully?" I asked, hoping for a better solution than murdering Kiran.

"Because of the f-ing Guard," Avalon shouted out impatiently.

"What Avalon means, is in our weakened state, most Immortals wouldn't stand a chance against the Titan Guard. They are too skilled in battle; the community as a whole understands that we would all die. Their combat skill is what sets them apart, what defines them as Immortals."

"And the Titan Guard is Ok with how things are being run?" I asked thinking of Talbott and his utter loyalty to Kiran.

"Well, if they aren't there's nothing they can do about it," Avalon interrupted again.

"When Derrick was first crowned King, the Guard gave a blood oath to protect the royal family as long as there was any living heir. If the Guard breaks their oath they will also all die. They have no choice," Principal Saint looked grim and tired. The lines in his face had become more pronounced, making him look ancient.

"But they definitely are the bad guys? I mean the royal family?" I didn't really need to ask the question, I knew the answer; but I was having a hard time accepting it.

"Of course they are!" Avalon nearly exploded. "They are the reason we are dying, they are the reason we live in fear, and they are the reason your friend Lilly is in jail!"

"Lilly?" I asked in a small voice.

"Yes, Lilly." Principal Saint replied with more control than Avalon. "When Derrick took the throne, he exiled all Shape-Shifters. He made their very existence illegal. If they were found in hiding, they were lucky to only get a prison sentence. After Lucan took the throne, their circumstances worsened extremely. They can barely call their existence living. Lilly was not hiding; she was very much out in the open. And to add circumstance to conviction she was not only attending the same school as the Crown Prince, but happened to be nearly alone with him in the middle of the forest, isolated. Thankfully for Avalon, the King currently blames her for the attack on Kiran's life. They have not even tried to look further for more details. In his mind, she was the traitor and the orchestrator of the attack."

"Thankfully for Avalon, but what about her?" it was my turn to get fired up and I stood up out of my stool, knocking it over behind me. My face flushed red and I turned humbly to retrieve it before sitting back down to listen to the answer.

"I don't know, my dear. I have been called to testify, but I'm sure my testimony will only feed the jury more evidence of her crimes, since I genuinely had no idea of her true identity either," Principal Saint looked truly distraught.

"But why? She fought against Avalon, she tried to help Kiran! It doesn't make sense that they would blame the attack on her. Kiran and Talbott were both there, I was there, can't we testify?" I struggled to understand what was so difficult about this. Lilly hadn't done anything wrong.

"I know that and you know that. But my standing in the community is very precarious; I have to be careful of the battles I choose. And you Eden, are absolutely forbidden to go anywhere near that trial. You're very fortunate Lucan hasn't discovered you yet. I can't say much for Kiran, but he seems to want to keep you a secret just as much as we do. I am afraid of his motives however," Principal Saint looked down at the counter he was leaning up against and said his last few sentences quietly, as if he were talking to himself and not to us.

"Why? Why can't I go?" I asked stubbornly.

"The simple answer," Principal Saint looked up from the counter straight into my eyes and said simply, "They would kill you without hesitation," I swallowed loudly, afraid to ask his reasons. By the look on Principal Saint's face, and the tone of his voice, I understood without any doubt that he was serious.

"Amory...." Aunt Syl rejoined the conversation and gave him a concerned glare. "She's just a child. There's no need to frighten her," as soon as she finished her sentence, Aunt Syl's cell phone buzzed and she flipped it open to read a text message. I watch her expression turn from concerned to disappointed. "They need me at the hospital. Avalon, make yourself comfortable, there are clean linens on the bed and I laid out fresh towels in the bathroom. Keep her safe," she winked in Avalon's direction and gave Principal Saint a kiss on the cheek before exiting the kitchen. I cringed a little at the familiarity between Aunt Syl and Principal Saint, not only because he was my principal and she was my aunt, but there had to be like a huge age difference.

"Well Ok, but what about Kiran and Talbott?" I stood up and began to put the leftover Chinese food back into their respective containers.

"Talbott is not allowed to testify because of his position in the Royal Guard. By law, Titans must remain loyal to the Crown under every circumstance. Since Lucan already has charged Lilly, Talbott's testimony would be in direct opposition to Lucan's charges, therefore making Talbott a traitor to the Crown. And Kiran has no backbone, no sense of responsibility; the last thing he would do, is to stand up to his father," Principal Saint accused Kiran like he was heartless and foolish. I flinched a little, refusing to believe the accusations were true.

"It's not like he would stand up to him anyway," Avalon yawned in the middle of his tirade. "There's no way in hell the Crown Prince is going to stand up for a Shape-Shifter like Lilly Mason. Trust me on that," Avalon slammed his hand on the kitchen counter to make his point.

"But why? Why do they hate the Shape-Shifters so much?" I asked out of ignorance.

"Lucan, like all of the royal family and much of the Kingdom, believe they are manipulative and untrustworthy. But even more, Lucan is extremely paranoid. He truly believes they are after his crown, and after his life. I don't think he's wrong to believe that now; but they weren't always. After Derrick outlawed them, he had hundreds of them executed in the worst ways to prove his point. Things settled down for a while, but during Lucan's reign they have escalated almost to the point of extinction. During the first several years he was on the throne, his main goal was to hunt every last one of them down. I don't think he would have stopped killing them either, if it weren't that...." Principal Saint suddenly cut off his sentence and shut his mouth as if he had said something he hadn't intended to.

"If it weren't what?" I asked hoping to glean more information.

"If he hadn't found the one Shape-Shifter he was looking for," Principal Saint coughed into his hand and walked over to the sink to work on the dishes. I gave Avalon a curious glance, but he shook his head as if he was just as confused as me.

"Well, you two, there is school tomorrow, so why don't you head off to bed. I'll finish cleaning up the kitchen," Principal Saint moved around Aunt Syl's chef's kitchen as if he knew exactly where everything was. He must have been using his magic.

"Goodnight," Avalon yawned again, raising his hands far above his head to stretch. He turned to leave and something finally dawned on me.

"You're staying here?" I blurted out, suddenly putting the random suitcases and Aunt Syl's instructions together.

"Yep," Avalon barely acknowledged me before making his exit. I heard him on the stairs and then into the guest bedroom where he slammed the door shut behind him.

"We thought it best if someone stayed here with you Eden. I think it's best that you have some protection," Principal Saint turned to look at me, and I found it strange that we are alone in the kitchen together.

"Why? Now that I know it was Avalon behind all of those attacks I'm not afraid anymore," I crossed my arms and fought back my own yawn.

"Yes, I know. But you should be afraid. Kiran could be very dangerous; you don't really know him, do you?" I held back a snotty response, realizing that they were the ones who didn't really know him. "It's just a precaution anyways," Principal Saint waved it off as if it was no big deal, "Besides wouldn't you like to get to know your twin brother a little more? I'm sure the two of you have a lot to catch up on," he gave me a genuine smile and I relaxed. After all of the information I just received I had almost forgotten that Avalon and I were twins.... actual twins.... actually related.

"I guess you're right Principal Saint," I conceded, sending him my own version of a genuine smile.

"Amory, please," he implored. "I'm so much more than your high school principal."

"Amory...?" I tried his first name a bit uneasily, "My first question never got answered. So what is the exact purpose of the Resistance?"

"Ah," Amory, took a moment to look out the window that sat above our kitchen sink. "Well, it has many purposes, such as to completely wipe out the royal line so that the Titans may have their freedom back. Also, to protect as many Shape-Shifters as possible so once we do have freedom again, our magic will not be missing anything and can be restored to its full glory. And then finally I suppose, to protect you my dear," he smiled at me gently, but also a little sadly. I took his reference to me as a general idea to protect the Immortal population as a whole.

I smiled again and nodded my head; but suddenly I had a very uneasy feeling about the true meaning of his words. I remembered back when my life as a human was so simple; all I had to think about was myself. Sure, I lived in fear of what I would blow up or burn down next, but even that seemed so much simpler than now. This whole fairy tale Kingdom came with a lot more baggage than you read about in Disney books. Not to mention the super powers; they had a different playbook all together. I stalked up to my room, exhausted and overwhelmed, hoping to forget it all in the sweetness of sleep.

Chapter Thirty-Two

"Eden, let's go!" Avalon yelled at me from the driver's seat of his oversized truck.

I took a final glance in the mirror, and applied another layer of lip gloss, before I grabbed my backpack and rushed out the door. Avalon revved his engine, accentuating his impatience. I flung the door open, and threw my backpack in before struggling to make the climb up into his cab.

"Tomorrow we are taking my car," I said, out of breath as I worked to buckle my seat belt, although Avalon had already taken off and was flying through the neighborhood streets haphazardly.

"Only if you let me drive it," he replied, swerving in and out of spaces I was convinced were much too small for this tank.

"Why can't I drive?" I whined, remembering my Land Rover with sentiment.

"First of all, you don't use magic enough for me to trust you," Avalon explained as if I was the unsafe driver, meanwhile I was pretty sure he just ran the last three cars we passed off the road. "Second, it's not safe. Eden, you are in real danger whether you believe it or not."

"I do believe I am in danger!" I folded my arms across my chest defiantly. "I believe your driving is the most danger I have ever been in!"

"You're such a human. Relax," Avalon demanded.

I laughed out loud. I was pretty sure Avalon meant "human" as an insult. He could insult all he wanted, but at least when I was a human I wasn't in life threatening jeopardy constantly.

"No, only everyone around you was at risk. Do you remember what you were like as a human?" Avalon answered my thoughts and I let out a small grunt of frustration.

"Just because you can read my mind doesn't mean that you should," I growled.

"Alright, alright," Avalon lifted his hands off of the steering wheel and held them up gingerly as if to say he conceded; but I knew it was only an act. He would be in my mind as long as we lived; and apparently that was going to be a very long time.

As it turned out twins were able to connect to each other's minds without letting their other defenses down. We could always communicate with each other and read each other's thoughts, no matter how far away we were. Amory said that to a certain extent even human twins had this ability; ours was just strengthened because of our other powers.

I was sure this would come in handy one day, but right now I found it extremely irritating. Since he moved in with us over two weeks ago, he was always there, always around and always in my head. I found it ironic that even though Avalon and I only just met we fell easily into the role of siblings without any extra effort by either of us.

"How did you sleep last night?" Avalon asked a little more sensitively than I was used to.

"Fine, thanks," I replied, not sure how to read his question.

"No weird dreams?" he pried further.

"No, not that I remember. Why?" I asked, suddenly suspicious.

"Just wondering," he turned sharply into a parking spot in the student section and I was convinced he was going to scratch the cars to either side of us. When he shut the engine off, I found myself clutching the seats and holding my breath. "Calm down, Eden. See this is why you can't drive, you rely too much on your human senses and forget to use your Immortal ones," he jumped down from the cab with ease and I followed behind carefully but awkwardly.

We were two of the last students to arrive, due mostly to my inability to be on time. Only a few other students hurried up the walkway to their respective classes. I watched Kiran and Seraphina from a distance. Her long blonde hair bouncing with every step she took. They seemed to be laughing about something and then he held the door open for her and let her pass with a small bow. Gross.

"Let it go, Eden," Avalon growled in my ear. He had obviously watched the same scene, but for completely different reasons. And I could guarantee his stomach didn't feel empty and his heart didn't tighten with jealousy after it happened.

"You're right. He's the bad guy," I sighed quietly,

watching him walk through the door to the English building with longing.

"And you're the idiot," Avalon nudged me with his hand, pushing me in the direction we needed to continue to walk.

"I just thought that... I mean he didn't even let me thank him for the night of the dance," I referred to the fight on the gymnasium rooftop. It had happened over two weeks ago, and Kiran had yet to say even two words to me.

"Told you. He's the bad guy," Avalon picked up his pace, and I had to run to keep up with him.

After the dance, it was days before Kiran returned to school. I had looked forward to each day, when I would hopefully find a chance to talk to him, to thank him for saving my life, and then to apologize to him for what happened next. But by the end of the week, when he finally came back to school, looking more beautiful than ever, completely unscratched and completely perfect, he did not pay me even an ounce of attention.

I expected to feel relieved; not only did his inattention appease Amory and Avalon; I thought I would be able to forget about him and therefore stop suffering from all of the mixed feelings I had for him. And although Amory and Avalon were quite pleased that he seemingly wanted nothing more to do with me; and although my feelings had become clear, it was not quite in the way I anticipated. I found myself missing him more and more every moment. Memories of our kiss, or the strange dreams I've had of him, flooded my thoughts and I realized that I had utterly, hopelessly and pathetically fallen for him in a way that must be categorized as much more than a simple crush.

"We're skipping after lunch, so be ready," Avalon whispered to me before opening the door to English class. I mumbled a reply, too wrapped up in my thoughts of Kiran to really understand what Avalon just said to me, and then prepared myself for the verbal lashing Mr. Lambert was sure to give me on the crime of tardiness.

"Where are we going?" I demanded of Avalon, as he once again controlled his truck carelessly. I gripped the door-frame and

234

whispered a silent prayer.

"I told you, it's a secret," I could hear the smile in his voice, but I refused to open my eyes and view the destruction ahead of us. Suddenly the road was very, very bumpy and I bounced around violently in the passenger's seat. If I had not been born and raised in Nebraska and realized the transition from pavement to gravel, I would have lost my lunch all together.

"Ok, fine. But why couldn't we go after school?" I asked, as the remorse set in for skipping class.

"Don't worry about that. We have permission," Avalon replied confidently.

"Sure. Sure," I decided not to argue the point as another wave of car sickness washed over me.

Just when I decided I couldn't take anymore and the car ride seemed endless; Avalon shut off the engine and let out a huge sigh of contentment. "We're here," he said as if referring to his home.

I opened my eyes and breathed a sigh of relief. I didn't know what I was expecting, but I was content with what I saw. We were surrounded on every side by corn and bean fields. The rows of farmland stretched on and on as far as I could see, rolling over hills and down into shallow valleys. The gravel road that got us here seemed endless as well, and I mentally calculated how fast Avalon had to be driving on it to get us here as quickly as he did.

Avalon was parked in front of a large two-storied farmhouse that looked as if it was just given a fresh coat of white paint; the black shutters also looked new. A long porch wound around the front of the house to the side and back where I couldn't see. A boy and a girl that seemed about the same age as Avalon and I, swung back and forth on a porch swing hanging from the ceiling.

A beautiful flower garden sat next to the house and I could see a woman working strenuously in it to pull weeds. Down from the garden was a large modern barn made out of steel siding. I noticed the green of John Deere tractors just inside the door. Behind the barn was a large fenced in area where I could see horses milling about inside its boundaries.

When Avalon jumped down from his truck, several teenage boys exited the barn entrance and made their way over to us. Avalon waved at me to come with him, and I obeyed, hesitantly. I tugged at my school uniform, embarrassed for some reason to be wearing it here.

"Well, Eden, welcome to the Resistance," Avalon gave me a roguish smile and gestured widely with his arms as I took my place at his side.

"No way," I said softly, but disbelievingly. I didn't know what I had expected the Resistance to look like, but a quiet farm, surrounded by all the beauty Nebraska had to offer, was not it.

The woman in the garden looked up from her work and smiled at Avalon. She took off her work gloves and sat them down before joining the others. Avalon leaned against his truck smugly and I took in the extraordinary view again. I was suddenly nervous and not sure what to do with my hands.

"Welcome, welcome," the woman reached us first. She walked straight over and embraced me. "We are all so happy to have you here, finally," she sounded as if they had been waiting for me to come forever. Magic buzzed all around and I could inwardly feel all of their Immortal power.

I hugged her awkwardly, musing at her energy. In fact, all of their magic seemed different than the magic at Kingsley. Their electricity felt lighter somehow, weightless. I hadn't even noticed the heavy feeling at Kingsley before, but now that I was surrounded by these people I felt a huge difference. It was almost as if their magic was somehow made of light. I was overwhelmed by the sensation, but I felt at home at the same time.

"We meet again," a very familiar voice greeted me next and I pulled out of the embrace of the woman realizing that I hadn't caught her name yet.

"Jericho," I mumbled with mixed feelings as I turned to greet the boy who was not that long ago trying to kill me.

"Eden," he mimicked with faux menace and I was able to pick him out of the gathering crowd.

He was definitely nothing I expected. Jericho seemed to be close to my age, maybe a year or two older. He had chocolate brown hair that hung roughly around his chin, a little bit shorter than Avalon's. His large hazel eyes gazed into mine with an expression I couldn't read. His nose was a little crooked as if it were broken in a fight and his sinister mouth, curved into an amused smile.

Jericho reached out a long muscled arm to shake my hand. He was almost as tall as Avalon, and each of his muscles were clearly defined underneath a white t-shirt. He was a little bit sweaty, evidence that he had been working in the barn. I took his hand tentatively, unsure what to expect.

He took my hand, firmly shaking it in his warm grasp. He smiled wider at me before giving me a playful wink and letting my hand go from his. My hand fell limply to my side as I stared at him with mouth half opened. He tucked his hair back behind his ear and I couldn't help but find him completely adorable.

"Oh, brother," Avalon sighed.

"You tried to kill me," I accused defensively, covering up my initial reaction and replacing it with mock defensiveness.

"No I didn't," Jericho was just as defensive, but I saw the playfulness behind his eyes. I was suddenly embarrassed at my outburst as the crowd around us stayed silent, listening to our diatribe. "I only tried to keep you out of the way so we could get the job done. It's not my fault you needed a little extra discipline," other boys around him snickered and I felt the heat rush to my cheeks.

"Oh really? I'm the one who needed discipline? If I remember right you were getting your ass kicked," I shot back out of pride and watched with self-righteousness as his tan cheeks colored quickly to match the shade of mine.

"Enough. You're both awesome," Avalon interrupted, if not sarcastically and pushed me towards the barn. I walked silently, brooding next to him.

Once inside the coolness of the barn, we took seats made of hay bales in the back, near the horses. A large white board was positioned on the wall with names and locations I didn't recognize. I stayed close to Avalon, using him as a security blanket. Jericho sat across the semi-circle from me and I noticed a glance from him about every five seconds. I couldn't tell if he was angry, or curious or what.

As everyone filed in to take their seats, Avalon stood up from the hay bale we were sharing and took his place in the front of the room. The woman from the garden filled his seat and placed her arm around my shoulders. At first I was uncomfortable with her closeness and the unfiltered flow of magic between us. Not a very touchy person myself, her lack of a personal bubble was hard for me take.

"Alright, everyone, let's give our attention to Avalon," the woman said authoritatively. She must have been in her seventies or eighties, but her hair was still long and flowed down in white curls from the low pony tail she wore. Her skin was hardly wrinkled, except near her eyes and smile. Her frame was anything but frail, and I could tell that she was strong despite her skinny bones.

"Thank you Angelica," Avalon smiled at her with an emotion on his face that I couldn't read. I remembered that Amory told me after Avalon moved in with me that he was raised by someone named Angelica after we were split up as infants. I realized this was her and I suddenly felt more comfortable around her. "First order of business today is Eden," Avalon turned to me and waggled his eyebrows. I was nervous, what did he mean me? "Well, this is it, this is the Resistance. Are you ready to join?" my mouth dropped open and I stood up instinctively.

I felt like I had just walked into a trap. What did it mean to join the Resistance? Did it mean I had to help them murder Kiran? Did it mean I had to plot against a King I knew nothing about? I turned from my standing position and walked as quickly as I could back the way I came. I could never hurt Kiran. Joining the Resistance was impossible.

Chapter Thirty-Three

"What is wrong with you?" Avalon asked half concerned, half pissed off.

He followed me immediately outside and didn't let me get nearly as far away from the barn as I would have liked. The sun was warm despite the cool autumn breeze of October. The trees surrounding the farmhouse had turned to brilliant shades of orange and red. The fields had been fully harvested and made ready for the winter coming soon.

"I can't be a part of this Avalon. I wish you would have given me some warning; maybe a head's up, like 'hey we're on our way to dig your grave,'" I rolled my eyes and folded my arms defiantly.

"Ok, first of all. You would have known what we were doing if you would use your magic just an eency bit. Second of all, it was nice of me to give you the option, but you don't really have a choice. And lastly, if you don't join this, then we are all going to die!" Avalon was animated in his very characteristic dramatic way, I fought back a smile and forced myself to focus on the fact that his surprise attack, really just pissed me off.

"Stop being the self-righteous martyr," I quipped harshly.

"And stop pining over the one guy that you can't have, the one guy who is only using you, the one guy whose sole purpose is to kill everyone you love," I closed my mouth sharply, not realizing it had been open. Tears welled up in my eyes and I watched Avalon flinch from remorse.

"I'm pretty sure he's not the only guy using me; and I can promise you he's not the only guy trying to kill everyone I love," I could barely get the words out before tears began to fall down my cheeks.

"Except if I am the one who gets me killed, at least it will be on my terms. I'm not going to live in oppression under a violent dictator only to die of a horrible disease that could strike at any moment," Avalon folded his arms the same way I fold mine, and I noticed the same defiant expression cross his face. I was kept in the dark so often that sometimes my biggest moments of revelation came through Avalon's side of the argument.

"What about the using me part?" I asked timidly.

"Maybe I'm using you, well not you, but, fine, your magic," he admitted. "But if I'm using you, it's with your best interest in mind." he gave me a playful grin.

"Sure it is," I stuck out my bottom lip in a mock pout.

"It's true. I'm not the only one who's stronger when we're together," he turned to walk back into the barn; he thought he had won the argument. *Please Eden, we need you.* His voice was in my head, and I could feel, more than hear the desperation in his emotion.

"I'm not saying that I'm joining. But I will listen to the rest of your meeting," he turned and bowed a little with his hands pressed together. I kicked a rock at him, sending it with extra force via magic and watched him duck out of the way just in time.

Instead of sitting down in my previous place I chose to stand in the back, hoping to remain anonymous. I knew that it was impossible since every person in the room was tuned into my magical current, just like I was tuned into theirs. Their lighter, brighter magic was unique and interesting. I felt their currents flow, each distinctive, almost illuminating their person. It was as if their blood was glowing from underneath their skin, only in an invisible way; like I could have seen it glow if I had held a black light up to them.

Avalon began the meeting by updating the group of twenty or so Immortals about the skirmish on the rooftop at Kingsley a few weeks ago. My cheeks burned hot as he recounted a little too in detail what went wrong and how lucky they were to get out of there discretely.

The five guys who were involved were all given pats on the back or some variation of a high five or fist pound. They were apparently all part of the reconnaissance team. Besides Avalon and Jericho, there were three other boys, all probably two or three years older than me. Avalon seemed to be the youngest and I found it odd that even though he was the youngest in the entire room he seemed to also be the leader.

Avalon then began to recount the positions of others all over the world. He named names and places I had never heard before. As small as this room of twenty appeared, it seemed there were hundreds of others all over the globe.

I had as much trouble taking the Resistance seriously as I did the whole Kingdom and Monarchy thing, but it might be more major than I could actually imagine. The way Avalon talked it appeared as if these five boys made up the most skilled reconnaissance team, but there were several others around the world. Avalon and his boys were in Brazil like he said; only he wasn't with his parents, but rather on a decoy and extraction mission.

Avalon continued to relay information and answer questions until the light began to soften outside the barn doors. I turned, a little bored, and a little lost to look at the beautiful sunlight outside. The sky had turned brilliant shades of orange, red and pink and the sun was a blazing ball of yellow as it set behind the rolling hills of the Nebraska plains.

A black sedan drove slowly across the gravel driveway and parked next to Avalon's truck. A tall man, dressed nicely and donning a bowler hat stepped out of the vehicle and walked with purpose towards the barn. As he got closer I picked up on his magical current and recognized Principal Saint, or Amory. The image was vaguely familiar and I had the strangest feeling of déjà vu.

I turned back around and forced myself to pay attention to Avalon. Amory stopped next to me, pulling me into a side hug and kissed the top of my head. I was surprised at his familiarity and couldn't help but feel a little uncomfortable. Avalon acknowledged Amory with a tip of the chin and a wide grin. I forced myself to relax and trust him.

"The trial is set for the 31st of October at the Judiciary Court's Citadel. Oscar, Ebanks, Jett and Ronan will all be charged. Another trial precedes theirs, a girl named Lilly Mason. She is a Shape-Shifter charged with hiding her identity, attending Kingsley illegally and threatening the life of the Crown Prince. She is not part of the Resistance, but in my opinion she is innocent," Avalon's latest update drew my attention back to the meeting.

"Will we try to extract her as well?" Jericho asked, and my heart fluttered with hope.

"We can try, but our first mission is to remove our members. I know you're afraid for your friend, but we have to

242

tend to our members first," Avalon turned to me with his last comment spoken sincerely. I lost hope immediately, realizing I was the only one willing to help Lilly. I also realized I was the reason the other members of the Resistance were going to be tried.

"And when did you say the trial was? Holy Eve?" Angelica asked with a look of disgust across her face.

"Yes, I'm afraid only Lucan would find that ironic. After the trial there is an evening feast to begin the celebrations for the festival of All Saints. Some of you will be invited and expected to attend," Amory interjected and all eyes turned towards him. I put two and two together and realized the 31st of this month was Halloween. "Conrad, Angelica, Terrance and I will attend the feast and leave the week before to make preparations for Avalon and his team. Jericho and the others will leave three days before the trial and connect with Ryder's team once they arrive."

"I will arrive last minute, because I have to take mid-terms," Avalon rolled his eyes and gave Amory a disdainful glance.

"Avalon, we have to keep up appearances. Nothing must look out of the ordinary. You will travel alone directly after your last test. The tests will all be given by substitutes since the professors of Kingsley will all be required to attend the trial and festival."

"How last is last minute?" one of the other members of Avalon's team asked.

"I should arrive the morning of the trial, if all goes as planned. But we will not pull them until the night of the feast. We expect they will be found guilty for seditious war crimes and conspiracy against the King; in that case punishment is death. Our intel suggests that Lucan will wait to execute until All Saints Day to set an example, so we will infiltrate the prison on Holy Eve while everyone else attends the feast."

"Surely the security will be enormous," Angelica interjected, clearly worried about the plan.

"Yes, the entire Guard is expected to travel," Amory took over again. "But the Crown Prince is also expected to be in attendance and so the Guard will be split between Kiran, Lucan, the royal family and then the prisoners. I'm sure during the feast they will require extra security as well," he cleared his throat as if

243

forcing the words out; as if he wasn't sure he believed them.

"So that will be our only opportunity?" the man Amory addressed as Conrad said solemnly.

"Yes, I'm afraid so," Amory looked at Avalon with a type of longing I couldn't define.

"So we better make it count," Avalon said with more enthusiasm than his older counterparts. "I have full faith in my team, and Ryder and his team as well," a plan spontaneously formed in my mind.

"I want to help too," I blurted out, focusing on my own plan to rescue Lilly.

"No!" The entire room yelled at me. Twenty pairs of eyes stared at me as if I had just said the most absurd thing.

"I mean, I won't mess anything up…. I promise," suddenly, I felt like the outsider I was. Obviously everyone blamed me for this mission to begin with. I was the reason their friends sat in prison awaiting death. "I know it's my fault that this mission is even necessary. But I think I can help…. I know I can help," I tried to explain myself, hoping for a better response.

"I'm sure you could help dear," Angelica looked at me with a deeply concerned expression and I didn't understand her emotion. "But we couldn't risk losing you, it's bad enough your brother insists on going," she turned to look at Avalon with the same pained concern.

"It's not necessary Eden," Amory put his arm across my shoulder again and I felt him try to use his magic to calm me down. I shrugged it off, persistent that I would go. "Really, our teams are trained in this type of mission; you would only slow them down."

"But Avalon gets to go. Wouldn't I make him stronger?" I asked, feeling naïve.

"You cannot go," Amory replied firmly. "It's too dangerous. I won't allow it."

"Can't I just tag along then? I could learn from this trip. I won't get in the way," I pled my case, desperate to save Lilly.

"Enough. You cannot go. That is the end of it," Amory said quieter, but with scary finality.

This time I kept my mouth shut, silently brooding, watching the other members of the Resistance nod in agreement with Amory. I knew I was wearing a scowl, frustrated at my lack of independence. It would have been nice to be treated as an equal, just once.

Chapter Thirty-Four

Avalon wrapped up the meeting, but I heard nothing else he said. I had to figure out a way to get to that trial. I had to figure out a way to save Lilly or at least testify on her behalf. I was determined to do it, even if I had to do it completely on my own. Avalon had said something about Kiran going, maybe he would help me.

"Are you ready for the mark?" Amory brought me out of my silent plotting and back to the center of the Resistance.

"What mark?" I asked, completely unaware of what he was talking about.

"She doesn't want to join," Avalon joined our conversation as the others milled about in groups of two or three. I got the impression they were all trying to listen to our discussion.

"Why is that?" Amory asked Avalon sharply; apparently not interested in any explanation I would give him.

"Why do you think?" Avalon replied sardonically.

"Eden, you have a lot to learn, young lady," he said it much like a parent, and I felt instantly resentful.

"What is the mark?" I tried to change the subject away from what I feared was a long lecture on responsibility.

"It's this," Avalon pointed to his arm; his school uniform was rolled up to the elbow and revealed the tattoo of a snake wrapped around his forearm eating its own tail.

"You want me to get that?" I exclaimed. There was no way I would cover my body in a hideous image of a masochistic serpent.

"No, not that," Amory shook his head. "Avalon is a little…. devoted. The usual symbol the Resistance wears is more subtle," he turned his head to the side and pulled his ear lobe away from his neck. I saw only clear flesh until he touched the part of his neck just behind his earlobe and injected a little magic to reveal the same serpent. The image was much smaller, almost miniscule, but was clear and obvious until he removed the magic. Once the magic was gone, the small tattoo vanished.

"And you all have those?" I asked, enamored with the trick. A dozen Resistance members turned to show me theirs, including Jericho and Avalon. Angelica's was a brilliant shade of orange, while Conrad and Terrence's were an army green color. Amory's was a deep crimson shade of red. And all of the members of Avalon's team wore ones in white, which stood eerily off their skin, except for Avalon whose tattoo was royal blue.

"What color would mine be?" I asked, with no intentions of actually getting one.

"I am guessing it would match Avalon's, but we won't know until you decide to get one," Amory answered my question, sounding slightly frustrated.

"What do you mean?" I asked, confused.

"The magic we use to apply the mark chooses your color. The magic, in a way, determines the color you deserve. Not that one color is greater than the other; rather it defines the magic you are made of," Amory put his hand on my shoulder one more time before leaving what had turned into a circle of people, containing mostly Avalon's team.

"You don't get to join the team until you have the tattoo. There will be no more fighting for you," Jericho said as if taunting me.

"She doesn't get to join the team. Tattoo or not," Avalon interjected threateningly. He gave Jericho a hard look that Jericho seemed to understand even though I didn't.

"Avalon doesn't want me to join the team, because I would easily replace you Jericho," I deflected my frustration, by turning it against Jericho.

"Oh you think so? Maybe we should have a rematch," his voice was sarcastic, but his eyes smoldered and I once again noticed how attractive he was. He was taller than Kiran, but his darker hair and darker eyes made him appear mysterious somehow. Any thoughts of attraction I had for him though were quickly forgotten once I remembered Kiran, and then my heart hurt with emotion and a type of longing I didn't expect.

"I'm sorry; I didn't catch your names?" I turned off the charm, and turned to face the other members of Avalon's team, but not before catching a confused look cross Jericho's face.

"Sorry. Eden, this is Xander, Xavier and Titus," Avalon made the introductions. I shook each of their hands consecutively, memorizing the magical imprint they left in my fingertips.

247

Xander and Xavier must be related somehow because they looked nearly identical and their magical current was only marginally different. Xander was slightly taller, but they both had to be close to 6'5 or 6'6. Their hair was long like Jericho's and Avalon's and dark like mine. They both had facial hair, but Xander seemed to be a little bit older than Xavier.

Titus was also an imposing figure, only a little shorter than the other two. He also wore scruff on his face; only his brilliant red hair and stockier stature made him look more like a lumberjack than a well-bred Immortal.

"Are you twins?" I asked with honest curiosity.

"We wish," Xander replied enthusiastically. "Unfortunately, only you two get to carry that cross," his eyes darted between mine and Avalon's. When I gave him a puzzled look he changed the subject. "This is my kid brother." He grabbed Xavier around the neck and pulled him into a headlock. Xavier zapped Xander's foot with a shot of magic forcing Xander to let go and let him stand up. They pushed each other playfully until Titus stepped in, grabbed both of their heads and slammed them together. I cringed when I heard the crushing sound the impact made. They seemed unharmed however and shook it off, rejoining the circle with smug smiles on their faces.

"So why haven't I met you before?" I tried to refocus the group away from physical violence.

"Technically you have met us before," Jericho spoke up. "Remember the rooftop?"

"I mean properly," I clarified my meaning, but I was sure they understood that from the beginning.

"Because we didn't know if we could trust you," Avalon said simply and the other boys averted their eyes at the awkward pause Avalon's comment caused.

"And yet they trust you," I said disdainfully, only half kidding.

"Cute," Avalon mumbled under his breath. "Eden, do you mind? We need to go over some logistics before we head back. I'll be ready soon though."

"Sure," I said a little disheartened. I offered a small wave and walked away aimlessly. Avalon was obviously important and Amory seemed to be mad at me; I wondered at the reason I even came to this meeting. I hoped they didn't expect me to really join their cause. How could they?

"You look just like your mother, dear," Angelica's soft voice summoned me out of my pity party.

"Do I?" I was instantly drawn into her conversation by the very mention of my mother. She patted the hay bale she was still perched upon and I joined her, pulling my skirt down behind my legs so the straw would not scratch me. "Did you know her?"

"Yes of course. We all knew her. Well, except for the young ones. But how brave they are? They have never known a time without tyranny and yet they are willing to fight for a freedom that is foreign to them," she sighed as if remembering something sad.

"I've never seen them before. Do Resistance fighters go to school somewhere else?" I asked, wishing I could figure out a way to bring up my mother again.

"Oh no, not here they don't. I suppose those boys have all finished school, except for your brother," she patted my knee familiarly. "You know, our numbers have never been this big. I suppose that means a war is coming soon." She turned her head, and for a moment I imagined I saw a tear run down her cheek.

"Was my mother in the Resistance?" I asked, hoping to glean something from this sentimental old woman.

"In her own way she resisted; I suppose she fought against both sides. You could say that she made her own path, much like you dear," she turned to face me again, searching my eyes for…. something. "Your brother is a good leader; much like your father and grandfather. One day I am afraid we will ask too much of you both," she shifted her eyes away from mine and to the circle of boys listening intently to Avalon's instructions.

"What happened to them, I mean my parents?" I asked feeling brave.

"Your brother is waiting for you, dear," she continued to look in the direction of Avalon who seemed to be still in the middle of conversation. I was about to ask her my question again, anxious for more information other than we just look and behave like our parents, but then Avalon was looking in my direction waving for me to follow him.

"It was nice to meet you Angelica," I stood up, and

reached out my hand to shake hers.

"Oh, it wasn't the first time we have met," she put her hand in mine and although I couldn't recall ever meeting her before, once our flesh met, the magic that flowed between us was familiar and sweet. Our currents mingled for a second before she let go of my hand and walked away.

"Eden, let's go," Avalon yelled at me, a little impatiently.

I walked passed him and towards the truck. I couldn't remember ever feeling more irritated with him than at that moment. As far as brothers go, I thought he stood up to the expectations just fine.

"I don't think it's fair you can't go," Jericho matched steps with mine.

"Oh yeah, why's that?" I asked, truly interested, "Everyone else seems dead set against it."

"Funny choice of words," Jericho looked at me curiously out of the corner of his eye. "I think you should be allowed to fight. Clearly you are capable. They can't hide you forever, especially with the way the Prince apparently feels about you."

My cheeks instantly flamed with the mention of Kiran and his feelings for me. I pressed my cool hands to my face hoping to calm my nerves. We reached the truck and Jericho lingered by the passenger side door.

"Well thank you, I guess," I forced myself to look him in the eye and carefully formed my next question. "Where is the feast anyway? What did Amory call it, the Judiciary something…?" I batted my eyelashes and gave the cutest confused look I imagined I was capable of.

"The Judiciary Courts Citadel," Jericho smiled shyly, aware that I was flirting with him. "Romania."

"How can we have our own Citadel without humans wanting to know more about us?" I asked innocently.

"The Citadel is not as large as you are probably imagining it, but it's also hidden in the mountains."

"It's like its own town? Does it have a name?" I pried.

"Yes, and yes. But that's all that you'll get out of me," he smiled shyly. He reached past my waist, bumping my side gently with his arm and pulled the door open behind me.

I waited for him to walk away before I struggled

250

awkwardly into the truck cab. No matter how many times I practiced the tall steps into the passenger's seat, I could never seem to accomplish the feat looking like a lady.

"You better change your mind," Avalon grumbled after buckling his seat belt and starting the engine. I understood that he was referring to joining the "cause" but I chose to ignore it.

"Avalon, do you know anything about our parents?" I asked softly.

"No," he replied quickly, but then took a long pause. "I mean, I know enough to know what kind of people they were and that they would have wanted us to join the Resistance," I caught his not so subtle hint, but chose to ignore that one too.

"What kind of people were they?"

"Strong.... Smart.... Powerful.... Kind. Just like me," he quipped.

"But they didn't join the Resistance?"

"Amory tells me, they didn't get a chance to." Avalon's voice was soft and far off. *Let me go with you.* I pled using our mutual telepathy.

"No," he said firmly and out loud.

I shut my mind off to him completely, angry at his stubbornness and at my own helplessness. I decided I must ask Kiran for help, I had no other option. Surely he would want to help Lilly, especially after she fought to save his life. He would have to help me.

Chapter Thirty-Five

"Ms. Matthews is there something you would like to share with the class?" Mr. Lambert called me out sharply in the middle of English class. I sat up straight and shook my head in a humiliated and ashamed "No."

Mr. Lambert returned to his lecture and I returned to my plotting, although anything else I attempted would not be done during first period. I looked over at Kiran who was now sitting two desks away from me, with Talbott in between. I had been trying to get his attention for days without any luck.

Any note I had passed, Talbott destroyed. Any attempt at suggestive looks, Talbott interceded. Any outright demands for attention, Talbott deflected. I didn't know many bodyguards in general, but I imagined Talbott was really good at his job.

My perfect posture turned to poor as I pouted in my desk, arms folded stubbornly across my chest. My last attempt at the "Pssst. PSSST!" obviously didn't pan out, and so I schemed silently, determined to have an audience with the Crown Prince almighty.

I refused to let Lilly face trial alone. She did a great thing by revealing her true identity in a fight for Kiran's life and she should have been rewarded, not punished. Besides all of the talk about execution and judiciary courts had me nervous. She was innocent as far as I was concerned and I was bound and determined to enlist Kiran in my cause.

And if he chose not to help, thereby destroying any hope I had that he actually had a soul, I would just have to do it on my own. I had to; I could not in moral conscious or as a friend to her, let her be found guilty. Kiran's privileged life wasn't the only life I was going to get into the habit of saving. I at least knew that I liked Lilly, and she liked me.

Kiran gave me so many mixed signals I couldn't even identify my true feelings for him. As soon as I thought I could not be more head over heels for him, he didn't talk to me for weeks on end and then I was confused once again.

He hadn't even spoken to me since the Fall Equinox Dance. In fact, he hadn't even looked me in the eyes since then.

He went to all of the trouble of getting me to the dance, and then let a little thing like a midnight battle and falling from a rooftop get in the way of all the progress we had just made.

I supposed I should figure out my facts about this whole trial thing just in case he was another dead end. I knew the trial would take place on Halloween. I knew that the trial would take place in Romania. I knew that the trial would take place in the mountains in Romania; which thanks to Google, I knew were called the Carpathian Mountains. I knew Lilly would be the first defendant tried, and would probably not be facing execution, although I was not very encouraged by that. I knew that there was some type of festival after the trial took place called the All Saints Festival; but only Immortals were invited.

Basically I knew nothing in great detail, and nothing that got me on location. I needed the exact location of the Citadel; but more than that, I needed to know where the trial was going to take place once I got inside the Citadel. I also needed to know who was representing Lilly so that I could convince them to let me be a witness. I needed a passport, and I needed a plane ticket. My heart sunk with despair and I was convinced more than ever that I needed Kiran's help.

The bell finally rung, but I chose to gather my things slowly. I watched Kiran out of the corner of my eye and noticed him glance in my direction several times before exiting the classroom in front of Talbott. I decided to pick up my pace and cut him off in the hallway. Talbott couldn't block him from every direction.

"Ms. Matthews, I would appreciate a more valiant effort for your attention in my class, if you please," Mr. Lambert interrupted my desperate plan with just a few snide remarks.

"I'll do my best," I mumbled quickly, and then thought better of it. "I really do enjoy your class Mr. Lambert. English is one of my favorite subjects," I threw on the charm, hoping to convince Mr. Lambert of what we both surely knew was a lie.

"Then pay attention," he retorted sharply before gesturing his arm towards the door.

I turned quickly on my heel and hurried out the door, still determined to catch up with Kiran before Drama. Mrs. Woodsen had us memorizing dramatic prose in preparation for mid-terms and I wouldn't have opportunity once we were inside the classroom doors,

"You are an enigma," Kiran's silky accent addressed me softly and my own version of a smirk rose to my lips. "A beautiful phenomenon I have yet to understand. Why can't you leave poor Talbott alone? He works so hard to keep you at bay, and yet day after day you persist. I'm afraid he is exhausted."

"Where is he?" I asked, afraid I had only seconds with Kiran, before Talbott appeared to whisk him away.

"I gave him the day off," Kiran's lips twisted into his smirk, sending butterflies fluttering about my stomach.

"You can't do that," I protested coyly, inwardly rejoicing.

"I can do whatever I want," his eyes hardened, and I began to doubt we were talking about the same thing anymore.

"Where are you going?" I asked bluntly as Kiran began to descend the stairs towards the lobby instead of ascending them towards Drama.

"We are also taking the day off today," I started to protest, but he beckoned me with a nod of the head and I obeyed.

"You're going to get into trouble for this aren't you?" I asked, catching up with him.

"Probably. But I imagine you will too," I couldn't argue with him there.

We left the English and Arts Building and I shuddered at the chilly wind. Although we'd had a mild autumn so far, the wind had turned cold and as we neared the end of October the temperatures were dropping. Kiran didn't say anything but led me towards the back of campus and the student parking lot.

"I didn't drive, so we'll have to take your car," he said matter-of-factly.

"I didn't drive either," I said, heart dropping into my stomach when I realized I rode with Avalon like every other morning since he moved in with us.

I heard Kiran curse under his breath and then eye the parking lot mischievously. For a moment I thought he was going to steal something, but he made no move towards any of the shiny black cars lining the parking lot. He cursed again and then looked around the campus. He stared at the Gymnasium for several minutes before seemingly making up his mind.

"What are the chances?" Kiran mumbled under his breath before he resumed walking.

"That we're attacked there…. again?" I asked finishing his thought.

"With you Love, one never knows," he slowed down his pace a little so that we walked evenly side by side. His fingers reached out and gently played with the tips of mine. He hadn't taken my hand fully, but the gesture was so sweet and so endearing that it sent electricity buzzing around my veins; not to mention the magic mingling between our fingertips.

"I don't think they were after me," I instantly regretted my comment, afraid of exposing Avalon.

"I know that," he replied simply. He led me past the Gymnasium and down the hill towards the football field and track. I wondered to myself if anyone used these facilities. I'd never been to a game here before. Maybe they were just for show.

"Lucky for you, I'm always there to save you," I turned to give him a playful smile, but he returned my look with an intense gaze that nearly stunned me. His aqua blue eyes sparkled, hypnotizing me as if reading my soul.

"Why is that?" We stopped walking and he waited for my answer.

"I'm beginning to wonder that myself," my breathing became shallow and I was afraid I had said too much. I tried to cover. "Maybe you're the one that attracts trouble."

"Maybe…." he said thoughtfully before we resumed walking. I cleared my throat nervously.

Despite our slow pace we eventually made it down to the gates leading into the stadium. Kiran tried the gate but it was locked. Once again I expected him to use magic, but instead he looked frustrated and I heard him curse again. I reached out my hand as if to just get on with it, but before I could use any magic, he reached out his own hand stopping me.

"They'll know where we are," Kiran said softly.

"If we use magic?" I asked, shocked. I hadn't expected that.

"Yep," he folded his arms and cocked his head to the side with a frustrated look on his face. I couldn't help but laugh a little.

"What did you do, run away to be with me?" I smiled

widely; pleased with the lengths he took to get us alone.

"Something like that," he looked around, clearly frustrated with our lack of options.

"Well, I guess we'll just have to do things the old fashioned way," feeling brave, I tossed my book bag over the fence and began the long, awkward climb to the top. "No peeking," I looked down at the amused face of Kiran, and held my uniform skirt close to my body, suddenly embarrassed.

"I'll be the perfect gentleman," he bowed his head a little and looked at the ground as if proving his point.

I did my best to climb the fence gracefully, but it was no use. The links were small, making the climb awkward and difficult. After finally making it to the top, I had to swing my leg over in a most un-lady-like fashion, flashing the entire world I was sure. My descent down was easier, but I cringed at the thought of having to make the climb again to leave.

Once I was safely on the ground and had fully entertained Kiran, he made the climb. Of course, he made it quickly and easily. Without even using magic he was to the other side in seconds. Once on the ground, he picked up my backpack and shouldered it.

"This thing is disgusting," he grimaced.

"What?" I reached for it defensively, but he moved out of the way quickly. "I love that bag," I pouted my bottom lip.

"Of course you do," We began to walk aimlessly around the track, shoulders and fingers in constant contact.

"What does that mean?" I asked, afraid of the answer.

"It means that you're different," when I looked at him horrified, he explained further, "I mean you're different than any girl I have ever met…. ever."

"Thanks?" I didn't know whether to be offended or flattered.

"I don't expect they thought we would ever meet," he said cryptically.

"What do you mean?" Who was "they?"

"I mean, I don't think it was in the plans. Neither one of us was ever supposed to come here, and I can guarantee that we were never supposed to find each other," his explanation didn't clarify anything, I was more puzzled.

"And why is that?" I hoped for a clearer answer.

"Star-crossed Eden, we're star-crossed," he gave me a very sweet smile; unfortunately I returned it with bewilderment.

"Romeo and Juliet?" I asked, giving it one more go.

"Unfortunately," he took his eyes off me to look down at the ground.

"Things didn't end well for them."

"Nope," he shook his head and kicked at a rock, sending it flying across the red, running track.

I wondered at his reference to one of the greatest love stories of all times. Despite the unfortunate ending he alluded to, I couldn't help but dwell on the fact that the story was all about unfailing love. I glanced over at him again, but he stared intently at the ground as if working something out in his head.

"Are you going to the Festival?" I asked carefully, although I already knew the answer.

"How do you know about the Festival?" He countered my question, amused once again.

"Everybody's talking about it," I tried to cover, realizing I shouldn't know about the Festival. "I'm just curious, since everything is so new to me."

"Yes, I'm going. I don't have much of a choice. I'll only be gone a week or so though," he finished his thought as if to assure me.

"Where is it? What is it?" I pried further, truly curious.

"The Festival? Basically the middle of Romania. In Transylvania; it's near a city called Sibiu. It's a three day long feast where we celebrate the dead," Kiran talked about it with small tones of disgust and my hopes were raised.

"Wait. It's a celebration?" I asked, confused again.

"Yeah, for like all of the Immortals who have died. Everyone comes from all over the world and we have this huge feast and remember the dead, or I guess during that weekend we call them the saints," he stopped walking near the bleachers and took a seat on the stairs leading towards the metal benches. He dropped my bag at our feet.

"Oh. But what about the trial?" A look of confusion passed over his face and I was suddenly nervous.

"How do you know about *that*?" Suspicion clear in his

257

voice.

"Lilly was my closest friend before she disappeared," I spat out with more venom than I had meant to.

"Lilly Mason is a liar, a manipulator and a Shape-Shifter," Kiran said with disbelief at my outburst.

"She fought to save your life," I accused.

"She lied to everyone, including you," he accused right back.

"She never lied to me! And she sacrificed everything when she decided to fight for you," I threw the facts at him again.

"Fine. But when she did that she also chose to face the consequences. There's nothing I can do about it now, she's at the mercy of the law," he calmed down a little. The initial shock of my outburst dulled.

"I'm sorry, the law? Who's law? It's not right, and I demand that she receive a fair trial," I folded my arms stubbornly.

"Who's law? Only the law that you and her and every other Immortal are bound to," suddenly he was very angry. "I'm sorry you're new to this Eden, but you of all people need to obey the law to the very letter. Do you even understand the consequences for an offense like Lilly's?" I could tell that he was as livid as me, but I refused to give up.

"Of course I understand. Obey the law or face the death squad," I replied bitterly.

"That's exactly what it would be like for you. But don't be ridiculous, they are not going to execute Lilly. They just want to make an example of her," his voice was still laced with anger.

"That's not fair. She helped save your life. She should be like rewarded or knighted or something else as ridiculous! Not be punished because of what your awful and outdated law says!"

"Listen, I am very grateful that she was there that night, but the law is the law, outdated or not," he quieted his voice, but hardened his tone.

"Then testify for her!" I said exasperatedly.

"I can't do that," Kiran replied stubbornly.

"Then I will," I stood up, determined.

"Absolutely not," he also stood up to face me, adamant. "There is absolutely no way you will go to that trial. You will not set foot in that country, or outside of this town. Do you understand?" his voice was raised and he ordered me around in a way I had never seen him behave.

"You have no say in the matter. If you are not willing to do what is right, then I will."

"I have every say in the matter. As your Prince I demand that you remain in your house the entire time I am gone. In fact, I am placing you on house arrest until I return," he was so angry and so determined that his face was red and I could see real emotion behind his eyes, but instead of trying to understand him, he only made me angrier.

"You can't do that," I shouted, stamping my foot.

"Yes I can, and if you push me I will leave Guards at every door and window," his voice once again softened, but the hardness to his tone was unmistakable.

"I wouldn't have to push you if you would do what any decent person would do! You have the power to save her, to give her another chance, but you're wasting your influence. Instead of placing me on house arrest, why don't you help someone who actually needs it!" I knew I had gone too far, the look that crossed Kiran's face was pure anger. I closed my mouth, unwilling to step down, but too afraid to say anything more.

"Do not question me," he seethed. When I opened my mouth to protest he held up one hand and I was silenced. "Do exactly what I say or I will have you thrown into prison. Do you understand?" when I didn't respond, his voice turned even colder. "Do you understand?" I nodded, but just barely.

Kiran brushed past me with a chilling coldness that made me regret everything that was just said. He blew open the gates with one blast of magic, sending the ten foot, chain link fence flying. I watched silently as he stormed back towards the school without ever glancing again in my direction.

Chapter Thirty-Six

I was there again; wandering the same beautiful and colorful forest, looking for the same person who was meant to share this place with me. My fingers slid over the wildflowers, their velvet petals bending to my touch. A warm breeze swirled around me, sending petals dancing through the air and invoking an intoxicatingly sweet aroma.

I heard the brook beyond the trees whispering sweetly as it ran over rocks and white sand. The sun shone brilliantly in the clear sky above, sending beams of light through breaks in the trees and making a sort of polka dot path of light for me to follow. Butterflies and fireflies buzzed around delicately, their presence was comforting.

I saw him in the distance, his strong build a stark contrast to the delicateness of the forest. The light played off his skin, illuminating him through the flowering trees. His blonde hair glistened and his blue eyes pierced my soul.

Even in this dream like state I was nervous and excited. My emotions flooded my senses, leaving me overwhelmed and confused. As I walked slowly closer to him I saw that he was only wearing a pair of baggy, gray sweatpants, his chest bare. The muscles from his neck to abdomen were clearly defined; I took in the sight of him and was left breathless.

Kiran waited patiently for me to approach. His face was a mixture of emotions, none of which I could define. He stood alone, a grove of trees encircling him. The space was too small to be called a meadow, but was hollowed out by a perfect ring of forest surrounding it. He leaned against a tree opposite me; and gave me a saddened version of his smirk.

I stopped short of entering the circle, a little afraid of him but more afraid of what he wanted. His eyes appraised my entire figure before he let them fall intently on mine, beseeching me with words not spoken. The silence was so beautiful that I was afraid to break it with even the smallest sound.

After several moments of what began to feel like a pained longing, Kiran approached slowly, gently. He closed the empty space between us, pulling me into his arms and holding me close.

The fears I had just felt, the apprehension that made me careful before, melted away and I let his energy consume me.

Our magic united together in an excited aura of frenetic energy. His closeness made me dizzy, his scent had me lightheaded and the warmth of his skin against mine felt as though my soul was strangely complete. I could never have left that moment and it wouldn't have been enough.

Kiran tipped my chin up so that I looked directly into his eyes. Leaving his fingers firmly on my chin, and with his other hand on the small of my back pulling me tighter to him, his lips found mine in glorious connection. Time stopped moving forward and the world stopped spinning and for the seconds my mouth was connected to his, I felt utter bliss.

"Eden!" Avalon screamed through the beautiful perfection of my dream, ripping me out of it in a most unpleasant way. "Eden!" he shouted again fully shaking me out of any sweet memories remaining.

"What?" I shouted back, groggy and disoriented.

"Wake up!" he said again loudly, too loudly.

"Why?" my voice was hoarse and scratchy and I could not get past confusion.

"Ummm…." Avalon struggled for a reason. "I need your help."

"What? With what? Can't it wait?" I turned over in bed, burying my face into my large feather pillows.

"Yeah, I guess," he started to leave my room, but then burst through the door again. "No, it can't wait. Come on, get out of bed," he ripped the comforter off of me, leaving me freezing and pissed off.

"Avalon! Get a life!" I yelled, fully awake and fully angry.

"Come on," he pleaded, not the least dismayed by my irate tone.

"What could you possibly need help with?" I asked, rubbing my eyes to make my alarm clock clear: 3:00 AM.

"Will you please help me pack?" he sounded like a little boy and I couldn't help but feel pity for him.

"Do you really need help? Can't this wait until tomorrow?" I sat up and pulled my knees to my chest. My teeth were chattering and my entire body had goose bumps.

261

"Yes, I really need help. And no, it can't wait, I leave tomorrow," he said the magic words. My eyes popped open and I was suddenly very awake.

He left tomorrow? That was impossible. But then again, tomorrow was the last day of mid-terms. Everyone else had already been long gone. The teachers hadn't been there all week and several students had been missing as well. One student in particular hadn't been at school since our fight in the stadium.

If Avalon left tomorrow that meant I had run out of time. Lilly's trial was only thirty six hours away and I had in no way been successful in my quest to rescue her. So far I was a failure. I crawled out of bed and grabbed a sweatshirt before following Avalon to his room.

"You can't be so careless when you're asleep. Geez, Eden," Avalon whined as we entered his room. At one time you could see the floor of the guest room, but that was before it officially became Avalon's. Clothes and shoes and who knows what else littered every inch from wall to wall.

"What do you mean?" I asked groggily, rubbing my eyes again. I did my best to bring the room into focus, but I was still fighting sleep.

"I can't save you every time you fall asleep. I need to sleep too!" Avalon was his characteristic dramatic self, but I had no idea what he was talking about.

"Save me? I don't need you to save me. Especially when I am sleeping," I touched my fingers to my lips remembering the sweet and intimate moment I shared with Kiran just before I was awoken. Our souls mingled as one, and our magic melding to form one powerful stream of unbreakable force; in my dreams we were meant solely for each other. "Um, until you can keep him out, you for sure do need me to save you." Avalon rolled his eyes and then walked over to his closet to dig out a black duffle bag.

"What do you mean keep him out?" my throat closed and my blood turned hot with nervous energy. It was not possible…. but then so many things I had assumed were impossible had proven me wrong.

"Out of your head. I mean you do a good enough job during the day, but come on. Really? No one wants to monitor that garbage," he threw the duffle bag on the bed and started

262

gathering random items off of the ground.

"Avalon I don't know what you're talking about!" I raised my voice impatiently and stomped my foot like a child. I was wide awake now.

"What? Are you telling me that Amory didn't warn you?" Avalon's face turned white as he spun around and gave me his full attention.

"No. Now explain," I demanded, arms crossed, glowering at Avalon like it was his fault.

"Kiran can Dream Walk. That wasn't just a dream you were having, that was real," Avalon spoke softly and slowly.

"What do you mean real?" I shrieked and then slunk down on the bed next to Avalon. We wore the same facial expression and our faces were the same color of white.

"He's a Medium. They have the power to call you out while you're sleeping. Your body stays where it is, but your mind goes to a place of their choosing. You are fully conscious, fully awake, and you should be fully aware. That is if you know what's happening to you," he finished quietly.

"So that place Kiran takes me to, is a real place? He is really there, he is really…." I couldn't finish my sentence, embarrassed to say out loud the memories I had thought were only vivid dreams.

"Well, kind of. It's a place he has created for you at least. But yes, he is there, not physically but mentally."

"Oh dear," I slouched lower, realizing I might have been sending mixed signals. Or was I receiving mixed signals? Now that I had to take into play not only our physical interaction but now our metaphysical interactions I felt more confused than ever. The last time I was with Kiran he yelled at me and then stormed off; however if you count the dream I just had it was our most intimate moment so far. I missed human boys.

"So you didn't know this entire time that it was real?" when I shook my head negatively, he began to flip through my memories. I let him, since I was as nervous as he was to find something I might have said that not only implicated him, but the entire Resistance. "From now on you have got to be more careful. You should be strong enough to protect your mind from him," Avalon said exasperatedly, but then breathed a sigh of relief when

263

he didn't find anything incriminating.

"He was definitely trying to get information out of me," I remembered the questions he asked about my identity and cringed; thankful I was as clueless as he was.

"That's not all he was trying to get out of you," Avalon mumbled under his breath. My face turned bright red, and I covered it quickly with my hands.

"I didn't know it was real," I defended myself. "I thought it was a dream!"

"Hmmm…. I wonder why Amory never told you. That stuff can be dangerous," Avalon's face had returned to his normal color and he bit his thumb nail in deep thought.

"What do you mean dangerous?" I asked as Avalon stood up and began to rummage through clothes and shoes, looking for items to toss into his bag.

"Well you experienced how real everything felt. I mean that is your consciousness. Can you imagine if he called you out and meant you harm? Think about it, he could create any scenario; he could create the inner most circle of hell if he wanted. And you willingly went, without the slightest hesitation."

I pouted my lip, ready to defend Kiran, but decided against it. The reality was he could have created anything, but instead of my own personal hell, he created the most beautiful place I had ever seen or been. And maybe I did go willingly, but I was never disappointed. Kiran was not the bad guy Avalon saw him as.

"It wouldn't be the first time," Avalon finished his thought and then sniffed several shirts before deciding if they made the bag, or returned to the floor.

"What do you mean?" my ears perked up, and a slow creeping sensation of jealousy made its way up my spine. If Kiran pulled this trick with every girl, I was going to be pissed.

"I mean with Mediums in general." Avalon shook his head as he simultaneously felt my jealousy. I relaxed and then felt foolish. There was no reason to feel jealous, he wasn't mine or anything, and in fact he was betrothed to another girl. "Remember that. But before, when the Monarchy took over, I guess they used their power of Dream Walk to torture all kinds of people. That's how the first Immortals died," his voice was sad but reverent and it was his turn to emote his pain on to me.

264

"Kiran's not like that," I said defending Kiran with my heart, but realizing with my head that I didn't really know.

"Sure, sure. You don't really know him though, do you Eden?" Avalon threw a dirty pair of socks at my face, but I batted them away quickly, afraid of all of the possible diseases they carried.

"So you really leave tomorrow?" I asked, sad that I would soon be alone, even if only for a little while. Even Kingsley would be empty. I hadn't even seen Kiran, well in person, since he left me on the football field and Avalon would be gone tomorrow. I knew it would only be for a few days, but the thought of being here alone and helpless to save Lilly made my heart hurt.

"Yeah, right after the Chemistry final," Avalon walked into his bathroom and I could hear him open and close cabinets until returning with a packed shaving kit.

"Why can't I go?" I whined in desperation. Avalon held up two shirts in my direction and I nodded to the one I thought fit him best.

"I don't know, but nobody wants you there," he said, not the least bit concerned. He walked over to his closet and pulled out the dark cloak and mask that were the final touches to his full duffle bag.

"There has to be a reason," I whined further.

"Of course there is. Amory doesn't do anything without a purpose and a reason; so if he says 'no' it's for a good cause," Avalon struggled with the zipper to his duffle bag for only a second before waving a hand over it and closing it with simple magic.

"Sure it is," I folded my arms across my chest and pouted my lower lip. "Promise me you'll save Lilly," I looked pleadingly at him and he rolled his eyes.

"My first objective is the team, and then yes, I'll do my best to save your friend." I knew that's the best I would get from him, and although I was glad he would try, I felt more discouraged than ever.

"I'm sorry Avalon, I'm the reason your friends are there to begin with," I looked at the ground and played with the corner of his comforter.

"That's alright. I'm the reason your friend is there,"

265

Avalon patted my head like a child, but I felt strangely comforted despite.

Chapter Thirty-Seven

The substitutes presiding over mid-terms were clearly human. Having been raised human my entire life, as I was reminded almost daily, I never noticed a difference between the two species. But after half a semester of Immortal teachers who not only knew everything, but saw everything, the humans they found to replace them were clearly blind and deaf to all of the activity around them.

Thankfully for them they were not actually teaching anything, otherwise I would have been afraid for them. The Immortal students left at Kingsley took advantage of the poor souls at every opportunity. They lied, they cheated and they just got up and left all together. It was a cruel joke to human teachers assuming they still had complete authority. The teacher monitoring our Chemistry final was particularly sad. A woman in her late fifties, and nearly blind to begin with, didn't seem to notice any of the chatter and foul play happening around her. I did my best to focus on my test, remembering that not too long ago that poor human was me.

It wasn't easy however, since Mr. Hayman had left a particularly nasty mid-term for us to take. To top it off Adelaide Meyer and Evangeline Harris sat behind me in constant conversation. Their high, excited voices scraped my nerves like nails on a chalkboard and it took everything inside of me not to turn around and give them a piece of my mind.

I did my best to focus on the test in front of me and refrain from magic. It would be easy to magically remember the answers, but that somehow seemed like cheating. I knew that the other students used magic for all of their classes, but I was determined to learn on my own.

"No way," Evangeline's shriek pulled me away from concentration once again.

"What?" Adelaide amazed me with her dramatic concern.

"We're not going now!" Evangeline was near tears and her voice found a painfully high pitch.

"What!" Adelaide repeated in an equally high voice.

"Dad and Mom have to fly to India instead. Apparently it's

on business for the King, but that means I can't go to the Festival!" I could hear her voice crack. I peeked over my shoulder to confirm the tears running down her cheeks. I saw her frantically typing on the small keyboard of her cell phone.

"But that's not fair!" Adelaide confirmed Evangeline's spoiled attitude. Maybe Evangeline and I should hang out while everybody else lived it up in Romania.

"I know! They said I can't go unsupervised. It's not like I'm flying coach, its first class for god's sake." Evangeline cried.

"You could go with us on Daddy's private jet. We have plenty of room! Daddy's jet is super posh; we don't even bother with customs!" Adelaide was bubbling over with excitement at the solution to Evangeline's problems.

"That would be so much better than flying on those dirty planes and standing in line!" Evangeline perked up and I heard her return to frantically texting. "They said that would be fine! Mom is going to call your mom," she shrieked again, only that time in an excited even more irritating way. "I even brought my things! We were supposed to leave right after this test. Where are you staying?"

Adelaide began rambling on and on about their swanky accommodations inside the Citadel, while I rolled my eyes. But then suddenly, a plan formed in my mind that was so ingenious I would have been a fool not to follow through. I glanced at the clock, only twenty more minutes left. I knew I said I wouldn't use magic on a human but this was different. It was life or death.

I quickly filled the rest of my test in, giving it a once over with magic before standing up to turn it in. The substitute shot me a curious look and opened her mouth as if to decline my gesture. I gave her a worried smile and walked quickly to her desk.

"Excuse me, but you need to sit down for the remainder of the hour," she said in a warbled, but firm voice.

"I'm so sorry," I gave her a frantic face and threw my test down on her desk. "I really have to use the restroom," I said in the softest voice a human could still hear. Several students, who had super-human hearing, snickered around me.

"You'll have to wait," she replied even firmer.

"You don't understand," I pled, and then pushed a little magic on her. I saw her think it over again before offering me a

269

pleasant smile.

"Of course, dear, if it's an emergency," she gestured with her hand towards the door, before returning to the erotic romance novel that was occupying her time.

I didn't even bother to smile back as guilt filled me. I reminded myself that this was for a good cause and picked up my pace as I sprinted across campus. The crisp autumn air stunned me a little as I burst out of the Science Building and towards the Administration Building.

Once I reached the Administration Building I flung the door open with magic, too excited to slow down. Mrs. Truance and Principal Saint had not been here all week, but thanks to Avalon, I knew that the students leaving directly after class today put their respective bags behind Mrs. Truance's circulation desk.

Out of breath, and jittery with nerves I leaped over the wide mahogany, frantic to beat the clock. Any minute students would be pouring through those doors excited for a long weekend abroad. I had to get out of there before Avalon or Evangeline were one of those students.

The floor was piled high with expensive designer suitcases and I realized I had no idea which one was Evangeline's. I did my best to calm my nerves and focus. I let the magic center my mind and drift through the Louis Vuittons, Tumi and Coach Travel Sets in search of Evangeline's carry on.

I felt my magic swirl around me, in and out of the piles of luggage. I sensed passport after passport and airline ticket or gate passes for private jets, but I forced myself to refrain from taking just anyone's. Eventually I felt it, deep inside a brown leather oversized purse sitting on top of Mrs. Truance's desk. I crawled over the chasm of suitcases and used magic to pull the golden zipper back. I couldn't have anyone dusting for prints.

I began to reach my hand inside of the bag ever so carefully, when the brass doors to the lobby slammed open and a torrent of students flooded the lobby. In my excitement and nervousness I knocked Evangeline's purse over, spilling the contents all over the floor. I joined them as quickly as I could, lying flat on my stomach and thinking as fast as my mind would work.

I had only seconds and my mind was reeling. Evangeline's

passport and airline ticket were conveniently tucked together in a discrete leather portfolio. The portfolio unfortunately slid underneath Mrs. Truance's desk due to my clumsiness. I focused my frenzied magic on the portfolio flipping it open quickly. I reached for the ticket but it was too far away.

With a quick nod, reminiscent of I Dream of Jeanie, the ticket flew into my hand along with the passport and I scrambled to my feet, tucking the precious papers into the middle of my backpack. I breathed a sigh of relief and shouldered my pack. Luckily, the students I was so afraid of were only underclassmen and completely unaware that I was committing theft. I slipped through the crowd and then the back door leading into the courtyard.

I smiled graciously as I passed Adelaide and Evangeline on the brick walkway; they returned my look with confusion and disdain. If only they knew they had just solved my most unsolvable problem. I walked quickly to the car, the weather was very cool and I hadn't bothered with a coat.

Normally I would have had to wait for Avalon and his keys before I could sit in the warmth and sanctuary of a car that would take me away from Kingsley; but since Avalon had to be dropped off at the airport today, I was in control. I pushed the button on my keyless entry and heard the glorious sound of the doors unlocking. I loved my Land Rover.

I shoved my backpack deep into the back seat and turned on the radio. I flipped through the stations, searching out something soothing and soft. I had to completely clear my mind in order to fool Avalon. If one small thought passed through my mind about what I had suddenly planned he would no doubt pick up on it immediately, if he hadn't already figured it out just by paying attention to our twin connection. But I hoped for the best, and repressed my magic and made it miniscule; hopefully I would also turn off the switch to our weird twin vibe.

I couldn't get rid of my nerves completely though and so I was still on edge when Avalon banged on the window in an attempt to scare me, it worked. I let out a blood curdling scream and nearly peed my pants. Pleased with himself, Avalon hopped into the passenger's seat all smiles and excitement.

"Chill out," he said, still laughing.

"Don't do that!" I scolded, heart beating wildly.

"How many times do I have to remind you to use your magic? If you were tuned into your surroundings I wouldn't be able to do that," he shook his head in mock disappointment.

"You're right," I tried to laugh it off, hoping to end the conversation immediately.

"What are we listening to?" Avalon made a disgusted face before taking over the seek-and-scan. He changed the university classical station to one that was more contemporary and…. loud.

I pulled out of the parking lot and filed in behind the long line of cars en route to the small airport Omaha had to offer. We merged onto the Interstate heading northeast in direction of Eppley Airfield. Some of the more expensive cars eventually made a turn for the northwest probably headed to the private airfields or who knows maybe their very own runways built into their very own expensive backyards.

The twenty minute drive was made in silence. Through the upbeat rap music I could tell that Avalon was focusing on the task ahead. He chewed on his thumbnail with his forehead creased together and stared out the window oblivious to anything around him. Although I was thankful for his less than interested approach with me, for the first time I realized he was nervous for the mission.

I had been so focused on Lilly and what her outcome at the trial would be that I completely overlooked the dangerous steps Avalon was about to take. If he was caught, I was sure he would share the same punishment as his accused companions. I glanced over at him and a pit began to form in my stomach. What was I asking him to do?

Avalon's mission to save the team I condemned was enough. I was selfish to ask him to carry out what should be my mission. I would save Lilly, if not by testimony then by extreme force. I didn't know these people, but I would be damned if I left my only friend's fate in their hands.

"When does your flight leave?" I asked, trying to focus Avalon's mind on the here and now.

"1:03, Southwest," he nodded in the direction of the drop off lane, but I had decided a long time ago I would at least walk my brother inside.

"No, I'll walk you in and say goodbye," I glanced at the clock and realized he was going to have to run to make his flight. I wondered if I would have to do the same, but quickly banished the thought before Avalon could catch on.

I parked the car in the multi-level parking garage and popped the trunk for Avalon. While he was transferring a few things from his backpack to his duffle bag, I grabbed my own backpack and dumped the books, leaving only the necessities. I took a glance at the ticket noticing my time of departure was 1:24, so I would have only minutes after Avalon took off to get where I needed to go.

I would need to wait until Avalon was in the air before I made any move for my plane, otherwise he would know. I glanced back at him; he was clearly still preoccupied with his mission. From the two missions I fought against him prior to this one, I had assumed he was fearless or at least enjoyed the fight, but by the expression on his face it was clear that he knew exactly what he was risking.

"Are you ready?" I asked, laying a concerned hand on his shoulder.

"Of course," he smiled, shaking his head a little as if to bring himself out of something.

"Then let's go. I want to see you take off," he rolled his eyes, but didn't object.

We walked across the drive way and into the airport. Omaha's Eppley Airfield was small and practical. Since Omaha didn't fly directly International, all flights would have to make a connection somewhere else. Avalon's was Minneapolis, mine was thankfully Atlanta.

I could feel Avalon's magic strong and purposeful as he checked in and handed his passport and ticket to the clerk. I took notes silently beside him. My first use of magic on a human happened today with the substitute and I was filled with guilt afterward. Avalon used magic seamlessly with humans and I could tell from his aura that he didn't feel the least bit guilty.

After a minute though, I could see why. Avalon's magic helped the human girl to focus. Everything with his check in went quickly and smoothly and neither one had anything to complain about. He only bent her mind a little bit, but it was for her sake, as well as his. He noticed my observation and then turned to give me a look that said, "And that's how it's done." I rolled my eyes, but was inwardly impressed.

I gave him a long hug at the top of the escalator leading to his terminal. He let me and didn't let go until I did. I tried to find the right words of encouragement but nothing poetic came to mind. He smiled at my efforts and then winked before turning to walk away.

Be safe. Do not do anything stupid while I'm gone. His stern voice was in my head, but inwardly I was too choked up at his show of affection to respond.

"Did you hear me?" he turned around to walk backwards towards the security checkpoint.

I nodded affirmatively and wiped a tear off of my cheek. He shook his head and then he was to security and having to take off his shoes and jacket; oh no, his jacket. I realized for the first time that Avalon changed clothes before he left school. He was dressed very nicely in a tailored black pin striped suit and white shirt with a green tie underneath. He put his shiny black shoes into the bin and I noticed that even his socks were fancy.

It was my turn to check in and I was standing there looking lost in a gross school uniform. I was apparently planning to storm the courtroom and demand Lilly Mason be freed from tyranny and unlawfulness in knee high socks and a plaid pleated skirt. Awesome.

Chapter Thirty-Eight

I took a quick glance at Evangeline's passport before handing it over to the desk clerk, a twenty something girl with too much make-up on. Luckily for me, Evangeline's passport picture was taken when she was ten and so there was a little leeway for growth.

Although she was still a brunette six years after the picture was taken, my shade of brown was not so nutmeg, but rather just straight black. And her eyes were definitely blue, and mine were definitely not.

The clerk looked at the passport picture and then at me, and then back at the picture and then again back at me. I gave her a nervous smile and tugged on my newly purchased red Nebraska football sweatshirt. I released my magic full force through my veins, knocking over a display a few feet away. I jumped, startled and realized if I didn't get my magic under control, they were going to call the police. Who knew magic could get nervous?

"I hate that picture," I cleared my throat and tried to sound confident. I attempted to send some magic her way again, but was afraid I would knock her over too if I didn't relax.

"Hmmm…." she frowned suspiciously. "Do you have another form of ID on you? A driver's license or something?" she put the passport and ticket on the counter and tapped her fingers impatiently.

"Y-y-yes I think I do," I stammered out, pretending to dig through my bag looking for it. My bag was not that deep, it was just a backpack and mostly empty since I had left all of my books in the car, but I needed to milk it for all it was worth.

"Isn't that your wallet?" she asked, as the item in question nearly fell from my hands. I gave her an irritated half-smile and handed it over. Once she saw not only the picture, but the name on it, this half-assed plan was over.

A creepy crawly feeling of irritation swept over me; I just wanted to get on that plane. I glanced over at the clerk and felt the same sense of irritation flood her, and that was when I realized I didn't have to be smooth. I didn't have to do what Avalon did. It was great that he could make other people feel safe and secure and smiley, but that was just not me right then. I was pissed, I was irritated and I was in a big freaking hurry. If nothing else, I could at least make her emote with me.

I released my magic a little too strongly and I saw the young clerk take a visible step backwards. I began to feel guilty for hurting the poor girl, but then she gave me a dirty look that reminded me a little too much of Seraphina. Suddenly she was looking at the clock and processing my airline ticket. She let out a huge huff of impatience, handing me my respective papers quickly.

"I assume you won't be checking any bags?" she looked disdainfully at my worn out book bag.

"Nope," I said, returning her irritation with a smile and breathing a sigh of relief.

She turned to the next passenger in line and I ran up the escalator. It could not have been that easy! Finally something was going my way. I didn't slow down until I made it through security, to my terminal and onto the walkway.

A pretty flight attendant with perfect posture greeted me at the doorway to the plane. I handed over my ticket grateful for assistance and she pointed just inside the doorway to a luxurious first class seat next to a window.

I sat down heavily and breathed another sigh of relief. I took a hair tie off of my wrist and knotted my hair into a messy bun on the top of my head. Per instructions of the flight attendant I stored my nearly empty backpack underneath my seat and buckled up for safety.

I looked out of my window at Omaha for one last time; I had never flown before, let alone overseas. I had no idea what to expect and less of an idea what to do when I got there. After my connecting flight in Atlanta I would be non-stop until Romania. The bright afternoon sunlight flooded my window and I relished in the warmth and security of self-righteousness. Lilly needed me and I refused to let her down.

I breathed in the smoke and smog that met me outside the dingy glass doors of the airport in Timisoara, Romania. The wide-lane street in front of me was full of small cabs in every color. Most of them were driven by middle-aged, olive-skinned Romanian men with mustaches and cigarettes. And all of the cars looked at least fifty years old.

I walked over to one of the parked Dacias, waiting to take me on the next leg of this exhausting adventure. I tugged at the oversized cruise wear I acquired at a gift shop in the Atlanta airport and realized that it was not nearly warm enough for the cold and dreary autumn of Romania.

"English?" I asked hopeful, to a gruff looking Romanian man wearing a worn out black leather jacket. He shook his head and grunted what I took to be an amused laugh.

I pulled out the English to Romanian dictionary I also purchased at the Atlanta airport and searched for the T section.

"Statie?" I stumbled through the word, using what I knew from my Spanish pronunciations to ask for the train station.

"Da, da. Timisoara?" he clarified our destination, since the airport was outside of the city a little ways.

"Da." I repeated the Russian "yes", most Romanians used.

He nodded his head towards the back seat and I climbed in. The springs underneath the well-worn upholstery dug into my sore legs. I yawned, but refused to close my eyes. Not that I necessarily trusted this stranger, nor did I know how long the ride would be exactly, but there was much too much to see as we made our way towards the western metropolis of Timisoara.

Communist block apartments rose on every side of me; the tall, simple, concrete buildings emoted a melancholy dismalness that was enforced by the incessant rainfall. Small corner shops and gypsy children begging for money lined the now narrowed streets as I held on for dear life. The driver swerved in and out of traffic more precariously than Avalon and not nearly as gracefully.

The olive skinned Romanians walked, or biked or took the tram, all with their heads down, minding their own business. In my Guide to Romania book I picked up along with my dictionary, I read that the Romanians fought their way out of Communism by a revolution started in this very city. What was once called the Paris of the East was only a shell of its former glory.

Timisoara was destroyed by Communism after World War II; the Communist dictatorship that enslaved the Romanian people

278

raped them of any technological or artistic advancement. And although they were well on their way to recovery after a Revolution that had happened over twenty years ago, there was still an oppressiveness that settled on the country's inhabitants.

I had yet to read anything in either of my books pertaining to an Immortal Citadel. In fact, the only folk lore of any kind related to vampires. I had no idea where I would end up or what to expect but for some reason entering Romania was like coming home. The desolate streets and war torn buildings held an eerie beauty I found captivating.

The cab slammed to a stop in front of an old building on the edge of a piazza or square. The driver tapped his finger on the meter, indicating the fare I owed him. I clumsily tried to count out the Lei, but in the end I threw a stack of bills at him, hoping he appreciated the tip.

I exchanged plenty of money in the airport, and was told that most places accepted my American credit card anyway. Hopefully, Aunt Syl wouldn't be too upset with the credit card bill this month. Who was I kidding? If it wasn't the bill that made her go ballistic, it would surely be my spur of the moment trip across an ocean to a third world country after I was specifically forbidden not to by more than one authority.

I shouldered my backpack once again; its weight had definitely increased throughout the trip, from old clothes to my new books, it was getting kind of heavy. I pulled the straps tight though, hoping to discourage any type of pickpocket and worked my way through the busy train station doors.

My travel guide had informed me that the Blue Arrow train was the only way to travel in style and I decided to take its word for it. I found the ticket counter without any problem, and pulled out my dictionary for the necessary terms. A stout, elderly woman who had seen better days sat behind a thick glass partition.

"Buna dimineata, doamna" I stuttered through, reading directly from a page marked Popular Phrases in my English to Romanian Dictionary. *Good morning madam.*

She grunted her reply, and I forged through another phrase.

"Un bilet la Sibiu va rog," *One ticket for Sibiu, please.* I gave her my award winning smile and she simply grunted back what I assumed to be a number, but I had no idea really. She could have said anything; she probably called me a stupid American.

I held up a small handful of cash, unsure of what any of it meant. Unfortunately, Kingsley didn't offer a monetary conversion class. Or maybe I just hadn't been forced to take it yet.

She took my handful of Lei and counted out what she needed; even if she took a little more for herself it didn't bother me. She passed me back the change along with a ticket and pointed in the direction of the platform, holding up her hand to signal five minutes.

"Multumesc," I tried again, saying thank you before walking away quickly to the platform.

I found the train I was assigned to and it was thankfully the Blue Arrow. The only modern and smooth looking ride among a line of trains that looked like they could be the first model of a train…. ever. Breathing my one hundredth sigh of relief I walked through the automatic doors, passed seats filled with all different social classes of Romanian.

The train was slightly deceiving in that I expected luxury once inside the automatic doors, but instead was met with a pungent smell that nearly made me hurl. I politely covered my mouth pretending to cough and collapsed into my seat, just in time to hear the whistle and feel the earth begin to move slowly beneath my feet.

On the long plane ride over I had time to plan and plot. I had gone over my speech a thousand times, and I was determined to give it once inside the court room doors. The only problem was that I needed to be able to find the courtroom.

The town of Sibiu was located in the central part of Romania and in the mountains; this was as far as I knew to go. I only remembered the name of the town Kiran had given me after I recognized it in the guidebook.

The biggest problem was that the festival was for sure not in the city, and apparently somewhere in the middle of nowhere. The train would take me directly into the city, but once I was there, I would have no other direction to follow. I was still determined; although regretful I hadn't pressured Avalon for more information.

The train left the city and wound through the breathtaking

Romanian countryside. I refused to sleep during that part of my journey too and watched as the train flew by fields being farmed by old fashioned horses and wagons and primitive gypsy villages with naked children running about.

Eventually someone came by to take my ticket. The train employee laughed out loud at my white, sleeveless sweater tank top and ocean blue capris. If only he knew the clothing options I was given in the middle of an Atlanta airport while trying to catch my international flight, I thought he might have been proud of me.

After he continued on his way, I realized how ridiculous I looked. I hadn't slept in two days; my long hair was greasy and knotted into an impossible mess on the top of my head. The cruise wear I purchased was obviously out of season, and then to top it off I was still wearing my school clogs. A cold shiver ran over my body and giving up completely I pulled out my bright red Nebraska Corn Huskers sweatshirt and threw it on over my tank top.

I remembered Avalon's expensive black suit and tie and cringed to think how out of place I would look upon arrival at the Citadel…. if I could find it. By my calculations the trial would be late this evening, and I had only precious hours until my time was up and all of this would have been for nothing.

I hugged my worn out back pack as if it were my last hope for success. I couldn't have come this far for nothing; I wouldn't have come this far and do nothing.

"You're one of them," An elderly woman took a seat next to me and spoke perfect English. I sat up shocked to hear my own tongue and even more shocked by her words.

"Excuse me?" A wave of nervousness washed over me, and I searched out a current of magic in the old woman but sensed nothing.

"One of the Old Ones," the woman smiled genially and revealed toothless gums. I did not know what to make of the woman who was clearly human and by the looks of things, a gypsy. She was dressed in layer upon layer of rags, her hair tied behind a dirty bandana. A large gold ring protruded from her nose, and larger golden rings dangled from her ears. Her hands were small and gnarled; the dirt under her nails prominent. Her eyes, a brilliant violet, were her only beautiful quality. They reminded me of Angelica.

"The Old Ones?" I asked, confident she meant Immortals, but unsure how she would know about us, or that I was one of them.

She reached out suddenly to grab my hands. Hers were warm and moist as they gripped mine firmly. I tentatively tried to pull them back, but her grasp was so tight and her gaze so intense I was honestly scared of her. I thought to offer her money, but she began to inspect my palms as if looking for something in particular.

"It can't be," she sighed softly taking my hands and holding them high above me towards the light.

"I'm sorry?" I pulled my hands away from her and tucked them under my arms, afraid of what she found. A chill worked its way up my spine.

"You are the next Oracle," she spoke with such awe and her gaze searched my eyes so intently that I looked down, once again afraid of this tiny old woman.

"Do you know where they are? The Old Ones?" I found my nerves and asked bravely; although I was unsure why I would trust this stranger.

"Do you not?" she pinched my chin tightly between her thumb and forefinger, and then moved my head in a circle, inspecting it for who knew what.

"No, I am…. I am trying to find them," I confided, still unsure if I could trust her.

"You are going to the mountain village?" she asked turning my head sharply in one direction and then letting out a loud giggle.

"Yes," I said, hoping she meant Sibiu.

"Then follow the magic," she suddenly stood up, then bent down and kissed my forehead with wet, sticky lips. I refrained from wiping off the slobber immediately. "They have waited for you for a long time."

The train suddenly lurched to a stop, sending me sliding forward in my seat. I looked up, expecting the feeble, older woman to be sprawled on the floor since she was standing precariously during the sudden stop, but she was already at the doors and gone before I could even get out of my seat. After she was safely on the ground the train began again as if it was scheduled to make that very stop.

Chapter Thirty-Nine

The gypsy woman still a mystery, the train came to a stop in the humble, but beautiful town of Sibiu. I exited the train, backpack in tow, to an outdoor platform. I breathed in the less polluted air of the countryside and lifted my face to the late afternoon sun, whose warmth I barely felt. I pulled the hood up on my sweatshirt and took in another big breath.

It was during that breath, that I finally felt it; the small hum of magic coming from some distance away. It was almost like a calling; the buzzing electricity beckoned me to find it.

I took another big breath and let the distant call of magic fill me. I may not have known exactly where to go, but at least I had a general direction to follow.

I looked around for cab drivers, but the smaller town wasn't as convenient as the booming Western city of Timisoara. In fact, the town looked nearly deserted. The tourist shops were all closed and the streets empty. I didn't know how far the Citadel was from this small town, but it was too far to walk, the magic could at least assure me of that.

I had no choice for now however, and began to jog in the direction of where I felt like the magic was located. The city was very hilly and I found myself walking up a very steep incline when I finally stumbled upon a cab driver taking a smoke and sitting on the hood of his run down Dacia.

"English?" I asked, not expecting much.

"Da. English," he smiled, and I could see rows of gold teeth behind dirty lips.

"Can you drive me?" I pointed in the direction I wanted to go in.

"Not that way," he shook his head rapidly and then spat on the ground.

"I will pay you," I said clearly and pulled out my stack of Lei again.

"Not enough to go that way," he looked back in the direction with an expression of fear.

"Please," I said plainly and when he shook his head no again, I resorted to begging. "Please, please," I cried out.

"Why do you want to go that way?" he asked with a thick accent.

"I have to save my friend," I begged, helplessly. "Please."

"I will not take you all the way, but I will get you close enough, da?" his expression was full of pity and I was so thankful that I rushed over and hugged the poor man. He spat his cigarette out and choked on the smoke, completely surprised by the affection.

Before he could recover I hopped into the back seat, a near replica of the first taxi I was in. I exhaled, but was unable to relax. Once the driver successfully started the stubborn car, my nerves only grew. I rehearsed again and again the case I intended to make for Lilly, my stomach turning into knots.

The cab drove out of the city and into the winding roads of the mountains. The countryside only became more beautiful; millions of trees in all different fall shades blanketed the horizon. Their loveliness stretched out across the rising hills and as the sun set lower in the sky, their reds and oranges melted into one extraordinary canvas of color.

The center of magic grew stronger and stronger the deeper we found our way into the lush forest; its call became more clarified. At this point I could have given directions to the driver, but he seemed perfectly able to find the way on his own. And as the magic intensified, the poor driver's speed decreased. The pitiable man was clearly terrified of a force I would not have expected him to be aware of.

I watched him become more and more agitated, lighting thin cigarette after thin cigarette, never allowing his mouth to sit idle. I wondered what sparked his anxiety, unsure if he was even conscious of exactly what he was afraid of.

Whether it was his nervousness that rubbed off on me or my own sense of foreboding I couldn't tell; but I did wonder if I shouldn't be proceeding with a little more caution. I thought of my purpose again though and my determination was renewed.

Lilly, who had done nothing wrong, who fought to save the very Prince who condemned her. Lilly, sweet Lilly, who had never said a hurtful word about anyone and befriended me when no one else would. She wasn't afraid of the consequences of her actions when she defended Kiran, why should I be?

As the sun took its lowest place on the horizon before it dipped below the never ending peaks and valleys, the driver finally slowed to a complete stop. He looked up towards the wilderness with mouth open, eyes wide, his cigarette hanging precariously from his lips.

"Multumesc," I mumbled quickly and threw my remaining stack of Lei in the front seat. He didn't respond to me, but as soon as the door was closed he performed a quick u-turn and sped off down the hill.

At this point the magic was so strong I knew I was only steps from the Citadel. Completely unsure what to expect next, I began my trek off the road and into the wooded wilderness. There was a steep hill I had to climb, I was hoping at the top I would be able to take in my surroundings a bit better.

Time was of the essence, so I did my best to hurry. Thankful for my devotion to yoga and the sudden necessity of magic, I scaled the vertical incline. Despite the electricity rushing through my veins, and the flexibility yoga had blessed me with, I fell several times and began to sweat despite the coolness of the evening.

By the time I reached the top of the hill I was covered in dirt and my hair was soaked with sweat. I did, however, get a better perspective once I could see more of what was ahead of me. I saw the low glow of lights in the distance, they encompassed a valley a few hills away from mine. The lights stretched out in a square of sorts and I took this to be the Citadel. I also felt the magic swirling about, indicating a large gathering of Immortals.

For a moment I was seized with anxiety and doubt. I forced myself to breathe, reminding myself for the millionth time my purpose. I picked up my pace; running down the next hill and doing my best to hike quickly up the following one. I became more and more dirty and I smelled a distinct odor not at all pleasing.

Eventually, I stood above the Citadel on a surrounding hill. I paused for a moment to take in the sight. The Citadel was huge, nestled into a valley surrounded by camouflaging hills. It was bordered by walls as if it was once a fort, or still was a fort of some type. Buildings lined three of the inside walls, with more buildings built into the center. The fourth wall was left as a type of

286

entrance, only with large doors that could be closed if needed.

The Citadel reminded me of some type of medieval village, with a castle positioned towards the back and clearly the most protected structure inside the walls. The spires of the castle wound towards the sky, each window lighted by a soft yellow glow. The streets of the city were littered with Immortals of every color and race. Several men stood at the entrance gates stopping people as they came or went.

I hiked down the hill and then around the Eastern wall to the gates. I took my time so that I could observe others enter through the wide doors, hoping to emulate their example. The Guards at the gate reminded me of Talbott and had a strict, military way about them. I noticed that they also carried both a gun and a sword attached at their belts. The people entering the gates were all stopped and asked to give their first and last name. They were then asked to hold out their palms so that the guards could grasp their hands firmly. The people were all clearly Immortal, I had no trouble reading that off of them, and it made me wonder if the guards were searching for something else.

I noticed one other fact about the people entering the gate, making my nerves skyrocket once again. All of the people, without exception were very well dressed. The women wore expensive ball gowns and the men were dressed in full tuxedos. Hair done, makeup done, expensive shoes, couture jewelry, it didn't matter, these people went all out.

I looked down at my pathetic shambles of clothing and took a sniff under my armpit; not pretty. I paused for a final moment to stop and reassemble my hair which was nearly impossible to unhinge from the hair tie. Eventually I succeeded, but not having a mirror around, I suspected I might have done more damage than good. I smoothed out my Nebraska hoodie and took a confident step forward. I'd made it this far....

"Name," a gruff Guard demanded when it was my turn. I could feel more than hear the Guards' confusion with my appearance.

"Eden Matthews," I said clearly.

The Guard looked over his list, and then over it again, clearly not finding my name. I hadn't realized there would be a guest list. The Guard looked me over skeptically at first, but then his expression turned to disgust and for a moment I thought I might be in trouble.

"Give me your hand," he grunted menacingly.

I obeyed, sticking out my palm and allowing him to grip it firmly between his.

"Your name's not on the list. Who are your parents? And why do you look like that?" two other Guards walked over to listen to my explanation.

"I go to school at Kingsley," I started to explain, realizing I knew nothing about this people group I belonged to. "I came with Seraphina Van Curen, we go to school together. My parents couldn't come, they're on business in India," lies tumbled out of my mouth built from random pieces of overheard information, and I forced my magic into submission, refusing to let it give me away. "I just went for a hike, but I am going to shower and change before I attend the feast tonight," I offered a wide smile, but then closed my lips quickly afraid of what my breath smelt like after not brushing my teeth since the airline bathroom.

"With Ms. Van Curen?" The guard asked skeptically. I nodded my head affirmatively and pushed a little magic his way, hoping he didn't notice. I knew it worked on humans, but I had no idea what the outcome would be on another Immortal.

"Please I would really like to be ready on time," I stared past the Guards as if I knew exactly where I was going once inside the gates.

"They just started the trial; you'll have plenty of time before the feast," the Guards made a path for me to fit through and the first Guard nodded his head for me to pass.

I rushed past them and into the narrow streets of the Citadel. If they had already started the trial, I didn't have much time. From the top of the hill I was able to see exactly where I had needed to go; but from the streets below I could not have been more lost. I moved in the direction of where I thought the castle was and let my magic lead the way.

I put all of my hope in the castle ahead of me. I didn't know for sure where the trial would be held, but logic encouraged me to examine the castle first. I sprinted full force through the mobs of people lingering about in the streets. My sole purpose was to get to that trial before a verdict was given.

Out of breath and out of willpower, I stumbled into a square by chance. Tall edifices surrounded a cobblestone piazza with an enormous fountain in the middle. The square was lit up with a thousand lanterns strung together and hanging from the buildings surrounding the fountain. Musicians played Beethoven and I glanced over expecting to see an orchestra, but was surprised by the eight or so Immortals that made up an intricate string ensemble.

With renewed vigor I took the remaining distance in strides and ran through the open castle doors. The floors of the castle were marble and I was suddenly sliding across the lobby trying to stop. Another Guard looked up at me from his post just inside the doors.

"Trial?" I asked, breathless and unable to slow down for a minute to listen.

"Through those doors," he pointed to a set of brass double doors that were almost an exact match for the ones at Kingsley. "But you can't go in there like that," he glared disdainfully at my red sweatshirt and I realized that he was probably right.

"Bathroom?" I patted my backpack like it had the answer to my disturbing appearance.

He pointed to a door positioned behind him and I rushed past. The bathroom was surprisingly modern, despite the old world appearance of the place. I didn't have time to take a good look however and I got straight to business.

I headed directly to the sink and mirror and was almost horrified to see the image staring back at me. My face was caked in mud and dirt and my hair was a big pile of tangles. My mascara and eyeliner had dripped down my face. I looked like a dirty raccoon. My clothing was completely ruined, not to mention the fact that it didn't match to begin with. I could only do so much and decided to focus on my face.

I turned the cold water on and splashed my face, scrubbing it roughly. Once it was clean, or at least clear of mud and makeup, I focused on my hair. I ripped the pony tail holder out and did my best to comb through the tangled mess with my fingers. Thankfully it was greasy enough that my frizz was actually more tamed than usual. I decided to leave it down, hoping the length and color would disguise the bright redness of my ridiculous sweatshirt that under normal circumstances I would have been proud to wear.

I finished quickly and turned to face the door. I decided the quickest route into the courtroom and then took one final breath before throwing the bathroom door open, sprinting through the lobby and bursting through the double brass doors.

"Lilly Mason is innocent!" I yelled at the top of my lungs, adrenaline and nerves getting the best of me.

Chapter Forty

The courtroom was silent, all eyes turned towards me; mouths fell open, a pin drop could be heard. After my outburst, I found myself speechless; I was disoriented. This was not at all what I had expected.

I took in the unexpected sight quickly, unsure what to make of my surroundings. I didn't know what I thought I would find, but the courtroom looked more like a cathedral than a place for judge and jury. The ceiling was vaulted all the way to the top of the castle spire; large stained glass windows extended two of the walls with elaborate and colorful designs reaching from floor to ceiling. The other wall, not containing the entrance doors was made of stone and practically bare, except for a large tapestry hanging in the center.

At the front of the room was a large imposing throne, at least twenty feet tall and made of what looked to be solid gold. An extremely good looking man of maybe thirty, sat straight edged, staring at me; his crown of more gold was slightly cockeyed on his head. The crown adorned with rubies and emeralds glistened on top of short golden locks, and matched his closely cropped goatee.

I stood there staring at him, wondering if I should bow or curtsy or continue with my testimony. He was obviously the King; unfortunately, I couldn't remember anything I had practiced to say. He jumped up suddenly and I took a step back; his simple gesture frightened me. He wore a long crimson robe and swept it back as he moved to stand. The entire room of people sat silently, waiting for him to say something.

My eyes finally fell on Lilly who was positioned in the middle of the room, surrounded by rows and rows of people forming a type of octagon around her. She was wearing a simple black robe with a hood, and her vibrant red hair stood out in stark contrast. She was boxed in on every side by what looked like a witness box, sitting on a stool in the middle. Our eyes met for only a second, but the gratitude she relayed to me in those brief moments made my entire trip worth it.

"Excuse me," Kiran's familiar voice nearly shouted his

apology and all at once he moved from his place next to his father and towards me.

I looked back over at the King, whose expression I couldn't read; something like anger, or surprise or a mixture of the two, but then there was something much deeper in his eyes. Kiran practically ran to me from his throne that was barely a smaller version of his father's. He too was wearing a golden crown adorned with colorful jewels and sitting crooked on his head. His longer locks, a little unruly underneath, gave him an almost wild appearance, but one I was infinitely attracted to.

"What are you doing here?" he whispered fiercely in my ear. He grabbed my arms firmly in his and shoved me forward to the base of the throne. "Curtsy," he whispered again even harsher and half pushed me into the position. I was confused enough not to fight him, although this was not exactly what I had planned. "Excuse us," he said loudly again, only this time he addressed the entire courtroom.

He turned to walk purposefully past the rows of people and through a side door, dragging me along with him. I tried to fight him off my arms, after all, I hadn't finished my testimony, but his grip was so tight I realized there was no use. Once we were through the wide brass door, he threw me out of his arms roughly. I struggled to regain my balance and when I finally was able to stand strongly I turned directly to give him a piece of my mind.

"Don't even start with me!" he spoke softly, but his voice was full of venom. "I told you not to come, I ordered you not to come. What the hell are you doing here?" he began to pace frantically, glancing at the door every several seconds.

"Somebody had to stand up for Lilly!" I felt like shouting, but I used the volume example he set instead, although I filled my voice with as much irritation as I could muster.

"Well you did that, didn't you? And made a fool of yourself! And now you'll probably be sentenced to a worse fate than she would ever have been! How could you be so reckless?" he continued to pace, and glance at the door, but eventually he added a nervous glance in my direction. His eyes were filled with fear and anxiety and the way he looked at me made my anger melt away despite the verbal lashing I was receiving.

"All because of a stupid interruption?" I asked, finally

taking the situation seriously.

"Because of who your parents are and because you look exactly like your bloody mother!" he finally stopped pacing and walked over to me, bringing me into his arms. I let him, confused once again, but comforted by his affection.

The door opened and he pulled me tighter into him, shielding me from the intruder. I could feel him hold his breath and when I looked up at him his eyes were shut tight, but as soon as the door closed and it was clear the only person that entered the room was Amory, he relaxed and exhaled. I was so confused by his behavior; I had no idea what to feel.

"What are you doing here?" Amory whispered, clearly enraged. "It doesn't even matter now. What are you going to do with her?" he turned his attention to Kiran, practically pleading with him.

"I can't...." Kiran's voice broke and I heard the emotion in his voice. Tears came to my eyes as my emotions were so tied up in his, I couldn't bear to see him so upset. "You have to take her; you have to get her the hell out of here. You have to save her, Amory," Amory stared, wide eyed and clearly in shock at Kiran's demands. "You can't let him take her. Please.... I can't lose her," his voice broke again and I saw that his eyes were full of tears.

"I don't know what to.... I won't. I won't let him anywhere near her," Amory's confusion disappeared and I watched him mentally set his mind to a plan.

"Do whatever Amory says, Eden," Kiran turned his attention back to me, gazing into my eyes and hugging my tighter. "You have to get as far away from here as possible."

"No," I said simply, unwilling to be as melodramatic as these two.

"Don't you understand what he will do to you if he finds out who you really are? He is most likely already suspicious, you look just like her," Kiran pulled me closer still, pressing my head against his chest. He rested his chin on the top of my forehead. I wondered at the "he" they referred to.

"I don't know what you're talking about," I said softly, but firmly. "There is no way I am leaving Lilly! Do you know what I went through to get here?"

"I don't care what you went through!" he pushed me away

with his arms to look me in the face; but his hands never left my body. "He will kill you, Eden, do you understand that?" Kiran whispered fiercely to me, and I was physically taken aback. I looked over at Amory hoping for answers, but he simply nodded in agreement with Kiran.

"Then you save her," I demanded, glaring at Kiran, firm in my solution.

"You can't be serious! I will be lucky if I can explain you away. My father will never allow that!" his accent was thick and crisp and every bit of irritation and frustration was evident in it.

"I am completely serious. If you can't protect Lilly, then I will stay and fight for her myself," I struggled from his grasp and folded my arms stubbornly.

"No, you will absolutely not," Kiran crossed his arms in an equally defiant pose.

A knock on the door leading to the courtroom startled Kiran and he once again took a defensive pose in front of me. Amory opened the door just enough to reveal a beautiful woman with long, dark auburn hair, adorned by a dainty golden crown. I watched as Kiran stiffened in front of me and I felt the surge of magic that flared beneath his skin.

"I'm sorry for the interruption," the woman began, "But your father has requested that you join us once again," she smiled congenially at him, never looking beyond him. Her eyes stared at the floor just before his feet.

"I'll be there in a moment mother," Kiran responded softly.

"Is that her?" the woman's voice was strained and almost too soft to hear.

"Of course not." Kiran's voice was masked by cheerfulness but he took another step backwards in my direction, shielding me further from sight.

The woman's eyes flickered once in my direction before she quietly shut the door and we were once again alone. Amory opened a wooden door parallel to the door leading to the courtroom and I saw that it led to a dim hallway. The floors and walls were made of the same stone as the courtroom.

"Take her to my room," Kiran announced loudly and suddenly.

Amory began to pull me out of the room, and I understood that Kiran's demand was only for show. Wherever Amory planned to take me would most likely not be Kiran's bedroom. I fought Amory, but only weakly, I knew I had no choice in the matter.

"Please, Kiran," I begged. "Please save her." Tears welled in my eyes and I wasn't for sure if they were for Lilly or Kiran.

He let out a soft grunt of frustration, but I could see that his eyes were resigned. He would help her. He put his hand on the door handle opposite ours, but turned around quickly as if he forgot something. He took the length of the room in two long strides and suddenly I was wrapped in his arms and his lips were against mine.

Kiran pressed his mouth on mine desperately. He dipped me back so that I was fully in his embrace. I gave up all fight and let his lips melt into mine. Our magic mingled together in a fervent, passionate, overwhelming force that left me breathless and wild. His hand grasped at my hair, tangling his fist into my dark locks.

When he finally released me, the emotion in his face was indefinable but I understood it since it was the emotion mirrored in mine. He pushed me out of the room towards Amory and I found myself swept up in Amory's tight grasp as I fought to return to him.

"Promise me nothing will happen to her," Kiran commanded Amory, and when Amory hesitated out of confusion, Kiran demanded louder, "Promise me!"

"I promise," Amory whispered quietly and with steady resolve.

Then the door was closed and I was running down a dark hallway, Amory practically pushing me to move faster. I was done asking questions. Nothing made sense; nothing was ever explained to me. For now I would do as I was told because Kiran asked me to, but there would come a time very, very soon when I would get my answers.

I glanced over my shoulder at the closed door and the room that only seconds ago housed the most intimate moment Kiran and I had ever shared. As I ran blindly in the dark, my feelings for Kiran were finally clarified. I loved him, with every breath I had, with all of my soul, I loved him. And I would do anything it took to be with him.

Chapter Forty-One

"Through here," Amory ordered, pushing me through another darkened passageway.

We had been running through the bowels of the castle for at least twenty minutes. Amory seemed to know exactly where he was going and I tried to trust him, but remained skeptical. I was once again a sweaty mess and wished we could stop for a moment so I could remove my sweatshirt. My hair flew wildly about me, sticking to the perspiration running down my face.

"Where are we going?" I asked, out of breath, stumbling a little in the dark.

"As far from here as possible," he responded, pushing me forward with his hands. "And through here," he suddenly turned right and took the lead. I struggled to keep up with him.

The passageway was dark and narrow, there was barely enough room for us to face forward between the cool stone walls. At one point we had taken stairs leading downwards, so I assumed we were somewhere underneath the castle. I was still unsure why we had to make this escape, but as long as Kiran kept his promise, I would keep mine and follow Amory without question.

"Stop," Amory whispered fiercely, pressing his body against the wall and thrust out his arm, forcing me to do the same.

We were quiet, both afraid of the unknown. The only sound I could hear was my own frantic breathing; I wiped the sweat from my brow, pushing my long hair behind my ears. Amory also breathed heavily, but I had been surprised at his level of fitness. He was awfully spry for someone of his age.

"Eden," he said softly, but gravely. "I need you to turn off your magic completely. I need you to repress it like you did before you knew what it was. Hold your magic in until we are safe. Can you do that?" he turned his head to give me a serious stare and I nodded my reply.

I pushed the magic down, making it dissolve completely from my veins. I was suddenly tired and sluggish. I hadn't realized how much the magic had kept me going; but after several days of no sleep and extenuating travel circumstances, any normal human would have been delirious by now.

At our stilled position and with our backs pushed heavily against the cool stone, the exhaustion began to take over. My knees became weak and without my permission my body started to slide down the rock wall towards the uneven floor. Amory pulled my exhausted body back into a standing position by the arm and shook me roughly.

"We have to keep going. Will you make it?" he asked, forcing me to look into his eyes by gripping the sides of my head firmly.

"I can make it," I mumbled weakly, not sure if it was possible, but determined to try. I shook my head feebly, trying to wake myself up.

"Think of Lilly," Amory coaxed, "Think of Kiran," he finally had my attention and I brought my body into a strong standing position.

"Let's go," I said with more energy.

Amory grabbed my wrist and pulled me along behind him. We ran, half stumbled in the darkness through the cool corridors. I never heard another footstep or sound other than ours, but I had no doubt that we were being hunted. I kept up with Amory the best I could; with my magic gone, normal, human adrenaline was forced to take over.

Suddenly we were faced with a dead end. The hallway had narrowed considerably and then came to a point where the two parallel walls met. I wondered what we were going to do now.

Amory let go of my wrist and I fell hard against the cool stone. I could barely keep my eyes open, but curiosity gave me a few more moments of consciousness.

Amory felt the point of the wall, letting his hands fall over every stone and every crevice. He started at the top of the wall and worked his way down to the floor, quickly and efficiently. He pushed firmly on random rocks, as if looking for one in particular.

Finally, he let out a small grunt of approval, and I watched his fingers disappear in what seemed to be the middle of the floor. He braced his body and then grunted louder removing a large block of stone from the floor and revealing a ladder leading further under the castle.

I forced my body away from the wall and began to descend the ladder without any instruction needed. Obviously this was our only option. I heard water beneath me, but was blinded by complete darkness descending slowly into the black abyss. I could still see Amory's face as I took the shaky ladder, rung by rung, deep into the blackness.

After I was far enough down the ladder for Amory to follow, he stood on one of the top rungs and slid the rock floor back into place. I saw a type of handle underneath the faux floor that made it easy to be returned home. Once the floor was in place we were completely in the dark and I was nearly paralyzed by fear of the unknown.

The ladder hung precariously from the ceiling of the cavernous hole and swayed back and forth with our body weight. Every move, every step, every breath we took evoked a rusty creaking sound that had me seizing up in fear. I forced my appendages to move and forbade my mind to consider the possibilities of this ladder crashing to the black chasm beneath us.

The sound of water grew stronger the lower we climbed, and I made the assumption of a creek or brook flowing through wherever we were headed. My eyes began to adjust to the blackness, but it was too dark to make anything out for sure. I wondered if Amory was using magic or if he repressed his as well.

Eventually my foot found the ground in an awkward step that made my knee give out. I didn't catch myself in time and fell to the solid ground in an uncomfortable heap.

Once on solid ground, I pushed myself up to my hands and knees and felt through the dirt as I crawled forward or at least in a forward direction until the ground ended and another stone wall ascended in its place.

I gripped the wall, using it to pull my body up into a standing position again. Wherever we were now was clearly far beneath ground because the temperature had dropped drastically. The water source was definitely a running stream of some type because I could hear the water moving purposefully. The air was clean and clear and I took a big breath in, happy for the moment to rest.

I heard Amory's feet reach the solid ground and the ladder ceased from creaking. I listened for his footsteps to move in a direction, but I heard only the sound of the water. I was afraid to call out to him, since he had yet to speak a word.

300

I heard a scraping sound and my heart jumped, but when sparks flew through the darkness I realized Amory had only lit a match. A small flame burned alone until Amory used it to ignite a larger torch. The darkness was illuminated and I finally made out my surroundings.

We were in a type of cavern, with rock walls on every side. A single river ran through the middle at a quick pace. The surface we stood on was wide, and the ladder leading to the castle above was positioned closer to the stone wall than the river and its dangerous current. I pressed my cheek against the cold stone one more time before joining Amory at the river's edge.

There was about a ten foot drop from the dirt surface to the rushing river below. I saw another rusted ladder built into the earth leading directly down into the water, with a small row boat tied to the orange metal. Two sets of oars lay on the bottom of the boat and a lantern was positioned at its stern. I looked at Amory with controlled fear, and he stared back with the same trepidation.

"Eden, we have to row upstream. It is very difficult, I won't lie to you. But if we follow the current it will take us straight back to the Citadel. We have to row against it, do you understand? I am not sure if you will make it," he was honest with me, and I saw the pain in his eyes through the flickering light of the torch.

"How far?" I asked, afraid he was right.

"At least two hours in the water, and then another three and a half hour hike after that. Can you repress your magic that long?" his eyes lost their pain and became determined. We both knew there was no other option.

"Yes," I said simply, I had no other choice.

"I can't do it alone. You will have to help me row," I nodded with determination and took off my Nebraska Sweatshirt stuffing it into my backpack, and then tossed it into the rowboat.

Amory rolled up the sleeves of his suit shirt, and I realized that he used his suit jacket as the kindle for our torch. Amory handed me the torch and lowered himself over the edge and onto the ladder. He pulled the boat towards him with his long leg and then slowly took his steps onto the bow. Using the ladder for balance the entire time, he was eventually able to take a seat on one of the small boat's two benches.

301

I lay down on the dirt floor and lowered the torch to Amory who had to stand precariously to reach it. Once it was in his grip he lit the lantern at the bow and put the torch flame out by dunking it in water. Instead of discarding the burned jacket in the river, he brought it back into the boat and set it at his feet. The wet clothing left a puddle of water at the bottom of an already damp floor.

Once Amory was able to give me his full attention, I swung my legs over the edge and found the ladder with my feet. I began my descent carefully, if not a little shakily. Eventually my feet ran out of rungs and my toe swept the river, flooding my navy blue clogs with ice cold water. I stretched my leg behind me until my toe bumped against the solid wood of the row boat and I used the force of my leg muscles to pull the boat closer to the edge of the dirt wall.

Gripping the lower rungs tightly with my trembling fingers, I placed one foot and then the other firmly on the bow of the row boat. I used my stomach muscles this time to pull the drifting boat closer still and took a step off of the bow and on to the wet, slippery floor. Sliding precariously, I let go of the ladder rungs and fell heavily onto the bench.

Satisfied with a somewhat safe landing, I gripped the sides of the boat tightly as it rocked roughly back and forth. I was positioned on the first bench near the front of the boat, with Amory behind me. He handed me my oars and I slid them through the paddle holes, so that I would not lose them. Their cold wood was wet and slippery. I regretted taking off my sweatshirt as the river water splashed over the sides of the boat and sprayed my bare arms and face.

"Are you ready?" Amory asked gravely. I took a quick moment to throw my hair onto the top of my head, securing it with my hair tie. I then gripped the oars, braced my body and nodded in agreement. "Start rowing now, and once I release the rope I will fall into a pattern with you," I nodded again and took a big breath. "Eden…." Amory paused, "however hard this may be, we have no choice but to succeed," his words held such gravity that I could not even respond.

I focused what little strength I had left and began to sink my oars deep beneath the turbulent surface of the river. I brought them high above the water and then deep beneath over and over again, fighting the strong current, determined to win.

I heard Amory struggle with the knot and then felt the quick release of the boat. At first we were taken violently downstream, and I forced my weak fingers to hold onto the oars. Amory joined my struggle and eventually we fell into a labored routine; the oars dipping under and over the water simultaneously.

I began to see progress as we forced our bodies to do the impossible. The cavern shrunk to only a rounded tunnel where the water was allowed to flow through. As we left the large grotto and began our journey against the current and through the narrow channel, I felt a glimmer of hope. No matter how difficult this flight may be, something deep inside warned me that it was necessary.

I glanced back at Amory Saint working with all of his strength to propel us forward. His face was set and his eyes were hard with determination. I may not have any idea what we were running from, but whatever it was, had scared the hell out of him.

Chapter Forty-Two

Amory and I rowed through the dark silently; the only sound in the narrow tunnel was our oars dipping in and out of the strong current and the rush of water against the stone walls. My body was shaking violently from weakness and my arms did their best to move us forward. I braced my body on the small wooden bench, using every muscle I had to row.

The lantern at the stern of the boat, the only light piercing the heavy darkness, cast eerie shadows on the rounded walls. Amory had clearly taken this exit before, but I was too exhausted to garner any details. I had no sense of time, and felt barely coherent.

Amory said we would row for two hours, he did not say we would be rowing in a dark and claustrophobic tunnel of death for two hours. I wished I was wearing a watch, because I was too afraid to ask Amory how much longer. Any extra effort, including talking and I was sure that would finally be it for me. I had never known such exhaustion in my entire life and I was positive I never wanted to know the feeling again.

The river's current stayed quick and I never noticed a change in depth, although there might have been one; it was impossible to tell without testing it for myself. My feet were freezing from the ice cold water that made its way over the side and I stopped feeling my fingers a long time ago. They maintained their grasp on the oars however, as if obeying a command I forgot I gave them.

Amory grunted suddenly with the effort of another oar stroke. The sound echoed off of the low ceiling and close walls making me jump. My heart beat wildly, and my already labored breath quickened. Normally easily scared, I was actually grateful my heart was strong enough to still have a reaction.

"Sorry," Amory panted and I heard the strained tone in his voice as our oars once again disappeared beneath the rough surface of the water.

I shook my head as if to say it was ok, but couldn't force words out of my mouth. I pushed the oars under the rushing ripples and fought with everything I had to push them against the pressure of a force much greater than myself. The river fought back, convincing me to let my oar fall easily into its grip and float away. One more stroke, I decided; and then again, just one more stroke.

My eyes were focused on the dim circle of light the lantern illuminated; I could only see maybe ten or so feet in front of me. I centered on what I could to ensure the boat maintained a straight path, although something told me that Amory could have made the entire journey blinded.

A cool rush of air wrapped itself around me and I shuddered violently. Already frozen from the ice cold water, I dreaded the idea of a draft. When another gush of air rushed by me again, I began to hope. Maybe it was not a draft but the wind.

And then finally, the darkness softened around me into the midnight sky and a thousand stars twinkled above my head. The night air was frigid, whipping violently through the trees. The river widened once outside of the cave taking two paths, one through the black tunnel and the other around it. We were at the bottom of a valley, with hills rising on either side.

"Row over to the left bank," Amory grunted. I obeyed, grateful to be finished with that part of the journey.

Once near the river's edge, Amory jumped over the side quickly, knee deep in the rough current. He pushed the row boat up the side of the bank and tied the rope to a nearby tree.

When finally the boat was secured, he returned to my side and offered his hand to help me out. I pried my overworked fingers from the oars and placed a shaking hand in his. I stood up weakly, and allowed Amory to sustain most of my weight, nearly tumbling over the edge.

My feet landed in three feet of water, the violent current still rushing wildly around my shins, doing its best to knock me over. Amory braced me against his body and continued his support until we were safely on solid ground.

I collapsed onto the river bank, thankful to be out of the boat. I still felt the strange sensation of the movement of water and clutched the cool grass to steady myself. The ground was rough, and littered with sticks and rocks. They punctured and scraped my skin, but I was too exhausted to care.

Amory walked back to the boat once again to retrieve my

backpack. He took the liberty of digging my sweatshirt out of the wet pack and tossing it to me. I made no movement for it, unable to find the strength to sit up.

"We still have a ways to go," Amory's voice was tired but determined. I opened my eyes to look at him, hoping I could form words but nothing came. His eyes deepened with anxiety while he looked around suspiciously.

"I can make it," I finally mumbled. I pulled myself into a sitting position and found the strength to put my sweatshirt on. Although my backpack was wet from sitting at the bottom of the boat, my sweatshirt remained mostly dry.

Once the warmth of my Huskers sweatshirt was wrapped around me, I began to feel better. I pulled the hood up and tied the draw strings tight. Eventually I found the energy to stand up and shoulder my backpack again.

"Let me carry that," Amory offered, referring to my bag.

"It's alright, I can carry it for now," I waved him off and then shook both of my feet consecutively. My shoes were full of water, and my toes ached from the cold.

Suddenly a jolt of electricity surged through my blood. I jumped, startled by the sudden burst of energy. My blood heated into a boil and my exhausted trembles turned into tremors of nervous energy. I did my best to dispel the unwanted magic, but it stayed persistent.

"They're here," Amory whispered. I realized the mysterious burst of magic was a warning sign that another Immortal was close. I followed Amory's example and hunched over, crawling silently up the vertical incline.

He gestured with his hand to keep moving. I stayed as low to the ground as I could without actually crawling and stepped carefully. I was embarrassed by how clumsy I was as only human. I repressed my magic, although the temptation to use just a little bit was strong.

Just like at Kingsley when the other students' magic would trigger my own, so this unfamiliar stranger had shot off a warning sign through my veins. I couldn't help but be thankful however, as the hot blood had not only warmed my body, but given me an extra burst of energy making it possible to escape quickly now.

"As long as we stay human, I doubt they will be able to

follow us. Stay close and stay quiet," Amory instructed in a soft whisper. I struggled to hear through the whipping wind and rustling trees.

We continued our trek through the Romanian wilderness. The wind was strong and with every current of air the autumn leaves were carried off in all directions. Despite the chilliness of the night, the sky was clear and the moon shone bright.

Amory led the way up one steep slope and down another, over and over again. We may not have been hiking entire mountains, but these foothills might as well have been. My arms were exhausted from rowing, but finally able to rest. It was now my legs turn to bear the weight of our escape.

The nervous buzzing of unfamiliar magic began to dissipate and I noticed Amory relax a little. He slowed our pace somewhat, taking his time and treading carefully through the more dangerous inclines. Never once did he look up to consult our direction, he seemed to take every step confidently, as if the path we walked had been traveled many times before.

Through our seemingly endless expedition my thoughts drifted to Kiran. My lips burned with the memory of his farewell; the frantic, determination in which he pressed his mouth against mine made me push through the pain and exhaustion. I remembered his aqua eyes deep and searching, begging me to run.

A shudder slithered down my spine, totally unrelated to the cold night. Whatever the reason I was running, Kiran was convinced it was absolutely necessary. I watched Amory take determined step after determined step and wondered at his reason for flight. What was it that had these two men so scared, so ready to risk everything to remove me from some mysterious danger?

"Here," Amory panted, bending over to rest his hands on his knees. "We can rest here," he struggled to catch his breath, while stabilizing himself.

I let out an exhausted sigh and sunk to the ground. The dirt and mud and damp ground had never offered such a comfortable resting place. I pulled my knees to my chest and rested my head wearily on them.

I licked my dry lips, realizing how thirsty I was. I thought back to the rushing river almost with regret. I shook my head quickly to rid my mind of the thought. I would survive.

"You can use your magic again," Amory said with a stronger voice and I saw him stand upright confidently. "Careful though."

The small buzzing of frenetic energy made its way over my body and I realized that Amory was bringing his back. He turned away from me and stretched out his arm. The buzzing grew stronger and Amory turned to shield his face.

A great white light followed by the sound of a tree exploding pierced the darkness and I let out a startled scream. I couldn't help but be relieved however, that I was not the only one with those kinds of issues. Apparently blowing things up was just what happened to those pretending to be human.

I followed Amory's example, allowing the buzzing to grow into a steady current of excited energy. I didn't bother to stand up, but rather positioned my hands as far away from my face as I could. The energy continued to build and build until I could no longer hold it in anymore.

The small sapling that took the brunt of my built up electricity exploded into a thousand tiny pieces. I covered my head with my arms as small splinters rained down on top of me. When they stopped, I took a big breath relishing in the renewed energy.

Although my exhaustion did not completely disappear I was able to begin the healing process. As the magic moved through my blood, my muscles could finally relax. My scrapes and bruises began to disappear along with the soreness in my muscles. I rolled my head in a circle, cracking my neck and then stretched my arms high above my head. I felt completely renewed.

"Better?" Amory smiled at me.

"Much," I smiled back.

"I don't know many other Immortals who could have pulled that off. In fact, I've only heard of two others besides myself that *have* pulled that off," Amory sat down beside me, resting his long arms on top of his bent knees.

"Oh really? Most Immortals can't do that?" I felt oddly proud of my accomplishment.

"Oh, no. Most Immortals are useless without their magic. You are very special, child," I blushed at his compliment.

"Who are the other Immortals then, I mean the ones who've done this before?" I asked, curious.

"You're parents," he said simply.

"Amory, I need answers," I demanded at the reference to my parents. Although I was thankful to be that much more like them, I was tired of feeling in the dark.

"And you will get them, but first we need to call your brother. Your journey is far from over," He looked out into the dark expanse with a distant expression on his face. I was not entirely sure if he meant my current journey or if he was speaking metaphorically. "Now that you have your magic back, I need you to connect with Avalon; he needs to come pick you up," he gave me a look that told me I needed to follow his orders immediately.

Avalon. I concentrated on my twin brother, filling my body with strong energy. *Avalon.*

What? I knew immediately that he was irritated by my interruption. I felt defensive until I realized he didn't even know we were in the same country.

We need your help. Now that our minds were connected, I felt every emotion, every thought he had, and I knew he felt the same with me. It was a very invasive experience.

Who's we? His thoughts were tight and constrained, much like the position his body was in.

Amory and I. We need you.

What? Amory? Where are you? The surprise in his thoughts was evident. He stopped moving completely to focus on our conversation.

Somewhere in the Romanian mountains. I'm not sure exactly, but we need you to come pick us up. I kept my mental tone light and I laughed a little when I realized that I was driving Avalon crazy. He was completely focused on his extraction mission, which he happened to be currently in the middle of. A pang of guilt hit me though and I was suddenly worried about Lilly and the team.

Can't it wait? I'm kind of in the middle of something. Although I could feel his irritation, I could also sense his concern for us. He would have easily given up the mission to come to our aid.

"He's in the middle of the mission. Can we wait until he's finished?" I explained to Amory out loud.

"No, we need to get you out of the country immediately. Tell him to bring Jericho and two cars. Ryder's team can finish the mission," Amory was stern and commanding.

Amory says to let Ryder take over the mission and come now. He says to bring Jericho and two cars. And he says I have to get out of the country immediately. I was embarrassed to admit the last part.

What are you even doing here? Fine. Where are you? I felt his body turn in the opposite direction then he was originally headed and signal to Jericho. Whatever he was in the middle of he had dropped it instantaneously to follow Amory's orders.

"Where are we?" I asked Amory in order to relay it to Avalon.

"He can follow your magic," Amory said without giving any more details.

Follow my magic. I relayed to Avalon and felt him internally irritated, but he didn't ask any more questions.

"I want answers," I demanded of Amory again when I could sense Avalon on his way.

"I will answer any question you ask," Amory continued to stare off into the distance. I folded my arms stubbornly and opened my mouth. He's damn right he would answer any question I had.

Chapter Forty-Three

"Ok, first of all, I'm glad we survived and all, but why on earth was that necessary?" I vented.

"You're survival is absolutely essential," Amory was quick to respond. "I'm afraid this war can't be won without you and your brother," Amory said firmly, although without actually answering my question.

"Yeah, I know; at least I've heard that before. But the question I am asking is why was my survival in question to begin with?" I turned to face Amory full on. I needed answers.

"Well that answer is a little more complicated. The short answer is because you look exactly like your mother; I'm sure you've also heard that before," Amory paused for only a moment; just long enough for me to give him an encouraging look. "The long answer is because your mother happened to be engaged to Lucan before she ran off and eloped with your father, Lucan's personal bodyguard. He would like nothing more than to find your mother and make her pay for a lifetime of sins."

My mouth dropped open in surprise. That wasn't exactly the answer I had been expecting. A million questions began to swirl around in my mind, but Amory, sensing my confusion, continued with his chronicle.

"Let's see, I suppose I should start from the beginning. Lucan became King at a very young age because his father, Cedric, died suddenly from the King's Curse. At that time Kings usually waited until they were 100 or so to choose a wife; Cedric had done exactly that, fathered a son and planned on living a long life. When he died, Lucan was only a teenager. His advisors tried to guide him, but he has always been stubborn. His personal body guard was a teenager as well, and although the Royal guard advised him to choose an older, more experienced Titan, he refused. You see, a King's personal body guard is chosen at birth; they are always the same age so that they grow together and learn to trust each other. They are naturally the best of friends. The same was true of Lucan and Justice, your father. Lucan at that time, not having finished school but not wanting to be alone, had a special group of students chosen from all over the world to study with him at the Royal Palace. Your mother was one of those students and I'm afraid Lucan fell head over heels for her the moment he laid eyes on her; I suspect Justice did as well. Your mother was a very special girl; beautiful of course, talented beyond any other Immortal and smart, very smart. So naturally, Lucan pursued her. I'm afraid she saw his faults from the beginning and although she tried to persuade him to find someone else, he was persistent. When all of his attentions came to no avail he finally commanded her to be his wife. You are so much like her in every way that I'm sure you can imagine how she would react to a direct order such as marriage. But like I said, Lucan is stubborn, and blind to all reason, and so he gave her no choice."

"But why didn't Lucan try to find someone who actually liked him back?" I asked, confused why anyone would fall in love with someone who didn't feel the same way.

"There are several reasons I believe; you see Lucan was scared. His father had died suddenly, leaving him the sole heir to the throne. Having no children of his own, and a fear of also dying young he was pressed to find a wife and begin a family. Since the Curse, no King has ever been able to produce more than one male heir. I believe that he is simply afraid of death; even still to this day. He is afraid of his precious bloodline dying. I believe he hoped your mother would cure all of that. You see, she is a very powerful Witch; probably the most powerful of her generation. And I believe that Lucan thought with their combined bloodline they would be able to save the line of kings."

"What does her blood have to do with anything?" I asked, trying to stay focused. I suddenly yawned and realize how exhausted I was.

"She is the daughter of the last remaining Oracle. If you remember, the Oracles were the most powerful Immortals before the King's Curse. Yes, that makes you the granddaughter of course."

"But I thought all of the Oracles were dead?" I was really confused now.

"One remains, but I believe his soul died a long time ago," Amory mumbled the last part, and I saw true sadness in his eyes. But then he continued quickly, "So, with that kind of magic mixed, Lucan was hoping for a super-child. He was hoping to bring back the old magic; the magic that disappeared when Derrick cursed us. Unfortunately though, for your mother, it was more than business that drew Lucan to her; he actually fell deeply in love with her. All of his attempts to win her over failed; and sometime during all of this Delia and Justice fell in love instead," he shook his head as if frustrated with the memory of it.

"Delia," I repeated softly, saying my mother's name out loud for the first time. "So, he killed them?" I asked, terrified of the answer.

"No, he didn't. They outsmarted him, but he hasn't stopped hunting them to this day."

"They're alive?" I was shocked and stunned. My entire life I had been told my parents were dead. How was it possible they were still alive? And where were they?

"Truthfully child, I don't know the answer to that question. Nobody has heard nor seen them since I received you and your brother on my doorstep when you were just infants, and even then you were the only proof I had seen that they were still alive. In all likelihood they probably are dead. I don't how anyone could still be hiding from Lucan after this many years," he looked at me with such sadness in his eyes that I was not sure I could bear to ask him another question.

"So how did they escape?" I forced myself to ask, remembering my interest in his story and accepting his answers so far.

"The same way we just did. They planned it very carefully. They must have practiced for months, maybe years, but they were eventually able to dismiss their magic and survive. They were the first Immortals to ever be able to live without magic. They conditioned their human bodies then to withstand the flight and one night they simply left. The wedding was planned and preparations were made, and then one night, when court was being held here, without a word to anyone they just left. Justice's mother was a Shape-Shifter, one of the old ones, when she discovered her son missing; she shifted to look like your mother and played the part of Delia until she believed they were given enough time to escape. When Lucan discovered what she had done he had as many Shape-Shifters as he could get his hands on, executed gruesomely until she finally came forward. Once she was dead, he

314

lifted the decree from execution to exile; but that is only part of the hell Shape-Shifters have lived through over the millennia. Your parents seemed to have disappeared forever, when about one hundred and fifty years later, you and Avalon showed up on my doorstep. Justice actually left you with Angelica and she brought you to me per their wishes, informing me that you were twins and that you were theirs. At that time they were still alive, but that was sixteen years ago. I do know she was healthy enough to bare twins, something that hadn't been done since before Derrick was King."

"And Lucan would kill me just because I look like my mother, although he thinks she's dead?" I clarified.

"I am certain Lucan believes they are alive; I don't doubt he has ever given up his search. If he were to uncover that you were Delia and Justice's daughter, he would not only have you tortured, but most likely use you to bait out your mother and father. If he ever found out you had a twin brother, then I'm afraid all hell would break lose."

"Why? Why does it matter that Avalon and I are twins?"

"Twins have always been rare within the Immortals, but since the King's Curse they have been non-existent. With the old magic, twins were unparalleled for strength and power and on top of that they have a telepathic connection so they work together flawlessly. I have yet to see yours and Avalon's true abilities, but the fact that you are twins is proof that you have all four types of magic in your recent genealogy, which is a miracle in itself. The interesting part is, you do not have the old magic, you have a new magic, something Immortals have never seen before. You are a rare and precious commodity Eden, something Lucan would do anything to possess…. and use," Amory spoke with awe in his voice, and I found myself embarrassed by all of these facts. I was not sure if I wanted to be the secret weapon in a war I didn't even know if I agreed with yet, for either side.

"How do I have all four types? I thought intermarriage was forbidden or whatever?" I asked, changing the subject a little.

"Let's see, your grandfather was a Witch and an Oracle; your grandmother was a Medium; they also married in secret, but she was later killed because of it. Justice, you're father, was a Titan and his father a Titan, but his mother was a Shape-Shifter;

315

something nobody knew until the fateful shift that began it all. That's all four types and Avalon too; but your strongest traits are Witch and Avalon's are Titan, although we try to make him play up his other ones. If he were to appear like a Titan, people would be suspicious why he isn't with the Guard," I lay back on the grass, unable to sit any longer and listened to the melodic tone in Amory's voice.

"Ok, so now I understand why I shouldn't have interrupted the trial. But why didn't you tell me all of this before? If I would have known this, I wouldn't have gone to all of the trouble of exposing myself. And Dream Walking to? Why didn't you tell me that was real?" I whispered quietly, rubbing my eyes to keep them open.

A million stars lit up the night sky; I pondered for a moment that although I was half way across the world this was the same sky I looked up to when I was home in the middle of America. The night was still cold, but the magic buzzing steadily through my veins kept my blood warm.

"I couldn't tell you this before because I wasn't sure if you would be able to hide it from Kiran. I was afraid that if he found any of this out that it wouldn't matter if you came to Romania or not. I have been waiting for Kiran to discover you this entire semester and turn you over to his father, but I'm afraid I underestimated him," Amory said with almost curiosity in his voice. "And the Dream Walking, I hoped it was harmless. I was afraid that if you knew too much, that if you protected yourself from Kiran too much, that would also make him suspicious."

"What do you mean?" I asked through another wide yawn.

"I think that Kiran has always known, or at least he's known for some time. I'm not sure how he would have recognized you, but after his reaction in the courtroom I am almost positive he is aware of your identity," I perked up a little by Amory's answer. If he knew this entire time, why didn't he ever say anything to me? Does that mean he was trying to protect me this whole time?

"So he knew who I was, but didn't tell his father? What does that mean?" I rubbed my eyes again, determined to keep them open.

"I think it means he had the same reaction to you that his

316

father had with your mother. He's obviously hoping for a different outcome," Amory replied, laughing a little.

"Star-crossed," I mumbled.

"What's that?" Amory asked, although I was sure he heard me.

"Nothing," I answered quickly. "If you were so afraid of Kiran finding out about me, then how come you had me enroll at Kingsley?" my questions would keep coming as long as I could stay awake. I finally had someone giving me answers, I was not about to give up now. But then I yawned again, and realized it was only a matter of time before I was able to fight my exhausted body.

"I never would have had you come to Kingsley had I known that Kiran would be attending. But by the time we got the call about his arrival, you were already on your way to school. I had intended to intercede, but I couldn't get to you before your run in with Kiran in the lobby of the Administration building. After that I had to hope for the best and protect you as best as I could. Kiran's interest in you however, made me a failure as it turns out," I expected Amory to be disappointed in what he considered a failure, but he sounded more entertained than anything.

"Why do you think he never told his father?" I asked again, not entirely sure what to think of the whole story. I closed my eyes, promising myself that I would stay awake and listen even if my tired eyes were shut.

"You said it best Eden…. star-crossed," and then I found the sweet surrender of sleep beneath a wide open Romanian sky.

Chapter Forty-Four

Eden…. Where are you?

Something stirred me from my unconsciousness. I fought wakening, and attempted to once again fall into the deep abyss of sleep.

Damn it. Eden, where are you?

A sharper, irritated memory lifted me once again from sleep's grasp. The memory felt strange, like it wasn't mine, and even stranger like it was stumbling through a wilderness. I rolled over, and concentrated fully on finding sleep again.

Sticks and rocks jabbed into my side, poking through my oversized sweatshirt. My cheek was wet and grimy from damp leaves that had become my pillow. Gross.

I sat up; realizing the memory that awoke me was not actually a memory but Avalon stumbling through the wilderness trying to find us. I rubbed my bleary eyes surprised by the light of morning. The forest was brightened by daylight, but it must have still been early morning because the sun was just barely shining from the peaks of the eastern mountain tops.

"Eden!" Avalon shouted through the trees. Apparently he got tired of waiting for me to figure out where his voice was coming from.

"Over here," I struggled to shout back through a hoarse and scratchy morning voice. I cleared my throat and tried again, "Over here."

I heard Avalon not far away, making his way noisily through the thick trees and underbrush. Someone was with him, although it was hard for me to determine the identity of their magic when I felt like I had just been run over by a bus. I was not sure how long I was asleep, but it wasn't nearly long enough.

I stood up to brush the leaves and dirt off of me. My legs and back were incredibly sore and I heard several of my joints make a cracking noise as I fought to get to my feet. I didn't have the patience to deal with tired muscles and aching bones this morning; I sent my magic surging through my body, heating my blood and relieving the tension in my exhausted appendages.

I felt instantly better, the magic did its job and my bones

and muscles felt better than normal; I wasn't sure if there was any hope for my external appearance however. I did my best to pick off the damp leaves and wipe away the dirt, but I began to think they had become a part of me. I reached my hand up to the top of my head in an attempt to deal with my hair, but after feeling around for a few seconds, brought it back down. There was no hope. I wouldn't be surprised if I had to shave it off when I returned to civility.

"Holy crap…." Avalon blurted out as he made his way over the top of the last hill that separated us. "What happened to you?" he confirmed my obvious suspicions.

"Ugh," I grunted back, not knowing where to even begin.

"Good morning, Eden," Jericho called in a very chipper voice, following close behind Avalon. I waved at him irritably, remembering I had been the one to tell Avalon to bring him and bent over to tug on my ruined clog.

"Where's Amory?" Avalon asked and I looked around confused. I didn't remember when he left, or if he left; I didn't remember anything. I must have been sleeping hard.

"I don't know," I said, feeling out of it.

"What do you mean you don't know?" Avalon demanded, his defenses suddenly on high alert.

"They wouldn't take him without her," Jericho, the voice of reason, chimed in.

"You don't know that. They could be hoping she leads them to the rest of us," Avalon retorted, irritated and anxious.

"If anything it would be the other way around and you know that," Jericho rolled his eyes and walked over to shake my hand. "Your brother is such a drama queen," he joked.

"Tell me about it," I agreed sarcastically. "And no more talking about me like I'm not here." I addressed both boys. "I'm as much a part of this thing as you two. From now on, I am always included and always informed," I folded my arms as if to strengthen my point.

Avalon rolled his eyes and began a search of the premises. I let him without any intention of joining him. I took Jericho's side in that I thought wherever Amory was, he was just fine.

"You look like you just came through hell," Jericho, still at my side, remarked.

"I pretty much feel like it." I remembered my stiff body before I used the healing power of magic and cringed.

"So, what are you doing here anyways? I thought you had been ordered to stay at home?" Jericho pried for an explanation; but I was not totally sure if I was emotionally ready to relive the last seventy two hours.

"I don't even know where to begin," I looked past Jericho at the breathtaking view of the Carpathian Mountains. The sunrise had painted the sky beautiful shades of pink and orange, and the soft light made the autumn hues of the trees brilliant.

"You better figure it out," Avalon grunted grumpily, while continuing his sweep of the perimeter. "I want a full debriefing, and I want a good reason why I had to leave my mission in the goddamn middle of the night," I let out a burst of laughter when I looked over at Jericho and watched him roll his eyes.

"Your brother thinks he's Napoleon Bonaparte," he shook his head and watched Avalon disdainfully.

"Seriously though, have you heard anything?" I asked a little more humbly. I was the reason Avalon had to leave his mission. What if they weren't successful and it was all my fault?

"No. We haven't heard anything," Jericho responded in a meek voice. "They've been incommunicado since before we left them."

"When will you find out?" I was more nervous now than I had ever been.

"Not sure. If all went as planned, hopefully soon," Avalon stopped his busy work to join us. He bit his thumbnail anxiously.

"Jericho and I are going to find out exactly what happened right now," Amory was suddenly involved in our conversation, making his way over the same rise that Avalon and Jericho had come by. He was carrying a cloth bag with him that smelled like a bakery. My stomach growled loudly and I realized that I hadn't eaten in days.

"Is that breakfast?" I asked, barely able to restrain myself from pouncing on Amory and ripping the bag open to find out myself.

"I thought you might be hungry," he gave me a timid smile and opened the cloth satchel to reveal several loaves of bread, apples and bottles of water.

I grabbed a loaf of bread and discovered that it was still warm; it must have just finished baking. Immediately I tore off a piece and shoved it into my mouth. I could not have been more unladylike, but I was having trouble caring. Jericho watched me devour a loaf of bread in seconds with his mouth slightly open.

"What?" I mumbled through a full mouth.

"Like I was saying," Amory also watched me with an expression that was both disgusted and amused. "Jericho and I will return to the Citadel to check the progress of the mission. If they failed last night without you, then most likely Jericho and I will have to do what we can alone this morning. The executions won't start until the afternoon, so we have a couple of hours yet to do the impossible. Did everyone go last night, are we alone?"

"We left Roxie and Fiona to run communications once the channels were open again," Avalon responded still chewing on his thumbnail. His stance was wide; he was totally in his element.

"Good, that will be good. Ok, so we will clean up in Sibiu. What about Lilly Mason? Is she with the others or in a different part of the castle?" Amory asked the question that had been gnawing at my heart since the boys arrived.

"Lilly Mason was released yesterday," Avalon said incredulously.

"She was!" I practically shouted; I almost didn't believe it was possible.

"Ok, good," Amory responded, more calmly than I had managed. "Avalon you will take Eden back home immediately. And under no circumstances is she allowed to make any decisions. Do you understand?" Amory looked directly into my eyes. "Your friend is safe; there are no more reasons not to listen. You will do exactly as Avalon says. Got it?" I nodded quickly, I had no intentions of ever stepping out of line again, although I couldn't help but feel like my efforts were worth it now that Lilly was free.

"How do you want us to go? Timisoara?" Avalon asked as if he were a travel expert.

"No, it's too exposed. You're going to have to go the long way. I believe our most efficient but incognito option is to cross into Hungary, ditch the rental and take a bus or train into Austria, once in Austria utilize the trains. I think the Zurich airport will be your best bet to leave Europe undetected," Avalon nodded along to Amory's directions, but I felt completely lost. I tried to conjure up a picture of a European map in my head, but couldn't trace the route mentally. I guessed I really would just have to trust Avalon. Oh boy.

"Do you want us to take our time?" Avalon asked all the right questions.

"No, get out of here as quickly as you can. The last thing we need is for you two to join the exiting traffic. Get home before the Festival is over," More instructions I felt like I just barely understood. "Where are the cars?"

"Sighisoara," Jericho answered.

"Good, good," Amory paused for several moments and appeared to be going over things in his head. "Ok, I think that's everything. We'll see you at home," Amory shook hands with Avalon and then Jericho and Avalon shook hands. The boys all began to walk back over the hill and I followed quickly behind them.

Once over the hill I saw that we were at the edge of the town they had just been talking about. The town of Sighisoara was spread out in a quaint and quiet cityscape that fanned over the smaller foothills of the Carpathian Mountains. The buildings were hundreds of years old and the still sleeping city had a very ancient world feel to it.

I kept pace with Avalon until we found the cars tucked away in the rustic village. Both vehicles were the classic Dacias that seemed to be the only style of car allowed in Romania. Avalon pulled out a set of keys and politely opened the passenger's side door for me.

"Oh Eden, take this," Amory walked over and handed me the cloth bag of food. I pulled out an apple and immediately took a bite. My grimy teeth were grateful for the natural cleansing the apple blessed them with. "There is a set of clothes at the bottom of the bag," Amory kissed the top of my head before returning to the other rusted Dacia where Jericho was waiting.

"What's wrong with what I'm wearing?" I asked sarcastically. Amory grinned happily back. "Hey Amory," I yelled quickly as he began to enter his car, he paused, looking up at me. "Thank you," I said, full of emotion.

"One day, I hope you return the favor," his smile turned

sad and then he was in the car and Jericho was driving away, leaving us in their trail of heavy exhaust.

"Let's go," Avalon yelled impatiently at me.

I sat down on the worn upholstery and thought longingly of my yellow Land Rover. I would never take it for granted again. I continued to munch on my apple, feeling very much at peace. Avalon gunned the gas and took off through the winding, hilly streets of another beautiful Romanian city.

I decided that I would very much like to come back to Romania under different circumstances. I couldn't help but be excited for the remaining leg of my journey. Compared to the last few days it sounded very relaxing. For my first trip to Europe, I felt like this was quite the crash course. At least for the second portion I would have company, and it sounded like Avalon knew where he is going. That would be a nice change.

"So Lilly was really released?" I asked, breaking the silence.

"I guess so. Apparently your boyfriend spoke on her behalf and she was given a second chance. They're going to let her return to Kingsley and everything," Avalon's voice was skeptical and I had a hard time believing the news as well.

I sat back, admiring the scenery, once again silent. Kiran did save Lilly. I made him promise he would, but after the fact I wasn't sure what to expect. Butterflies attacked my stomach as I remembered the emotion in his eyes during our farewell.

The depth of longing I felt for him didn't seem possible for someone my age. My heart was gripped with clarity; completely full of adoration for the boy I could officially consider the love of my life. My magic was stirred with the memories of our energies mingled and wild together. My cheeks blushed at the thought of my mouth once again pressed against his.

Against all reason and circumstance we had found each other in a world torn apart by our very existence. In order to be together we would have to defy all odds, defy all logic, and defy all influence. I saw two battlefields in front of me; the one that pinned Kiran against me, and the one that we would have to forge in order to be together. I understood the purpose of the Resistance, but the battle I chose to fight would be the one that brought me closer to the man I loved with every fiber of my being.

Chapter Forty-Five

I stretched my arms and lifted my head off of the cold glass window. I yawned wide and shook my head, making the crick in my neck disappear. Looking out at the Austrian country side flying by, I smiled. Europe had captured my heart; if only I hadn't been on the run to save my life.

Avalon seemed in deep thought as he too stared out of the train window in silence. Field, farm, field, farm, lake, field, farm, mountain.... Austria was breathtaking. Of course I said the same thing about Romania, and then again about the rustic beauty of Hungary. Austria was a different kind of beauty however. The clean and contemporary buildings and more modern farms made it clear that this was a different side of Europe.

I pulled my ivory cardigan closer around my waist; the train air was frigid and although I was grateful for the new set of clothes Amory picked out for me, they were obviously picked for convenience and practicality, and not necessarily style. A pair of baggy, brown work pants clearly meant for a man, a plaid red colored shirt and an ivory cardigan felt like the nicest clothes anyone had ever given me after what my cruise wear had been through. I also had had to retire my Nebraska sweatshirt; but I promised myself I would buy another one paying tribute to the Huskers when I returned home.

I wiped my fingers beneath my eyes, self-consciously. I remembered what I looked like when I was finally able to assess the damage in a Hungarian train station bathroom. I did the best I could to rinse out and wash my hair in the small sink; I at least had gotten it out of the hair tie and into a neat bun on the nape of my neck. It wasn't pretty, but at least I didn't look crazy anymore.

My face, arms and legs were covered in dirt and grime and I would definitely need a long, hot shower to feel completely clean, but I was much improved, although my legs needed a good shave.

My face took the longest to scrub clean; besides the dirt, I had to deal with a mess of makeup plastered to my face. Never again would I travel wearing non-waterproof mascara and black eyeliner. By the time I exited the small bathroom, my face was bright red and swollen from all of the scrubbing.

I sent a burst of magic through my body, heating my blood and awakening my senses. Avalon naturally felt the surge himself and sat up a little straighter. I smiled at him, hoping to draw him into conversation, but he stared past me in a dreamlike state. He was so worried about the outcome of the mission he could barely function. And even though he carried an international phone and glanced at it every other second, we hadn't heard from anyone since we left Romania.

Avalon was skilled at international travel and clearly used to being followed. He had taken every precaution necessary to ensure we were alone. After ditching the Dacia on the Romania/Hungary border, he set it on fire, making sure any physical evidence we left behind would be destroyed. We then took a bus through most of Hungary, changing only once we were close to the Austrian border. Since Austria we had changed trains as often as we could while still moving in the general direction of Switzerland.

I couldn't help but enjoy the trip however. Riding a European train was like truly riding in style. The glory of the Austrian Alps was like nothing I had ever experienced before; and I would gladly ride a train through them until I had every mountain memorized.

The game plan was to fly home from Zurich; who knew how many trains that meant before we were in the heart of Switzerland. Only Avalon was concerned about our timing though. I was too swept away with Europe to be in any hurry to leave.

Avalon's phone buzzed gently and suddenly he sat up completely alert. I noticed the tension in his body and felt his anxiety as he opened the cell phone and answered quietly.

"Hello?" he asked softly, discretely.

"Oh, thank God," I saw his body visibly relax and felt the apprehension turn to silent joy. "Is the package in the mail?" he asked, using code. I couldn't help but laugh; he was like the obvious cliché for a 1950's spy. Next thing you knew, we would be on our way to Russia to stop the Kremlin.

"What?" he asked, suddenly exasperated. "You can't be serious! I'm not doing that. No way. I might as well send her to

325

the London palace with instructions on how to find the rest of us. No way…." whatever he was so upset about, he had dropped all pretense of code. "No way…." he repeated over and over to whatever the other line was saying.

"Where?" he asked eventually, with a softer but more frustrated tone. The hostility in his voice was unmistakable. "How do we know it's not a trap?" he listened a little longer, his magic growing stronger and stronger every second. I wouldn't have been surprised if the humans could feel it for themselves. "What happens if you're wrong?" Avalon listened longer, but did not seem appeased.

"If I do this, I want some type of insurance; some type of trade off…. We would have gotten her out of there even if he didn't do anything. That doesn't make him a hero; it just makes him look like an idiot!" Avalon stopped talking to get an earful from whoever was on the other line. I found myself sitting on the edge of my seat, totally engrossed in Avalon's side of the conversation.

"Fine…. I said fine. I guess we'll see you in Geneva," Avalon snapped the phone shut and glared at me. I was almost too afraid to ask what that had been about.

"Geneva?" I asked tentatively.

"I guess so," he mumbled.

"Switzerland?" I tried again.

Avalon nodded affirmatively.

"What happened to Zurich?" I finally asked bravely.

"We've been ordered," Avalon paused and cleared his throat irritably, "asked…. if we would oblige the Crown Prince by joining him in Geneva," he couldn't even look at me, but turned to glare out the window.

"It's not a trap Avalon," I said quickly but quietly; my stomach filled with butterflies.

"I do not want to talk about it," Avalon responded grumpily and I knew better than to push it.

A black sedan pulled up in front of the train station and Avalon took the initiative to approach. I followed behind, shouldering my backpack once again. A man exited the driver's side to open the back door for us. Avalon stuck his head menacingly into the back seat before entering the car fully. I smiled apologetically to the driver and climbed in behind Avalon.

Avalon sat with arms folded and his back turned to me. I knew he was mad, but I also didn't think I really deserved the silent treatment for the last eight hours. I elbowed him roughly in the kidneys before the driver had returned to his seat, but he didn't respond.

I was irritated with Avalon, but soon my bad feelings turned to adoration as we drove silently through Geneva at night. The streets were lit in the soft glow of streetlamps and from the bright windows of buildings built before America was even a recognized country.

Our ride took us past Lake Geneva, glistening in the moonlight. A large fountain sprayed a cascade of water from the middle of the lake, and the Alps sat as a backdrop to the perfect postcard picture. The streets were narrow, with historical buildings rising to either side. I marveled at their intricate architecture, and embellished building fronts.

When the car finally came to a stop in front of a charming palace, I was somehow not surprised. After witnessing the grand architecture and style of the Citadel, I was finally able to wrap my head around the words "Monarchy" and "Crown Prince." I hadn't really been expecting quite this grandeur however.

"Is this one of their palaces?" I whispered, hoping Avalon would answer.

"This is a hotel," Avalon responded irritably. I blushed, feeling very ignorant. "Ok, it used to be one of their palaces; now it's just a hotel," After feeling my embarrassment, Avalon conceded the truth.

The palace turned hotel was exquisite. I was dumbstruck by the beauty and elegance of what was formerly Kiran's family's home. I followed Avalon out of the car and stayed timidly behind him. I glanced down at my ill-fitting, makeshift outfit and felt embarrassingly under-dressed.

As we entered the foyer of the grand hotel my mouth dropped open in awe. We were surrounded by marble pillars that reached from expansive marbled floor to vaulted marble ceiling.

Intricately, upholstered furniture with golden thread filled the entrance hall. The only evidence that this was not a palace but indeed a hotel was the circulation desk with uniformed employees standing behind it.

My nerves were on edge thanks to Avalon; although he appeared relaxed and calm, his magic was surging at high alert. Because of our connection my senses were heightened with his and our magic circulated in unison. He bypassed the hotel clerks and headed straight up a wide, winding, ivory staircase.

After walking up several flights of stairs, Avalon led me into a long hallway. The hairs on the back of my neck rose suddenly when I felt the strong presence of other Immortals. Avalon slowed his pace and I noticed him clench and unclench his fists regularly.

We walked the hallway slowly and I didn't complain. I was not sure what to expect but Avalon was so uncomfortable and tense that I regretted him coming. I felt like it was my fault and therefore also felt guilty and blameworthy; but then remembered we were ordered to come here and I was even ordered specifically not to make any more decisions. I sent this thought poignantly to Avalon; he returned it with a dirty look.

At the end of the hallway Avalon paused and took a big breath. He raised his fist to knock on the cream colored door but paused again as if he couldn't make himself do it.

"I don't know what's behind this door Eden," Avalon whispered fiercely to me and I was surprised by the apprehension in his voice. "We could be walking into a trap…. Eden," He paused again and I waited nervously, expecting some type of brotherly declaration, instead Avalon continued, "Eden, let me have Kiran; I'll enjoy killing him much more than you will."

Before I could think of any response Avalon knocked forcefully on the door. He gave me another nervous sideways glance and shoved his hands deep into his pockets to appear casual. I wished he felt as calm as he was working so hard to look; his nervous energy was making me edgy.

Talbott opened the door and for some reason that surprised me. He was dressed casually and his hair was a little messier than at school. When he opened the door he was laughing and involved in a conversation. Avalon stared at him suspiciously, until he gestured with his hand for us to enter.

I was more than a little surprised to find Amory in the extravagant room. He was sitting on a plush, periwinkle sofa, holding a snifter full of a golden brown liquid. He was the one involved in conversation with Talbott, and it appeared they were having a very animated but pleasant conversation.

Avalon grunted grumpily before taking a seat close to Amory. Although he relaxed his magic a little, he was still in a sour mood. Avalon reclined in his seat and slammed his feet cross-legged onto the gold, inlaid, glass coffee table. His movement made a terrible crashing sound although he managed not to shatter the fragile antique.

The attention of everyone in the room was now on Avalon who smiled smugly in reply. Amory relaxed on the sofa and put an arm around Avalon in a very paternal way. I stood in the middle of the room not entirely sure what to do.

"I'm glad you're safe, Eden," Talbott said out of the blue. I was not the only one surprised by his statement.

"Thank you," I replied humbly.

"Eden?" Kiran appeared out of the bedroom and said my name almost reverently.

I turned to face him and was struck ferociously with emotion. He stood in the doorway, hair tussled and eyes piercing. His hands fidgeted nervously, but his gaze never left mine and never softened in intensity.

Moments ago, I hadn't known whether to sit or stand, but once I saw the look of pure desire cross Kiran's face I knew there was only one place I wanted to be. I closed the distance between us in seconds, sprinting across the expansive suite and leaping into his arms.

He caught me instinctively and found my mouth immediately. My legs wrapped around his waist and my hands held his face firmly to mine; our magic mingled together in a perfect symphony of all consuming power.

At this most passionate moment there was no one else besides Kiran and nothing else existed besides our love. I was thrilled to find his feelings as intense as mine. My thoughts, my consciousness, my very blood filled with a desire bigger than me, bigger than I could even hope to understand.

I could have lived in that moment forever, but like all good things it had to come to an end. After several throat clears from our audience and then a pillow to the back of my head thanks to Avalon, I relinquished my hold on Kiran. He set me down gently and then kissed me one more time sweetly on the lips.

"Ok, that's enough…. seriously," Avalon interrupted in an irritated voice. "The rest of us are trying to exist here; we don't need your crazy magic suffocating us."

I turned around embarrassed, heat flooded my cheeks. Avalon could not look more disgusted and Amory and Talbott couldn't even look in our general direction. Kiran intertwined his fingers through mine and pulled me closer to him protectively.

"Excuse us, gentlemen," Kiran addressed the room politely; his crisp, English accent perfectly enunciating every consonant.

Chapter Forty-Six

Kiran walked backwards into one of the bedrooms of the massive suite, pulling me with him. If I thought I felt humiliation before, that was nothing compared to the sweeping embarrassment of being taken into Kiran's bedroom with three sets of suspicious eyes following my every step. Luckily, Kiran closed the door quickly behind us.

The bedroom looked like some place a prince would stay. A huge four poster bed with royal blue and gold striped silk comforter sat in the middle of the room facing an enormous flat screened TV. Kiran's suitcase and clothes were laid haphazardly on a royal blue divan. I noticed a golden crown half buried underneath a pair of designer jeans.

Kiran walked across the room, pulling me behind him, and out onto a balcony overlooking Lake Geneva. The moonlight glistened off the black water and I saw the outline of the Swiss Alps in the distance; their tall peaks turning white at the top, billowy clouds resting on them, melting into mere extensions of a vast midnight sky.

The mid-autumn night air was frigid and I sent a burst of magic through my blood to warm up.

"Did you know that you can use your magic for more than an occasional space heater?" Kiran asked softly but sarcastically, while leaning back against the outer wall of the hotel.

"I'm cold," I responded, a little defensively.

"Here…." he replied, pulling me against his body. I laid my head against his chest and listened to the soft beating of this heart.

"Thank you for saving Lilly," I mumbled into his warm embrace.

"My pleasure," he replied, amused. "And thank you for nearly getting yourself killed. Thank goodness your grandfather was there to help you escape. I don't know how I would have survived losing you," he held me tighter, kissing the top of my head.

"I'm sorry, did you say grandfather?" I asked, wishing I could just dwell on Kiran's sweet sentiments, but instead I found myself unable to move past the next big mystery of my life revealed. Would it never end?

"Yes, you're grandfather…. Amory." Kiran paused to look me in the eyes. "Are you telling me you didn't know that he is your grandfather?" he asked incredulously.

"I had no idea…." I laughed out loud a little. "But I guess it makes sense," I could now explain away all of the times Amory seemed so paternal, apparently he was just being grandfatherly.

"I'm sorry; I didn't mean to spoil anything," Kiran gave me his signature smirk and I swore I fell even more in love with him.

"It's alright; something tells me he was waiting for me to figure it out on my own," I returned my head to Kiran's chest, butterflies flooding my stomach.

"He should know better than to wait for that," Kiran joked lightly.

I couldn't help but agree with him. I hadn't figured anything out on my own yet, what made Amory think I would start with that?

"God only knows what I have left to figure out," I mumbled.

"Yes He does, but He's gotten you this far…." Kiran surprised me with his answer.

"Do you believe in God?" I asked, confused.

"Of course. Don't you?" I pulled my head away from his chest to look him in the eye; for some reason I found it hard to believe he was serious.

"I mean I guess I did when I was human, but now I don't know what to believe," I left the closeness of his embrace, feeling slightly embarrassed and walked over to the balcony's edge.

"That seems backwards to me," Kiran responded and joined me. We stood silently for a moment enjoying the beauty of Lake Geneva before he continued, "You believed in God when you thought you were human; when you suffered pain and hunger, tyranny and war. But now that you live above that, with unlimited power and unlimited life you doubt that there is an entity greater than you? Someone created all of this, all of the beauty of the earth, all of the fragility of human life and all of the extraordinary existence of us. Choosing to believe in God only when you are surrounded by death and destruction is to truly not know God at all."

Kiran put an arm around me and kissed the top of my head again. Despite his point, I knew his feelings for me were as strong as ever.

"Am I not still surrounded by death and destruction?" I asked, feeling characteristically defensive.

"No, you're not. Believe me. I've done my homework; you could not have a stronger genealogy. But the rest of us, yeah.... maybe.... But isn't that where we find our substance? I think there is a certain beauty to death; a macabre exquisiteness that brings meaning to life."

I stood there gazing at Kiran with so much emotion I felt like I would explode. Avalon was right, I had no idea who Kiran was, but the more I learned, the more I fell madly in love with him.

I threw my arms around his neck and pulled him into another passionate kiss. He gladly reciprocated.

"Excuse me, sir," Talbott interrupted, like usual. "It's time for Eden to go."

Kiran paused for only a second to wave Talbott away before returning to me. He pressed his lips against mine fervently; lifting me off of the ground and making me forget the world around me. Our magic became an intense force; rising around us with an almost visible presence.

Eventually he returned my feet to the ground and my mind slowly returned to reality. He smiled at me as if holding onto a secret and my heart fluttered with the sweet memories of his mouth against mine.

"You just got here and now you have to go," Kiran gazed at me with all of the intensity of a boy madly in love. "I just had to know that you were all right. I had to see you," he kissed the top of my head sweetly and continued, "Before we join the others, I have something for you," Kiran led me back into his bedroom and pulled out a black, square, velvet box from his suitcase.

He opened the box to reveal a necklace and pulled out the long silver chain to expose a pendant intricately woven with several black stones placed throughout. He clasped the beautiful, complex accessory around my neck and the stones turned from black to a brilliant shade of blue. I fingered the pendant in my hands, amazed by the color and loveliness of the stones.

"I thought so," Kiran said cryptically and kissed me on the cheek. "Eden, when we return to Kingsley things are going to be difficult. We won't be able to see each other or be together, at least not easily. I am going to continue my engagement with Seraphina and go on like nothing has changed. You will have to stay far away from me," he cupped my face in his hands and I saw the pain in his eyes.

"But why?" I asked, scared and upset.

"I'm so sorry, Love. But you have to go on playing the part Amory created for you. As of now, my father is convinced that you are not your mother. After several interrogations, the most convincing of which was Seraphina's, he agreed to let it go. She was pretty adamant that you are no one special, especially not Delia Saint. But that doesn't mean he will stay pacified. We cannot draw any unnecessary attention to you. I am determined to keep you to myself. His suspicions are small, but you've raised his curiosity and so we have to keep you as far under the radar as possible without making you disappear completely," he held me closer to him as if to prove his point.

"So I can't see you at all?" I asked, afraid of the answer.

"No, I will find a way for us to be together, I will. But we will have to be extremely careful. You can't show that necklace to anyone; but I wanted you to have it as a token of my love."

"Your love?" I said the words religiously.

"Yes, my love. Because Eden, I have loved you avidly from the first moment I saw you and I will love you completely with all that I am until the day I die," his eyes had hypnotized mine and I was transfixed by their passion. He grinned sheepishly at me and I realized he didn't grasp the seriousness of my feelings for him.

"Kiran Kendrick, I love you too," I whispered, my throat closed and my eyes full of emotion.

He swept me into another passionate kiss and I melted into his embrace. When he finally released me I felt weak from my expended magic. Kiran led me back into the living room, but not before I tucked his gift beneath my plaid work shirt.

Avalon and Amory stood near the door waiting anxiously.

Kiran kissed my hand sweetly and mouthed "I love you," I blushed and joined my grandfather and twin brother at the door.

"Thank you again, Kiran…. for everything," Amory said humbly before we made our exit.

"Scoot over!" I demanded irritably while shoving my elbow into Avalon's ribs. Sitting between Avalon and Titus on the eight hour flight home was not ideal for anyone. But it was Amory's great idea of added protection; although in my personal opinion totally unnecessary.

"That's it!" I declared loudly, and stood up as dramatically as the small coach cabin would allow. "Move!"

Avalon obeyed and slid his knees into the aisle so that I could pass. I walked unsteadily between the rows of seats and passed several members of the rescued Resistance team, until I found Amory staring out his window pensively.

I fell heavily into the seat next to him, not really caring if I bothered him or not. He looked up at me and smiled. I grinned back, pleased that I had the upper hand, if only for a moment.

"What happens now, grandpa?" I asked, barely able to contain my laughter.

His expression turned anxious and then relaxed when he saw my smile. He laughed a little himself and I was glad that at least it didn't seem he wanted that information to remain a secret.

"When did you figure it out?" he asked, still smiling, but not quite able to look me in the eyes.

"Kiran told me, kind of on accident. He assumed I already knew…. silly him," I said sarcastically. Amory's face flushed with embarrassment. "So you're the last remaining Oracle. You seem pretty alive to me," I joked.

"For now," Amory flushed deeper with embarrassment. "That's a much longer conversation, for a more private setting," he cut me off when my I opened my mouth to ask a million questions.

"Ok, but I'm going to hold you to that," I paused for a moment before continuing, "So really what happens when we get home?" I decided on a different topic that I had just as many

336

questions for.

"Well first we explain everything to Sylvia. That will be our first battle. She has been worried sick. You're lucky I was able to talk to her yesterday, I hopefully softened the blow," he gave me a stern, parental glare and it was my turn to blush from discomfort.

"Then what?" I asked timidly.

"I'm not sure; I'm afraid most of this is now out of our hands. For the first time, in a long time, our futures lay in the hands of someone I don't know what to expect from," he turned his head to return his thoughtful gazing out the window and I realized he was referring to Kiran.

"But we're not going to try to kill him anymore, right?" I sounded more casual than I felt. My throat closed with emotion and my hands trembled a little at the thought. Even though I was on the side of the Resistance, I had no idea if it was a place I could stay, especially if they tried to continue with their original plans.

"No, my dear. I could never hurt someone you cared about so deeply. You don't need to be worried anymore," he put an arm around me, and continued to look quietly out of the small window.

I sunk into my own personal pensiveness, wondering if Lucan would really leave me alone or if he would hurt me in pursuit of my parents. If they were still out there, where were they? I doubted I could help Lucan find them anyways; I certainly had no way to look for them.

A hundred questions swirled through my mind, but the questions that kept demanding to be answered first were when would I get to see Kiran again? When would we get to be alone again and when would I feel safe once more in his arms?

As unlikely as our love affair might have been, loving Kiran was the only concrete path I could imagine. I was wholly consumed with a love that would probably get me killed, but I would never have chosen any other way. I could not have chosen any other way. We were truly destined for each other, fated to be together…. we were star-crossed.

About the Author

Rachel Higginson was born and raised in Nebraska, but spent her college years traveling the world. She married her high school sweetheart and spends her days raising their growing family. She is obsessed with bad reality TV and any and all Young Adult Fiction.

Reckless is her first book, and the first part in a four part saga, The Star-Crossed Series. Hopeless Magic, the second installment of the series is currently available.

Follow Rachel on her blog at:
www.onedaysomedayeveryday.blogspot.com

Or on Twitter:
@mywritesdntbite

Or on her Facebook Pages:
Rachel Higginson
And
Reckless Magic

Keep reading for an excerpt from Hopeless Magic, the second installment of The Star-Crossed Series.

Acknowledgements

I am so grateful to get to write an acknowledgement section that I just might start back as far as I can remember and start thanking everyone I've ever met! Ok, maybe I won't. But there are so many people that have helped bring me to where I am today that I should probably start naming them!

First of all, this gift of writing that sometimes feels more like a miracle at the end of the day came from God alone and to Him I give the glory. He has had a plan since the beginning and I am so blessed to be invited along on this wild ride.

Thanks to my loving family, who have put up with my sleepless nights and all of my "Not right nows…" and "In a little bits…." You've put up with a dirty house, dirty laundry and let's face it a dirty mommy, but you have supported me through it all and I thank you for that.

Thanks to my parents, who promised me from childhood I could do and be anything that I wanted. To my dad, who although might be disappointed I'm not a missionary in the jungles of Africa, would be proud to know I followed my dream. And to my mom who has spent endless hours babysitting, encouraging me, spreading the word about my books and even done my dishes and laundry a few times! Thank you for your support.

Thanks to Kylee who sat by me for hours and hours while I bounced ideas and thoughts off her. To Pat: who let us exchange yard work for cover art. And to Carolynn for going through the first, very, very rough versions and donating her editing eye.

Thanks to Jenn Nunez who took me under her wing and walked me through this whole crazy process step by step, holding my hand and answering all of my millions and millions of questions!!

Finally, thanks to my amazing husband, Zach. Without

him, I would never have taken the plunge and published, or continued to publish, or maybe even continued to write. He has been a constant source of encouragement, always helping me be better and pushing me to do more. Love you Zachary.

I followed Lilly through the other side of the barn and around the large white farmhouse. A small group of other Immortals walked silently with us. All of them were the older generation except Avalon, whom I noticed was allowed more of a leadership role than anyone else our age, including me.

Angelica led our small group behind the farmhouse and down into a storm cellar. Lilly and I followed Conrad, Terrance, Amory and Avalon down a set of worn stone steps. The men all carried fiery torches and as we walked through a surprisingly long tunnel, they stopped and lit suspended torches along the wall.

What I expected to be a typical Nebraska tornado shelter, meant to protect from seasonal storms, had turned into a long, but wide tunnel, leading further and further into the earth. The already cold November night continued to stiffen the frigid air the farther into the passageway we walked.

Lilly's hand in mine, I could feel her tremble with anxiety. The look on her face was sheer determination, etched with near panicked hysteria. Her already pale skin had turned translucent by fear and her vibrant red curls framed her face in a haze of frizz. I squeezed her hand, hoping to comfort, except I couldn't help but empathize her same fears.

Eventually we came to a thick stone door. The small group ahead of us mounted their torches into frames already nailed to the walls. Through the dim firelight I could see small markings bordering the outline of the door and then another large symbol set exactly in the middle at eye level: a snake, wrapped in a circle, swallowing its' own tail.

Angelica was the first one through the door. She put her finger, just below her ear, where her jawbone met her neck and I watched the faint flare of light. I realized she was illuminating the same symbol of the snake eating its own tail, the same symbol Lilly was on her way to receive. Angelica carried the magic in her finger, from her neck to the symbol in the door. She placed her index finger ever so softly on the serpent and I watch with quiet awe as the door glowed in the same color as Angelica's magic before opening into a circular room.

The door closed behind Angelica and Conrad was next in line. He repeated the same procedure as Angelica, only this time the door illuminated in army green, to resemble the brand of magic he carried. I realized at that moment that I may not be able to keep my promise to Lilly, since it seemed to enter the secret room of the Resistance, one must already be a member or on their way to become one.

I squeezed Lilly's hand tighter as I watched Terrance and then Avalon both enter the room in turn. Amory turned towards us, his expression pure excitement. He held out his hand to Lilly and she accepted the offer silently.

"I'm afraid you won't be able to join us, Eden dear. Unless you are also willing to join our humble cause tonight," I saw the hope in his black eyes and felt ashamed when I shook my head no.

"Then you had better wait out here," his smile softened into a sadder version of happiness and I was struck with guilt. Some small part of me understood that I could not waver in the middle much longer. Sooner or later I would have to make a choice; I would have to join a cause that would eventually lead to the death of the person I loved with all of my soul, or I would have to turn my back on this cause and alienate myself entirely from the only family I would ever have.

I squeezed Lilly's hand one more time before letting go and gave her an encouraging smile. She returned my smile with renewed confidence and I suddenly felt envious. Her brilliant emerald eyes shone with sheer determination and something more, something much like victory. Then, Amory was lighting the door and I watched them disappear behind the thick wall of stone.

Can I watch? I spoke to my twin brother telepathically, hoping he would understand my need to be involved. Although I could have easily opened our twin sense and made the decision for myself, I felt obligated to ask Avalon for his permission. I had a hard time invading his privacy unannounced. He, on the other hand, had absolutely no problem spying on me.

As long as you don't interrupt. Avalon replied, slightly exasperated. I loved my brother dearly, but when he was in super commando leader mode, I couldn't help but find him more than a little irritating.

I leaned against the cool stone wall in the wide passageway. On this side of the door the torches flickered, casting long shadows on the rough floor. I closed my eyes and melted my mind with Avalon's, opening my senses with our similar magic. I saw through his eyes, heard through his ears and felt through his senses.

Although my vision was limited to what Avalon was looking at, I could still take in the room. The space behind the thick stone door was smaller than I had imagined it to be. A large, dark wooden chair sat in a circular area, illuminated only by candle light. Hundreds of tiered candles sat on long, low tables circling the rooms. They took up most of the wall space, except where a door was located.

There were four other doors besides the stone one blocking my path. They were wooden, and not made from stone; however, the same symbolic snake crested them as well. A deep pot of sorts sat not far from the lone chair that Lilly had now taken. The large cauldron was full of some type of iridescent liquid and although I couldn't see any fire beneath the pot, it seemed to be bubbling as if boiling.

Avalon stared at Lilly intently. I could see the tension in her eyes and she gripped the armrests of the chair tightly with both hands. Amory was asking her a series of questions and she nodded confidently despite the terror I could tell she was feeling.

Avalon was also tense; I could feel that he was afraid she would back out. I could feel him admire her beauty, which felt a little bizarre coming from Avalon, and that he would desperately like her to join the cause. In part, but not entirely, he felt that way because he thought Lilly would have influence over me. I smiled on the outside of the door, wondering if he was right.

"Lilly Elizabetta Mason, you are about to join a cause that stands directly opposed to the Monarchy and King and if you are found out the price is your life. Are you sure you want to give up your rights as an Immortal, your eternal life as an Immortal and your fate as an Immortal, surrendering them all under the cause of the Resistance?" Amory asked Lilly gravely.

She responded with a strong "Yes."

"Then Lilly, through any trial, tribulation, torture and trap the Resistance will always give you aid, always give you support and always give you sacrifice. You are, little sister, one of us, wholly, and forever."

Amory paused to smile benevolently and reassuringly at Lilly before gesturing toward Conrad and Terrance. They moved

343

towards Lilly in slow but swift movements and then began to strap her down with restraints I had not noticed before, attached to the chair.

I stood up straight, overcome with anxiety for my dear friend. Why on earth would they need to strap her down? She looked like she was about to be electrocuted by some old school torture tool, something straight out of a fifties era death row chamber. And although I could see that Lilly was willfully allowing them to tie her to the chair, and through it all she seemed to have significantly calmed down, I could not believe she really understood what she was about to go through.

I began to pace the hallway nervously, doing my best to find a way into that room. If things went badly for Lilly, I refused to do nothing. I did not risk my life to save her in Romania from Lucan, only to bring her back to Omaha and watch her die at the hands of my brother and grandfather.

Calm down. You're so dramatic. Avalon sent me a thought and I inwardly cringed, realizing I had promised not to interrupt him.

You better not hurt her. I seethed through my thoughts, finding it slightly ironic he was the one calling me dramatic. He rolled his eyes, not only inwardly but physically as well.

Eden, the whole process is hurt. She's going to be in a lot of pain in just a few seconds and there is absolutely nothing you can do about it. Just remind yourself that she chose this path, and this path comes with a price. Avalon's words hit a nerve and I was suddenly agitated. I knew that he didn't mean to hurt me, but he was right. She chose this path willingly and there was absolutely nothing I could do about it.

When I tuned back in to the events unfolding beyond the stone door, Lilly was completely buckled down, from the top of her head to the soles of her feet. She looked painfully uncomfortable even if this was her choice. Besides the chair restraints, Conrad, Terrance and Amory had also taken hold of her as if adding to the support of the buckles.

Angelica stood in the corner near the bubbling cauldron of shimmering light. She had put on a pair of long, thick work gloves and held a lengthy, cylindrical glass tube with a bulb on one end and a narrowed point on the other. When Amory nodded his head,

Angelica dipped the cylinder into the vessel point side down. She stirred the flickering illumination around until the tube itself seemed to be full of the same mystery; something not quite liquid, not quite light.

When the glass bulb itself began to glisten, she pulled the cylinder out of the cauldron. Angelica walked carefully, methodically over to Lilly, holding the glass cylinder by the point. Once she reached her, she took a long moment to breathe and maybe meditate before pressing the bulb against Lilly's neck and jawbone just beneath her right earlobe.

Suddenly I understood the restraints. As soon as the glass tube touched Lilly's skin she let out a blood-curdling scream that engulfed the small room. I covered my ears instinctively, although technically no sound reached beyond the stone door.

Lilly began to thrash aggressively, despite the fact that she had three grown men and numerous buckles holding her down. Her eyes rolled into the back of her head and I could see her seize violently. She continued to scream, loud and menacingly, a sound that would haunt me for a very long time.

Despite Lilly's struggle, Angelica continued to hold the glass cylinder to her neck, never faltering, never moving. I noticed the light inside the tube begin to drain, and Lilly's skin begin to shine a shade of shimmering violet. Her entire being was engulfed in the beautiful lilac, shining and glistening.

If my friend wasn't in so much terrifying pain I would have found the effect absolutely captivating. Unfortunately, despite her beauty, Lilly seemed to be in an insurmountable amount of hurt. She continued to scream and shake long past the last drops of light had drained into her skin.

Suddenly the shimmering lavender intensified into a deep and bright purple, painting everything in the small room with its concentrated color. As quickly as the color grew bright, it diminished into a small snake eating its tale just below the earlobe of Lilly's right ear. And finally there was silence; Lilly slumped, unmoving in her chair.

I relaxed, exhaling a breath I had not realized I was holding. Apparently my relief was premature however, as only seconds after Lilly had calmed down, she began again with another round of screaming and thrashing. I left Avalon's head unable to withstand the sight of my dear friend enduring so much pain. I cowered against the wall and let out a choking sob.

The door opened slightly and Avalon slipped through to my side of the stone. His face was etched with the same pain that I imagined mine was, minus the tears. He stood facing me with a mixture of sorrow and exhaustion that aged him for a moment. For only a moment, I didn't see my sometimes irritating and always overdramatic twin brother, in his place I saw a great leader, and a great man. I shook my head quickly, reminding myself of the here and now.

"Where is she?" I peered around Avalon, expecting the door to open again at any second.

"She has to stay here for a while. She has to recover," Avalon spoke softly and with compassion.

"What do you mean? We have school," I said plainly, as if the choice Lilly just made shouldn't interfere with high school.

"Lilly won't be able to come to school for a while Eden. You don't need to worry about her though; she's in very capable hands," Avalon began walking towards the exit and I followed, realizing he was right.

"She will be alright?" I asked timidly. I wanted to trust him, I knew I needed to trust him, but the image of Lilly facing so much physical pain would give me nightmares. I could not imagine going through the same torture myself willingly.

"Of course. I'm just fine, aren't I?" Avalon replied and I held back a sarcastic thought. "Just fine," was pretty relative. "Besides don't you have a rendezvous with what's his name? You better forget about Lilly for now, until that kid isn't around anymore. Eden, he can't know anything about her induction, got it?" his compassion had turned into hard lecturing, although I did understand his point.

"I got it," I replied, confident that it wouldn't be a problem, but uncertain Lilly's induction wouldn't cloud my thoughts the rest of the evening all the same. "And you can use Kiran's name. Amory's not going to kick you out or anything."

Avalon only grunted his reply. We both knew Amory was not the problem. Avalon hated Kiran with a passion and never missed an opportunity to remind me.

Despite Avalon, I blushed at the thought of seeing Kiran

tonight. I hadn't seen him alone since before we came home, at his hotel suite in Geneva, Switzerland. Our time there was so intimate and special I had been nervous about seeing him again since.

Kiran sent Talbott over late last night to inform me of our date tonight. Well, I didn't really know if you could call it a date, but we would finally get to be together…. away from school, away from Seraphina and away from Talbott. The horror of Lilly's induction faded quickly when replaced with the sweet thoughts of our upcoming moments together.

"You mean booty call? I'm coming by the way," Avalon interrupted my daydreams and I stopped dead in my tracks.

"What?" I squealed.

"Eden, seriously?" Avalon turned around to give me his best chastising glare. "Prime surveillance opportunity. Wouldn't miss it for the world," he turned quickly on his heel, leaving me gaping after him. A date with Kiran, might be more than a little awkward if Avalon was planning on chaperoning.

Made in the USA
Middletown, DE
19 May 2018